"Grisly, gripping, and riveting. Two brilliant law enforcement pros join forces to hunt a twisted serial killer. Elliot and Leigh have created a page-turning, edge-of-your-seat, cat-and-mouse thriller that kept me up late. I recommend!"

—Robert Dugoni, *New York Times* bestselling author of the Tracy Crosswhite series

"One ruthless serial killer plus one FBI agent plus one homicide detective equals a propulsive game of cat-and-mouse that kept me glued to the page and checking my locks. *Echo Road* maps the darkness of a human heart and the light of female friendship."

—Tess Gerritsen, bestselling author of *The Spy Coast*

"What do you get when you pair up two genre masters? A double-barrel blast of crime fiction awesomeness."

—Lee Goldberg, #1 *New York Times* bestselling author

"Elliot and Leigh bring their formidable talents to this addictive thriller, their voices blending seamlessly to create a provocative page-turner with heart. Suspense readers have won the lottery with this one!"

—Jess Lourey, author of *The Taken Ones*

"Intense. Propulsive. Exhausting, but that good can't-stop-reading kind of exhausting, the rooting-for-justice kind of exhaustion, the kick-ass-women-kicking-ass kind of exhaustion."

—Rachel Howzell Hall, *New York Times* bestselling author

ECHO
ROAD

ALSO BY KENDRA ELLIOT

COLUMBIA RIVER NOVELS

The Last Sister

The Silence

In the Pines

The First Death

At the River

MERCY KILPATRICK NOVELS

A Merciful Death

A Merciful Truth

A Merciful Secret

A Merciful Silence

A Merciful Fate

A Merciful Promise

BONE SECRETS NOVELS

Hidden

WIDOW'S ISLAND NOVELLAS

Close to the Bone

Bred in the Bone

Below the Bones

The Lost Bones

Bone Deep

ALSO BY MELINDA LEIGH

BREE TAGGERT NOVELS

Cross Her Heart

See Her Die

Drown Her Sorrows

Right Behind Her

"Her Second Death" (A Prequel Short Story)

Dead Against Her

Lie to Her

Catch Her Death

On Her Watch

MORGAN DANE NOVELS

Say You're Sorry

Her Last Goodbye

Bones Don't Lie

What I've Done

Secrets Never Die

Save Your Breath

SCARLET FALLS NOVELS

Hour of Need

Minutes to Kill

Seconds to Live

SHE CAN SERIES

She Can Run

She Can Tell

She Can Scream

She Can Hide

"He Can Fall" (A Short Story)

She Can Kill

MIDNIGHT NOVELS

Midnight Exposure

Midnight Sacrifice

Midnight Betrayal

Midnight Obsession

ROGUE RIVER NOVELLAS

Gone to Her Grave (Rogue River)

Walking on Her Grave (Rogue River)

Tracks of Her Tears (Rogue Winter)

Burned by Her Devotion (Rogue Vows)

Twisted Truth (Rogue Justice)

WIDOW'S ISLAND NOVELLAS

A Bone to Pick

Whisper of Bones

A Broken Bone

Buried Bones

The Wrong Bones

ECHO ROAD

KENDRA
ELLIOT

MELINDA
LEIGH

Published by Montlake, Seattle

www.apub.com

Amazon, the Amazon logo, and Montlake are trademarks of Amazon.com, Inc., or its affiliates.

ISBN-13 (digital): 9781662522017
ISBN-13 (hardcover): 9781662522000
ISBN-13 (paperback): 9781662521997

Front cover design by Olga Grlic
Back cover design by Logan Matthews
Cover image: © sharply_done / Getty

Printed in the United States of America

First edition

To Ladybug,
the best girl ever.
You'll live forever on the page.
I wish you could have lived forever with me.
Miss you, girl.
—ML

Prologue

HIM

The first time I saw her, I knew I would kill her.

Why did I do it?

Because our relationship didn't turn out the way I wanted? Because she didn't please me the way I'd intended?

No. Those were all excuses. I killed her because I wanted to.

In the moment, I called it an accident. But was it really? I'd already kidnapped and beaten her. I could hardly let her go, but I hadn't planned her end. I didn't wake that morning and decide the time had come. The truth is, I lost control. Even though I'm alone right now, the heat of embarrassment rushes up the back of my neck. Once the killing started, I couldn't stop. I became no better than an animal. Worse, even. Because not only did I lose control, I *liked* it.

I shake my head, trying to banish the memory.

But it seeps through my resolve.

The deafening rush of my pulse in my ears.

The convulsing of her body under my hands. Squeezing. Harder and harder. I hear animallike noises. Her or me?

Maybe both of us.

Grunting. Gasping. Choking.

SHUT UP SHUT UP SHUT UP.

My hands jerk toward my ears, but the sound isn't external. It's inside my head.

Despite my initial frenzied reaction, the act itself was euphoric. In fact, I'm left with an adrenaline rush like nothing I've ever experienced. I feel alive, which is ironic considering the circumstances. I have no regrets. What bothers me is the fumbling way it came about. In hindsight, I should have savored the moment. The breaking of her will—of her—had just happened. The quiet after had been almost disappointing.

She had been disappointing.

At this moment, I know I will need to do this again. The next time, the act won't be an impulse. It will be deliberate.

I'm done with her, but the next one—she will be perfect.

Chapter 1

BREE

Day 1

Sheriff Bree Taggert heard the drone of flies as soon as she opened the door to exit her vehicle. In her experience, an excessive number of flies was never a good sign. The heat enveloped her as she stepped onto the pavement. Summer in upstate New York was generally pleasant, but they always had to suffer through a sweltering week or two. They were smack in the middle of that annual heat wave.

She grabbed a water bottle from her county SUV and closed the vehicle door. The blacktop radiated heat, amplifying the temperature and humidity to sauna level.

Ahead, county maintenance worker Edmund Hoyt stood on the shoulder of the road, staring into the knee-high weeds. Sweat soaked his long-sleeve T-shirt and gleamed on his lean, tanned face. Bree walked past the tractor Edmund had been using to mow roadside vegetation and stopped next to him. The flies sounded like a remote-controlled plane.

She handed him the water bottle. "What did you find?"

"Thanks." Lifting the bottle, Edmund pointed into the weeds with it. Five feet down the roadside embankment, two discarded suitcases lay in a patch of tall grass. "Didn't expect the sheriff to respond."

"I was nearby, on my way to a county budget meeting." Which Bree was more than happy to miss. Township meetings were about as pleasant as sticking a fork in her eye.

He laughed, twisted off the bottle cap, and gestured toward the suitcases again. "When I first spotted them, I was going to take them to the county dump. Then I got closer, saw the flies, and smelled . . . whatever that stink is." He paused to take a long drink. "I decided not to touch them and called your office."

"Good thinking."

Edmund usually started his day early and had likely been working in the heat all day, but his body odor couldn't compete with the stench wafting from the luggage. The muggy, still afternoon intensified the unmistakable scent of decay. With no wind, the odor rode the humidity like fog hovered over damp ground.

"I didn't get any closer." Edmund removed his hat and wiped his face on the sleeve of his shirt. In his midfifties, he sported a few days of salt-and-pepper scruff and the deep crow's-feet of a man who worked outside. "Feels sketchy to me."

The situation felt sketchy to Bree too. But someone had to see what was in the suitcase. Was she paying the price for bailing on the budget meeting? Karma could be a real bitch.

In this heat, flies would be drawn to any decaying organic matter. The suitcases could contain rotting food. On the other hand . . . dead things attracted the most flies.

She used her phone to take pictures. Then, with one eye on the ground for tracks, debris, or other evidence, she picked her way down the slope. A sticker bush ensnared her boot, and she carefully extracted it, picking a bur from her laces.

The wheelie bags were the larger size you had to check for a flight. One lay partially open, the zipper's teeth gaping apart. The other stood upright, propped on a rock. She could imagine them pushed or tossed out of a vehicle, tumbling down the embankment, and one breaking open before they came to rest in their current location.

She turned and scanned the incline up to the road. With the weeds and the slope, the luggage wouldn't be obvious to the average car driving by, but Edmund had a better view from the tractor's elevated seat. Even if a passerby spotted the suitcases, from a distance they would appear to be nothing more than luggage. Discarded debris wasn't unusual. Bree had seen everything from mattresses to old appliances dumped on the roadside. One had to get closer to these to realize something was amiss.

The sun beat on the top of her head, and sweat had already saturated the T-shirt she wore under her body armor and uniform. The odor from the suitcases grew stronger. As she moved closer, the flies' incessant buzzing raised goose bumps on her arms, even in the oppressive heat. Staying a few feet away, Bree crouched to get a better look inside the partially open suitcase. Even after spending years as a homicide detective in Philadelphia, flies gave her the creeps.

She leaned closer. The point of what appeared to be a black lawn-and-leaf bag protruded from the broken zipper.

Maybe it's just garbage.

Mentally, she crossed her fingers but snapped a few more pics, just in case, because she'd learned to be prepared for the worst.

Bree removed her expandable baton from her duty belt, snapped it to full length, and gently used the end to widen the opening. The smell that poured out made her eyes water. Bree recoiled, turning her head and coughing as the thick odor filled her sinuses, mouth, and throat.

She used the baton to lift the edge of the plastic a little farther, taking care not to tear it. She widened the opening another inch, and something fell out, landing at her feet and creating a puff of dry dirt.

Bree rocked backward on her heels. Horror crawled through her. The object was dried and decayed, the shriveled flesh mottled black and brown. Odd patches of white coated the skin. But she still recognized a human forearm and hand, reaching out of the suitcase as if asking for help.

Too late. The victim had likely been murdered. People who died naturally or accidentally didn't generally end up in suitcases.

Bree stood and took two steps backward. Her legs felt weary from more than just her morning run. She collapsed her baton and returned it to her duty belt. She wouldn't disturb the body any further. The medical examiner would want to see the remains *in situ*.

She brushed off her hands, which hadn't touched anything, and turned back toward the road, climbing the embankment on the same path she'd used on the way down. She joined Edmund on the road, the pavement feeling solid under her boots.

Edmund squinted at her. "From the look on your face, I assume the suitcase isn't filled with trash?"

"No. Not trash. Give me a couple of minutes." Bree returned to her vehicle, started the engine, and turned the air conditioner on high. The tepid air that blasted from the vents was an improvement over the environment outside. She called for backup, the medical examiner, and a forensics team, though she predicted not much evidence would be gleaned from the scene. Based on the fly activity, the suitcases had likely been sitting there for a while.

She thought of the second suitcase. Until proved otherwise, she would assume a second body was inside.

Two suitcases. Two bodies. Two murders.

Chapter 2

BREE

Forty-five minutes later, additional patrol vehicles were parked nose to tail on the shoulder of the road. Bree's deputies had marked off the perimeter of the search area with ground stakes and crime scene tape. To minimize the impact of searchers on the scene, they'd left a walkway for law enforcement personnel.

Edmund had looked wrung out, having been outside in the heat and sun since early morning. Bree had taken his statement and sent him on his way, with the request that he not discuss what he'd seen with anyone. The case had the potential to be a media spectacle.

One of Bree's young deputies, Juarez, took photos. Another sketched the scene on a notepad and took measurements.

A car approached, slowing as the driver craned his neck to see what was happening. Bree sent a deputy to the road to keep passersby moving, but it wouldn't be long before the media noted the police activity.

"Call the station. Have someone bring a tent out here ASAP. I want those suitcases blocked from view of the road and the sky." Bree sensed the oddness of the scene would draw attention. She shielded her eyes and scanned the horizon. No helicopters. Yet.

"Yes, ma'am." Juarez lowered his camera and surveyed the area. "This is a lot of ground to cover."

"Outdoor scenes are always challenging. Weather and wildlife disturb evidence." Bree scanned the extensive cordoned-off area. "I like to mark a scene larger than I think will be necessary. Once searchers have trampled all over the ground, it's compromised. You can't go back and uncompromise it." Every person who entered a scene left their stamp on it, potentially shedding hairs or skin cells and making footprints.

"Where's Flynn?" Juarez asked.

"Out in the woods doing a K-9 training exercise." Bree was missing her part-time investigator—and full-time live-in boyfriend—Matt Flynn. Matt was determined to train K-9s. He'd found the sheriff's department's current K-9 through his sister's dog rescue organization. He was always on the hunt for a new recruit and was working to improve his handling skills. Being out in the wilderness with a bunch of dogs was his idea of a dream vacation.

Juarez surveyed the scene with a frown. "That's unfortunate timing."

"It is." She couldn't even call Matt to ask for his input on the case. He'd been out of cell phone range since the previous day.

The medical examiner's van rolled up and Dr. Serena Jones stepped out. A tall Black woman, she wore green scrubs and rubber boots. Her assistant busied himself retrieving equipment from the back of the van. Med kit in hand, Dr. Jones approached with long, athletic strides, descending the embankment with much more grace than Bree had managed.

Stopping a few feet short of the suitcases, Dr. Jones propped a hand on her hip. "This is a first for me."

"Same." Bree pulled her shirt away from her neck, hoping some air would reach her skin. Sweat had gathered under her uniform at the armpits, beneath her body armor, and under her duty belt.

Dr. Jones squatted next to the hand and studied it for a minute. She slipped on a pair of gloves and then lifted one of the fingers to examine it. "The nails are painted."

Bree leaned closer and craned her neck. The color was a bright shade of pink that instantly reminded her of her nine-year-old niece, Kayla. After Bree's sister had been murdered, Bree had moved from Philadelphia and given up her career with the Philly PD to assume guardianship over her niece and seventeen-year-old nephew. Kayla wasn't exactly a girly girl, but she had a few Barbies. Most of Barbie's accessories were this color.

The distinctive color instantly humanized a victim still mostly hidden to Bree. Had Barbie Pink been her favorite color? A wave of sadness passed through Bree, followed immediately by anger. She quelled both. Emotions clouded judgment.

"I'm making assumptions here. I won't know for certain until I perform the autopsy, but the polish color and slender structure of the forearm and hand suggest the remains are female." Dr. Jones studied the suitcase. "The bugs have been busy. Overall, insect activity suggests the remains have been here at least five days, probably longer."

Juarez pulled a bandanna from his pocket and mopped his dripping face.

Dr. Jones leaned back on her heels. "My initial impression is that the remains have been out here from five to fifteen days. The entomologist should be able to narrow that window considerably by aging the insects."

Juarez looked equally fascinated and horrified.

Dr. Jones asked, "Has anyone looked in the other suitcase?"

"We left that honor for you," Bree said.

"Good. Good," Dr. Jones muttered, clearly focused on the suitcases. "We could have one or two bodies, then." She pulled out a flashlight. She spread the edges of the plastic bag a few inches with her fingers and shined the light inside. "I see long brown hair." She adjusted the angle of the flashlight. "The body is on the small side." She turned her head to eye Juarez. "You wouldn't fit in that suitcase, not even in pieces."

Beneath his heat-flushed cheeks, Juarez paled. "The body could be in pieces?"

Dr. Jones's mouth twisted as she turned back to the opening in the plastic bag and adjusted the beam of her flashlight. "I believe this one is intact. She appears to be folded up in there."

Dr. Jones duckwalked to the second bag and gently unzipped it a few inches. Shining her flashlight inside, she exhaled. "Looks like a second body. This one is not in a plastic bag. I see a foot, slender, with what appears to be the same shade of nail color on the toenails." She closed the zipper, straightened, and backed away two steps from the suitcase.

Bree turned to her deputy. "Details stay under wraps. Don't even discuss them among yourselves."

"Yes, ma'am," Juarez said.

"Will you open it in the morgue?" Bree asked the ME.

"Yes." Dr. Jones nodded.

Juarez exhaled, as if relieved.

Dr. Jones contemplated the luggage with a tilt of her head. "It'll be best for evidence preservation to open everything in the lab. We'll sample insects here, though."

Juarez's throat shifted as he gagged, then swallowed.

Bree said, "Don't vomit here."

His head bobbed in a tight nod.

The ME's assistant approached with his camera.

Dr. Jones began issuing orders. "Photograph everything. I want samples of the soil under the suitcases and all the bugs."

With a nod, the assistant went to work photographing the suitcases. He started at a distance and worked every angle, slowly spiraling in to shoot close-ups from multiple perspectives. There couldn't be too many photos. The scene couldn't be reconstructed after the bodies were removed.

Bree's chief deputy, Todd Harvey, arrived, and pulled a tent from the back of his patrol vehicle. He and Juarez set it up over the suitcases and arranged the side flaps to block the view from the road.

"Just in time." Bree heard the distinct *thwap thwap thwap* of an approaching helicopter. A few seconds later, a news copter passed overhead. "Get a grid search going. Also, I want deputies to walk the sides of the road for a quarter mile in every direction in case our killer tossed anything else out of his vehicle."

Two hours later, the ME and her assistant placed both suitcases on gurneys in black body bags. A couple of deputies helped carry the gurneys up the embankment to the road. A news van parked on the shoulder. The cameraman focused on the gurneys as they were loaded into the back of the ME's van. A tall blond reporter filming a sound bite looked Hollywood worthy, but also familiar, though Bree couldn't think of his name.

"Sheriff!" the blond man called, smoothing the sleeves of his dark-blue suit and straightening his silk tie. How was he not sweating?

"I can't talk to you right now. Please stand back. This is an active investigation." Bree summoned one of her newest hires, Deputy Renata Zucco, to ensure the media kept their distance. Zucco was petite but tough, even mouthy to a fault at times. Former NYPD, she wouldn't allow anyone to bulldoze her or compromise the scene.

Todd reported back. "Roadside search is complete. We found the usual litter: water bottles, soda cans, cigarette butts, take-out bags, et cetera."

Every scrap would be photographed next to an evidence marker, bagged, and transported back to the forensics lab for analysis. Each bag would contain the glove used to recover that particular piece of evidence. Each label would document the current link in the chain of custody. Any break in that chain would render the evidence inadmissible.

Bree said, "I wasn't expecting much because the victims clearly weren't killed here. This is a dump site. But you never know. This is a strange case."

After the bodies were removed, Bree and her deputies photographed, sampled, and searched the ground where they'd lain.

"The lack of evidence is frustrating," Juarez said.

"We'll have plenty when the autopsies are complete." Bree mentally crossed her fingers the remains and/or suitcases would help them identify the victims and solve the murders.

Chapter 3

BREE

It was early evening before Bree returned to the station, where media vans clogged the main parking lot. Bree drove around back and used the employee entrance. She stopped in the break room to fill a stainless-steel bottle with water, downing half of it on the way back to her office. She dropped into her chair, leaned back, and closed her eyes, letting the air-conditioning waft over her.

"You are a mess."

She cracked an eyelid. Her administrative assistant, Marge, stood in the doorway. In her sixties, Marge wore black slacks and sensible shoes. Her dyed brown hair was sprayed into submission. Her sole concession to the heat was the lack of her usual cardigan.

Bree sat up. "I am." She looked down. Her uniform was stained with sweat, dirt, and grass. The sun and heat had left her exhausted and dehydrated. Her face felt hot and tight, probably sunburned. No doubt she'd sweated off her sunscreen. She drank more water, then fished a packet of electrolytes out of her drawer, added it to the bottle, and gave it a shake.

"You should shower. There's a fresh uniform in your closet."

Bree nodded. "You're right." Nothing would feel better than hosing off the grime.

"The lobby is full of press. You don't want to address them like that." Marge waved in Bree's direction.

"Actually, I do. Maybe if I smell bad, they won't stay long." Bree grinned.

Marge gave her a Look.

Bree's grin shifted into a scowl. "I've been out in the heat all day. I'm in no mood for niceties." Her skin felt like fruit leather.

Marge said nothing, but one penciled-on eyebrow rose a millimeter.

Bree met her gaze head-on. "I'm too tired to play politics."

"There's a maggot on your boot."

Bree quelled the urge to fling it across the room. That's what crawling around a crime scene will get you. She tapped her foot on the floor. The maggot dropped off, and she crushed it under her boot. "I'll shower." She heard the grumpiness in her voice but didn't care.

Marge didn't actually smile, but the corners of her eyes crinkled. "I'll bring a fresh uniform and clean boots to the locker room."

Marge had worked for the sheriff's office for forever. She knew every dirty detail that went into law enforcement, including the nasty things that often inhabited crime scenes. Cognizant of Bree's elected-official status, Marge always had a fresh uniform and a clean pair of boots ready.

A sudden wave of paranoia swept over Bree. She glanced down at her body. She didn't see any more insects, but she swore she could feel them everywhere. Bree was on her feet and stripping in the locker room within two minutes. Leaving her filthy uniform on the tile and her body armor on the bench, she hurried into the shower.

She stepped under the spray, grateful for the recent renovations that had added a locker room for female employees. Prior to Bree taking office, there had been only a male locker room. But then, the previous, corrupt, now-dead sheriff hadn't employed any female deputies. Everything had changed when Bree had been appointed to the office.

She'd cleaned house. Those first months had been rough. She'd dealt with lingering sexism, and close to half the deputies had quit. But in the long run, everything had worked out, and she was pleased with the deputies who had stayed and her new hires. The boys' club had been shown the door.

After scrubbing down multiple times, she emerged from the shower. A fluffy towel sat on the bench next to a fresh uniform. She dried off and dressed. She gave her hair a quick blast with the dryer, then pinned it into its usual professional bun. Ever hopeful, Marge had left a makeup bag near the sinks. Bree ignored it. Usually, she'd appease Marge and apply a bit of concealer and lipstick. But today, she was done. After dealing with the callous discarding of two women, the heat, and the bugs, Bree had not a single fuck left over for her personal appearance.

Clean and tidy was the best anyone was going to get this evening.

She used the deodorant and toothbrush she kept in her locker before exiting.

Marge gave her an up-and-down appraisal, with barely a frown at her unmade-up face. "Better."

Was she giving up?

Bree hoped so. She caught up with Todd in the squad room. His damp hair and clean uniform indicated he'd also showered.

Todd tilted his head. "Do you want me to talk to the press?"

"No. I'll handle them."

"Thank God." He looked as exhausted as she felt. "What can I do?"

"Get Juarez to help run queries in NamUs, ViCAP, and NCIC. Start looking for females with long brown hair reported missing in the last six months."

ViCAP was the FBI's Violent Criminal Apprehension Program, designed to analyze and collect information on violent crimes. Records included murders, sexual assaults, missing persons cases, and unidentified remains. NamUs was a searchable national database of unidentified remains and missing persons cases. The National Crime Information

Center was a nationwide clearinghouse for missing persons and crime information. More than twenty-three thousand missing persons cases were currently open in the US. Querying all three databases gave them a better chance of identifying their victims.

They'd update the search after the ME supplied more information, but they could get lucky. The victims could be ID'd quickly. It was much harder to solve a murder without knowing who had been killed.

"Will do," Todd said.

Bree checked the time. "After that, both of you go home. The investigation will ramp up tomorrow after the autopsies are complete. May as well get some sleep while we can."

For now, they had very little information to work with.

"Yes, ma'am." Todd turned toward the desks and computers.

She went out into the lobby and faced the press. She spotted only local stations and crossed her fingers that the case hadn't generated national media attention. A circus-tent atmosphere didn't help any investigation.

The moment she stepped into the lobby, the media erupted with questions. Bree stood in front of the crowd and waited. They settled and she began. "This afternoon, the remains of two bodies, likely female, were found by the side of Echo Road." She described the circumstances of the find.

"Is it true the bodies were stuffed into suitcases?" a reporter yelled.

Bree cooled a quick flash of anger. She couldn't expect such a juicy detail to elude the media. The crime scene was a public road, and numerous cars had driven by, observing the activity, before they'd erected the tent. "Yes. The remains were contained inside two large suitcases."

Another reporter called out, "Do we have another serial killer in Randolph County?"

Bree raised a hand. "It's far too early to make any such assertions. These people could have been victims of a number of other crimes."

She could think of many possibilities, from gang violence to human trafficking, but the press did not need any further speculation. "When I have more details, I'll pass them along."

"I heard both victims wore pink nail polish. Is this true?" the blond reporter who had been at the scene earlier asked. He was in a fresh suit, and his face and hair looked perfect, which irritated Bree almost as much as the information he'd just spilled. Bree had wanted to keep the polish detail in-house, to help determine real leads from false, but clearly that was no longer possible.

With effort, Bree maintained her poker face. "Yes."

The blond continued. "And one of the victims has long brown hair?"

Bree tamped down a primal scream. The media was already sabotaging the case, and she'd barely begun the investigation. This was not a good sign.

"Correct." She skirted a few more questions with vague answers and then ended the session with "I'll schedule another press conference after I've heard from the medical examiner." She turned to the nearest camera. "If anyone saw suitcases being dumped on the side of Echo Road or has any information about the case, please call the sheriff's department." Bree gave the general number and thanked the public for their assistance.

Closing the secure door to the lobby behind her, Bree walked back to her office. The bodies had been in suitcases, which were inside black body bags when they were transported to the ME van. It wasn't possible for passersby or reporters on the road to have seen the remains through the Russian-nesting-doll effect. There was no possibility any unofficial personnel saw the nail polish or long dark hair. Those details had been leaked.

But by whom?

Angry and exhausted, she gathered her files and left via the back door in the fading dusk. After tossing her bag across the console, she slid behind the wheel. The gate barrier rose, and she drove out of the fenced lot.

The radio chattered softly as she made the turn onto the main road. An object sailed toward her windshield, hitting with a wet smack. Bree's heart slammed into her throat. She stomped on the brake pedal, her heart jackhammering against her breastbone. Red liquid oozed across the glass.

Someone had thrown something at her car.

She could have crashed her vehicle.

Outside, someone yelled, "Fucking useless cops."

Bree couldn't see anyone. The red liquid blocked her view through the windshield. Blood?

She jerked the gearshift into park, wrenched open the door, and jumped out of the vehicle, her hand on her weapon. A piece of thin latex waved from her wiper. *A balloon?*

Her head pivoted toward the sound of running footsteps. She spotted a figure in a hoodie bolting away. The height and gait suggested a male suspect. She used her lapel mic to call for assistance, hoping a patrol unit was nearby and could cut off the assailant at the other end of the block. But no such luck. On-duty deputies were either at the station or out on patrol.

She bolted after him, anger fueling her stride. Her thighs and lungs burned, but she gained on him. Ahead, he turned into an alley. Bree skidded around the corner. The alley was empty. She aimed her weapon into the darkness. Was he hiding? Easing past a dumpster, she checked between it and the brick wall. Then she rose onto her toes and flipped the top open. The smell of garbage poured out, but the container was mostly empty. No one was inside. She closed the lid, scanned the alley, but saw no one.

A chain-link fence rattled, feet hit the ground hard, and then running footsteps faded into the distance.

Fucking fuck fuck fuck.

She holstered her weapon, rested her hands on her knees, and wheezed for a minute.

Frustrated, she returned to her vehicle and suspiciously examined the red liquid on the windshield. It was thick and appeared sticky. Not blood, though. After her day, she expected a terrible smell, but a sweet and tangy odor wafted to her nose. Barbecue sauce? A patrol car came toward her, lights blazing.

Juarez rushed out of the driver's seat. "Sheriff?"

"I think someone threw a balloon filled with barbecue sauce at my vehicle."

"Barbecue sauce?"

"I assume it was intended to look like blood."

"Oh, wow." He stared at the mess.

"Yeah. Everyone needs to take extra care leaving the station. Someone is angry." She texted Todd to put the word out to all the employees. "No one was hurt, but this"—she gestured toward her windshield—"could have caused an accident."

Then she slid back into the driver's seat. The windshield was completely obscured. She lowered the window. With her head sticking out, she drove back into the parking lot. Juarez followed. He took a few pictures, then hosed off her SUV for her.

She picked the small piece of latex from her wiper. "This is going to be the most ridiculous report ever."

"Yes, ma'am." Juarez coiled the hose.

Thankfully, the vehicle was undamaged. But her hands trembled from the adrenaline dump as she slid behind the wheel.

Barbecue Sauce Balloon Man wasn't wrong. She did feel useless. There was another killer in Randolph County. Two women were dead. It was her job to keep the public safe, and she had failed.

———

Still shaken, Bree drove home in the falling darkness. She'd been in no rush to get back to the farm. The usual home vibe was noisy and chaotic. When Bree had moved to her sister's farm in Grey's Hollow, her former homicide partner had retired and moved upstate to serve as an unofficial nanny and pseudoaunt to Bree's niece and nephew. Dana had taken the kids to the Jersey Shore to vacation with her extended family.

The farm was also home to two dogs: Matt's former K-9, Brody, and Bree's pointer-mix rescue, Ladybug. Five horses and one territorial tomcat were also in residence. This week, with Matt away pursuing his K-9 adventure badge, and the kids at the beach, Bree had the farm all to herself.

For a woman who'd spent the majority of her adult life alone, being thrust into a frenzied family environment had been disconcerting. But now that she'd adjusted to living in chaos, the sudden quiet was just as disarming.

She opened the back door, but instead of going inside, she let the dogs out. Ladybug slammed into Bree's knees, demanding attention before trotting onto the grass to pee. Brody waited his turn for a head scratch like a gentleman. With the dogs at her heels, Bree detoured to the barn. Her younger brother had fed the horses and dogs at dinnertime. Five huge heads peered over the half doors of their stalls. Bree checked each animal, spending a few extra minutes with her paint gelding. He'd been her sister's horse, and his company gave her comfort. She ran a hand over his sweaty shoulder. Even with the doors open, the barn was hot, and Bree turned the horses out into the pasture for the night. Her boots crunched across the dry grass. How long had it been since it rained? Too long, considering the scorching temps.

In the house, she and the dogs stared at each other.

"I know. You're bored." Bree should have been exhausted, but instead, she was unable to settle. The quiet felt unnatural. She poured a glass of iced tea and took it out onto the back porch. The dogs lay at her feet. Together they watched the dark shapes of the horses grazing in the pasture. Her phone rang, and Dana's number appeared on the screen. Bree answered.

"Hey." Dana sounded breathless. "Kayla wanted to call."

"Aunt Bree!" Kayla yelled.

Bree put the call on speaker. "Whatcha doin'?"

"We went to the boardwalk and we got pizza and ice cream and I rode the roller coaster and Luke went with me and tomorrow we're going to the beach," Kayla said in one sentence and one breath. She inhaled. "Dana's brother has two girls and he promised to take us to the water park."

"I'm glad you're having fun." Bree wished she were with them, but the trip had been last minute. She already had too many deputies on vacation to take time off herself.

"Gotta go," Kayla said. Over the connection, children giggled.

After a clunk, Dana came back on the line. "Sorry about that." She laughed. "She's going to pass out the minute she gets in bed."

"Are you exhausted yet?" Bree asked.

"Nope. My brothers' kids are all here. They're tiring each other out."

"Luke?"

"He's mini golfing with my nephew," Dana said. "They should be back soon."

"He doesn't need to check in, but he can call if he wants."

"That's what I figured."

Bree would be happy to talk with Luke, but she hoped he didn't feel the need. She hoped he was enjoying himself. But damn, she missed them much more than she had expected. But she was glad the kids weren't in Grey's Hollow while dead bodies were turning up in suitcases.

Chapter 4

Him

They found the suitcases while I was at work.

I probably should have concealed them better. Like my first kill, the act had been impulsive, but the smell had been getting worse.

I replay the press conference on my laptop. I'm not worried about being discovered. I'm too smart. No one would ever suspect me. But a female sheriff? I almost want to laugh at the absurdity.

The bitch is obviously incompetent. *She* won't get in my way.

I open the fridge and stare at the contents. I'm low on food. I grab a pack of bologna, a bottle of ketchup, and a beer from the door compartment. Wishing I had better options, I close the door, drop the food on the table, and assemble a sandwich. The ketchup looks a little like congealed blood.

I bite into the sandwich. The bologna tastes weird. I check the expiration date, which is fine. The meat must have absorbed odors in the refrigerator. I make a note to add a box of baking soda to my shopping list. A swig of beer washes the taste from my mouth.

What doesn't kill me, right?

I watch the press conference again while I finish my dinner. The cops' confusion amuses me. They're a bunch of bumbling idiots. My attention focuses on the sheriff. She has dark hair. I wonder how long it is? Long enough to wrap around my hand and give me a great grip? I pause the video and enlarge the image, but her hair is pulled back. I can't judge its length. Her nails are bare and cut short. Too bad. I prefer them manicured.

I push aside the paper plate and drain my beer. A noise from the next room catches my attention. I freeze, listening. The soft whimper sounds again.

I told her to be silent.

Equal parts anger and excitement course through me. She's led a privileged, spoiled life and thinks she's important.

She needs to be taught a lesson.

Chapter 5

MERCY

Two weeks earlier

FBI Special Agent Mercy Kilpatrick paused on the front walkway of the Holcrofts' huge Oregon house, scanning for security cameras. She spotted two. One covered the entrance, and another pointed at the wide driveway, where three Deschutes County Sheriff patrol vehicles, a black Ford Explorer, and her Tahoe were parked.

The entrance camera was at least twelve feet off the ground. She stepped directly underneath it and squinted.

Is that tape?

Black electrical tape covered the lens.

"Shit."

Seventeen-year-old Paige Holcroft, the daughter of Senator Adam Holcroft, had been missing for twenty-four hours. The tape was an ominous sign.

A kidnapping?

The daughter of a US senator would be a valuable victim.

"Mercy." Deschutes County Sheriff detective Evan Bolton had opened the front door and stood watching her. "You got here fast." The detective followed her gaze. "Yeah. I don't like the tape either," he said. "The senator didn't have it placed there. And the camera covering the driveway is blacked out, but none of the other ones are."

"Good to see you, Evan."

The detective was a close friend, and she was pleased he'd caught the case. Evan was smart and committed. She'd worked a number of cases with him in the past and was confident in his skills.

Mercy took a few steps back to study the house, a sprawling new home that sat on a two-acre lot at the top of an exclusive subdivision. The home was a twist on the Craftsman style, adding modern and high-desert influences. The result was simultaneously representative of the forested Pacific Northwest mountains and the rugged, dry Central Oregon vistas. Stacked-rock columns, massive windows, a variety of different shades of wood. It harmonized with the landscape.

The architect nailed it.

The only things out of place were the two deputies walking the property and another standing behind Evan in the doorway.

And black electrical tape.

She turned around and was gifted with a perfect view of the Cascade mountain range. The snowy areas on the peaks were few and far between, but that was normal for the middle of the hot, dry summer. Winter snow would soon blanket the mountains.

"Anything new?" she asked the detective as she entered the home, nodding at the silent deputy as he stepped outside. Mercy froze. "Wow," she mumbled, staring at the soaring high crossbeams and two-story walls of windows. The sight was magazine perfection.

"I know." Evan clearly enjoyed her reaction. "I felt the same when I stepped in. And to answer your question, I've only been here a few minutes, so I don't know much more than you. I spoke a bit with the parents. The senator is trying to calm his wife, who is understandably completely rattled. Their son, Finn, was dropped off twenty minutes ago. He spent the night at a friend's house."

"You'd said Paige's phone and laptop are in her room?" Mercy asked.

"Yes. I found them hidden under her pillows. Her parents assumed she had them even though she wasn't showing up on their family location app. I powered on both devices, and they appear to have been wiped and reset to factory settings."

"That has to be deliberate." Mercy reevaluated her kidnapping theory. "Let's send them to the RFCL lab immediately. You'd be surprised what the technicians can find. Wiped devices are never as clean as people think," she said, referring to the FBI's computer forensics lab in Portland. "Does Paige have a car?"

"It's in the garage. I went over it briefly—same as I did with her bedroom—but both need a deep search."

"Let's see if the parents are ready to talk yet. Lead the way." She gestured at Evan, who strode through the great room and past a custom kitchen—that Mercy tried not to ogle—to tall glass doors that had been slid aside, opening an entire wall to the outdoors. The parents, Adam and Denise, sat at a table on the large patio, protected from the hot sun by a gabled roof that blurred the line between indoors and outdoors. Fans spun overhead. Mercy noted the outdoor kitchen, complete with a high-end grill and mini fridge. The covered patio was the size of her living room and kitchen combined.

The senator stood and held his hand out to Mercy. "Adam Holcroft. Thank you so much for coming quickly."

"Special Agent Kilpatrick," she answered. She recognized the man from news coverage. He'd been a state senator for two years before jumping successfully into the race for the US Senate. She was slightly startled to discover that he was shorter than her—many people considered her tall, but Adam Holcroft had come across much taller on TV. He was forty-five and bald with a graying goatee. He had a powerful, kind, and intelligent presence. She'd noticed it on TV, and it carried over to meeting him in person, explaining why he had swept up Oregon's votes.

His eyes were bloodshot.

"Do you have any news?" he asked Mercy. Still seated, his wife leaned forward at the question.

"I'm sorry, I do not." She'd barely dipped a toe into the case. "But things have been put in motion. We should know something soon."

"I've filed a request for Paige's cell phone records," said Evan. "And a forensics team is on its way to collect evidence from her bedroom and car."

"What *kind* of evidence? Did you find blood somewhere?" Denise Holcroft asked abruptly. A Kleenex box sat on the table in front of her, several crumpled tissues next to it.

"I haven't seen blood anywhere," Evan said firmly but kindly to the woman. "They'll collect prints, hair, and anything else they see fit to check." He gestured for Mercy and Adam to sit and pulled out a chair for himself. "Like I told you earlier, since there is no obvious crime scene, the most important thing to do this early is talk to family and friends."

"You should be out looking for her!" Denise wiped her nose, her eyes angry. She was petite, but Mercy sensed her strength and fire. Her brunette hair was slicked tight in a high ponytail, and she wore a red sleeveless top. Denise Holcroft was tan, fit, and polished—she looked like a senator's wife. The photos of Paige that Mercy had reviewed showed a younger version of her mother. The resemblance was striking. Both were petite with long dark hair. But all Paige's photos showed a wide, genuine smile—unlike her mother at the moment.

"I've issued a BOLO with Paige's description," said Evan. "And we kept her name out of it as requested."

On a phone call during Mercy's drive to the home, she and Evan had discussed releasing Paige's name. They didn't want news media to swarm the family after learning the senator's daughter was missing. Not yet. The deputies on the scene had been ordered not to mention the family's or victim's name.

But someone always talked.

Their window of anonymity would be short. The news of a senator's missing daughter would bring the nuts out of the woodwork and trigger a rash of false leads. They had to move fast before being hindered by the media and a curious public.

And before something horrible happened to Paige.

Assuming she isn't holed up in a motel with a boyfriend.

But she'd left her phone behind. That fact alone raised Mercy's concern.

Teenagers were rarely separated from their phones.

"Where is your son?" asked Mercy. "I'd like to talk with him too."

"He's in his room. I'll get him," said Denise. She picked up her phone and sent a text.

It's a big house.

"Let's start with when you last saw Paige," said Evan. He had a small notebook and pen in hand, ready to take notes. Mercy opened her bag and pulled out the same.

"Around noon yesterday," said Adam. "She was here when Denise and I left for a fundraising event. She was eating lunch." He looked at his wife for confirmation, and she nodded. "Neither of us checked in with her after that. It was a whirlwind of a day, which included a late dinner and then cocktails with supporters. We didn't get home until almost midnight. I saw her car was in the garage and her bedroom door was closed—which is normal at night."

"The cat bothers her if she leaves the door open," Denise cut in. She blotted her nose. "Nothing seemed out of the ordinary."

"And your son, Finn, was at a friend's?" asked Mercy.

"Yes, he's been there the last two nights."

As if on cue, french doors opened and a lanky teenager stepped outside at least fifty feet away from where they sat. His dark hair was shaggy and he slouched as he walked, his hands shoved in his shorts' pockets. Mercy watched him approach, noting his worried eyes, but his strides and posture stayed casual. Finn sat down in the chair next to his mother, who put an arm around him, briefly pulling him to her side and pressing a kiss to his temple. He didn't seem bothered by the kiss or that his mother held his hand after the hug.

Mercy's gaze went to the senator. His hands were clasped before him on the table, watching his son. The two feet of space between him and his wife suddenly seemed like yards.

I haven't seen them touch each other.

"How did you discover she was missing this morning?" Mercy asked.

Denise gave an embarrassed half shrug. "I didn't check on her until eleven. It's the weekend," she explained, her eyes begging Mercy to understand. "Sometimes both kids sleep until noon. I've often done my workout, gone for a run, eaten breakfast, and showered before they appear."

"And you, Senator?" Evan asked.

"Adam, please. I had an early tee time. Denise called me after she couldn't find Paige."

"I checked our app for her location and couldn't find it," added Denise. "I texted Finn but he didn't know where she was."

"Boyfriend?" asked Evan.

"She hasn't dated anyone in at least six months," said Denise. "Right now she takes summer classes at the OSU-Cascades campus in Bend and just hangs out with her friends. No job at the moment."

"Did you call her friends?" asked Mercy.

"She has two very close friends, but Finn had to contact them for me," said Denise. "I didn't have their numbers."

"You have your sister's friends' phone numbers?" Mercy asked the teen, thinking that was odd.

"I don't know their numbers," he said, briefly meeting Mercy's gaze. "I messaged them on Snapchat. Both said that they hadn't seen her or heard from her since yesterday morning. Paige didn't show up on Snapchat's locator either. They're worried."

Mercy knew from her niece, Kaylie, that Snapchat allowed users to share their location with trusted people. "I'd like to talk to both friends," said Mercy, glancing at Evan, who nodded. "Can you ask them to come to the house?"

Finn focused on his phone and started tapping.

"Tell them not to talk to anyone about this," Adam told Finn. "I don't want it spread around yet."

Mercy eyed the senator. "I agree with you, Adam. But this will eventually get out. People talk. For all we know, Paige's friends have already told their parents and other friends that she's missing. You need to be prepared."

"Telling the public could help us locate her quicker," added Evan.

"I want this kept quiet for now," Adam said firmly, meeting their gazes. "I don't want a public uproar and then discover my daughter is out hiking with a friend."

That's the strong senator I've seen on TV.

Denise said nothing, her focus on the tissue she was systematically tearing.

"You said you'd checked the camera feeds and saw when they went dark, correct?" Evan asked the senator.

Adam pulled out his phone and touched the screen. "I have ten cameras covering the property and house. Only the entrance and driveway cameras were blacked out. Both views show tape being applied around one p.m., but the person doing it is out of sight. I've sped through the footage before that. No one but Paige was in the house all morning." He slid his phone over to Evan and Mercy, who watched as the home entrance view was suddenly cut in half by a strip of tape. Another strip was applied a few seconds later, obliterating the scene. The driveway camera showed the same. Whoever applied the tape had known exactly where to approach and stand to avoid being seen on camera.

"Have you ever used security guards on the property?" asked Mercy.

"No, I've never felt the need. We've never had a problem in the past with trespassers or protesters. My home security system sends alerts to our phones," he said, gesturing to himself and his wife. "We don't use an outside service to monitor it. Protecting our privacy is important."

"I assume you can also view the camera feeds on a computer," said Mercy.

Adam nodded.

"Can we review them that way, please?" The images on Adam's phone were crystal clear but small.

"I'll be right back." Adam strode into the home.

"Paige's friends will be here in a half hour," said Finn, staring at his phone. "Sophie's picking up Jordyn." He looked up, distress in his eyes. "Neither have told anyone."

"They're good kids," added Denise. "I guess they're not kids anymore . . . but they've been friends with Paige since middle school. Nice girls."

Adam reappeared; an open laptop balanced on his forearm as he typed with the other hand. He paused at the table for a moment to finish typing and then set the computer down where everyone could see the screen.

"Much better," said Evan, watching the tape be applied to the entrance camera again.

The view from the driveway camera wobbled just before the black strip appeared.

"Wait!" Denise leaned forward, her eyes wide. "Back it up. Slowly go ahead."

Mercy studied the video as it moved in slow motion, wondering what Denise had seen.

"There!" Denise pointed at the corner of the screen as the first piece of tape was applied. Adam paused the recording and backed up. A tiny pink blur appeared and quickly vanished. "That's Paige's nail polish," she exclaimed. "I'm positive! I was with her when she bought it, and I didn't like the color—it looks like Pepto-Bismol. She's been wearing it for a few days."

Mercy exchanged a look with Evan.

Why did Paige cover the cameras?

Chapter 6

MERCY

Later Mercy stood in the center of Paige's huge bedroom, disappointed by their lack of clues to the young woman's whereabouts. She and Evan had done a thorough bedroom search and were still waiting for Paige's friends to arrive.

After identifying the nail polish, Denise and Adam had been stunned to realize their daughter had hidden her disappearance from them. Denise fell into a bout of crying, upset about an argument she'd had with Paige two weeks ago. Adam had finally put his arms around his wife, reassuring her that Paige wouldn't leave because of a fight.

Mercy wasn't so sure.

Paige was seventeen. Mercy had witnessed the odd things teens did when upset. She lived with her nineteen-year-old niece and her husband's son, Ollie, who was twenty. Young people that age often didn't think logically.

And did irrational things as a result.

Adam had turned to Evan and Mercy as he held his wife and asked, "Does this mean she wasn't kidnapped?" His gaze had searched theirs.

"It's not ruled out yet," Mercy had said.

But why cover the cameras?

"She left her car," Mercy said quietly to Evan in the teenager's bedroom. "Unless she walked away, she was picked up in front of her home by someone she didn't want her parents to see." Her gaze went to the phone and computer on the bed. "But why leave those behind?"

Evan didn't have an answer.

Mercy entered Paige's walk-in closet again—it was the size of her niece's bedroom. She and Evan had checked all the clothing pockets and slid their hands into shoes, and then opened and searched the twenty-plus purses and bags. There were enough clothes in the closet to open a boutique. If Paige had taken clothing with her, it didn't show.

"We've been looking for evidence that might have been left behind, but what we need to know is what's missing," Mercy said, staring at the shelves of shoes.

"Paige's friends are here," announced Finn.

Mercy stepped out of the closet to see him at the bedroom doorway. He eyed the electronics on the bed. "Finn, could you look in Paige's closet with me for a moment?" She wasn't optimistic that the teen could help. She suspected teen boys paid no attention to an older sister's belongings.

Except their electronics.

Finn awkwardly stood by Mercy in the big closet and ran his hand through his shaggy hair. "Do you see anything missing?" Mercy asked.

The teen scanned the packed racks of clothing. "I wouldn't know."

I was right.

"But her suitcase is missing." Finn pointed at a corner under a shelf of bags where four shallow dents appeared in the carpet.

How did I miss the wheel dents?

"She packed stuff," Finn said to himself, and moved to riffle through some dresses.

Mercy stayed silent. The teen clearly had thought of something.

He finished the dresses, then moved to check the shoes, nodding to himself. "Her slut dress and shoes are gone."

Taken aback, Mercy couldn't speak for a moment. She finally blurted, "Slut dress?"

"Yeah. It's black and tight and too short. She looks stupid in it. I saw her try it on here a week ago. Told her it was slutty. The red shoes were stupid too. Heels so high she could barely walk." His voice cracked as he wiped his eyes.

His words were rude and sexist, but Mercy suspected they were a result of strong emotions about his sister's disappearance.

She'd ignore the offensive language. This time.

"Finn," said Evan from behind Mercy. "Would you tell Paige's friends we'll be out in a minute?"

The teen nodded and left.

Mercy studied Evan's stony expression. "What is it?"

He held out his hand. Paige's driver's license sat on his palm. "I took the case off her phone. This was inside."

"Kaylie does that too," said Mercy. "She never carries a purse." She paused, letting the implications sink in. "You heard what Finn said about the dress and suitcase?"

"Yes," he said grimly. "More evidence that she chose to leave." He looked down at the license. "But this doesn't make sense. Same with leaving her phone behind."

"Maybe her friends can shine a light on some things. The missing dress and heels point to a mystery man in her life. Friends usually have the inside scoop."

A few minutes later Mercy and Evan sat outside across from the two young women. They had long, loose curls that hung halfway down their backs, but one was blonde and the other brunette. Both wore crop tops and high-waisted shorts—the current uniform of their age group. Mercy had asked Paige's family to give them privacy for the initial interview.

"The last time I talked to Paige was the day before yesterday," Sophie was saying. "I'd commented on one of her Instagram photos, and she replied."

Mercy didn't think an Instagram comment qualified as "talked to." "How about when you last saw her in person?"

"The Basement club three nights ago," stated Jordyn, and Sophie nodded in agreement. "The three of us went together. We were out pretty late." She glanced at Sophie.

Mercy knew the local dance club didn't serve alcohol, and you had to be at least seventeen to enter. It was always packed on the weekends.

"I didn't get home until one," said Sophie. "But first I dropped off Paige. Jordyn drove herself."

"Was your last communication with her at the club too, Jordyn?" asked Evan.

Jordyn thought. "Let me look. I checked our texts and looked for her Snap location when Finn messaged me, but I forgot about Insta." She touched her phone screen a few times. Her brows came together, confusion filling her face. "I can't find her. Her Instagram account is completely gone."

"Let me look." Sophie studied her phone. "You're right."

"Her Snap is gone too," stated Jordyn, her eyes wide as she looked up at Mercy. "This morning I noticed that she wasn't on the map—which usually isn't a big deal because it's not very accurate—but deleting her accounts isn't a good sign."

Phone, laptop, and license left behind. Social media accounts deleted.

Mercy agreed with Jordyn. Not good signs.

"Her parents said she attends the OSU-Cascades campus in Bend," said Evan. "Do either of you go there?"

The girls exchanged a look and both seemed to deflate slightly.

"We just graduated high school. Paige got early admission to OSU—she started last fall—and skipped her senior year. She had the grades and credits to finish. But she dropped out of college this past spring," said Jordyn reluctantly. "She doesn't want her parents to know. Now I feel like they should be told."

"Definitely," agreed Mercy.

Kaylie would be in big trouble if she tried that on me.

"How can Paige pretend to be in school?" asked Mercy. "I know her parents check her location sometimes. Wouldn't they find it odd if she's not on campus? And what about tuition? I'd notice if a tuition bill didn't show up."

Sophie grimaced. "I think she told them most of the classes are online. I know she hangs out on campus like one day a week. She sits in the coffee shop and just plays on her phone in case they check."

"Her parents transfer money to her bank account for tuition," said Jordyn. "She told me she tells them the amount and they just do it, believing she'll make the actual payment."

"She pocketed her tuition money," stated Evan.

"And she got a partial refund from last spring after she dropped out," added Sophie.

Mercy eyed the large expanse of green grass and the two water features near the patio. A good acre of the property had been elaborately landscaped: trees, boulders, flowers.

Every element of this home was expensive. These were wealthy people.

Do the parents have enough money that they wouldn't keep track of a tuition payment?

"Roughly $3,000 for summer tuition at that campus," said Evan, looking at his phone. "Spring term was closer to $6,000." He looked at the young women. "How long was she in school this past spring?"

"Maybe a week or two?" Jordyn glanced at Sophie, who nodded.

Evan didn't say anything, but Mercy knew he was thinking that Paige had a good-size chunk of money in her pocket.

"Who's her boyfriend?" Mercy asked, her gaze going from one girl to the other.

Both shook their heads emphatically. "No one," said Jordyn as Sophie said, "She's not seeing anyone."

"Then she didn't tell you about him," said Mercy. "Is that the Paige you know? Would she keep secrets?"

The heads shook again. "Never," said Jordyn. "We tell each other everything."

Something flickered in Sophie's eyes and vanished.

Not everything.

Mercy wondered if she should interview Sophie alone.

"Why would she keep a guy secret from her friends?" Mercy asked, continuing to question them as if the mystery man existed. "Could she be seeing a married man?"

Jordyn's jaw dropped open and distaste crossed Sophie's face. "No," they said simultaneously.

"Surely she's talked to one of you about someone she's interested in or attracted to. Maybe someone at the college. That could be part of the reason she continues to go to campus."

Jordyn scowled but concern filled Sophie's eyes. "I think she's texting someone," Sophie admitted. "She was smiling at her phone when I was late to meet her at Starbucks a while back—a special smile, you know? I asked who it was, and she said 'No one.' I didn't really believe her—it wasn't the first time she's recently sorta tipped her phone away after getting a text. I figured she'd just started talking to a guy, and she'd tell us once she got to know him better. It's like that sometimes." She turned to Jordyn. "I don't tell either of you about guys I've met until I think it could go somewhere."

Now we're getting some answers.

"Did she spend time with a particular guy when you went to the club recently? Did she seem especially interested in anyone?"

"No, we stuck together almost the entire time," said Sophie. "If she's met him in person, I don't know about it."

"What about new interests? Has she mentioned a new activity she hadn't done before?" asked Mercy. "Like suddenly taking up tennis or hiking."

The young women considered, but neither could think of anything.

Evan leaned toward Mercy. "Can I talk to you a minute?"

She stood. "I think we're done for now, girls. But I'd like both of you to stay longer in case we have more questions. Please don't talk about this to anyone until we say so, OK?"

The girls solemnly nodded in unison.

Mercy followed Evan out to the middle of the perfectly green lawn, approving that he wanted to talk away from the house. And away from the ten cameras.

He stopped and faced her, his brown eyes serious. "Paige definitely decided to leave."

"But not on her own," said Mercy. "I'm convinced someone was here. Someone she wanted to hide from her parents and everyone else, which is why she taped the cameras."

Evan was grim. "How much older do you think he is?"

"I don't want to guess—hopefully he's a seventeen-year-old she met at the club."

"Someone older could have manipulated her into leaving so they could get to the senator. I wouldn't be surprised if he got a ransom call."

"I'll get his office phones covered," said Mercy. "That would be the most likely place for a call. I'll take care of their cell phones too. Even Finn's. I don't want to leave anything uncovered."

"Paige could have been manipulated for the money," added Evan. "She has nearly ten thousand dollars. That could be his motivation."

"A lot of possibilities."

"Let's check in with the parents again," said Evan, turning back to the house.

Adam and Denise were on the patio, watching them. Adam had his arm around his wife's shoulders. From this distance, they appeared to be a happy couple. But as Mercy drew closer, the pain in their eyes and stiffness in their postures told a different story.

Those poor people.

We've got to find Paige.

Chapter 7

MERCY

Late that evening, Mercy joined Evan in a small conference room at the Deschutes County Sheriff's Department.

"I haven't worked in this room before," she said as she walked in. "You've got sofas!" She dropped her bag on an overstuffed gray sofa.

"Don't sit on that one," Evan warned.

Mercy studied the piece of furniture, not seeing a problem. "Why?"

Evan made a sour face. "Trust me."

She removed her bag, joined him at the table, and pulled out her laptop. She was tempted to press for more information about the sofa, but she suspected it had something to do with vomit, semen, or urine. She didn't want to know.

"The senator sent me all his recorded security camera video for the last forty-eight hours," Evan told her. "Ten cameras. They're not motion activated, so they record all the time."

"Four hundred and eighty hours of video. How fast can we fast-forward?"

"I've started, and it's going pretty quick," said Evan. "Most of the time there is no one in the footage, so I only slow it when someone enters."

"Did your deputies find any neighbors that had security cameras with a view of the senator's road?" asked Mercy. The homes were far apart and sat back from the main road, but deputies had been sent to knock on doors.

"I received one that has a distant view. The deputy said a few vehicles go by in the window of time, but license plates and car makes and models aren't clear, so I'm not optimistic. We can watch it after we finish the senator's coverage."

"Did you hear from the wireless carrier about Paige's cell phone records yet?" Mercy asked, reviewing a to-do checklist.

Evan checked his email. "Not yet."

"Paige's laptop and phone are on their way to the lab. I marked them priority."

"But did you slip in a hundred-dollar bill for the lab director? Everyone wants priority."

"No," Mercy admitted, knowing how busy the lab was. "I should have sent Kaylie's lemon bars as a bribe."

Evan immediately eyed her bag. "I thought I smelled something. What'd you bring?"

Her niece, Kaylie, owned a coffee shop known for its baked goods. The day-old leftovers were a hot commodity at Mercy's office and her husband Truman's police department.

"Lemon bars, of course." She took one out of a container and then slid it to Evan, enjoying how his eyes lit up. "Did you ask the senator's team about any issues with constituents or hate mail?" she asked, then bit into a lemony piece of heaven.

"Yes." Evan brushed away the crumbs on his shirt. "Hate mail is a daily thing. I asked if any specifically mentioned Paige, and they showed me some of the most disgusting things I've ever read. What is wrong with people? She's a child."

"She's beautiful and comes from wealth," said Mercy. She Googled the senator's family and studied the photos. "That makes some people very bitter and angry. Especially if they hate the senator's politics." She clicked on a photo of Denise Holcroft, which took her to a women's fitness magazine article about Denise's workout routine. Mercy marveled again at how Paige was a dead ringer for her mother. She scanned the article and immediately felt tired after reading the amount of time Denise spent on fitness.

Mercy was a believer in maintaining fitness and health. Her father had emphasized it as long as she could remember. She had grown up in a family of preppers and survivalists who spent their lives preparing in case the world fell apart. Besides stocking up on food and fuel, taking care of personal health was important. Doctors, hospitals, and medications might not be around if TEOTWAWKI (the end of the world as we know it) occurred.

But Denise Holcroft took fitness to a different level.

Mercy browsed her Google results, skimming quickly, looking for anything beyond what would be expected from news outlets. There were several pictures of the family at official events. Dressed up, smiling, and raising their arms in perfect waves. Paige seemed to be enjoying herself in most of the photos. Denise looked happy but slightly stressed, and Finn appeared a little robotic—as if he were only doing what his parents wanted.

That's what I'd expect from a teenage boy.

She continued to scroll, quickly passing through ten pages of results. The websites grew a little more obscure and the posts older as she scanned.

Do I expect to find a personal diatribe against the senator?

Maybe.

"I dug into the family a little bit," said Evan. "There are no records of police calls to the home. I can't even find a traffic ticket. The kids appear to be good students. It's a squeaky-clean family."

"As a senator's family needs to be. Otherwise every wrong move is amplified and dissected in the media. I wonder how much pressure that puts on the kids. They must live with a perpetual fear of screwing up."

"Maybe Paige got fed up with the stress and left."

"Possibly." Mercy thought Paige's friends would have said if she struggled with the constant need to walk a narrow line. "Can we divide up the surveillance videos? Make it go twice as fast?"

"They're on the department's server. You won't be able to access it with your laptop." Evan's gaze was glued to his screen. "Come look at this."

Mercy rolled her chair next to Evan's. He was simultaneously fast-forwarding four video feeds on his screen. In the lower right one, Paige sat at the counter in the kitchen, speedily eating a sandwich, her gaze never leaving her phone. The senator suddenly dashed through the kitchen. Evan halted that feed, backed up, and they watched the senator walk through the kitchen at a normal pace. He said something to Paige, who nodded but didn't look up from her phone. Evan and Mercy continued to watch Paige eat at a normal speed. A minute later Paige put her plate in the sink, took a bottle of water out of the fridge, and left the kitchen. The time on the video showed 12:17. Evan sped it up again.

In the camera view of the driveway, an SUV shot backward out of the garage, reversed, and then sped out of view toward the street. Evan backed it up and they watched the SUV move at a normal pace. The senator wasn't visible, but Denise Holcroft was easy to spot in the front passenger's seat.

In the living room camera, Paige briefly flashed in and out of view in the bottom corner, and Evan backed up and froze on her image. "She changed her clothes," he said.

Paige had been in a tank top and shorts as she ate in the kitchen. Now she wore a little sundress and had a large pink flower behind one ear. Her hair was down instead of the earlier ponytail.

"She dressed up," said Mercy. "Definitely going to meet someone. To place the tape over those cameras, she'll need a ladder. I guess she'll climb it in that dress."

"If she's the one who places the tape."

"Run it again."

Evan advanced the living room video bit by bit, stopping for several seconds to study the brief flash of the girl. Neither of her hands were in the video, disappointing Mercy, who wanted to see the nails. The camera in the kitchen had been too far away to see fingernail polish.

Mercy turned her gaze to the driveway and entrance cameras, watching the time, knowing they would go black sometime after one. "What do the other six views show?" she asked Evan.

"Two cameras cover the backyard and patio, and then the other two sides of the home each have one. There's an inside view of the front entrance and foyer, and another is of a long hallway. I'm not sure exactly where that hall is in the house."

"I have the home's floor plan," Mercy said.

Evan's surprised gaze met hers. "How did you get that?"

"I nicely asked one of the senator's assistants." She opened the email. "Looks like there are a couple of long hallways. This one leads to a wing with a huge primary suite. This other hallway leads to four bedrooms. We'll have to view the video to figure out which hallway it is."

The outside entrance camera suddenly went dark. Evan paused the other views, enlarged the entrance one, and backed it up. In slow motion, they watched the scene they'd already seen with the senator.

"Definitely a pink fingernail," said Mercy. "I can't see the color in the other views of her, but it does coordinate with that dress she just put on. And the flower in her hair."

Evan closed out the video and they watched the same thing happen to the driveway view—but no fingernails came into sight. "Assuming it's her, she knew how to approach both cameras without being seen." He closed out the cameras that had gone black and replaced them with two new camera views. One was the hallway and the other was an outdoor view of one of the sides of the home. "I doubt the outside will show much," Evan said. "There's no walkway or doors."

Mercy studied the number of doorways in the hallway view and compared it to her floor plan of the home. "The hall is the one with multiple bedrooms, not the primary suite."

Paige was seen passing through the hall dozens of times. Mercy kept expecting to see Finn until she recalled he'd spent the two previous nights at a friend's home. She made a note to contact the friend and his family. Once the clock passed 1:15, Paige wasn't seen again. The next day near eleven a.m., her mother knocked several times on her door, finally opening it and stepping inside. She then checked the other rooms in the hall. Her husband did the same an hour later. Then Evan showed up in the hall, soon followed by Finn strolling to his bedroom with a backpack, returning from his friend's. Then the view showed Mercy and Evan moving down the hall to check Paige's bedroom.

Something pricked at the back of Mercy's brain as she watched people move through the hallway, but she couldn't put her finger on it. They watched the rest of the views. Denise paced through the living room and kitchen, her phone to her ear, constantly in motion, agitation growing in her expression. The outdoor views of the home's sides showed nothing, but the parents were seen occasionally on the backyard patio, and eventually Mercy and Evan appeared there too.

"Go back to the hallway," said Mercy. "You can speed it up." She watched again as people dashed up and down the hall. She frowned as the realization hit her.

Where's Paige?

"We don't see Paige in her dress," said Mercy. "She walks to her room after her lunch, steps into the bathroom two doors down, and then goes back to her room still wearing shorts. We know she changed her clothes—we saw the dress, but she's not seen coming out of the room in it." She turned to Evan. "Could this feed have been edited?"

He shook his head. "I was watching the clock. Nothing is missing."

Mercy looked at the floor plan. "Oh, I see. Her room has a door that connects to a bonus room. I knew that. I opened the door when we searched her room."

"The room with the pool table and TV," added Evan.

"She must have gone through there after she changed." Mercy studied the floor plan. "But she used the hallway at least a dozen times before that. It's a much longer walk to the living room, where we briefly saw her. She didn't—"

"Want to be on camera in the dress for some reason," Evan finished. "Do you think another person was in the house with her?"

"I don't think so," said Mercy. "All outside doors were covered by cameras. We would have seen someone enter. I think she was alone until she taped over the cameras. She must have misjudged the angle of the camera in the living room, accidentally letting us see that flash of her in a dress. I bet she was also pulling her suitcase and didn't want it seen. Next she could have made it to the garage, opened the rolling doors, brought out a ladder, and covered the cameras—all without being on camera."

"So her parents wouldn't immediately realize that she left on her own? She's a senator's daughter. She had to know that simply vanishing would create a quick law enforcement response."

"Maybe that's what she wanted for some reason." Mercy shrugged. "Let's see the neighbor's coverage of the street. It's about a mile from Paige's house."

Evan made a few clicks and opened a video. Mercy watched an Amazon delivery vehicle go by. The deputy was right. The distance was too far and the angle was wrong to catch any plates. Several minutes passed. Then a smaller SUV and a pickup went by. A driver was visible in each one, but Mercy couldn't even tell if they were male or female.

"Wrong direction anyway," Evan commented. "The street dead-ends just beyond the senator's home. Paige had to go south."

Unless she went to a neighbor's home and never passed this camera. Could she be that close?

Three vehicles passed in the right direction. Mercy checked the clock. All three were in the time window. Evan managed to zoom in slightly but lost too much clarity. Both watched silently, and Mercy realized the video wouldn't be helpful until they had a vehicle description to compare to the passing vehicles. A sedan drove by. "Back it up," Mercy said, but Evan had already moved to do so.

They leaned closer to the screen as it restarted in slow motion.

Something pink was on the side of the passenger's head.

Paige's flower.

Chapter 8

BREE

Day 2

Late the next morning, Bree parked at the ME's office next to a beat-up SUV with a license plate that read BUG GUY.

In the passenger seat, Juarez asked, "Who is that?"

"I assume that's the entomologist," Bree said. The young deputy had promise, but he needed experience. So Bree had brought him along.

"You've seen an autopsy, right?" she asked.

"Uh. Not since the academy." He glanced out the side window, as if embarrassed.

She remembered him gagging at the scene. "Don't vomit in the autopsy suite. If you need to step out, do so before it gets to that point. No one will care if you leave. There's no shame in it. Witnessing an autopsy can be overwhelming, especially if you're not used to it. The important thing is that you don't contaminate any evidence."

"But there's only one way to get used to it, right?" he asked in a grim tone.

"Unfortunately."

"Is it OK if I ask questions?"

"Definitely," Bree said.

They signed in, suited up, and entered the autopsy suite. The bodies occupied two stainless-steel autopsy tables. On a long worktable against the wall, the suitcases, plastic bag, and several sections of cut rope had been laid out on white sheets.

Dr. Jones was conferring with a chubby man in PPE from booties to cap. Unlike Bree and the ME, he wore only a face shield, no mask. Did the smell not affect him? Considering the level of decomp, Bree was grateful for her N95 respirator.

"Sheriff," the ME called. "This is Doug Nimoy."

"Call me Spider," he said.

Okaaay. Better than Maggot.

"Spider." Bree nodded as she approached but didn't offer a hand.

He held a small plastic container, the kind you'd use to transport a hermit crab. This one contained maggots feeding on a chunk of meat. "These are great." He bounced on his toes with enthusiasm, then turned bright eyes to Bree. "Dr. Jones gave them liver. They love that." His voice held affection, as if he were talking about his pets.

"Glad to hear it," Bree said. "You'll be able to narrow our postmortem interval?"

Spider raised the container. "The insects develop on a predictable schedule. So I'll be able to tell you how long the body was exposed to insect activity. But Dr. Jones isn't so sure these remains were dumped right away. If a body is kept in some kind of protected environment for a while, those time periods might not match."

Standing at Bree's flank, Juarez cleared his throat. "How will you do that? Do you dissect them?"

Spider set down the container and faced them, clasping his hands in excitement. "Fly pupae are opaque, so determining the age of the metamorphosing insect inside is hard. It's evidence. On principle we don't want to destroy it by cutting it open. Instead, we use a micro-CT scan."

Juarez nodded. Behind the face shield and mask, his olive skin looked gray.

"I'll just take these back to the lab." Humming, Spider loaded the containers in a cardboard box and carried them out of the suite.

Dr. Jones waved a hand toward the worktable. "The suitcases are unremarkable, common brands. One is Samsonite. The other is American Tourister. Both are empty except for the remains. No luggage tags. No other identifying marks."

Bree scanned them. They didn't look new, but then they'd been sitting outside. Both were large bags, black, with zipper closures and spinner-type wheels. She doubted they'd be traceable, but they'd try.

"The autopsies are almost complete." Dr. Jones gestured for Bree and Juarez to approach the bodies. Bree walked to the first table. Juarez shuffled forward but stayed two steps behind her shoulder. "I'll give you the highlights before I get back to it."

The ME indicated the first body, a small figure of rotting flesh. Bone shone through in places, gleaming under the glare of overhead lights. "The victim is definitely female. As expected, when we removed her from the suitcase, she was curled in a fetal position." Dr. Jones indicated a wheeled stand, where a laptop computer displayed digital photographs. "Her hands were bound behind her back. There was also a rope around her neck. We clamped the rope on each side of the knots and then cut the rope outside those clamps to preserve the knots themselves. The rope itself is a natural fiber, unfortunately a very common type."

Bree's gaze was drawn to the finger- and toenails, both painted the same shade of Barbie Pink. The nail polish again brought Kayla to mind, and Bree's gut twisted.

"She currently weighs seventy-seven pounds. I estimate she was one hundred to one hundred five pounds when alive." Decomposition and insect predation had consumed a good portion of her flesh. Dr. Jones pointed at the chest, where the Y-incision had been stapled closed. "She has a unique tattoo."

Bree leaned closer. "A heart formed by chain links?"

"That's what it looks like to me," Dr. Jones said. "The other body has the same tattoo, in the same location."

Bree glanced over, then turned back. "Would you forward photos of the tattoos?"

"Of course." Dr. Jones pointed to the mouth. "As you can see, there's a ball gag in her mouth."

The nail polish and the ball gag seemed incongruous. One appeared girly, almost childish, the other sexually deviant. The juxtaposition evoked a swirl of emotions.

Next to her, Juarez gagged and bolted for the door. Bree heard the door swing open and shut.

Dr. Jones didn't miss a beat. "Given the rope and ball gag, erotic asphyxia comes to mind, as does strangulation, but she's too decomposed to determine cause of death. Manner of death is, clearly, homicide."

Dr. Jones gently worked the rubber ball out from between the teeth. Setting it aside, she repositioned the gooseneck light to shine inside the mouth. "Teeth are in good condition. She had dental work, probably braces, some composite fillings."

"So, middle- or upper-class economic status," Bree said.

"Probably," Dr. Jones agreed. "It also means she'll have dental records somewhere."

"I might have them right here," a woman said.

Bree pivoted to see a tall woman in PPE standing just inside the door. She must have come in when Juarez exited. Her face was obscured by the N95 mask, but her eyes were an intense green.

Dr. Jones didn't look up. "And you are?"

"FBI Special Agent Kilpatrick. I'm looking for Sheriff Taggert."

"That's me." Bree straightened. She didn't recognize the agent's name. "You're not from the Albany FBI office."

"Oregon." Behind the mask, the agent's gaze sharpened.

What's going on?

Why would an agent from Oregon be looking for her? Bree's gaze dropped to the body on the table, the only possible reason Agent Kilpatrick would be here. "Since you brought dental records, can I assume you're here about this case?"

Kilpatrick's eyes went flat. "Yes."

"You're looking for someone," Bree said.

"Yes." The agent looked at the ME. "Do you have an age?"

Dr. Jones glanced at Bree, who gave a small nod. "I estimate sixteen to twenty-five."

"How long has she been dead?" asked Kilpatrick.

"I'm not sure yet," Dr. Jones said. "Waiting on some tests."

"Could she have died within the last two weeks?" asked Kilpatrick.

The ME's head waggled. Then she said, "It's possible."

Kilpatrick went very still.

"Who are you looking for?" asked Bree. *Do I have to drag every fact out of this agent?*

"I can't tell you," she said after a pause.

Bree bristled. *What the fuck?* The FBI didn't normally insert themselves into murder investigations. A sense of foreboding washed over Bree. "This is related to a case you're already working?"

"Maybe," Kilpatrick said.

They stared at each other for a long breath. *Is she really not going to say any more?*

Dr. Jones broke the awkward silence. "You checked in with your credentials out front?"

"Yes," Kilpatrick said.

"Then you two can work out your business later. I need to get back to work. We have another body to discuss, and I have more dead waiting their turn." Dr. Jones stepped over to the second table. Bree followed, and Kilpatrick approached to stand next to Bree.

Reluctantly, Bree put aside her irritation and turned her attention back to the case. But the agent would have plenty of questions to answer when it was over.

Chapter 9

MERCY

Mercy studied the Randolph County sheriff out of the corner of her eye as they stood next to the second body. Though of average height, Bree Taggert stood tall and confident. Mercy couldn't see much of the sheriff, but she guessed they were close in age. Randolph County appeared to have its share of rural areas, and Mercy suspected Taggert had dealt with a lot of sexism during her career. But she had made it to the top.

Not many women become sheriff. Good for her.

Mercy felt guilty—but not very—that she couldn't share the details of Paige Holcroft's disappearance with the sheriff. Not yet. Taggert's gaze had turned to stone when Mercy refused to answer her questions. But Mercy knew nothing about the type of person the sheriff was. She wouldn't risk Paige's case getting to the media.

She hoped these autopsies would provide answers.

Mercy had taken a hard look at the face on the first body, seeking hints of Paige in the features, but the decomposition was too advanced. The long brown hair was matted with gunk, its length hard to determine.

On the table before her, the second victim's face was also not identifiable.

Dr. Jones caught Mercy's gaze. "This body has been dead much longer than two weeks."

Mercy looked at the pink nails that matched the first victim's. And the shade Mercy had seen on the Holcrofts' security camera.

If Paige is the first body, she's tied to this woman somehow.

"I'm still interested," Mercy said. "But before you tell us about the second, could you compare these dental films to the first victim?"

"I haven't taken dental films yet," said the medical examiner. "I was waiting to remove the ball gag so Sheriff Taggert could watch." She gestured at her assistant. "Could you start the films?" He nodded.

Mercy clenched the file in her hands.

I'm so close to an answer.

"I'm not an odontologist," Dr. Jones said firmly, looking Mercy in the eye. "That exam will be done later this afternoon. How current are your films?"

"Three months."

Dr. Jones nodded. "That will be helpful. Teeth usually don't change much in three months."

"Now can we discuss the second vic?" Sheriff Taggert asked.

Dr. Jones launched into a briefing, and Mercy tried to pay attention.

Mercy's last two weeks had been a blur of digging for leads and scrambling to keep Paige's disappearance out of the media. She didn't believe the senator was doing the right thing refusing to go public—they needed more leads. His wife had begged him to take it public too, but he'd held firm. The lead Mercy was currently following had come from Paige's cell phone records. Numerous calls had been made to and from an upstate New York phone number. But the number had led nowhere specific. It'd belonged to a burner phone and a dead end.

Mercy had been focused on other leads when her office's data analyst had discovered an online article about a Randolph County news conference yesterday announcing two dead women found in suitcases.

When Mercy heard about the nail polish, hair color, and the fact that the women could be young, she got on a plane.

She'd rented a car at the Albany airport, made some calls, and learned that the sheriff was at the medical examiner's office for the women's autopsies, so she'd driven straight there.

Mercy glanced back at the first body. If that was Paige, she was a long way from home.

Mercy's team had combed reports and video from Oregon airports and bus and train stations with no results. It had been frustrating work since Paige was most likely using a different name and had possibly acquired new ID.

Mercy studied the second body. She was shrunken and leathery, her skin in shades of black and brown with some white patches that looked like mold. She looked as if she'd been baked.

"Like the first body, we cut off the ropes, protecting the knots for forensics," Dr. Jones was saying as she worked the second woman's ball gag out of the mouth. "Her hands were bound behind her with the rope coiled around them several times. She is eighty-four pounds and around five foot two. I think she's a little older than our first victim. I estimate her to be in her late twenties to late thirties. And as I said earlier, she has the same tattoo in the same place as the first victim."

"Where?" asked Mercy, realizing her late arrival had made her miss something important.

"Right over the heart," said Dr. Jones, indicating a darker area.

Mercy moved closer to see. The tattoo was made of chain links in the shape of a heart.

Why do they have matching tattoos?

Paige's mother had said she didn't have tattoos. But Paige could have kept one a secret.

"Can you tell the cause of death?" asked the sheriff.

"Her hyoid bone was broken," said Dr. Jones. "So strangulation is a strong possibility."

"How long has she been dead?" Mercy asked.

"I don't know yet," said the doctor. "She's partially mummified. That's why she looks so dried out. Testing will help, but I don't know how accurate it will be at this advanced stage of mummification."

"How does mummification happen?" asked the sheriff.

"Usually dry air," said the ME. "Extreme cold can do it. Or hot temperatures and an arid environment. We're too humid around here. Most likely this happened in an enclosure of some sort."

"They were found outdoors in the same location," said Mercy. "But they came from different types of environments?"

"Yes. The decomposition of the first woman is what I would expect to find on a body that had been abandoned in our current weather."

"What happened to this woman's hands?" asked Mercy. The second victim's fingers were swollen and much paler than the rest of the body.

"We rehydrated her fingers. The mummification simply dried her fingers; they didn't decompose," said Dr. Jones. "So we managed to get fingerprints. We'll run them soon."

"Nice work," said Mercy. The woman had died too long ago to be Paige, but Mercy still cared and hoped that she could be identified.

The sheriff turned to Mercy. "This can't be your girl," she stated.

"Correct."

"But the first one could be?" Taggert asked, impatience in her tone.

"Maybe." Mercy did not like keeping her cards so close to her chest. *I have no choice right now.*

Taggert's hazel gaze bored through her. "Let's talk in my office."

"Gladly."

But I can't tell you much else.

Chapter 10

Bree

Bree stalked into the sheriff's station, irritation fueling her stride, with Juarez and Kilpatrick in her wake.

"Juarez, show Agent Kilpatrick to the conference room, then update the NCIC, NamUs, and ViCAP queries."

"Yes, ma'am," he said.

Bree turned to the agent. "I have to check in with my admin. I'll join you in a few minutes."

Juarez led the agent away. Bree spotted Todd at a computer and stopped to give him a quick recap on the autopsies.

Todd's gaze tracked the agent's exit from the squad room. "What's the deal with the FBI?"

"I don't know. Yet." Bree went into her office to check her messages. Marge appeared in her doorway before Bree's butt hit her chair.

Marge closed the door. "Who is that?"

"FBI Special Agent Kilpatrick."

Marge didn't respond.

"I've never had an agent show up with no notification." And Bree didn't like it. Not at all.

Marge said, "I'll dig up some info on Agent Kilpatrick."

"Thanks, Marge." Bree scanned her email and fanned her pink message slips across the desk. A year and a half into the job, and the number of people in Grey's Hollow who wouldn't use email or voice mail still amazed her. "Do I need to address any of these right now?"

"The fire marshal initiated a complete fire ban until this weather breaks. No campfires, brush burning, fireworks, et cetera."

"Good."

"The rest of the messages can wait." Marge disappeared as stealthily as she'd appeared.

Bree pushed off her desk and walked to the conference room, where Todd had already started the murder board. He'd hung a row of crime scene photos with magnets. She poked her head into the room. Agent Kilpatrick was studying the board.

"Coffee?"

Kilpatrick turned and nodded. "Please."

"Sugar, cream?"

"Heavy cream if you have it."

Bree almost laughed. "We aren't that fancy here."

"Black is fine."

Bree went to the break room, poured two mugs of coffee, and carried them back to the conference room. Handing a cup to Kilpatrick, she stood next to her and scanned the photos. Neither spoke for a few minutes. Full-color glossies emphasized each element separately: the scene as photographed from the road, the fly-covered suitcases, the outstretched hand.

Bree turned to the long table, where Todd had stacked printed reports and more crime scene photos. She eased into the chair at the head of the table. Kilpatrick selected a seat on Bree's right, facing the board.

Bree flattened a palm over the short stack of reports. "You can't tell me who you're looking for. What can you tell me?"

Kilpatrick didn't answer for a full breath. "It's a missing girl, but her disappearance isn't in the system."

Bree mulled that over for a few seconds. Her knee-jerk reaction was to demand information, but she sensed there would be no point. "She went missing in Oregon?"

"Yes."

Why would an FBI agent be unwilling to divulge details on a case she was working? Withholding information made the investigation more difficult for both of them.

"The case is politically sensitive?" Bree asked.

Agent Kilpatrick's poker face didn't budge, nor did she comment.

So Bree guessed the answer was yes. She reminded herself that her case wasn't a pissing contest. She had two dead women who deserved justice. While she didn't entirely trust the tight-lipped agent, she was a resource and Bree would use her.

She reached for the pile of crime scene photos and began dealing them out on the table. "Hopefully, the ME will be able to tell us if the first body is your missing woman. Until then, I have a complicated case and my investigator is out. This is a small operation here. So, while we wait, I'm going to pick your brain."

Surprise flickered in the agent's eyes for a nanosecond, then her poker face slid back into place. She shifted her attention to the photos.

Bree described the crime scene. "Have you ever seen anything like this before?"

Kilpatrick gave the photos her full attention. Her impassive expression yielded to interest as she flipped through the images. When she'd finished, she set them down. "No. I haven't."

"Thoughts?"

Kilpatrick lined up the edges of the photos. "The weight of a suitcase is about ten pounds. Loaded with a body, they would have weighed about ninety pounds each. Lifting them in and out of a vehicle would have taken some strength."

"Or multiple people." Bree got up and went to the board to write *strong killer or multiple killers.* "The matching tattoos suggest the killer inked them or had them done."

"Or at least chose the design," Mercy suggested. "My missing girl could have taken a design to a tattoo parlor in Oregon before she disappeared. The design looks pretty simple."

Bree had two extensive tattoos she'd designed to cover scars from a childhood dog mauling. She knew ink. "Simple, yes, but the fine-detail work is well done. Quality ink takes practice. My gut says these were done by an experienced artist." She wrote *matching tattoos* on the board. "If we show tattoo artists photos, they will recognize their own work. I'll assign a deputy to that. Maybe we can find someone local who inked at least one of these hearts."

"Tell me about the area where the bodies were found," Kilpatrick said.

"Echo Road is a back road. Some farms, a campground, and Echo Lake are within a few miles. The lake itself draws people for fishing, swimming, canoeing, et cetera. It's not one of the larger, popular lakes for tourists. This one is mostly used by locals. The suitcases sat below the road's grade."

"So possibly visible but not obvious."

"Yes. Keep in mind, the area is semirural, but we're only a few hours from New York City and Philadelphia. The area is more densely populated than it seems. We have our share of drugs, gang activity, human trafficking . . ." Bree wrote those three items on the list.

"Given the way these women were discarded like garbage, any of those would be plausible," Mercy said.

Bree's phone rang, and she glanced at the screen. "It's the ME." She answered the call. "You're on speaker, Dr. Jones. Agent Kilpatrick is also present."

"Good, that saves me a call. One, we have the results of the fingerprint comparison on the partially mummified body. The victim is

Vanessa Mullen, age thirty-one. She has a record. Two, the odontologist says the dental records Agent Kilpatrick brought do not match the other victim."

Mercy

Relief and disappointment hit Mercy simultaneously.

Paige is not that decomposed body.

Paige is still missing.

She noticed Taggert watching her closely, and she struggled to keep the emotions from showing on her face.

Taggert cleared her throat. "So neither woman is your victim," she said to Mercy.

"Correct." But Mercy suspected she was in the right place to find Paige. The cell phone records and the two victims' nail polish were impossible to ignore.

"Dr. Jones, is there anything else?" asked Taggert.

"That's all I've got for now. You'll receive my preliminary report in the morning." The ME ended the call.

Mercy sent Evan a quick text, letting him know the body wasn't Paige. She'd call him later to discuss the details.

Taggert opened her laptop. "I'll see if I can find relatives of Vanessa Mullen for a death notification. I prefer to do them in person."

"Look for a current photo," said Mercy. Taggert nodded, her focus on her screen. Mercy turned back to the board with the photos. She wanted to see what Vanessa Mullen had looked like before someone put her in a suitcase and left her on the side of the road.

Someone did a lot more to her than that.

Mercy peered closer at the hands of the two victims. The polish was definitely pink. But was it the same as Paige's?

Her gut said yes.

"I guess since neither are your victim, you'll be taking off?" Taggert said as she tapped on her keyboard.

"I'd like to stick around," said Mercy.

"Why?" Taggert raised her eyes, her gaze curious. "This is a dead end for you."

How much can I tell her?

"There's too much here that lines up with my victim. It's possible she may be with whoever dumped those women."

The sheriff stopped typing. "Start talking."

Mercy took a breath. "I'm looking for a seventeen-year-old girl. She's petite with long dark hair. In her cell phone records are dozens of calls to and from a burner phone with an upstate New York area code."

Taggert was listening closely.

"She vanished two weeks ago. She packed a suitcase but left her cell phone and laptop behind along with her ID. We have video of her as the passenger in a car. I believe she left willingly or else was threatened enough to hide it from her family. We started keeping an eye out for anything in this area that could involve her. When we read about the victims' details given at the press conference, I got on a plane."

"Sounds a little thin to send you across the US," said the sheriff.

"She recently started wearing nail polish that matches your victims'. She was wearing it when she vanished." Mercy raised a brow at Taggert.

"Jesus." Surprise lit up her face. "That'd be a clincher for me too. Now can you tell me who she is?"

"I can't. I'd like to, but I can't yet. You'll have to trust me on this. As soon as I get approval, you'll be the first to know."

"You stroll in here and ask me to trust you? I don't *know* you," said Taggert.

"I don't know you either."

The women eyed each other for a long moment. Mercy was starting to sense she could trust the sheriff. Taggert was showing herself to be capable and clearly cared about finding out what happened to her victims.

But what does she think of me?

Mercy's mouth quirked. She was a fed who'd shown up without notice at a murder investigation and refused to share details. Mercy would be annoyed and suspicious too. "I'm offering FBI resources to help you find who murdered these women. I'm not here to take over your case. You are the lead, but I want to be on scene and informed of developments."

She watched Taggert weigh her offer. She suspected the sheriff would like to tell her to step back, but the opportunity for extra manpower from the FBI was too good to pass up.

"I think my missing girl is here," Mercy said softly. "I don't want her to end up like those other women."

If she isn't already dead.

The sheriff looked back at her screen. "I have an address for Vanessa Mullen's husband. You can go with me to notify him in the morning."

I guess that means she accepted my offer.

"Vanessa Mullen is thirty-one and has an extensive arrest record," continued Taggert. "Prostitution, drug possession, shoplifting. Her booking photos show a gaunt woman with a lot of facial sores."

Mercy moved to look over the sheriff's shoulder. "Meth. Face picking."

"Yep." Taggert opened another window. "Her driver's license photo from six years ago is better."

Mercy agreed. Vanessa's face was fuller and she had a sincere smile.

What happened to you?

"Is there a missing persons report?" she asked the sheriff.

"Her husband reported her missing six months ago. He reported it to Scarlet Falls PD. Here it says there were a couple of follow-ups but no results."

"He's her *ex*-husband," Mercy noted, reading over Taggert's shoulder. "Is that a restraining order?"

"Yes. He filed it nearly three years ago *against her*. She was required to stay away from the house and their two kids." Taggert tapped her fingers on the table. "Tomorrow's conversation should be interesting."

Mercy silently agreed.

I have several questions for the ex-husband.

Chapter 11

PAIGE

This isn't what he promised.

He promised fun. He promised love. He promised forever.

It was good for the first week as we drove across the US. He was caring and funny, and I felt like the only woman in the world. The dinner at the nice restaurants, the new sexy dresses. I saw the gleam in his eye as I modeled for him at the store. His touch thrilled me, and he promised to ease me into the life we both wanted.

The world was new to me. I'd read about it and then gone searching for it online.

And I found a culture of people who excited me and stoked my dreams. I wanted more than anything to belong to him, be controlled by him, submit to him. He'd care for me, give me the attention I never received at home. I craved the pain with the soft kisses of healing. And he told me he'd do that for me, but I had to stay with him forever—as his wife.

It took a few weeks of phone calls and promises, but once I agreed, I realized I wanted to be with him *now*. And I wanted that symbol of his devotion on my skin, proof we were committed.

When I reached his home, I knew he'd lied.

His home was disgusting, the furniture stained, and the place reeked so bad it made me gag. After he took all my cash, he immediately made me strip and tied me to the bed. I don't know how many days went by before he let me get dressed. He ordered me to put on the dress he'd bought. I obeyed with shaking hands, struggling to look him in the eye. Once it was zipped, he tied my hands again, thrust the ball gag in my mouth, and forced me to my knees. Then the pain began again.

The safe word was ignored.

Nothing about this is safe.

Chapter 12

Bree

Bree returned to her office after the FBI agent left the station.

She stopped at Todd's desk. He was reviewing reports on his computer. "Where's Juarez?"

"Out on patrol."

"I need to track down a tattoo." She showed him the photo forwarded from the ME's office. The fact that it was on a dead body wasn't apparent in the close-up. Despite the darkened skin, the tattoo details were clear.

Todd squinted at her phone screen. "Looks original."

"That's what I thought. Check NamUs, ViCAP, and NCIC for similar tats." Bree headed for her office.

Marge poked her head in the doorway. "I emailed you some articles about Agent Kilpatrick."

"General consensus?" Bree woke her computer.

"Seems like the real deal," Marge said. "I made some calls and double-checked her credentials."

Bree suppressed a smile. Of course she had. Marge trusted no one she didn't know personally, and she'd been working in the sheriff's office for more than three decades. She had more contacts than Bree did.

Marge had worked for a corrupt sheriff. She wouldn't completely trust formal channels. She'd want a variety of sources to get beneath FBI reports, official statements, and bureau speak. Marge would want to know what wasn't on the record.

If Marge said Kilpatrick was the real deal, then she was.

Bree opened the first link. Kilpatrick had spent five years with the Portland FBI office, mostly working domestic terrorism cases. She was currently assigned to the Bend satellite office, where she'd been for a couple of years. She had an excellent closed-case percentage and had been awarded the FBI Medal of Valor for an undercover assignment at an off-the-grid militia compound, which had led to Agent Kilpatrick going missing for ten days. During that time she was held captive and severely beaten, and barely managed to escape with her life. More recently, Agent Kilpatrick had caught domestic terrorists targeting electrical substations, for which she had received a commendation.

The FBI didn't hand out commendations like participation trophies.

Bree read more articles. From all the information, it seemed Marge's assessment had been accurate. Kilpatrick was an intelligent and effective agent. Whether Bree liked her on a personal level was irrelevant—and to be determined—but there was nothing to suggest Kilpatrick was corrupt.

Bree closed her computer. The agent had offered FBI resources for the investigation. She might not have told Bree who she was looking for, but she'd shared the information about the nail polish, hair, and local area code. Bree sensed she was doing what she could to cooperate, and clearly someone ranked above her was the reason she was holding back. The lack of information irritated Bree, but she would try not to hold it against Kilpatrick. The agent hadn't seemed happy about the situation either.

"Headed home?" Todd asked.

"I'm going to stop and see what my tattoo guy says about this photo." Bree packed her messenger bag with reports and her laptop, then went to the locker room to change into jeans and a tank. She drove to Hardcore Ink, a tattoo parlor that squatted on the edge of Grey's Hollow. The bell sounded as she walked in the front door.

Carlos, the owner, got up from his stool behind the counter. He set aside a sketchpad and pencil. He was skinny, with droopy pants and a black T-shirt. She knew him to be nearly thirty, but with almost no facial hair and the pasty-white skin of a person who never went outdoors, he could have passed for a teenager. He tugged on his waistband. The toothpick between his teeth bobbed when he talked. "Bree! Let me see how that touch-up looks."

Bree turned to show him the back of her shoulder. The dragonfly tattoo was brilliantly colored in shades of green and blue that almost appeared iridescent. Every now and then, the colors needed refreshing.

Carlos whistled around the toothpick. "That is gorgeous."

Bree looked over her shoulder. "You did a great job deepening the greens."

"What do you need? Please tell me you want a new tat." He smiled and rubbed his hands together. Excitement rolled off him in palpable waves. "I would love to design something for you."

"No. Sorry."

"Well, shit." His face fell.

"I need your professional opinion on a case."

Carlos brightened. "Always happy to help."

She pulled out her phone and showed him the screen.

He tilted his head. "It's not my work." His tone was defensive.

"Does it look familiar?"

He shook his head. "It's not the most original design I've ever seen." He sounded almost snobbish. "Pretty ordinary for a bondage tat. Themes usually involve chain links, thorns, whips, things like that."

Bondage as a theme made sense considering the killer also liked ball gags.

He looked closer. "But the work itself is good."

"A professional, then."

"Definitely."

"Can you ask your friends if they've done anything like this?"

"I can. You're looking for someone local?"

She thought about the fact that Kilpatrick had traced her missing person to a burner phone with a local area code. "My hunch would be within a reasonable driving distance, but I don't know for sure." She was just guessing.

Carlos twisted the toothpick, then pulled it out of his mouth and gestured with it. "Here's an idea. I can put this out on social media. Instagram is a good place to look, and there are private Facebook groups for artists. That will be the most efficient way of tracking this down. Can I post this pic online?"

"Yes, and thank you."

"No worries. I got you, Sheriff."

"You'll let me know if anyone claims the ink?"

"Yep."

Bree drove home, turned the horses out, and spent the next hour mucking stalls. When she'd finished, she was soaked with sweat, but the physical exhaustion felt good. She showered, dressed in shorts and a tee, and paced around the empty, too-quiet house for a while before settling on the back porch with the dogs once again.

Her phone buzzed, and she pulled it from her pocket, stupidly excited when she saw Matt's name on the screen. He'd been gone for only two days. She rolled her eyes at herself. "Hey."

"Hey yourself." His deep voice made her warm inside. "It's good to talk to you."

"Same," she admitted. "How's the trip?"

"Great." Enthusiasm rang in his voice. "We rappelled with the dogs in harnesses today. Tomorrow, we have a mock hasty search."

"I've missed you," she said. Usually he said it first.

"I miss you too, but I haven't showered since I left, so . . ."

She laughed. "Sounds awesome."

"What's going on there?"

She gave him a quick summary of the bodies found in the suitcases.

"This is bad timing. You need help?"

"Here's the thing. An FBI agent turned up out of the blue. Special Agent Kilpatrick."

"Huh?"

"Yeah," Bree said. "But she seems smart, so I'm going to use her."

"May as well."

"Right?"

"Kids are OK?" he asked.

"OK enough that I've only had one call from Kayla."

"That's great."

"I miss them too, though." Bree didn't say it was too quiet because she didn't want to jinx her life. Cops were ridiculously superstitious about their workloads.

"I miss you all." Matt's voice went husky. "But I'll see you next week."

The connection broke up, and they said hurried goodbyes. Bree lowered her phone. Sitting on her back porch with Matt at her side and the kids in bed would have seemed peaceful. Tonight, she was simply lonely.

Brody let out a long breath with a hint of whine.

"Seriously." Her hand trailed on Brody's thick ruff. "How did I live alone all those years?"

The big shepherd turned understanding brown eyes on her. At the sound of her voice, Ladybug bumped Bree's other hand, clearly jealous. Bree scratched behind her ears.

The answer was all too clear. In her single, childless previous life, she hadn't known what she'd been missing.

Chapter 13

MERCY

After unpacking in her motel room, Mercy opened a box of crackers, sat on the big bed with her laptop, and leaned against its headboard to work. She'd dumped the clothes she'd worn to the medical examiner's into a plastic bag and knotted it. Even though she hadn't been at the autopsies that long, the smell lingered. Her hair was still wet from the necessary shower to get the scent off her skin.

I don't know how that odor tunnels through the protective gear and into clothing.

She opened her computer. She had two goals for the evening: to call her husband, and to see what she could find about Sheriff Bree Taggert. Since Mercy would be working closely with the sheriff, she wanted to know what kind of person she was.

She propped up her cell phone on a book beside her and FaceTimed Truman. As it rang, she put the sheriff's name into a Google search.

Governor Appoints Former Philadelphia Homicide Detective to Replace Randolph County Sheriff was the first headline. Mercy's eyebrows rose, and Truman's face popped up on her cell before she could read any further.

"Hey," he said. Truman was in his office at the police department.

As usual, her stomach got little fluttery butterflies at the sight of him. Her husband was a good-looking man. Not to mention smart and kind and a hard-ass when needed as chief of police for their little city. The combination worked for her.

"What'd you find out?" he asked.

Mercy gave him a rundown of everything she'd learned that day. "I'm glad Paige wasn't one of the victims, but now I'm even more worried about her. She has to be connected to these murdered women."

"Is the sheriff helpful?"

Mercy looked at the article about Bree Taggert on her laptop. "So far she seems very competent." Scanning the story, she was surprised to learn the sheriff before Taggert had killed himself after serving for two decades. The story strongly alluded to long-term, deep-seated corruption during his time in office.

"She?" asked Truman. "The sheriff is a woman? That's impressive."

"I thought so too. She's about my age, and from what I've seen so far, she's good at the position." Her interest piqued, Mercy wanted to continue the deep dive into the sheriff's background, but instead she focused on Truman's face. "How are the kids?"

He grinned. "Ollie got sunburned real bad, which put Kaylie in *I told you so* mode, and he's not appreciating it. How are you liking New York?"

"The humidity is ridiculous, and they're in the middle of a heat wave. I haven't experienced this sort of weather since I was at Quantico. And the mosquitoes!" She shuddered. "I swear some are the size of hummingbirds."

"Any new leads from Detective Bolton out here?" Truman asked.

"No. Last I talked with him, he was waiting on computer forensics from Paige's laptop. The senator still wants silence about her disappearance. I can't believe the story hasn't leaked yet. It's been more than two weeks."

"You think they should go to the media to ask for sightings of Paige?"

Mercy shook her head. "I don't feel that way anymore. I'm nearly certain she's not in Oregon. I think she's in New York."

"It's a US senator's daughter. The story would be national, not local."

Mercy cringed. "Can you imagine trying to work a case with national media attention?"

"Yes," Truman stated, a wry look on his face.

"That's right. You've been there." Truman's tiny town had been over-run with national media during a past investigation. It'd made his work near impossible and threatened his sanity.

"Does the sheriff know who you're looking for?" he asked.

"Not yet." Guilt tightened her throat. "I feel horrid keeping Paige's name from her. I'd want to know who it was if I was in her shoes. I don't know how long her patience will last."

Truman glanced away from the camera. "I'll be right there," he told someone off-screen and then looked back at her. "Gotta go."

"I love you," she told him, feeling a tiny pang in her heart.

I miss him already.

"Love you too." He vanished.

Mercy turned back to her search on Sheriff Taggert, clicking on link after link as she munched on her crackers.

How did the sheriff go from Philadelphia to New York?

Reading further, she discovered Taggert had grown up in Randolph County and then returned after her sister's murder—which she solved, catching the attention of the governor. Her number of closed cases in Philadelphia was impressive. Surprise shot through Mercy as she read that Taggert was the guardian of her sister's kids.

Just like I became Kaylie's guardian when my brother was killed.

Her admiration for the sheriff grew. She read on, skimming articles about Taggert's recent cases. Mercy paused on an article, reading that

Taggert's father had shot her mother when the sheriff was eight and then killed himself. The eight-year-old had called 911 and then hidden her younger siblings under the back porch. Investigators were convinced that the father would have shot the entire family if he had been able to find the children.

Jesus.

Mercy closed her laptop. She'd read enough. She set aside her crackers, her appetite gone, haunted by a vision of a young girl cowering under a porch, protecting her siblings as her father raged through their home.

She exhaled, seeing the sheriff in a new light.

I think we'll get along just fine.

Chapter 14

BREE

Day 3

In the sheriff's station parking lot, Bree waited behind the wheel of her official SUV while Kilpatrick slid into the passenger seat. At eight in the morning, the sun already beat down like a heat lamp. Bree handed a take-out coffee cup across the console. "Heavy cream."

Kilpatrick smiled. "Thank you."

Bree did not comment on the fancy concoction, as she was currently drinking a cappuccino dusted with cinnamon. She followed the GPS directions, and they sipped in contented silence for a few minutes. Vanessa Mullen's ex lived in Scarlet Falls, about fifteen minutes from the station.

Bree stopped at a traffic light. "Rick Mullen is thirty-two. No criminal record. He is squeaky clean. Doesn't even have a parking ticket on his license." She reached behind the seat, pulled a file from her messenger bag, and gave it to Kilpatrick.

Kilpatrick opened it and skimmed the pages. "Vanessa looked normal until three years ago."

"Makes you wonder what happened." Bree parked at the curb in front of a tidy yellow bungalow with freshly painted white trim. She stepped out of the vehicle and came around to join Kilpatrick on the sidewalk. They both glanced down at daisies drawn on the concrete with colored chalk. A child-size bike lay on its side, training wheel up, on the small, dandelion-spotted lawn.

Bree started up the driveway, passing a bottle of bubble solution with a pang in her chest. On the front porch, the door opened before she could knock. A little girl of about seven blinked at them through the screen door, then turned and screamed, "Daaaaad!"

A man with curly blond hair approached the door with a younger boy still clad in Spider-Man pajamas on his hip. Both children had dark hair and eyes like their mother.

"I'm Sheriff Taggert, and this is FBI Special Agent Kilpatrick." Bree hesitated. She didn't want to mention Vanessa with the children in earshot. "Are you Rick Mullen?"

"Yes." The man's face shuttered. Did he know or guess why they were there? He glanced at the children and then back at Bree. "Give me a moment?"

"Of course." Bree stepped aside.

He pulled a phone from his pocket, turned, and walked away from the door. A few minutes later, a young brunette woman in yoga pants and flip-flops came out of the house across the street. She eyed Bree's uniform as she went inside, gathered the kids, and led them back to her own place, distracting them with, "How about some pancakes?"

The little girl glanced back at Bree as the boy said, "Yay!"

When the kids disappeared into the neighbor's house, Mr. Mullen opened the screen door. "Come in. Can I assume this is about Vanessa?"

"Yes." Bree stepped over the threshold. The house looked like two small children lived there. A double jogging stroller was parked by the door. Wooden train tracks formed an oval on the wood floor. The kitchen table was strewn with coloring books and crayons. Bree walled off her emotions. Two children were going to learn their mother was dead today. She had to focus on the case, but the kids broke her heart. *Damn it. Kids don't deserve this.*

Mr. Mullen turned to press his back against the pantry and looked at them expectantly.

Bree said what needed to be said without preamble. "Vanessa's remains were found yesterday. We're sorry for your loss."

He seemed to deflate. "How did she die?"

"We're not sure. Have you watched the news?"

He shook his head.

"Her body was found in a suitcase on the side of Echo Road."

"Jesus." He pulled out a chair and sank into it. Bending at the waist, he buried his head in his hands for a long minute. He straightened, then exhaled. "What do I tell my kids?"

Bree had no answers.

"When was the last time you saw Vanessa?" Kilpatrick asked.

Mr. Mullen shook his head. "Seven, eight months ago. We were supposed to meet to make a plan for her to see the kids at Christmas and she never showed up or returned my texts."

"You're not surprised she's dead," Kilpatrick said.

"No." But he did look sad. "She'd sunk pretty low. She destroyed what we had a long time ago, but she's still my kids' mother."

Bree scanned a wall of framed photos and spotted one of Vanessa holding an infant. "What happened to Vanessa?"

He followed her gaze. "About a year after Billy was born, she started to act erratically. I found drugs in her purse. I didn't even know what it was. Had to ask a friend whose brother is a state trooper. Crystal meth." He shook his head, as if he still couldn't believe it. "I put her in rehab. But it didn't stick. One day, I came home and found her passed out. The kids were two and four. Billy had a plastic bag of meth in his hand. The bag was wet. I knew it had been in his mouth. I was done. I couldn't have her in the house anymore. It was too dangerous for the kids. I kicked her out and filed for divorce." He scrubbed both hands down his face and stared at the wall.

"That's a hard situation," Bree said.

"I found out later that she'd been on drugs in high school. She never told me." He sat back, his shoulders slumped. "She would stalk the day care center and show up at my mom's house. I had to switch from working in-office and go remote. Luckily, I'm in accounting, so it wasn't that hard. I was afraid to leave the kids with anyone. Then one day, she just disappeared. I knew something was wrong, so I filed a missing persons report, but the cops were honest. There was no proof anything bad had happened. Vanessa was an adult. They assumed she'd finally just moved on."

Kilpatrick sighed in empathy. "Where was she living at the time?"

"At a motel with some scumbag drug dealer named Jimmie." He sounded exhausted.

"Do you know the name of the motel?" Bree asked.

Mr. Mullen nodded. "Shady Acres."

Bree knew it all too well. "Do you know Jimmie's last name?"

"Elkins. I never met him. While the cops were dragging her away from the house for violating the restraining order, she yelled she was going to send Jimmie after me. Jimmie was going to beat my ass. Jimmie was a real man. Jimmie loved her. Things like that. The cops told me who he was. I just wanted to keep them both away from my kids."

"Does Vanessa have any other family who should be notified of her death?" Bree asked.

Mr. Mullen shook his head. "Her parents are dead, and she is—was—an only child."

Kilpatrick asked, "Did she have any friends?"

Mr. Mullen dragged a hand through his hair. "Years ago, yes. But after the meth . . . she was a whole different person."

Bree had seen the photos and agreed. She'd certainly looked like an entirely different person. "So there's no one she would confide in."

"No."

They left him alone in his kitchen, thinking of how he would tell his children their mother was dead.

Back in the vehicle, Bree glanced over at Kilpatrick. "You up for finding this Jimmie Elkins?"

"Oh, yeah."

Chapter 15

MERCY

As they drove to Shady Acres Motel, Mercy had an image stuck in her head of Vanessa's two-year-old sucking on a baggie of drugs. Vanessa was lucky she hadn't murdered her child.

Lucky? Vanessa is dead.

Mercy studied the screen of the sheriff's computer console in the SUV. Jimmie Elkins's weathered face stared back at her. For someone in his thirties, Jimmie showed a lot of mileage. The lines around his eyes and mouth were more common for a fifty-year-old, and his gaze was full of disdain and suspicion.

His record was extensive. Possession, dealing, domestic assault. He'd been in and out of prison since he was nineteen. He was not who you wanted your wife—or anyone else you knew—hanging around with. He was the type to drag his friends into deep water and then climb on their shoulders, not caring if they drowned.

Taggert turned off the rural highway and into the motel parking lot. Brown streaks ran down the plastic face of the Shady Acres sign, and it had a big, jagged hole that looked as if someone had shot at it. The run-down motel sat alone, a skinny, two-story building surrounded by scrubby fields that stretched on for miles. Mercy had seen dozens of its kind on rural roads in Oregon.

The SUV bounced through the potholes in the parking lot; they were impossible to avoid. The sheriff swore under her breath, and Mercy grabbed the handle above her door. Taggert parked in front of the office, a squatty protrusion from the motel. An OPEN sign hung crookedly on the dirty glass door.

It looked like a motel that simply brushed off the sheets before making the bed for the next occupant and then used the same sponge to clean both the toilets and sinks.

"Lovely," Mercy muttered, thankful she had hand sanitizer in her bag.

"I know," said the sheriff. "And I swear there's someone different working in the office every time I'm out here. They can't keep staff."

"Come here often?" Irony filled her tone.

Taggert cracked a grin. "More than I'd like. It's a cesspool."

They stepped out of the vehicle, and Mercy fell in behind the sheriff to let Taggert handle the desk clerk since she was in uniform. Mercy had considered wearing an FBI jacket but decided it was best to keep a low profile to avoid questions about her presence. Instead she'd dressed in her usual black pants and black lightweight blazer—necessary to cover her shoulder holster. The sheriff pulled open the door, and the scent of mildew slammed into them as they entered.

No one was working the counter. Behind it was an old TV with two Kardashian sisters arguing on-screen. Three Big Gulp cups with tall straws sat beside the TV. Scanning the room, Mercy spotted an ancient coffee maker on a rickety table at the far end of the lobby, a stack of Styrofoam cups beside it with a handwritten sign: *one cup of coffee per person!!!*

I wouldn't drink anything out of that machine. Or the cups.

The sheriff tapped the rusty service bell. It clanked.

A large young man sucking on a Big Gulp appeared from a doorway and approached the desk. His gaze narrowed on the sheriff's uniform. "Help you?" he said around the straw.

"We need a room number for Jimmie Elkins," stated the sheriff.

He sucked noisily before answering. "That's private. I can't do that."

"Because this place *always* follows the rules," said Taggert. "We can go pound on all the doors and bother your guests, or you could keep everyone happy and tell us the number."

"Get a warrant."

Mercy took a half step forward and held out her ID. "FBI, asshole," she said politely. "Maybe knowing that federal law enforcement is interested in Jimmie Elkins would change your mind?"

The man's gaze narrowed, and he stopped sucking.

"You up to date on your taxes?" asked Mercy. "I can have a word with a good friend at the IRS if you continue to block our investigation." She'd found that mentioning the IRS encouraged a certain type of person to cooperate. The agency was more alarming than the presence of the FBI.

He slammed down his Big Gulp. "One twelve."

Mercy smiled sweetly. "Thank you so much." The two women turned and left.

"You've had people harassed about their taxes?" asked the sheriff as they walked across the parking lot.

"No." Mercy shrugged. "We have no influence with the IRS. And of course I don't know anyone there."

Taggert chuckled. "Think he gave us the right room number?"

"We'll find out." She scanned the motel doors. Room 112 was three-quarters of the way down the building. They were about thirty feet away when the door opened a few inches and someone peered out.

That looks like Jimmie.

It opened wider, and a man tore outside.

"He's running!" Mercy shouted, and the women darted after him.

That asshole at the desk warned him.

"Stop! Randolph County Sheriff!" yelled Taggert.

Jimmie disappeared around the corner of the building, heading behind the motel. Mercy was full-out sprinting, the sheriff matching her pace.

She has the added weight of her tactical vest and belt.

A split second of panic raced through Mercy. No vest. She had her Glock in her holster but no protection. The panic vanished quickly as she recalled that Jimmie had dashed out of his room wearing nothing but baggy athletic shorts and shoes. No shirt. His shorts had flapped around his thighs—nothing in a pocket to weigh down one side. If he was armed, it wasn't with a gun.

The women turned the same corner and spotted Jimmie racing away from the motel across a large stretch of dirt spotted with bushes and tall, dry grasses.

Mercy panted, her feet pounding the ground. It was only mid-morning, but the heat and humidity were in full force, and it felt as if she were in a sauna. "Stop! FBI!" she shouted. Jimmie took a glimpse over his shoulder and turned up his speed.

Shit.

She scanned the landscape. Far ahead the field gave way to densely packed trees, which seemed to be Jimmie's target. Taggert continued to match her stride for stride, apparently used to running through saunas.

Ahead Jimmie suddenly yelped and dropped out of sight.

Did he fall?

As they drew closer, Mercy realized he'd tumbled into a deep gully and was now running awkwardly along the bottom, heading to their left. His back and hair were coated with dirt from his fall.

It's a dried-up creek bed.

It wasn't completely dry, and Jimmie's pace slowed as he tried to avoid areas of thick mud.

Without a discussion, Mercy jumped and sidestepped down the embankment as the sheriff stayed at the top, sprinting parallel to the dry creek. Mercy ran after Jimmie, careful not to plant a foot where he'd left deep prints in the boggy mud. "Stop! FBI!" she yelled again.

He didn't stop.

Mercy turned on a burst of speed and drew within ten feet of the running man. Up top, Taggert passed them and rapidly shuffled down the embankment to cut him off. Jimmie dashed to the opposite side to climb out of the gully.

Bad choice.

He had picked a steep spot and had to scramble, his hands clawing the dirt to keep his balance. Mercy lunged. She caught the waistband of his shorts and used her weight to yank him backward, hurling him to one side. He tumbled out of her grip and into the mud, landing on his stomach directly in front of Taggert. "Don't move!" the sheriff yelled, her weapon trained on him. Jimmie raised his head, one side of his face covered in sticky mud. He peered up at the sheriff and then back at Mercy, who now had her weapon aimed his way as well. He sighed loudly and clasped his hands behind his head.

He knows exactly what to do.

Panting, Mercy met Taggert's gaze, and a wide grin filled the sheriff's face. "That was fun!"

Mercy laughed.

She's right.

◆ ◆ ◆

Ten minutes later, they were in Jimmie's motel room, where Mercy had cranked up the air-conditioning. The machine was pitiful, puffing out weak breaths of mildly cool air.

Jimmie sat on the edge of the bed, his hands cuffed behind him. He'd asked to wash his face, and Mercy told him he could once he'd answered their questions. She enjoyed watching the mud rapidly dry and crack on his cheeks.

The room was a pit. It smelled of ancient cigarette smoke mixed with the skunk scent of weed. Mercy eyed the bed, wondering how long it'd been since the sheets were washed. Clothing was scattered about the room. Men's clothing. She saw nothing that would belong to a woman.

"What's all this water on the floor?" she asked, moving toward the bathroom. "You got a leak?"

"Huh?" He craned his head to see past her. *"Shit."*

Mercy stepped carefully around the small lake that extended into the bathroom and found the source of the problem. The toilet had overflowed, and floating at the top of the bowl were several plastic baggies. Pills, crystals, and powders. She looked closer and recognized an imprint code on the pills that filled three of the baggies. Opioids. Clearly the hundreds of pills weren't just for personal use.

He tried to flush his drugs and clogged the toilet. Then ran.

Idiot.

While examining the bathroom she decided she wouldn't bring him something to wash his face even after they talked. There was no way she was touching the rusty sink faucet or any of the graying, limp towels. The dark mildew stains in every crevice and the sheets of scum on the tub walls made her want hazard gear.

The drugs give us grounds to arrest him.

She stepped out. "Can you call someone to take him in?" she asked the sheriff. "There's a pharmacy of drugs floating in his toilet." Taggert nodded and spoke into the mic at her shoulder.

"Am I under arrest?" he asked, sourly looking from one woman to the other.

"Yep," answered Taggert.

"Why did you run?" asked Mercy.

Jimmie shrugged, his bony shoulders nearly touching his ears. He was thin, and Mercy could see every rib. He had the same type of facial sores she'd seen in the last photo of Vanessa. Another meth user. Mercy recalled her discussion with the sheriff about their suspect being able to lift a suitcase with a body in it. If Jimmie was their man, he must have had help. He didn't look strong enough to lift a bag of dog food.

"We're looking for Vanessa Mullen," she said.

"Ain't seen her in months. Whatever she's done has nothing to do with me," he said emphatically.

"Can you be more specific about the date you last saw her?" asked Taggert.

Jimmie screwed up his face in thought. "She bailed on me for Christmas. We had plans to hang with some people, and she didn't text or nothin'. I called her and kept getting voice mail. She never called back or came around." He shrugged again. "Guess she found something better."

Mercy exchanged a look with the sheriff. "She'd been living with you? Here?"

"Yeah. Sometimes she'd take off for a few days."

"You didn't ask where?"

"None of my business. She doesn't ask what I do, and I don't ask her. We're free adults."

Mercy noted he spoke of Vanessa in present tense.

"She in trouble?" he asked.

He had the smallest note of concern in his voice, and Mercy suspected he had some feelings for the woman no matter what he claimed.

"Did she take her belongings?" asked the sheriff.

"Yeah, she packed up everything. Stole my money. Took my stash too." He straightened and blinked rapidly, probably realizing what he'd admitted. "It was *her* stash, not mine."

Mercy tried not to laugh. Maybe he'd forgotten she'd found a toilet full of drugs. She jerked her head for Taggert to follow her to the bathroom. As the sheriff wrinkled her nose at the overflowing toilet, Mercy said in a low voice, "He's more concerned about a drug charge than anything else. He seems clueless about Vanessa."

"I was thinking the same. But he could be a good actor." Taggert looked skeptical, and Mercy agreed they'd found nothing to rule Jimmie out as a suspect in Vanessa's murder.

"For now let's take him in," said Mercy. "We can search the room once he's gone. Maybe something will turn up."

Taggert surveyed the bathroom. "Better double glove."

"You read my mind."

Maybe something will lead us to Paige.

Chapter 16

BREE

"Well, that was disgusting." Standing behind the open cargo hatch of her vehicle, Bree sprayed disinfectant on the soles of her boots and offered the can to Kilpatrick.

"Agreed." The agent used the spray generously. "And we didn't find anything useful."

"Jimmie is going to jail, though." A fact that cheered up Bree. "He'll be available if we need to question him again."

Bree's phone buzzed. Carlos's number popped onto the screen. "This is my tattoo guy." She pressed the phone to her ear and answered the call. "Hey, Carlos. You have something for me?"

"You betcha." He sounded proud. "Dude from Albany recognized the tattoo. The name of his shop is Freedom Body Art. It's on Central Ave."

Bree pulled up the address on her dashboard computer. "Thanks, Carlos."

"Goes by the name Picasso."

"OK." Bree made a note. "Thanks again."

"Anytime." The call ended.

"How far is that from here?" Kilpatrick asked.

"An hour."

"Let's roll."

Bree glanced at the time on her phone. "We'll grab food and eat on the way?"

"Sounds good."

"Burgers, subs?" Bree suggested.

Kilpatrick made a face. "I have some protein bars."

"Suit yourself." Bree stopped at a deli and grabbed a roasted chicken sandwich and two bottles of water. She scarfed her sandwich while she drove. Her phone buzzed again, and the name *Cruella* showed on the screen. A quick laugh burst out of her mouth before she could stop it. Matt must have changed the contact name on her phone. He'd compared the county administrator to the Disney character, and the nickname had stuck.

Kilpatrick glanced over, raising a brow.

Steering with her forearms, Bree wiped her hands on a napkin. "The county administrator and constant pain in my ass."

Kilpatrick put away her protein bar wrapper. "Politics?"

"My perpetual nightmare." Bree answered the call on speaker. "Sheriff Taggert."

"This is Madeline Jager."

"Sorry I missed the budget meeting." Bree was not sorry. "Duty called."

"That's not what I called about," Jager snapped. "Those bodies in the suitcases are all over the news."

"And?"

"And the press is now saying we might have another serial killer in Randolph County."

"I'm aware, but I can't stop them from speculating."

Jager's voice went shrill. "We can't have another serial killer."

Bree had no response.

"It looks bad for the county," Jager said.

"It does," Bree agreed.

"You need to handle the press, Sheriff."

"You're right," Bree said. "I'll call a press conference today."

Jager stuttered. "Well, OK, then . . . You do that."

"I'll do it when I get back to the office this afternoon. Have a good day." Bree ended the call.

Kilpatrick chuckled. "She expected an argument?"

"That is our usual pattern, but I'd planned to hold a press conference today anyway." Cutting off Jager before she'd had a chance to go on a rant had been a bonus, which sounded petty. So she didn't admit that to the FBI agent.

"I don't know how she expects you to control the killer's motivation," Kilpatrick said.

Bree turned up a palm. "Politicians don't operate on logic. We had some young women killed recently. Everyone is understandably still on edge." She had no idea how she would manage the situation.

They listened to radio chatter for the remainder of the drive. The GPS directed her toward a strip mall. Freedom Body Art was a glass-fronted store on the end. The plate glass bore a detailed painted mural of a field of American flags waving in the wind.

Bree spotted a security camera pointed at the front door as she pushed it open.

An old-fashioned bell hanging from the door handle rang as she and Kilpatrick stepped inside. The shop was small and cluttered, with a counter at the front, a doorway in the back, and tables and equipment clustered in the middle. An old man maneuvered through the tight space. He was anywhere from sixty-five to a hundred years old, with a wiry body and skin the color and texture of old leather. His jeans sagged, and the arms that hung out of his white tank sported nautical-themed tattoos on nearly every square centimeter of skin. A few wisps of white hair stuck out from under the bandanna tied on his head. "Can I help you?"

"We're looking for Picasso," Bree said.

The old man thumped his chest with a fist. "That's me. What can I do for ya? I'm always happy to help the boys—er, gals—in blue."

If he'd been younger, Bree would have been offended. But she gave him some latitude considering his age. She introduced herself and Agent Kilpatrick. "I'll need your full name for my report."

"Cyrus Van der Cleese." He snorted. "Ridiculous, right? Now you know why I go by Picasso. I'm too broke to have a snooty name."

Bree scanned the inside of the shop. The walls were covered with close-up photos of intricate, clearly custom tattoos. She nodded toward one of a wolf's head drawn on an impressive biceps. The animal's face looked realistically feral. "Did you do all of these?"

He beamed. "Every single one."

"We're here about this tattoo." Bree showed him the image on her phone. "Carlos posted about it?"

Picasso wobbled to the counter on bowlegs, stiff-gaited as if he needed a double knee replacement. He picked up a pair of reading glasses from the counter and slid them onto his nose. "Like I told him, I remember it."

"What can you tell us?" Bree leaned a hip on the opposite side of the counter.

Picasso eased one butt cheek onto a stool. "The girls came in with the heart drawn on paper. I didn't design it, not that there's anything wrong with it. People are free to put whatever they want on their bodies. My style just runs more to the unique and intricate."

"Each of the women came in alone?" Kilpatrick asked.

Picasso nodded. One palm rested on an open binder of simple tattoo designs, the kind drunken groups of college girls got after too many shots of tequila.

"Do you have surveillance videos?" Bree asked.

"Yep." He pointed to the front and back of the store. "I got a camera on each door. They hold a rolling thirty days of videos."

Only thirty?

Kilpatrick stepped up beside Bree, her presence sharpening with her interest. "Did any of the women come in within the last thirty days?"

"Yep. The last one came in about . . ." Picasso stared at the ceiling and waggled his head back and forth for a few seconds. "I'm gonna say ten days ago."

Ten days? If so, then it wasn't likely she was the most recent victim. Was she Kilpatrick's missing girl?

"Can you show us the video?" Bree asked.

"Sure." He slid off the stool and waved for them to follow him into a tiny office at the back of the store. The old wooden desk looked like it had been used in a school in the 1950s. Picasso slid into a squeaky chair and booted up a desktop computer. He opened an app and scrolled by date, muttering to himself. "Not her. Not her. Nope. Here she is." He turned the monitor to face them. On the screen, a girl opened the door and walked into the shop.

Bree groaned inside. The video was horribly grainy.

Picasso dragged the cursor backward, rewinding the feed, until the girl was in the center of the open door. Then he clicked PAUSE.

Kilpatrick said nothing, staring at the girl.

Bree could feel her disappointment. The girl wore a baseball cap that blocked most of her face. Between the cap and poor video quality, the image would not lead to a definite ID.

"She looks young," Bree said. The girl had long dark hair and was petite. Her tank top, short shorts, and spiked sandals looked expensive-trashy.

"She had ID." Picasso sounded defensive. "It said she was eighteen."

"Did you copy it?" Kilpatrick asked.

Picasso shook his head. "No. But I looked at it real good."

"You don't have any cameras inside the store?" Bree stared at the screen. The camera was focused, showing a small scrap of concrete walkway and a few feet of asphalt parking lot behind the girl. There were no cars in sight. If their killer had brought her, he'd parked out of camera range.

"Nope. That would be an invasion of privacy." Picasso drew back as if offended. "Tattoos are personal, and sometimes people want them in very personal places. My clients wouldn't be comfortable if they were being recorded."

"Understood." Bree soothed his professional ego. "We were just hoping to have additional images of her."

He relaxed and waved toward the monitor. "This is it."

Kilpatrick squinted at the screen. "Where did the women want these tattoos?"

"Top of the left breast." Picasso tapped his own chest with his forefingers.

Bree jerked her chin toward the computer monitor. "I'd like a copy of the video."

"I can do that." He slid a thumb drive into the USB slot and clicked a few buttons.

The FBI agent held out her phone to the artist. "Is this the most recent woman?"

Bree shifted so she could see the screen.

She's so young.

The picture looked like a high school senior photo, the girl wholesome and happy with long dark hair.

Picasso peered at the photo and then enlarged it. He shook his head. "I can't say. Maybe? She wore a lot of makeup. Probably needed a spatula to scrape it off."

Kilpatrick showed him another. This time it was a girl with her family, but the family's faces were blurred out.

He shook his head again.

She put her phone away, clearly discouraged.

The agent needs to tell me who she is.

Kilpatrick sighed. "When did the other women come in for the same tattoos?"

Picasso's face scrunched up. "One was maybe three months ago. Another maybe six or eight? I'm guessing. And the fourth was in between those."

"The fourth?" Kilpatrick's spine snapped straight.

Bree and the agent shared a quick glance.

Another victim?

Picasso pulled out the thumb drive and handed it to Bree. "Yeah. I did four of them."

"Can you describe any of the other women?" Bree mentally crossed her fingers.

"They all looked like they were under thirty-five. Long dark hair, thin." He shook his head. "One looked like a junkie. Had tracks on her arms. I wore two pairs of gloves for that one."

"Do you have records that would show the dates they came in?" Bree asked.

"Nah," Picasso said. "I'm not that organized. I keep a calendar of appointments for major design consultation and work, but not the small stuff. Most of those are walk-ins. Plus, the women paid in cash."

Ten minutes later, they walked out into the hot parking lot.

Bree faced Kilpatrick over the hood over the vehicle. She raised the thumb drive. "Do you think the FBI can eliminate some of the graininess?"

"I'm not sure. It's worth a try. I can show it to the missing girl's parents too. Maybe they'll recognize her clothes or the way she moves."

"She didn't look like someone who's being held against her will," Bree said. "She strolled right in."

"True, but if she's my missing girl, she's a minor."

"I get it, but I wonder if all the women were this willing."

Kilpatrick said, "Maybe they were willing until they weren't."

Was the girl still alive? And who got the fourth tattoo?

Fuck. Bree slowed as they approached the sheriff's station.

Mercy whistled. "That's not good."

Picketers marched up and down the sidewalk holding signs. Bree read a sign aloud. "Sheriff lies while girls die."

"Do you know that lie they're talking about?" Kilpatrick asked.

"I have no idea." Bree turned into the driveway that ran behind the building. The barrier rose, and she drove into the fenced parking lot. The protesters were out of sight, but she could hear them chanting as she and Mercy crossed the asphalt and entered through the back door.

Marge met them in Bree's office. "You saw the protest?"

"Couldn't miss it." Bree rounded her desk. "What are they talking about?"

Marge leaned over and turned on the desktop computer. "That blond reporter accused you of covering up another active serial killer."

Bree dropped into her chair. "Covering up what? We have a press conference scheduled for today."

Marge tipped her head at the screen. "Reality has nothing to do with clickbait headlines. The clip went viral."

Marge clicked PLAY. On the computer, the blond reporter stood in front of the station. He rehashed the information about the finding of the bodies in suitcases, the nail polish, and the long dark hair on the victims in a sensational tone. Then he finished with, "Two young women are dead, and there's been no update from Sheriff Taggert. What is the sheriff's department hiding? Is there another serial killer in Randolph County? Why doesn't the sheriff want you to know?"

Bree wanted to scream. She checked the time. "The best way to combat this nonsense is with the truth. Let's move up the press conference. I'll be out in fifteen minutes. Have Juarez print a photo of Vanessa Mullen and a close-up of the tattoo."

Marge exited with a slight bow of her head.

Bree faced the FBI agent. "Do you want to be in on this or not?"

"I'm going to head back to my motel and check in with my office," Kilpatrick said. "I don't want to be on camera."

Considering the media attack, it would have been nice to have an FBI agent at her back, but Bree didn't make it an issue. "I'll catch up with you tomorrow."

After the agent left, Bree checked her appearance in the locker room, tucked a few stray hairs back into her bun, and decided that was good enough. She went out to the lobby. Reporters were crammed into every inch of space. They shuffled camera equipment and presented microphones like flags as Bree took her place. Juarez stood at her flank, the two photos tucked under his arm.

Bree spotted the blond reporter in the front row, but she looked over the entire crowd before beginning. "I've called you here for an update on the women found in the suitcases. The medical examiner has completed the autopsies. One of the victims has been identified as Grey's Hollow resident Vanessa Mullen, age thirty-one. Vanessa was reported missing six months ago by her ex-husband. The medical examiner was unable to determine the cause of death. She has likely been dead for several months, but we do not have a specific time frame."

Juarez turned an eight-by-ten copy of Vanessa's driver's license photo to the press.

Bree continued. "The second victim is as of yet unidentified. Her time of death is pending test results. She is believed to be age sixteen to twenty-five, approximately five foot two, and had long brown hair."

The blond reporter interrupted, yelling, "The autopsies were conducted yesterday. Why did you wait so long to bring the public this new information?" The question was delivered like an accusation.

"Because the next of kin deserves to be notified first," Bree said.

The blond was not swayed. "The public has a right to know."

"No one wants to learn the fate of their missing loved one on the news or social media." Bree let the point stand for one breath, then continued. "Both victims had matching tattoos. We doubt this is a coincidence. This is where we'd like help from the public." She motioned to Juarez, who showed the second photo. "If anyone has seen this tattoo or has any other information about the case, please call the sheriff's department." Bree recited the phone number.

Reporters clamored for attention. Bree ignored the blond and pointed at a different reporter. "Go."

"Is this the work of another serial killer?"

"It's too early in the investigation to make that assertion, but I won't rule it out either." Bree nodded toward a man in the second row.

"How did the women die?"

"The medical examiner isn't one hundred percent sure," Bree said. "But it's possible that the unidentified woman was strangled."

The blond, clearly frustrated, called out, "Is Vanessa Mullen's ex-husband a suspect?"

"We have no reason to believe he was involved in her death," Bree said. "In fact, Mr. Mullen is the one who reported her missing."

A commotion at the door caught everyone's attention. Heads swiveled, and the crowd parted. Madeline Jager strode through the crowd. A cream-colored pantsuit fit her thin frame, and her unnaturally red hair was fresh-from-the-salon fluffy. She looked like a cherry lollipop.

Bree made an effort not to show her displeasure as the county administrator made a place for herself at Bree's side, forcing Juarez to move. Jager did nothing accidentally. Her presence at the press conference was deliberate as fuck.

Most of Jager's face was Botoxed into immobility, but she gave Bree a hairy eyeball.

Reluctantly, Bree yielded the mic. What else could she do? Jager was going to address the press no matter what Bree did. Lack of cooperation between county agencies was a bad look.

"The sheriff's department is working hard to find this murderer, and it's up to you to help bring him to justice," Jager said with as much fanfare as the reporter. "To that end, we are offering a five-thousand-dollar reward for any tip that leads to the arrest of the killer."

Bree's jaw dropped open a half inch as bedlam broke out in the room. She quickly snapped her mouth shut. Best to appear as if she knew about the reward. But holy hell. This was not a wealthy county. The fake tips would be flowing in like floodwater.

Chapter 17

MERCY

Mercy closed her motel room door and pulled out her cell phone. She flung her bag onto a chair as she scanned her texts, impatient to inform Detective Bolton about the video from the tattoo shop. But Kaylie had sent six pictures of her foster kittens, and Mercy couldn't resist rapidly scrolling through them all first.

It helps to look at kittens after seeing Jimmie's motel room.

Truman had texted a heart, and she sent one back.

Evan's message asked her to call. She tapped his photo, hit the CALL button, and checked her email as she waited for him to answer. Her gaze locked on an email from the NW RCFL, the FBI computer lab that had Paige's laptop and phone.

"Mercy?" Evan answered.

"Yes. I was about to open the computer lab's email," she said. "Is this why you called?"

"It is."

"Evan, I've got some rough video from here that might be Paige."

"That's great!"

"It's ten days old and it's grainy and the face is hard to see. But I'd like her parents to look at it. See if they can identify her."

"I'm at their home right now. I was about to discuss the computer lab's findings with them when you called. Can you send me the video?"

"Yes." She quickly opened her laptop and uploaded the video. "There's something else."

"What?" Evan asked.

"The video is from a tattoo parlor. If this is her, then the tattoo she got was also on the two murdered women. A heart made of chains and in the same location over the heart. And the artist said he'd done four of them. So there's another woman out there somewhere."

Evan was silent a long moment. "Paige might be one in a line of missing women? And two are known to be dead?"

"Yes."

"Will the FBI send more agents out there?"

"I need to call my boss, but I don't think so. Several agents are following leads in different states—these are possible Paige sightings too. I'll continue to be the only agent in town unless I can confirm that Paige is here."

"I can hear it in your voice . . . you think she is," Evan said.

"I'm considering all options."

Damn, I hope I'm close.

He exhaled. "With your tattoo news, the results from the laptop make more sense."

"Explain."

"You might as well hear about it as I update the Holcrofts. But let's give them your news first."

"OK. Switching to video." Mercy tapped her phone screen, and Evan's face appeared. She recognized the senator's yard in the background.

"They're in the house. I stepped out to take your call." He opened a door and moved into the home. "Senator, I've got Agent Kilpatrick on video from New York. She has an update, which I'm going to show you on my laptop."

The senator and Denise came into view. They were seated side by side on a sofa in the huge living room. They looked exhausted, their faces strained. It'd been more than two weeks without news of their daughter. Evan propped his phone against something so they could see Mercy.

"What have you found?" asked the senator, his tone cautious. Hitting dead end after dead end had trained him not to get his hopes up.

"Ten days ago, a girl that *could be* Paige got a tattoo in Albany, New York," said Mercy. "I just sent Detective Bolton a video from the tattoo parlor. It's very grainy," she warned. "And the woman is wearing a hat. I can't be sure it's her, but maybe you can tell."

Denise reached over and clenched her husband's hand. "Ten days ago," she repeated in a flat tone. "That's so long."

"Here it is," Evan said.

The parents turned their attention away from Mercy, both of them leaning forward as they focused on Evan's laptop. Mercy watched, slightly pained by their faces full of hope.

Please say it's Paige.

"Back it up," Denise told Evan. "Stop it right there." She squinted and then turned to her husband. "I can't tell." She looked about to cry.

Adam continued to stare at the video. "Do you recognize the shoes?"

"No," whispered Denise. "I don't recognize any of the clothes or the hat. And those heels make her walk awkwardly, so if it is Paige, she doesn't move how I'd expect." She covered her face with her hands.

"Are there more videos or photos?" asked the senator.

"That's it," said Mercy. "I'm sorry I don't have anything else for you." Her heart dropped.

Is this another dead end?

Adam dragged his gaze to Evan. "What were you going to tell us about her computer?"

Denise grabbed a tissue, blotting her eyes and then her nose.

"This is the first Agent Kilpatrick is hearing of the results too," said Evan. "The FBI lab discovered that Paige spent a lot of time on a site called CuffMe.com."

Mercy caught her breath, remembering the ball gags and bound hands of the two dead women.

Paige appeared to be into BDSM.

That would explain the tattoo.

There's a good chance that is her on the video.

The senator froze but his wife frowned. "What is that?" she asked.

"It's a site about BDSM," Evan said carefully. "Which is bondage, domination, sadism—"

The senator cut him off. "I know what it is! What the hell are you trying to say?"

"And masochism," Evan finished. "There were extensive Google searches on her computer about all aspects of BDSM, but she spent hours on this site for several weeks."

"She's a teenager!" Denise's voice was shrill. "She's curious about things. I wouldn't be surprised if Finn's Google history is full of sex things too."

"Mrs. Holcroft," Mercy began delicately. "The reason we went to the tattoo parlor in the first place was to track down a tattoo found on two murdered women here in New York. These women were found with . . . elements of bondage on their bodies. And the tattoo could be interpreted as representing that too. The girl in the video received the same tattoo."

Denise stared, her mouth slightly open.

"You think Paige is in New York *doing that*?" The senator's face was stony.

"I'm not positive," said Mercy. "But I think we're getting closer."

Evan cleared his throat. "The CuffMe site has a place for users to make personal connections and have conversations," he said. "It's well known for bringing people together who are interested in the same things."

Maybe that's where he found the women. And Paige.

"She met someone on there. That's who she was in the car with," stated the senator in a flat tone. "And then he took her to New York." Beside him, Denise sat very still, shock on her features.

"It's a possibility," said Evan. "The FBI computer lab believes she has an account, but they aren't able to access it to see who she talked with. We're putting together a subpoena for CuffMe's parent company to let us into Paige's account."

"How long will that take?" asked Denise. "Once you get that you'll know who the man is, right? You'll find an address for him from that site?" Her hopeful gaze went from her husband to Evan and back.

"I don't know how long," said Evan. "And we need to be prepared that whoever she spoke with didn't use any traceable information. Often people who use these sites use fake information."

"Except Paige," Denise said bitterly.

"Which was good for us," Mercy added. "It's led us to this point." Her brain was rapidly processing the information Evan had shared. "I think we can say this information has greatly reduced the possibility that her disappearance is politically related to the senator."

"Because Paige got herself into this," said the senator slowly. "No one sought her out to get at me."

Denise pulled her hand out of his and started to cry.

His words made Mercy see red. "She's a child, sir. This is not her fault," she snapped. "The man involved is a predator and most likely an adult. This is squarely on him, not Paige. She made some bad decisions, but I suspect she did *not* leave your house on her own. She was manipulated."

Shame flickered across his face. "I didn't mean it that way. It's just that for two weeks my brain has been working overtime, blaming my job, blaming my voting record, analyzing every little word I've ever said, looking for the *why* of Paige's disappearance. Now I just learned I've been obsessed with the wrong angle."

"Your position hasn't been ruled out as a factor," said Mercy, cooling a bit after his explanation. "It's still on the table. But it's looking unlikely that this was about politics." She paused. "I think this is about power. A man hunting for power and control. A need to dominate."

By holding and abusing these women.

Chapter 18

HIM

I'm barely in the door when I reach for the laptop. Anxious to see if I've made the news again, I set down my Coke, open Google, and search for *the serial killer in Randolph County NY*. Pages of results appear on my screen. So many articles.

I'm famous.

The very first result is a YouTube link that leads to a clip from WSNY. The like button shows 15K thumbs-ups, 115K views, and 965 comments! That is some impressive engagement.

Ken Wells, you handsome devil. You are The Man.

The clip is going viral. *I'm* going viral. It's almost too bad no one will ever know I'm the one.

I know. That should be enough.

I think of the woman in the next room. *She definitely knows.*

I scroll through the search engine results and read a few articles. They aren't as exciting as the videos. People like the sensational aspects of media attention, and the written word just isn't as grabby. Still, I save every hyperlink.

Halfway down my screen, I click on another YouTube link. The sheriff gave another press conference today. She is boring. All facts, no fun. She can barely handle a few softball questions, but she acts as if someone is putting the screws to her.

Come to think of it, I wouldn't mind putting *actual* screws to the sheriff.

I watch the press conference twice more. Sheriff Taggert tries to keep a straight face, but she is out of her element. She will never figure it out. She barely has any information, and what little she has came from the medical examiner. Sheriff isn't a job for a woman. Females don't belong in positions of power. It's unnatural. She's another impostor, a wannabe man.

Someone should show her the truth.

The reward is huge, though. I can't contain my laughter. I copy the link, adding it to my list, so I can watch it as many times as I like.

They can't decide if I'm a serial killer. Maybe I should make that clear. Steering the investigation might be fun too. I can fuck with Sheriff Taggert. It'll be entertaining. I write down the number for the hotline, then watch the whole event again.

Why haven't they named me? Every serial killer needs a name, right?

This is my only chance to be famous. I hope they come up with something spectacular.

Chapter 19

Bree

Day 4

"CuffMe.com?" Bree stared over her desk at the FBI agent. Kilpatrick had come in bright and early with a lead from the FBI computer forensics department in Oregon.

"The bondage angle makes total sense, given the state of the bodies," Kilpatrick said.

"Let's hope the subpoena comes through quickly." Bree wanted a solid lead. So far, the investigation had felt like they were chasing smoke. Thanks to Jager's announcement the evening before, today promised to be more of the same. "Until then, we can work with leads from the tip line. Did you watch the press conference?"

Kilpatrick made an irritated face. "That was a total shit show—no offense. It wasn't your fault."

"None taken." Bree agreed with the agent's assessment. Circus clowns were better prepared than she'd felt when Jager had dropped her bomb.

"The reward was the politician's idea?"

"Yep." Bree exhaled hard through her nose. She still wanted to scream at Jager. "Which she didn't mention before offering it, live on television."

"Wow. That's . . . that's something." Kilpatrick's forehead furrowed in disbelief. "I don't even have a word for that."

Bree had several, but none could be repeated in a professional conversation.

"Have the phone lines been swamped?" Kilpatrick asked.

"We set up a dedicated tip line and assigned a deputy to man it full-time." Bree tapped a printed sheet on her desk. "A hundred and forty tips came in overnight. I've pulled the ones that seem the most promising, and I've assigned deputies to work lists as well." She stood. "You're welcome to join me in following up on mine."

"I'm in."

"Let's go." Bree folded the paper and rounded her desk. She opened a small closet and removed a Kevlar vest with SHERIFF printed on the front and back. "I pulled a spare vest for you. I've no idea what today will bring. Assuming you didn't fly with yours?"

"I didn't." Kilpatrick accepted the vest, removed her shoulder holster, and tried it on. "It's a decent fit. Thank you. I'll switch to a belt holster."

They left the building via the back door and climbed into Bree's SUV. Bree drove out of the lot. She stopped at the end of the driveway and waited for the picketers to move. The group had shrunk since the press conference. A few diehards still carried signs. "At least they've stopped chanting."

Kilpatrick fanned her neck. "Maybe it's too hot."

One of the protesters, a young woman with a spiky blonde pixie cut, bent over to glare through Bree's driver's-side window. She screamed, "Liar," her face screwing up with hate, her mouth opening wide enough for Bree to see her tonsils.

"She seems fun," Kilpatrick said.

Bree inched forward, maneuvering her vehicle through the small crowd. "It feels bitchy, but I hope she gets sunburned."

Kilpatrick laughed.

Bree turned the corner, leaving the hostility behind with a deep breath. "The first stop is the mall. A security guard phoned in saying he recognized Vanessa."

"Good. A security guard isn't likely to completely waste our time."

"Fingers crossed."

The mall was a small, sad establishment with one vacant anchor store. The exterior needed refreshing, and clumps of weeds sprouted through wide cracks in the asphalt parking lot. Bree parked near the security office. The blacktop seemed almost sticky under her boots from the heat. Inside, she pushed through into a tiny reception area. Kilpatrick followed, sliding her sunglasses onto her head.

"Hello?" Bree called out.

A man stepped into the doorway behind the counter. About forty-five, he looked fairly fit in a standard mall security guard uniform: white shirt, black pants, and a few badges and logos meant to convey a feeling of authority. His hair was buzzed short, and he sported a neat salt-and-pepper goatee. His duty belt contained a radio, flashlight, keys, and a canister of pepper spray.

Bree checked her list. "I'm looking for Don Dutton."

"That's me." He approached the counter.

Bree introduced herself and Kilpatrick. "Thanks for calling the hotline. You recognized the victim?"

Don nodded. "We had several encounters with her. Had to ban her for shoplifting."

"When was this?" Bree asked.

"Last December. We're always busy in the preholiday season. Shoplifters think they can blend in with the crowds." He waved them forward. "Come on back to my office. I'll show you the paperwork."

Bree and Kilpatrick followed him into a larger room. A desk faced six wide-screen monitors, each divided into a dozen views of the mall. He opened a file on his desk. "I printed the reports for you." He separated two papers. "In the first incident, Vanessa Mullen shoved a sweater into her handbag. We gave her a warning and banned her from the mall. Unfortunately, she came back two weeks later and tried to steal a designer handbag and some socks."

The mall was in the town of Scarlet Falls, which had its own police department. Though it fell within Bree's jurisdiction, normal policing would be addressed by the locals.

"Did you follow up?" Kilpatrick asked.

Don shook his head. "I don't know what happened to her. Usually, minor charges are pleaded out."

"What made you remember her?" Bree asked.

He set a pair of reading glasses on his nose and read something on the page, as if refreshing his memory. "In the second incident, she tried to run with the merchandise. I had to chase her down. When I caught up with her, she was belligerent. From her erratic behavior—and frankly, her appearance—I suspected she was high on something. I called the SFPD and let them deal with her." He dropped the glasses on the blotter. "Usually, people are pretty cooperative when they're caught red-handed leaving the premises with the merchandise. There are cameras everywhere. We almost always have videos. The ones that run or fight stand out."

Don swept the pages into the manila folder, closed it, and offered it to Bree.

"Thanks." She took it and scanned the report inside. There was a black-and-white photo of Vanessa attached. The image was clear enough to capture her pocked skin and dark circles. "Everything seems to be in order." She handed the file to Kilpatrick, who looked it over.

Dutton lifted a thumb drive from his desk. "I also copied the security footage for both incidents."

"Thorough." Bree pocketed the drive.

"SFPD should have an arrest report."

"I'll get a copy from them," Bree said. "Thanks for the info."

"Not sure how it helps your case, but you're welcome." Don escorted them back to the tiny lobby.

The sun blazed on Bree's head the second she stepped outside. "Now we have corroboration of the ex's statement that Vanessa was alive in early December."

They got back into the car.

"What's next on our list?" Kilpatrick fastened her seat belt.

Bree handed the sheet to the agent. "You tell me."

"The manager at the Burger Palace—Carl Simmons—recognized Vanessa too. He says he'll be at work from eight to five." Kilpatrick read off an address.

"I know it. It's only a few blocks from here." Bree drove to the burger joint, and they went inside. They were between the breakfast and lunch rushes, and the restaurant was mostly empty. The lingering smell of bacon made Bree's stomach rumble. She stepped up to the counter.

A pimply-faced young man asked, "What can I get you?"

"We're looking for Carl Simmons."

A man in brown polyester pants and a short-sleeved dress shirt stepped out from the kitchen. "This way, Sheriff."

Bree and Kilpatrick followed him to a corner booth. He slid onto a vinyl bench, and they took seats opposite him.

"You called the hotline?" Bree asked.

"Yeah. I recognized the dead woman. She used to come in here all the time. She'd use the bathroom without making a purchase." He paused for a breath. "She'd stay in there way too long. I asked her not to come back. But she did anyway, snuck in through the side door. One day, she wouldn't come out for over thirty minutes. Eventually, I unlocked the door with a key. Thought she might be dead in there or something." He made a face. "She wasn't. She ran off the second I opened the door."

"Did you chase her?" Kilpatrick asked.

He patted his generous stomach. "Do I look like I can chase anyone? No. I didn't run after her, but I found a needle on the floor afterward." He grimaced. "We get some gross stuff, but needles freak me out. I disinfected the whole bathroom myself after that."

"Do you have any video or a report?" Bree asked.

"I didn't bother. We were really busy." He shook his head. "She was long gone, and she never came back." He shrugged. "We get plenty of homeless in here. It's not like we have security or anything."

Bree pulled out a notepad and wrote a few notes. "Do you remember when this happened?"

He jerked a shoulder. "It was before Christmas. That's all I remember."

"OK. Thanks for your help." Bree got up.

"Will do." His eyes brightened. "You'll let me know about the reward, right?"

Bree sighed. "If this information leads to the apprehension and arrest of the killer, we'll call you." She used a *don't call us* tone.

"I doubt that information will be very helpful," Kilpatrick said as they walked back to the vehicle.

Bree sighed. "Right? Guess he figured he had to try."

"I hope the rest of the day isn't this pointless."

"One foot in front of the other," Bree said. "And we're narrowing down Vanessa's last known appearance to sometime in December."

They'd work every lead until they ran out.

Chapter 20

MERCY

Mercy glanced at the list in her hand to verify Taggert had driven them to the right address for the next tip. "This looks abandoned." They'd pulled into the parking lot of a small strip mall that looked as if it had been empty for decades. All the windows were boarded up. Trash and weeds covered the parking lot.

It looked like a place to make a drug deal.

"There's a car," said the sheriff after driving to the far end of the parking lot. The front half of a newer Mercedes sedan was visible behind the strip mall. Taggert cautiously drove closer and stopped a dozen feet away. A man in sunglasses stepped out of the car, and he hesitated, eyeing the SUV.

"Hang on." The sheriff popped the plate into her dashboard computer. "Registered to Pete Conrad." She pulled up his license. "Does that look like him?"

Mercy studied the license photo and then the man waiting for them. "Think so. Hard to tell with the sunglasses, but he's tall. License says six three."

"Agreed. Did he really think his tip would be anonymous when he shows up in his own vehicle?"

"He's not what I expected," muttered Mercy, studying him. The man had claimed to have information about Vanessa Mullen but had refused to give his name or come to the station. Mercy had suspected it would be a false tip or that they would meet someone from the dregs of society. Instead the man before them was in a suit and tie. His hair was neatly trimmed and his shoes shiny. Light glinted off his sunglasses as he took quick looks to the left and right.

"Someone doesn't want to be seen with us," the sheriff said quietly.

The women got out of the county SUV and approached. The sun was hot on Mercy's head and back, her black vest immediately soaking in the rays.

"Morning," said the sheriff. "You called the tip line about Vanessa Mullen?"

"I did," said the man, shifting his weight from foot to foot, discomfort on his face.

He does not want to be here.

"What's your name?" asked Taggert.

"I'll tell you in a minute," he said. "Maybe. I need assurances first."

Someone watches too many cop shows.

"Can you take off your sunglasses?" asked Mercy. "We can move into the shade." She jerked her head to the shade near the empty building. He stepped to the side but didn't remove the glasses until Taggert and Mercy stared at him silently for a long moment, waiting. He sighed and took them off, reluctantly meeting their gazes.

Definitely Pete Conrad.

He was in his forties. The suit was nicely tailored, the tie expensive, and his nails perfectly trimmed.

"I'm facing a legal charge. I want it dropped in exchange for the information I'm about to share," he stated.

Mercy exchanged a look with the sheriff.

Yep. Too much TV.

"You must have some awfully important information about this young woman's horrible murder," said Mercy.

You selfish prick.

He toyed with his sunglasses. "Not about the murder per se, but I have the name of a possible suspect."

"Tell us what you know, and if it's strong, I'll see what I can do," said the sheriff. "But no DA will make a deal before hearing what you have to say." She paused. "What are you charged with?"

Mercy had a hunch. This upper-income man who wanted to meet behind a building and not give his name meant it'd been a crime he wanted to keep secret. Since their meeting involved Vanessa, she placed money on drugs or prostitution.

"It wasn't my fault," he started. "It wasn't fair—"

"What are you charged with?" Taggert repeated.

He looked away, tightening his grip on the sunglasses. "Solicitation of prostitution." His gaze shot back to them, fury in his eyes. "It was a fucking sting operation. Totally unconstitutional. My attorney says—"

"We don't care what your attorney says," said Mercy. "We want to know what you have to say about Vanessa." She stared at his wedding ring, and then met his gaze.

I knew it. And it was not his fault, of course.

Frustration filled his face. "I need to know you can get the charge dropped."

"You're looking at up to a year in prison, aren't you?" said the sheriff. "Sorry, can't promise a deal without knowing what you have." In unison, she and Mercy turned away and took a dozen paces back to the SUV.

"Wait!"

They paused and looked back.

His shoulders slumped. "I'll tell you. If it's valuable, I want a deal."

"I'll try my best," said Taggert. They rejoined him.

"I used to . . . used to see her." He swallowed hard, struggling to look at them.

"You mean you paid Vanessa money for *sex*," said Mercy, loudly emphasizing the word *sex*. "We know her history. What about it?"

"I used to go to her motel, and a guy stayed there with her." His eyes turned hopeful. "I know his name. She'd always say I had to leave before he returned."

Another useless tip.

"We know that Vanessa stayed at the Shady Acres Motel with Jimmie, who at this moment is sitting in jail," said the sheriff. "We're not convinced he's involved, so what else do you have for us?"

Anger and disappointment flashed across his face.

"That's it?" asked Mercy. "Sorry we aren't able to help you out." She looked at Taggert. "We done here?"

"Yep. Have a nice day, sir," the sheriff told him in an upbeat voice. "The county appreciates your help." The annoyance in her eyes contradicted her tone, and she headed back to the vehicle.

Mercy lingered. "Here's a *tip*," she said quietly, leaning closer to the man. "Don't screw around with prostitutes. Who knows what you've taken home to your wife and kids, Mr. Conrad."

His mouth fell open at her use of his name.

Before he could speak, she spun around and strode away to join Taggert in the SUV.

"Asshole," Mercy said as she climbed in. "Can you imagine meeting a prostitute in Jimmie's nasty motel room? I saw the sheets; they were disgusting."

Taggert shuddered. "A condom wouldn't be enough. Full-body latex coverage would be needed."

Mercy chortled. "Moving on." She checked the list. "Next tip is also anonymous." She sighed. "I hope your deputies are having more luck running down tips."

"What's the address?" asked Taggert, who wrinkled her nose after Mercy told her. "That's in a sketchy part of town."

"Makes sense. The caller claimed Vanessa hung out there a lot and that the people in the home know her really well. Caller didn't think they'd contact the police, so he was doing it." Mercy's stomach rumbled. "Can we get something to eat first?" she asked. Her breakfast was long gone.

"On it."

Thirty minutes later, Mercy felt much better. The sheriff had taken her to a little hole-in-the-wall Mexican restaurant with surprisingly authentic food. Two enchiladas and a ton of chips later, they were back on the road.

"I wish the heart tattoo had brought in some tips," said Mercy.

"It's early," said Taggert, watching the road ahead. "We might get information on it. Or our next stop could be the tip that blows everything open."

"That's optimistic of you."

The sheriff shrugged. "If it's not, we'll continue moving forward. Crossing off each lead."

"And knocking on doors."

Taggert went silent, and Mercy noticed her knuckles whitened on the steering wheel. She waited a few seconds, but the sheriff didn't volunteer her thoughts.

None of my business, I guess.

A few minutes later, Taggert turned down a gravel road and drove by several run-down homes.

"You were right about it being sketchy," said Mercy, spotting two chained-up dogs, who barked their heads off as they passed a home.

"We get calls on this road all the time," said the sheriff. "Usually domestics." She pulled to the side of the road and nodded toward a house set back from the road. "That's the one. It's owned by someone out of state and is a rental. No recent calls at this specific address, but it racked up a lot a few years back. Those people must have moved out. We'll see how cooperative the new occupants are."

The house was a faded-brown ranch style with an attached single-car garage. The front door was a cheery bright yellow with a small awning overhead. Three steps led up to a wide concrete porch at the door.

"No cars," commented Mercy, wondering if anyone was home. "Yard hasn't been touched for a while." The grass was a dry yellow with bare spots.

"Yard looks pretty normal for around here," said Taggert. "Not worth it to water during this summer heat. You'd have to constantly drown it to keep it green." She touched her holstered weapon and tugged on her vest under her shirt. "Ready?" There was an air of apprehension around her that Mercy hadn't noticed before.

It's a sketchy location. She's being prepared.

They climbed out of the SUV and took a good look around. Mercy saw curtains shift at the home directly across the street.

Someone is curious. Or nosy.

The neighborhood was quiet as they moved up the crumbling walkway. Taggert had sweat on her temples, and the hot humid air made Mercy feel as if she were in a tropical country. At the front door they each stepped to one side. Taggert met her gaze and then knocked.

The home was silent. A few moments later the sheriff knocked again. "Randolph County Sheriff's Department!"

Mercy strained to hear any noise from inside. "Check the back?" she whispered.

The sheriff nodded. "Go."

As Mercy turned away, the crack of a weapon reached her before a bullet crashed into her back, hurling her off the porch. She body-slammed onto the ground, her lungs not functioning. She fought for air.

I'm shot!

Chapter 21

BREE

Gunshot!

Whipping her gun from its holster, Bree dived off the porch, crawled two feet, and crouched between the downed agent and the direction where the bullet seemed to have come from. Bree turned to face the hidden shooter, using the porch steps for cover, leveling her weapon over the concrete stoop. Scanning the opposite side of the street, she saw no movement, no glint of sunlight metal, no shooter.

Without lowering her gaze, she nudged Kilpatrick's foot with a boot. "Are you alive?"

Prone, face down on the ground, Kilpatrick wheezed out a response halfway between "Oof" and "Yes." Her next inhalation sounded rough.

She's still breathing.

But Kilpatrick's head and shoulders were potentially exposed. Bree turned, grabbed the agent's feet, and dragged her farther behind the steps. She yelled into her lapel mic, "Shots fired. Officer down." She barked out the address. "Requesting backup and an ambulance."

Dispatch responded, but another gunshot commanded Bree's attention. She ducked. The bullet struck the porch railing. Bits of wood flew, and a hot sting hit the side of her neck.

Just debris.

But still a solid reminder of their vulnerable position. Images of the kids and Matt flashed in her mind before she banished them. As much as she loved them, she couldn't afford any distraction. She breathed. Forcing her lungs to expand and deflate with almost painful deliberation, warding off the tunnel vision that could result from the unchecked rush of adrenaline.

She touched her radio mic again. "We're pinned down next to the front steps and under fire!" Dropping her hand, Bree peered over the stoop, aiming her weapon at the home across the street, the white bungalow where curtains had moved when they'd arrived. The curtains shifted now, but Bree saw only a face, no gun barrel.

Where is the shooter?

They'd both been focused on potential threats coming from behind the door. Bree had been fired on from inside a home in a very similar circumstance. Neither had expected a shot to originate from behind them. She scanned the windows and roofline but saw nothing.

A third gunshot rang out. Bree ducked again as the bullet pinged the dirt just beyond the porch steps. Her heart hammered. Her breaths came short and fast. "Kilpatrick, are you bleeding?"

"Don't know." The agent barely choked out the reply.

Bree glanced over her shoulder. The agent hadn't moved, but Bree didn't see any blood. She could either defend them or provide first aid.

Deciding that a second bullet wouldn't improve the agent's health, Bree turned her attention to the houses that flanked the bungalow. A beat-up old pickup was parked in the driveway of a dark ranch-style house. To the right, a two-story brick home looked vacant. Overgrown weeds crawled up three feet of the brick sides. Several windows were broken. Something moved behind the broken glass of an upstairs window. Bree took aim and waited. A shadow appeared in the window, and light glinted off the barrel of a gun. Another shot rang out. Ignoring the ping of the bullet hitting a concrete step, Bree squeezed the trigger, returning fire.

The shooter yanked the weapon back into the house.

That's right, asshole. I'm shooting back.

Bree pulled the trigger again. She wanted him to know they weren't completely helpless. Movement behind the broken glass ceased. Had he moved? Would he fire again from a different direction? They would be sitting ducks if he moved to the other side of the steps they were hiding behind.

She updated dispatch with the potential location of the shooter. She didn't want her deputies shot as they drove up.

Next to her, Kilpatrick shifted on the ground. In her peripheral vision, Bree saw her move her arms and legs, as if checking to make sure they still worked. Then the agent rolled onto her side, exhaling painfully with the effort, and vomited into a patch of weeds. The enchiladas in Bree's stomach did a slow, sour roll.

The worry that the agent could have internal injuries or heavy bleeding made Bree turn away from the steps. She put a knee to the ground and bent over the agent. She gave Kilpatrick's limbs and head a quick scan. No visible blood. "Where were you hit?"

Bree pivoted her head and checked the brick house again. No movement. No shadow. No glint of light on metal. She scanned the roofline and the approach to the porch they were hiding behind. When she didn't see anyone, she turned back to the agent.

"My back." Kilpatrick wriggled, turning her head to attempt to look over her own shoulder. Every movement elicited a grimace, but her breathing no longer rattled like a subway train.

"I've got you." Bree ran a hand across the back of the vest. She felt a hole in the stiff material on the back of the agent's ribs. "Right here."

The vest should have done its job. But with them still under fire, Bree didn't want to remove it to check. She patted the agent's shirt at the bottom of the vest. If there was a wound underneath the vest, the shirt should be saturated. "I don't feel any blood."

Kilpatrick nodded, her face strained. Even if the bullet hadn't pierced the vest, the shot would have hurt. Kilpatrick would have a massive bruise and potentially some broken ribs. Both of which were better than a big hole.

Satisfied the agent's death likely wasn't imminent, Bree turned back to the shooter. The street was empty and still. People in this neighborhood knew to duck and cover when gunshots rang out. The only sound she could hear was the barking of the dogs down the street.

Bree's skin itched, and the hairs on the back of her neck waved in alarm. Was the killer watching them? Had he moved to a new location? Maybe one on this side of the concrete steps, where he'd have a better shot at them?

She put her back to the concrete and widened the area she was covering. Seconds ticked by. Sweat dripped down Bree's back. The tank top she wore under her body armor was soaked through. Her gaze returned to the brick house. Nothing. Behind her, Kilpatrick coughed and grunted in pain, but she managed to wriggle closer to the base of the steps.

"See him?" Kilpatrick asked in a tight voice.

"No. I think he moved." Or left. He had to know the police would be coming. She breathed.

The sound of approaching sirens could have been a chorus of angels. Nothing had ever sounded sweeter. If he hadn't fled, he surely would now.

Kilpatrick struggled to a sitting position and pulled the Velcro strap of her vest free. She shifted the heavy material and felt her back. "It didn't go through."

"Still going to leave a mark."

"I'll take it." Kilpatrick dropped her hand and leaned back against the steps. "Thanks again for the vest."

"You're very welcome."

Two Scarlet Falls PD units screeched to a halt in front of the brick house. A Randolph County Sheriff's vehicle turned the corner. The air was filled with the overlapping wails of sirens.

Kilpatrick squinted at her. "You're bleeding." She pointed to the side of her neck.

Bree felt the corresponding spot on her own body and found a big wooden splinter lodged under her skin. "I'll take it." Her hand came away sticky with blood. She wiped it on her pants, then met the FBI agent's troubled gaze. "Chance encounter or intentional ambush?"

"Intentional." Kilpatrick clutched her side. "We've pushed someone's buttons."

Chapter 22

PAIGE

Something has changed.

I watch him stalk around the room, his attention turned inward, his mouth curved down in concentration. Usually he constantly stares at me, challenging me with his gaze. Now he seems to have almost forgotten about me.

I shift in the large dog crate, my legs starting to cramp and my stomach twinging with hunger pains. He's forgotten my breakfast; that hasn't happened before. He gets a lot of pleasure out of feeding me. His favorite way is to cover my eyes and tie up my hands, putting me at his mercy for food. I clear my throat and his gaze shifts to me. I glimpse the surprise in his eyes before I look down.

"I'm hungry, Master," I say in a docile voice, staring at the floor.

"Good girl," he says. He strides to the crate and unlocks it with the key from his pocket. He flings open the little door. "Get your own breakfast today," he says. "There's yogurt in the fridge." He stalks out of the room.

Relief and fear swamp me.

Is this a trick?

He's played tricks on me before, testing my obedience, punishing me when I misunderstand. I stay in the crate for ten minutes more, running his command through my head, analyzing it from every direction, searching for a hidden meaning. But I can't find one.

Am I really able to get my own food?

I inch out of the crate and automatically slip on the high heels. The shoes are a rule. I touch the pink bows in my two ponytails, checking that they are straight. There are no mirrors in the home, and I wonder if I look acceptable. I apply the required pink lipstick by feel, then I stand and blood rushes back to my legs, making me waver.

Will he punish me?

I've never been allowed to move about the house on my own. A TV show sounds from the living room, and I take a few unsteady steps to the doorway and recognize the voices from a rerun of *Modern Family*. Tears smart as memories of my family watching it together wash through me. Dad would do perfect impressions of all the characters, making Finn and me roar with laughter.

Why did I leave home?

Because I'd thought my parents were overprotective bores. But now I'd give anything to hear my dad imitate Mitch and Cam.

I take a deep breath and move down the hallway, one hand bracing against the wall. As usual, I'm naked except for the dog collar. I pause at the hallway's end, scanning the large room with the kitchen to my right. All the windows have indoor shutters, which are locked. No chance of a neighbor seeing me wave for attention. He is on the sofa, the back of his head to me, his bare feet propped up on an ottoman.

He ignores me.

But I have no doubts that he knows exactly where I am.

My gaze goes to the front door with its three heavy bolts, and I imagine making a dash for the door, tearing down the street, screaming my head off.

Someone would stop for me, right?

Heat fills my face as I realize I'd be naked in the street. Strangers would see me.

Do I care?

His focus is on his phone as he taps rapidly on its screen.

Jealousy surges through me.

Is he messaging another woman the same promises he made me?

Anger at myself sweeps away the ridiculous split second of jealousy. I hate him. I don't care what he does. He abuses me and lies to me. If he's distracted by another woman, that's less focus on me.

Will he send me home if he finds someone else?

For the first time, a flicker of hope appears, and I urgently pray that he is finished with me. I'll call my parents and get money for a flight home. I could be back in Oregon for fall term. Optimism fills me as I walk silently to the fridge, careful not to disturb him. I can stick out the situation a little longer if it means going home soon.

I open the fridge door and stare, reality sinking in.

I'm going to die.

Chapter 23

MERCY

"I don't need a hospital," Mercy said for the tenth time, glaring at the EMT.

She sat on the bumper of the ambulance, a shiny Mylar blanket draped over her legs even though it was as hot as Hades outside. Air-conditioning from the back of the ambulance blew across her neck, and she wished it would blow everywhere. Especially down her back.

"You probably have cracked ribs," said the young EMT, the image of patience.

"You know what they do for cracked ribs?" asked Mercy. "Nothing. They point them out on an X-ray and then say there's nothing to do except bind them."

"You might have internal bleeding."

"I don't." She wasn't positive, but she knew what to keep an eye out for.

He's doing his job.

She forced a smile. "I appreciate your concern."

The shooting and Bree's call of "officer down" had brought every law enforcement officer for twenty miles. The neighborhood was now crowded with county deputies, state police, and officers from three cities. Not to mention the two fire trucks and an ambulance.

Mercy hated the attention.

Worse, the media had also swarmed. Apparently it was a slow news day.

She was still rattled from the shooting. A few years ago she'd caught a bullet in the leg, but the impact of the bullet to the back of her vest hurt worse. Her entire spine and rib cage would ache for days. She couldn't imagine what the bruise would look like—probably a huge black-and-purple starburst. Breathing already hurt like a bitch. She'd taken ibuprofen and acetaminophen, but so far the pills weren't doing shit.

Who fired at us?

Bree appeared, checking on her for the third time. "You good?"

"Yes," Mercy said between clenched teeth. "But don't you dare make me laugh. My ribs are on fire."

The sheriff raised a brow. "This isn't a laughing matter."

"Our tip house was empty, wasn't it?"

Bree looked grim. "Correct. It appears to have been empty for months. We're trying to contact the owner, but the neighbor across the street said the renters moved out in the early spring and she hasn't seen anyone in the home since."

Mercy shifted her gaze, not wanting to move her head, afraid it would cause pain up her spine. "Does the neighbor live in that house?" She indicated the home where she'd seen curtains flutter when they arrived.

"Yes. She's in her late eighties. Not our shooter."

Mercy snorted and then bit back a cry as pain raced through her ribs. "Don't be funny," she snapped.

"You should get those x-rayed."

"I'm fine."

The look on Bree's face indicated she knew Mercy was lying, but she didn't press the issue. "I have deputies canvassing the neighborhood," said Bree. She leaned closer. "I didn't find any shells in the house next door where I saw the gun barrel—he took the time to clean them up. A busted-out window near the back door indicates he may have broken in. He must have known the house was abandoned when he called in the tip. There's a path behind the home that leads through the woods to a dirt road, and I suspect that's where he parked. I didn't see any footprints or tire tracks, but they're still looking. The dirt's too damn dry."

"He knew where to send us so he could take a shot," said Mercy. "He must be a local—possibly a longtime local if he knew the dirt roads out here."

A clamor of voices pulled their attention. More media had arrived and were pestering the stony-faced deputy assigned to keep onlookers behind the yellow tape. Mercy subtly shifted backward, trying to use the ambulance to hide from the prying cameras.

Bree noticed. "Get over it. You're now part of a police-involved shooting. I've already turned away questions, citing medical confidentiality, but that's not going to last. Your days of hiding from the limelight here are done."

"Shit." Mercy wasn't surprised but she would have liked more time. "How will you explain my presence?"

"Federal assistance on a case."

"And when they ask why an agent from Oregon is helping on a New York case?"

"Maybe tell them that the FBI doesn't see fit to explain its decisions to me?"

Mercy controlled her laugh this time, but a simple deep breath made her eyes nearly roll back in her head.

Truman is going to hit the ceiling when he finds out about the shooting.

She'd feel the same way if it'd happened to her husband. But the risks came with the job, and neither of them would ever ask the other to quit.

This is who we are.

"Is Jimmie still in jail?" asked Mercy in a low voice. He was the first person she'd thought of who might have an issue with their investigation.

"I'm way ahead of you. I already made the call. He was bailed out last night."

"We need to pay him another visit," muttered Mercy.

Bree looked thoughtful. "Frankly I don't get the sense that he'd do this. But I'll have a deputy pick him up for questioning."

"Until I have proof he didn't, he's on my list," said Mercy. "Who else have we stirred up?"

"I don't trust that Mercedes guy we just met—Pete Conrad—but this tip was called in overnight."

"He could have called in two tips. Both were anonymous. He may have called in the second as backup in case he didn't like how the first encounter went." Mercy recalled his angry face. "He definitely didn't get what he wanted."

"But to risk a murder charge when all you have at the moment is soliciting a prostitute? Is he that dumb?"

"The guy had sex in Jimmie's motel room; he's not bright."

"True. Who else?"

"It could be someone we haven't talked to yet," said Mercy. She stiffly leaned forward, peeking around the ambulance but quickly pulled back. Numerous lenses were pointed her way. "This is going to explode, isn't it?"

"You saw the ridiculous mess of people protesting outside the station. The media loves that sort of thing."

Mercy winced. It simply hurt to breathe.

Bree noticed. "I don't think your motel has sufficient security measures. You've been shot at and now your face is probably going to be plastered across the local media. Once they get your name, they'll find where you're staying. Who knows what kind of person will come looking for you."

"I know how to deal with idiots."

The sheriff didn't look convinced. "I'm not worried about curiosity seekers. I'm worried someone will be mad because he didn't finish the job."

"Maybe he meant to hit you."

"Uh-huh." Bree scowled. "Are you ready to tell me the identity of your girl yet? After this fuckup I *really don't* like being in the dark. For all I know, this shooting was completely about her—and you."

Mercy briefly closed her eyes. It was time. The sheriff deserved to know. "I'm looking for Paige Holcroft. She's the seventeen-year-old daughter of US Senator Adam Holcroft."

"Damn it." Bree stared. "That is worse than I expected." She glanced back at the cluster of reporters. "How the hell have you kept it from the media for more than two weeks?"

"A lot of luck," said Mercy. "I'm grateful it's lasted this long."

"And she might be in the hands of a killer." Bree rubbed the back of her neck. "Does he know who Paige's father is?"

"I assume so. She was picked up at her home. As you can imagine, the house is rather grand. If he didn't already know she was the daughter of a senator, the house would raise questions."

"But no ransom. No political threats."

"Not even a whisper."

"So it looks like he took her because she offered what he wanted. Especially if they met on that website," said Bree. "I assume he didn't like that we're investigating Vanessa."

"Don't assume," said Mercy. But she didn't have any other ideas. Besides Jimmie.

"I'm open to all possibilities," said Bree. "Which also means you are checking out of that motel and staying with me. The security at my place is top of the line, and I'm the only one at the house this week."

"I can't have you do that."

"Well, I can't have you staying in a motel with a single camera and door locks I can bust with one kick."

Mercy knew the sheriff was right, but imposing on anyone made her uncomfortable.

"I have a fancy coffee machine." The sheriff raised one brow.

Mercy blinked.

"And I have horses."

Mercy imagined running her hands along the smooth neck of a horse and the sweet scent of hay. She'd been raised on a farm, and she missed the animals.

"Deal."

Chapter 24

BREE

It was almost dark when Bree opened the rear cargo area of her SUV, grabbed Mercy's bag, and realized that she now thought of the agent by her first name. Being shot at together—and Mercy confiding in Bree about the senator's daughter—had put them on different terms.

"I can get that," Mercy protested as she eased out of the SUV like a ninety-year-old.

Bree ignored her outstretched hand. "You just get yourself to the door."

Mercy walked gingerly across the grass.

"Let me go in and contain the dog. We have two. Brody is a former K-9. His manners are impeccable. But Ladybug is less . . . I hate to say she isn't smart, but she isn't. She is, however, aggressively friendly."

Mercy waited on the porch while Bree opened the door and stepped into the kitchen. Ladybug slammed into her legs. Behind her, Brody seemed to sigh. Bree set down Mercy's bag.

"OK, girl. Chill." Bree grabbed the dog's collar, asked her to sit, and opened the door for Mercy. "It's safe."

Mercy walked into the kitchen. Brody greeted her gently. Mercy stroked his head. "He's a beauty."

"He's a very good boy." Bree pulled Ladybug toward the door. "I'm going to take the dogs outside for a few minutes. Why don't you get settled? Top of the stairs, first bedroom on the left."

"Thanks." Mercy picked up her bag, clearly trying to cover the pain of lifting it.

Bree called Brody and released Ladybug on the back porch. Both dogs trotted onto the grass to do their business. She headed for the barn. Adam had once again handled feeding time. Bree went from stall to stall, checking each animal for cuts or lameness. Horses had a unique ability to injure themselves doing absolutely nothing. Everyone seemed fine, and Bree turned them out into the pasture for the night.

She returned to the house to find Mercy in the kitchen with her black cat, Vader. "The cat seems nice."

"He likes women. Men, not so much," Bree said. "You're probably hungry since you lost your enchiladas."

"I am." Mercy patted her stomach. "The Mexican seemed like a good idea at the time, but maybe something a little milder would be better now."

Bree opened the freezer. "You're in luck. My unofficial live-in nanny, Dana, likes to cook, and knows I won't. She left meals in the freezer."

"Where is the family?" Mercy asked. "I saw a little girl's room."

"My niece, Kayla, is nine. Luke is seventeen. They went to the beach with Dana's extended family. It's a good time for them to escape the heat here." Bree pulled a glass baking dish from the freezer and read the label. "Chicken piccata?"

"Homemade?"

"Dana would be offended to be asked that." Bree put the dish in the microwave. "Oh. I found a loaf of her french bread." She turned on the oven, then went to the pantry and scanned Dana's stash of red wine. "I'm not a big drinker, but tonight might call for a small glass."

"I agree wholeheartedly."

"I don't know much about wine. You want to pick a bottle?" Bree put the bread on the baking sheet.

"Glad to." Mercy emerged from the pantry and held up a bottle. "Pinot noir."

"OK." Bree pulled the cork and filled two glasses.

Ten minutes later, the piccata was hot and the bread crisp. Bree piled the food on plates and brought them to the table.

Mercy tasted the chicken. "This is amazing."

"Wait until you try the bread."

They cleared their plates in minutes.

"That's almost embarrassing." Bree piled the dishes in the sink. "Let's take the wine outside. I think some fresh air would help clear my head. It's been a day." She grabbed an ice pack for Mercy.

The dogs followed them onto the back porch, lying down with deep sighs and the thunk of bones. Bree settled back in her chair. The wine was mellow.

"What kind of horse is that?" Mercy pointed to Beast grazing just beyond the gate.

"Matt's Percheron. He was an Amish workhorse. He's a big one but very gentle. Loves the kids and all human attention like a giant puppy. They're all rescues, from the kill pen."

Mercy sat down slowly, placing the ice behind her and leaning on it. "This is nice. How long have you lived here?"

"Since my sister died about a year and a half ago."

"I'm sorry."

Bree sipped. The pain still bloomed fresh whenever she thought about Erin's death, but with time, it was becoming more of a blunt ache and less of a sharp stab. "She was murdered, which made things even harder on the kids."

"I've been raising my niece since my brother was killed."

"That's not something I'm thrilled that we have in common," Bree said.

"No."

"I used to work homicide in Philadelphia." Bree waved a hand toward the pasture, where the dark shapes of the horses moved. "This is a whole new life for me. Sometimes I feel guilty for being happy here."

"I get that." Mercy inhaled. "I miss the country. I even miss the smells of a farm."

Bree snorted. "I was raised here until I was eight. I adjusted to city life, but manure still smells like home to me."

Mercy laughed, winced, and then quieted. "I hate to bring up work, but do we have a plan for tomorrow?"

"Finding out who shot you would be awesome. I'm assuming it's our killer."

"Seems the most likely possibility," Mercy agreed.

"Are we also agreed we're dealing with a serial killer?" Bree asked. "We'll have to answer to the press tomorrow."

Mercy stared out over the dark pasture and drank more wine. "I don't see how we can deny it any longer. We have two dead women, one kidnapped teen, and a potential fourth victim, so I'd say yes. We have a serial killer here."

"It's up to us to stop him."

"And find Paige," Mercy added.

"You know she's here."

Nodding, Mercy flattened a hand at the base of her throat. "I can feel it."

Bree felt it in her bones too. "Then we need to find her."

Before he kills her.

Chapter 25

Him

I scan today's articles. A headline in the middle of my news page reads: FBI AGENT SHOT IN RANDOLPH COUNTY HUNT FOR SERIAL KILLER.

I skim the content. A thrill zooms through me. I'd thought I was shooting someone in the sheriff's department. After all, her vest was emblazoned with the word SHERIFF on both sides. As it turns out, I shot an FBI agent.

Cool.

I'm pleased that my plan worked as well as it did. The sheriff followed my "tip" and walked right into my trap. I took a few potshots at what I'd thought was a deputy or plainclothes detective. I'm not ready to kill the sheriff outright. Not yet. I'm not done playing with her.

I add *think of new ways to fuck with the sheriff* to my mental to-do list.

But shooting an FBI agent? Could my luck have been any better?

Hell no!

Good thing I am an excellent shot.

There's a photo of the agent receiving medical treatment from an EMT at the scene. I was long gone before first responders arrived. I zoom in on her face and her lovely long dark hair. She's taller than I like, but I still take a moment to imagine her wearing just a collar.

I think of the girl in the next room. She's been easy to train, to mold.

To break.

Is she too easy? I thought a senator's daughter would be more defiant. After all, she's been raised to think she's better than everyone else. But it seems that spoiled life made her soft and naive instead.

I've become a better teacher through the last few experiences. It is a learn-by-doing activity and requires practice. But with greater skill I might want to try a more challenging subject. I'll let that idea marinate. So far, I've lured my conquests. Then again, I lured the sheriff to that vacant house too. I just did it in a different way. I like it when *they* come to *me*, when I manipulate them and they are unaware.

I scroll through more headlines, almost surprised that no one has named me yet. The public and press haven't come up with anything interesting. They've been a disappointment. I read the list I've been working on.

Randolph County Killer? Nah. Boring.

Echo Road Killer? I roll my eyes at that one. Sounds cheap.

The Suitcase Killer? Too sensational and obvious. Not original at all.

I want something clever. The name is how I will be remembered forever. It should be both clever and catchy, like Ted Bundy's nickname, the Lady Killer. Dennis Rader named himself the BTK Killer, his own clever take on *bind, torture, kill*. Maybe naming myself is the way to go. If I leave it to chance, an embarrassing name might catch on, a name not worthy of my accomplishments.

If you want something done right, do it yourself.

I vaguely remember that Rader taunted the police and kept them at bay for many years—until he lost control and made a mistake that led to his capture.

Control is the most important aspect of this game. Control is what I seek. Control of the women, control over myself. I think of the excitement I felt watching the sheriff arrive at the location where I'd led her, of lining up the sights on my gun, of choosing my target, of pulling the trigger, of my bullet knocking the FBI agent to the ground. I play the shot over and over in my mind like a GIF.

Control over the press and police investigation is critical. Soon, they'll realize I'm in charge, not them.

My gaze roams to my anonymous email account, and my name comes to me. Why didn't I think of it before? It's so obvious. I already know who I am. I've been using the perfect moniker forever. It says everything about me and what I want to accomplish.

I am the Master.

Chapter 26

MERCY

Day 5

The next morning, Mercy pressed some random buttons on Bree's fancy coffee machine and then washed down her ibuprofen with steaming-hot coffee, burning her tongue.

Her back hurt. Her ribs hurt. And now her mouth hurt.

It was almost six a.m., and Mercy had slept like shit. If it wasn't her back waking her up, it was the unfamiliar pillow or her brain in fast-forward. The house was still silent as she quietly moved in the kitchen. Bree seemed like the type to start her mornings early, so Mercy expected to see her soon.

She peeked in the fridge, and her gaze locked in surprise on a small carton of whipping cream. Mercy suspected it had been bought by the nanny—the one who made that amazing chicken from last night. The carton was open and the expiration date had just passed, so she took a strong sniff and then poured it in her coffee. She headed outside.

She sat in the same chair on the porch as last night, leaning back carefully into a faded cushion. The morning light was soft and the skies clear, promising a warm day. She sighed and tried to relax. The faint smell of horses reached her, and Mercy fought the urge to explore the barn. *Can't take the farm out of the girl.*

Her thoughts returned to yesterday. Late last night she'd told Truman about the shooting, worried the news would somehow make it across the US before she could call him. He'd been silent as she spoke rapidly. At least she'd been smart enough to open with "I'm not hurt, but . . ."

"Are you in danger out there?" he'd finally asked.

"You and I are in danger every time we step out the door. Comes with the territory."

"Doesn't mean I can't get upset. Thank God that sheriff gave you a vest. Keep wearing it," he'd said.

"I'll ask for a new one. That one is damaged." She'd been pleased to hear him nearly laugh at that.

"Do the investigators out here know about it?" he'd asked.

"I plan to call Evan after you."

"I'll tell Kaylie and Ollie what happened. Neither one is going to be happy."

"I know." There'd been a long moment of silence as she thought about the kids. "I love you," she said.

"I love you too."

They ended every phone call with the words, too aware that their future wasn't predictable.

Bree opened the back door. "You OK?" She came out and pulled up another chair, scanning Mercy up and down, searching for signs of pain. She wore pajamas and her phone was in hand.

Mercy wasn't used to seeing Bree with her hair down. It'd been in a bun every day. She held up her cup of coffee in salute. "I'm good. Sore. It'll get better."

"Have you been online?" Bree looked grim.

Something's up.

"Not yet. Still trying to caffeinate. Is there something new about our case?"

"Yes and no." Bree looked at her phone. "You've been identified."

Damn it.

"We knew that would eventually happen," said Mercy. "More time would have been nice, though. Who broke it?"

"It's all over the local news' social media. That reporter, Ken Wells, shot a segment asking why the FBI has an agent involved and implying again that we haven't been fully truthful about the murdered women. As if he hasn't stirred up the community enough."

"Nothing about the senator or Paige Holcroft?"

"Not yet." Bree looked grim. "That's inevitable, though." She held out her phone and Mercy watched the reporter's video.

It had been posted just after midnight, filmed in front of the home where Mercy had been shot. "He's pretty, isn't he?"

"He knows it," said Bree. "I wonder how he got the information."

"I bet he asked one of the deputies or even the EMT about the officer who'd been shot and someone corrected him that I was FBI. Maybe they even said my name. A little digging and he found me." She eyed Bree, thinking about their little chat last night. "I didn't thank you for saving my butt yesterday." Her throat grew tight. "I'd have you back me up anytime."

It was the ultimate compliment in their profession. As law enforcement they always knew who they wanted as backup—and who they absolutely didn't. You had to trust them with your life.

Bree nodded, her gaze on Mercy. "You're welcome, and the feeling is mutual."

"I know it's early, but can we go find that killer now?" asked Mercy with a half smile.

"Breakfast, shower, then go."

"Sounds good. Say . . . can I get a new vest?"

"Abso-fucking-lutely."

The women exchanged a grin.

◆ ◆ ◆

A few hours later, Mercy and Bree were in the conference room sorting through more tips.

"Damn that reward. It's bringing in all sorts of junk," said Bree. "Everyone wants to say something even if it's not related. I swear they just want to mess with us."

Mercy agreed. She'd made a follow-up phone call on a tip only to hear the caller swear that she saw Vanessa Mullen two weeks ago at the grocery store.

Mercy didn't tell her that was impossible. She thanked her and hung up.

Marge had been turning away call after call about the presence of an FBI agent on the case. She said most of them had been from more media.

Mercy had made a quick call to Evan, waking him at six a.m. Pacific time, to give a heads-up about her status. They'd had a quick discussion—again—of whether it was time for the senator to publicly announce that his daughter was missing. There were pros and cons. Mercy wanted more investigation time before the national media got the news; the local media was causing enough problems as it was. Evan argued that they might get more leads. Two leads that had led agents to Utah and Washington had been a bust.

"That makes it all the more important that we are able to investigate here," Mercy had told him.

"Do you need to ask for more agents?"

"Nothing is concrete yet," she'd told him. "But I feel I'm close."

In the conference room, Bree looked at the pictures they'd put up on their board. "Who do we like?"

Mercy went to stand beside her and pointed at Vanessa's ex. "Jimmie turn up yet?"

"Not yet. We're still looking. He's probably under a rock somewhere."

"I'd say he's our strongest suspect. It doesn't look good that he was out of jail when I was shot."

"True. How do you feel now about Mr. Mercedes, Pete Conrad? His background check came back clean." Bree studied the man's photo.

Mercy eyed the tall man. "He's still not high on my list. I suspect he's just guilty of bad decisions. But I want to know where he was at the time of the shooting." She made a note on her yellow pad. "I'm curious what his alibi will be."

"We haven't considered the ex-husband," said Bree, gesturing at Rick Mullen. "Seems like a normal guy. With those kids, I don't know how he has time for anything else."

"He seems unlikely too. Damn it. Why isn't anyone jumping out at me?"

"Possibly because the right guy isn't on our board yet."

We'll keep digging.

Bree's cell phone rang and she checked the screen. "It's Dr. Jones." She answered immediately.

It took Mercy a long second to connect the name to the medical examiner.

Bree listened briefly. "I'm going to put you on speaker, Doctor. Agent Kilpatrick is in the room with me." Her eyes danced with excitement.

"Morning, Agent Kilpatrick. I have an identification on the other woman from the suitcases," said the doctor.

Yes!

"I received a call yesterday from a Naomi Binney that the woman might be Tisha Talbot. Age twenty-five. Naomi had heard about the press conference and called me instead of the tip line. She stated they had been close friends since high school, and she hadn't seen her for a few months. She tried to call Tisha and went to her apartment with no luck before contacting me. Naomi even knew the name of Tisha's dentist—said they went to the same one. I called the dental office yesterday, got Tisha's films, and my odontologist says it's a definite match."

"Tisha Talbot isn't on our list of missing women within a hundred miles," said Bree.

"I just got back Tisha's lab reports, which say she's been dead about a month. Agent Kilpatrick, you'd originally asked if she could have died within the last two weeks, and I'd said yes, but now we know that's not what happened."

"A month? Why did no one report her?" asked Mercy.

Was she a recluse?

Bree was already tapping on her computer.

"Naomi said that the police should contact Tisha's father," continued Dr. Jones. "She wouldn't be specific, but she said he's got a record and had hurt Tisha at one point."

"Hurt?" asked Bree.

"She didn't expand," said Dr. Jones. "I pressed a little, but she wouldn't give any details. She said there's a police report."

"Thank you, Doctor. Anything else?" said Mercy.

"Yes. You should be aware that Rick Mullen contacted my office today. He needs documentation of Vanessa's death for her life insurance."

Mercy met Bree's stare.

Motive.

"Thank you for telling us," Mercy forced out, still processing the new information.

"Glad I could help." The doctor ended the call.

"Holy shit," said Mercy. "We'd just talked about him. I'd say life insurance moves him up the suspect list a bit."

"Especially since they've been divorced for three years," said Bree.

"I'll make a note to follow up on that," said Mercy, adding to her yellow pad. "I'm interested to know how old and how much the policy is for. But for now let's get back to Tisha. I want to know why no one reported her missing."

Bree refocused on her computer screen, a small frown on her face.

"Well?" asked Mercy. "What did you find on her?"

"At the moment I'm more interested in Neal Talbot, her father. He is on the registered sex offenders list as a level two and has about ten domestic assault charges over the last decade. Prison time twice. Appears the older charges were filed by his wife, but there are a few other women in the last few years. Girlfriends maybe? I'll guess the wife got away from him at some point."

"Is there a current address for his wife?" Dread built in Mercy's stomach.

Did his wife vanish too?

"Yes. And she got a speeding ticket last month." Relief flashed on Bree's face.

"Did Tisha file a report against her father?"

"I don't see one." The sheriff frowned. "Did Naomi lie about the report to Dr. Jones, or did Tisha lie to Naomi?"

"I suspect the latter. What got Neal Talbot a level two on the registered sex offenders list?" Mercy knew the three levels were determined by points assigned to various aspects of the crimes. Any combination of actions could have landed Talbot there.

"Armed. Forced. More than one victim. And physical injury."

"He sounds like a nice man." Anger was building in Mercy's chest.

"He also sounds like someone who'd force a ball gag into someone's mouth," said Bree. "I want to see him. Today."

"The friend too . . . Naomi Binney. And maybe Tisha's mother." Mercy winced. "Shit. We need to do a notification, don't we?"

"The mother lives in Maine. I'll find someone local to do it in person. Then we can call her." Bree spun the laptop around so she could see.

Several booking photos of Neal Talbot were on the screen. He was bald on top and had a thick porn stache. His eyes were angry. Mercy noted he had a bloody nose in one and scratches on his cheek in another. *Somebody fought back.*

"No charges filed against him in the last two years," said Bree. "I guess that's good."

"Let's pay a visit right now," Mercy said. "I'd like to hear what he has to say about his daughter's fate."

"I'll grab a deputy for backup," said Bree.

A random pain shot through Mercy's ribs. "Good idea."

Chapter 27

MERCY

Neal Talbot's apartment building looked new and well cared for. The landscaping was perfectly manicured, and someone had put thought into paint colors for the apartments, using a palette of grays, greens, and blues. As Mercy and Bree got out of the car, they heard children splashing and shouting in a pool.

"Nice place," said Mercy.

"It's not very old," said Bree. "One of the more expensive complexes around here."

It wasn't where Mercy expected a man to live who had been convicted of domestic assault and appeared on the sex registry.

Don't assume.

They went up an open stairwell to the second floor and found the right apartment. Mercy tapped her vest, reassuring herself that it was in place. Even Bree was scanning their surroundings more than usual, her jaw set. "We decided to come here," Mercy said softly as they stepped to the side of the door. "No one directed us here."

Bree gave a sharp nod and knocked on the door.

A few seconds later it was opened by a young woman in shorts and a tank top who appeared to be in her twenties. Her dark hair was cut short in a pixie cut that perfectly framed her face. Her smile faltered as she took in Bree's uniform and Mercy's vest emblazoned with SHERIFF. She wrinkled her forehead. "Can I help you, officers?"

"We need to speak with Neal Talbot," said Bree.

Something flashed in the woman's eyes, and her chin rose the smallest bit. "May I ask what this is about?"

"It's about his daughter, Tisha," said Mercy.

The woman's perfect brows shot up. "Is she OK?" She looked from Mercy to Bree, concern in her gaze.

"Is Neal here?" asked Bree.

"Yes. Come in." She stepped back and waved them toward a nice sectional in the living room. She moved to the base of a stairway that led to the upper level of the apartment. "Neal? Can you come down? The police are here and want to ask you about Tisha."

"Coming," came the faint reply.

"What's your name?" Mercy asked, studying the woman. "Do you live here?"

"Colleen Bell. And yes, I do." The slightly defensive expression returned.

Protective. Is she a girlfriend? Relative?

Mercy couldn't remember if Neal Talbot had other family.

Feet thudded on the stairs, and Neal came into view. Mercy did a double take, and noticed Bree had sat up straighter at his appearance.

Neal Talbot barely resembled his booking photos. The porn stache was gone, replaced by a neatly trimmed goatee, and his face was lean. He'd lost the roundness from the pictures. He looked like a healthy and relaxed fifty-year-old. He no longer had anger in his eyes, only concern.

"What's happened to Tisha?" he asked as he entered the room. Colleen moved to stand next to him, as if she knew he would soon need support.

"Can you sit down, Mr. Talbot?" asked Bree. "We need to talk."

The couple sat. Mercy noted Colleen took Neal's hand and her leg pressed against his.

Definitely girlfriend.

She wondered about the age difference. It had to be at least twenty years.

"I'm very sorry, Mr. Talbot. And there is no way to break this easily, but Tisha was murdered about a month ago. Her remains were found just this week."

Neal's face fell and he exhaled, his shoulders drooping. Colleen rubbed his upper arm. "I'm so sorry, sweetie." She turned to the women. "Are you sure it's her?"

"She was identified through dental records," said Mercy. "There is no doubt."

"What happened?" asked Colleen.

"We'll get to that in a moment," said Bree.

Neal buried his face in his hands. "I told her," he blurted, his face hidden. "I warned her so many times that she needed to put it all behind her."

Mercy exchanged a glance with Bree.

"Put what behind her, sir?" Bree asked. "If you could give us some background on Tisha, we'd appreciate it. We are looking for the person who did this."

He blew out a breath and raised his head, meeting their gazes. "The drugs. The alcohol. Her life rotated around them. I told her it'd come to no good." His face crumpled. "And now it happened."

"When did you see her last?" asked Mercy.

He wiped his nose and looked at Colleen. "Two, three months ago?"

Colleen nodded. "Nearly three months. It was the day before my birthday when she came here." Distaste flickered in her gaze.

He turned back to the women. "She wanted money. That was the only reason she ever came around. She looked like hell and I could tell she was high. She threw a fit when I said no, yelling and screaming at both of us."

"You didn't think it odd that you hadn't seen her since then?" asked Bree. "What about a phone call or text?"

"Not odd at all," said Neal, pulling a phone out of his pocket. "She'd come begging, I'd send her away, and she'd vanish for weeks at a time." He scrolled on his phone. "No calls. That's normal. And the last text was two days before she came here. Asking for money, of course."

"May I see that?" asked Mercy, holding out a hand. He gave her the phone, and Bree leaned to look. The last text was from Tisha, calling him an asshole and rapist. The conversation before that was her asking for money and Neal refusing. She noted the date and gave the phone back.

"Rapist?" asked Bree.

Neal sighed, resignation in his eyes. "I assume you know my past."

"Maybe we should talk to you alone," said Mercy, eyeing Colleen. Neal might not want her to hear certain things and would hold back information.

He shook his head. "Colleen knows everything. *Everything*," he emphasized. "She knows about my record and prison time and the fact that I'm on the sex offender registry. I have no secrets from her."

Point for Neal.

"I assume you know too," he said. "But I'm a different man now. I've been in recovery for two years. Once I gave up alcohol, my life changed—all for the better. It's been a bitch, but I've done it. Day by day."

Colleen squeezed his hand. Mercy didn't know what to think of the look of pride on Colleen's face. Given Neal's past and what he'd done to other women, it was hard to believe she had chosen to stand by him.

Has she been manipulated? Brainwashed?

Even serial killers in prison attracted attention from women. Seemingly normal middle-class women who wrote them love letters and sent money. It was a state of mind that Mercy couldn't comprehend.

"What happened to Tisha?" he asked, his voice breaking on her name.

"Did you see the news about two murdered women found alongside a rural road this week?" Bree asked gently.

He shook his head. "I don't watch the news. Or read much of it either. I may have my head in the sand, but it helps keep me steady. What I see on the news . . . can anger me," he admitted. "And when I'm angry, I want a drink."

Colleen nodded. "I pay attention. I tell him if there's anything newsworthy that he should know. I heard something about two women and suitcases?"

"That's correct," said Mercy. "Sadly, Tisha and a woman named Vanessa Mullen were murdered, packed in suitcases, and left along Echo Road."

Neal blanched. "Jesus Christ." He swallowed hard and rubbed a hand across his mouth. "Who would do that?" he whispered.

"Do either of you know Vanessa Mullen?" asked Bree, showing them a photo on her phone. Both shook their heads.

"Did you physically harm Tisha at one point?" asked Mercy, closely watching his face.

Guilt flashed. "I did," he said quietly. "It was before I quit and I was drunk at the time—which is no excuse for what I did. I take full responsibility for my actions that day, and I've asked Tisha's forgiveness for it. She was high, and we got into an argument. She'd accused me of some things I *didn't* do. She swung at me and I grabbed her arm, wrenching it behind her back." He shuddered. "I can still hear her scream. I bruised her arm pretty badly and pulled something in her shoulder. She threatened to call the police, but I managed to talk her out of it." He met Mercy's gaze. "How did you know about it?"

"She told one of her friends. But also told her friend a police report had been filed."

"Tisha probably thought the friend would be angry if she didn't file a report. So she lied about it," said Colleen, giving Neal a questioning glance.

"Probably." He looked grim.

"You'd heard before how he'd hurt her arm?" Bree asked Colleen.

"Yes. He's not that man anymore."

"How long have you been together?" Mercy asked.

Colleen tipped her head, thinking. "Nine months. I moved in two months ago. We both work at Home Depot."

"Just to confirm," said Bree. "Neither of you have heard from Tisha in three months."

Both nodded.

"Do you know of anyone who would do this to her?" asked Bree.

Mercy watched their eyes. "Do you know where she was living?" she asked Neal. "Or who she was hanging out with?"

"No. I haven't been a part of her life in a long time." He met Mercy's gaze. "I assumed she hung around with people like herself, but I don't know who they are or where she's been. As far as I know, I'm the only person who physically hurt her. Until now." His gaze was steady, but Mercy heard pain and regret in his voice. "Has her mother been told?" he asked.

"Probably not yet," said Bree. "I've asked her local PD to notify her in person. I plan to talk to her later." She stood and Mercy joined her. "We'll be going. Here are our cards if you think of anything we should know." They accepted the cards and a minute later the women were headed down the outdoor stairwell.

After they got in Bree's SUV, she asked, "Believe him?"

Mercy took a deep breath. "I don't know. I hate to admit I prejudged him before we met. I like to think I approach people unbiased."

"Hard to not be biased after reading his record," said Bree. "Do you believe he's turned over a new leaf or not? And what is with Colleen? The man is made of red flags. Most women would be headed for the hills."

"I don't know," said Mercy. "I don't understand her thinking, and I don't know if I believe everything he said." Her brain was spinning with doubt.

Bree's phone rang, and she sighed loudly. Mercy glanced at the screen. "Cruella again?" She wasn't a fan after the county administrator had announced the reward without first discussing it with law enforcement.

Bree touched the screen, answering the phone on speaker. "Sheriff Taggert."

"There you are," said Madeline Jager.

"What do you need, Ms. Jager?"

"I wanted you to know I've organized a town hall. A gathering where our residents can express their safety concerns in an orderly fashion. I expect you to be there. And that FBI agent too."

Mercy doubted any town hall about a serial killer would be orderly. According to Bree's expression, she'd had the same thought.

"Are you sure that's—"

"It's in one hour," announced Madeline, cutting her off. "I'll see you there." She ended the call.

Bree blew out a breath. "Why the fuck does she do shit like that?"

"Sounds like an interesting evening," said Mercy.

"You have no idea."

Chapter 28

BREE

Bree maneuvered the vehicle around a crowd of people in front of the Randolph County municipal building. "Looks like we're going to have a full house."

"The protesters followed you here." Mercy gestured to a group carrying signs and marching in a circle.

As soon as the protesters saw the sheriff's vehicle, they surrounded it, thumping on the car and chanting, "Sheriff Taggert lies!"

Bree eased off the accelerator but kept the tires rolling. "Plenty of press too."

Vans were lined up at the curb. Reporters delivered sound bites from the sidewalk with the building in the background.

Bree nosed the SUV toward the electronic arm that blocked the entrance to the fenced county employee parking lot. Once the yellow barrier rose, she entered the lot. They might have left the protesters behind, but she could still hear the chanting. The impending town hall seemed to have invigorated their enthusiasm.

They used the back door to avoid the worst of the crush.

"Are town hall meetings usually this well attended?" Mercy asked.

"It's hit or miss." Bree gestured toward a double doorway. "You should have seen the uproar when the board of supervisors wanted to tighten regulations on backyard chickens. People lost their minds."

"I believe it."

To avoid the main crowd, they used the side door to access the community room, which was already packed. Reporters flanked the room. Residents filled every seat and stood in the back. At the door, Deputy Zucco warned people, "It's standing room only."

Two members of the board of supervisors sat at a long rectangular table that faced the room. A podium stood just off-center of the large projection screen mounted on the wall.

As Bree and Mercy took seats at the table, the crowd hushed. A microphone on a stand had been placed at the head of the center aisle. Clothing rustled, conversation hummed, and shoes squeaked on tile. Somewhere, a baby cried. Jager made her grand entrance and people focused on her, which was clearly what she wanted. She strode down the aisle as if she were the queen.

Bree scanned the antsy crowd. Many of the faces were familiar. She recognized people from around town: The grocery store clerk who'd rung up her order over the weekend. A nurse from the pediatrician's office. The manager of the Burger Palace, Carl Simmons, was in the third row. *Interesting.* A group of mothers from Kayla's school clustered together. Also notable, Vanessa Mullen's ex-husband sat in the same row as the mall security guard, Don Dutton.

Jager went to the podium. "This is an informal town hall. We're here to update you all on the double-murder investigation and to answer your questions." She introduced the two county supervisors. Bree didn't know why they were there, except to show support for Jager and get their faces in front of the cameras. "And here we have Sheriff Taggert and FBI Special Agent Mercy Kilpatrick."

Someone booed. Another yelled, "Liars."

In the back a man shouted, "Shut it, people. Let them speak."

Thank you.

"First, I'd like to have Sheriff Taggert give you an update on the investigation. Sheriff?" Madeline smiled almost sweetly, but Bree saw the challenge—and warning—in her eyes, an unspoken command for Bree to smooth the situation over and make everyone feel better.

But it wasn't Bree's job to make nice. It was her job to catch a killer and protect the residents. She also didn't take commands from a bureaucrat.

A microphone sat on the table in front of Bree, clearly intended for her use. But Bree rose and strode to the podium instead. Jager was forced to step aside and cede the position to her.

Bree leaned over the mic and gave the information about Tisha Talbot. "The medical examiner has estimated that she's been dead for about a month. Since we now know that our two deceased women died in separate events, we can confirm that they were likely victims of a serial killer."

Bedlam broke out. People shouted over one another, the pitch of the combined conversation rising in panic. Jager looked like she was grinding rocks into dust with her molars.

"Quiet, please." Bree raised her voice. "We are here to answer your questions."

A bottle blonde in an expensive white sheath dress shoved people in her row to get to the microphone. "How did two women die without you knowing about it? How did that happen, Sheriff?"

How did I let something happen that I didn't know about?

Since Bree didn't have an answer to a nonsense question, she merely said, "The sheriff's department has been working on the case 24/7 since the victims were found. And we will continue to do so until the killer is caught."

The blonde didn't seem satisfied, but a man in wire-rimmed glasses, a black T-shirt, and baggy jeans took the mic. "Why is the FBI here? Are you going to take over the case?"

Mercy joined Bree at the podium. "In cases like this, the FBI provides resources that most local municipalities don't possess. We're here as a supportive role—not to take over the investigation. I can assure you that Sheriff Taggert is doing everything possible to catch this killer."

People began to line up at the mic. An older man waved his cane in the air. "The wrath of God is raining down on this town because of ungodly behavior. Satan is using smartphones to tempt our children into unholy deeds. We need Jesus back in the classroom."

"OK," Bree said. "Next."

Vanessa's ex-husband, Rick Mullen, stepped up to the mic. "I had to tell my children that their mother is dead. I'm grateful they're too young to ask details, but someday they'll want to know what happened to her. I don't know what I'm going to tell them." He broke down with a sob. "What are you doing to make sure other women—and their families—don't meet the same horrible fate as my wife?"

Why did you have an insurance policy on your ex-wife?

"I'm sorry for your loss, Mr. Mullen. My department is working nonstop to apprehend your ex-wife's killer." Bree turned toward the closest camera, addressing the killer in case he was watching. "We will find him."

People stirred. The air-conditioning couldn't handle the outside temps and the crush of warm bodies. A bead of sweat dripped down the back of Bree's neck.

An attractive brunette appeared at Rick's side and led him away. The way she touched him and leaned her head toward his suggested intimacy. Was that the neighbor who'd watched his kids the day Bree notified him of Vanessa's death?

I wonder how long that's been going on.

As Rick Mullen stepped away, Bree noticed the manager of the Burger Palace watching intently, as if he needed a bucket of popcorn. This did feel like a spectacle.

"Liar!" someone in the back of the room shouted. "What are you hiding?"

Deputy Zucco signaled to Bree, asking by gesture if she wanted the heckler removed. Bree shook her head. Having residents thrown out of the town hall wasn't a good look. Instead, she decided to address the vocal resident directly. "What would I hide and why?" A minute of silence went by with no answers. "Seriously, I am baffled when I hear these accusations because I can't figure out what my motivation would be."

"You're all about politics!" the woman retorted, but her weak response lacked steam.

Bree ignored her. "I hear you. You're all upset, and you have every right to be. This is horrible and frightening. But you all know the two women were murdered, and that we haven't caught the killer yet. What else is there? Trust me, I want nothing more than to tell you we've solved the case—or even that we're closing in on a suspect. But I can't, because that wouldn't be honest."

She made as much eye contact as possible, shying away from no one's gaze, even the hostile ones.

Don Dutton approached the mic. He must have come directly from work because he was still dressed in his uniform. "I work security, and people are worried. How should people keep themselves and their families safe?"

Finally, a productive question.

"People should keep their doors locked. Go out in groups. Carpool. Be aware of your surroundings. When you're in an empty parking lot, keep your eyes up, not on your phone." Bree cited the usual safety precautions, which felt woefully inadequate.

"Do you know how he took the women?" a woman called out without bothering to approach the mic.

"We don't," Bree admitted. "So be aware all the time."

When the handsome blond reporter took the mic, Bree felt heat build at the base of her neck. This forum was for the public, and he was up to something. She could read it in the cocky set of his shoulders and the triumph in his eyes.

"Ken Wells, WSNY," he said in a deep voice that was as Hollywood as his face. His cameraman worked a flattering angle from the sidelines. "When are you going to tell the public that the serial killer might have claimed four victims, not two?"

People went ballistic: talking, yelling, and gesturing angrily. From the smug smile on Ken's face, Bree was sure that sowing chaos had been the plan.

She kept her face impassive, but what the actual fuck? How did he know about that? But she did need to respond—and quickly. She tapped the mic, but the crowd wasn't having any of her attempts to wrestle back control of the meeting. Instead, she raised her voice into the mic. "We have no evidence of that, and we don't operate on conjecture."

The noise settled to murmurs.

"But four identical tattoos were done, right?" Ken pressed. "And two of them were on the dead women."

"We showed you the tattoo that was on the victims. But—again—we don't have any means to identify other people who might have wanted a similar or the same tattoo."

The reporter's bombshell had made the crowd angry and restless. No one was listening. Bree tried to think of information that would settle them but came up with nothing.

Jager bumped Bree's elbow and leaned across her body to speak into the mic. "The meeting is adjourned."

Bree covered the mic. "Why would you end the meeting on that note?"

"Well, you certainly weren't winning anyone over, were you?" Jager glared, then muttered, "That was a disaster."

Disgusted, Bree turned away from her. She wanted to talk to Ken Wells. Scanning the room, she saw that Mercy was already on it. She was cutting through the crowd on her way to the reporter. Bree signaled to Deputy Zucco at the door and pointed to the reporter. The deputy nodded. When Wells tried to pass, the deputy pulled him aside. But Wells shook her off and glowered back at Bree before bolting for the door. Deputy Zucco flashed angry eyes at Bree, but Bree signaled to let him go. They had no legal cause to detain him by force. Zucco looked unhappy but complied.

Waving at Mercy to follow her, Bree went out a side door. They jogged around the building. "I think the WSNY van was parked over there." They rounded a county transport vehicle and cut off the reporter fifty feet from his van. He must have been separated from his camera crew because he was alone.

"Hey, Ken!" Bree called out.

He stopped, a small flicker of annoyance on his face. "Yes?"

Bree stepped between him and the van. "Where are you getting your information, Ken?"

"So, you admit it's true?" He sneered.

Bree didn't give him anything.

He crossed his arms. "My source is anonymous. Even if it wasn't, I wouldn't be able to tell you. A journalist protects his sources or he doesn't have any." He sauntered toward the waiting crew and van.

Mercy huffed. "I don't like him."

"Me either. He knows things he shouldn't. The tattoo artist information would only have appeared in my report."

"Do you trust your people?" Mercy asked.

"I do, or I did." Doubt washed over Bree. This wasn't the first leak she'd experienced on a case. But damn it, she couldn't imagine any of them betraying her and jeopardizing the case.

"I hate to ask, but is there anyone in your department who's experiencing a financial hardship?"

Bree scrubbed a hand down her face. "It's a valid question, and one I should be asking myself. The answer is, not that I know of. But not everyone likes to make embarrassing situations known."

People keep secrets.

"I want to know who is feeding Ken information." Mercy pronounced the reporter's name with venom.

Bree nodded. "Most definitely."

Chapter 29

MERCY

Day 6

Mercy poured her third cup of coffee from the sheriff's department pot. After the disaster of a town hall last night and the fact that her back looked like a gigantic purple flower, she'd barely slept. This morning she'd asked Bree for help taping her ribs. Mercy had thought she could get away with ignoring them, but breathing and any torso movement still hurt.

The tape helped a little. A very little.

In shock, Bree had stared at her back. "Christ, Mercy. It looks like you got kicked by a horse with giant hooves."

"Or shot," Mercy had added, sarcasm in her tone.

Now she and Bree were digging into more tips and checking Ken Wells's background. The reporter had no record. He'd been working in the area for six years but was originally from Ohio. She was still annoyed that he had fired up the audience with his mention of four tattoos. And she wanted to know where he'd gotten his information.

Is there a leak in Bree's department?

Mercy's phone chimed with a text from Detective Bolton.

Can we FaceTime?

Mercy sat down at her laptop and called him with the app. "Evan wants to talk," she told Bree. The sheriff immediately rolled her chair next to Mercy's.

Evan appeared, and she recognized his office in the background. His eyes were grim.

"What happened?" Mercy asked.

Instead of answering, he narrowed his gaze on her. "You look like hell."

"Thanks."

He looked at Bree. "She taking care of herself?"

"No."

"What happened?" Mercy repeated, in no mood for either of their opinions. "Was Paige's identity leaked?"

"No," said Evan. "But it's been hard keeping a lid on it. I've been reminding her friends daily that they can't talk to *anyone* about it. Her mom has received some inquiries about where she is, but told people that Paige is visiting cousins out of state. I've also posted several memos in the sheriff's department, referring vaguely to an extremely sensitive case where someone's life relies on silence from the people who worked on it. So far, it's been successful. But every morning, I'm surprised that it hasn't made the press."

"You and me both," said Mercy.

"I'm going to tell you what I found before I talk to the Holcrofts," Evan said. "I'll take it to them next. CuffMe.com finally allowed us access to Paige's account." He winced. "It's what we expected. She was talking with a few men and the conversations aren't pleasant reading. Basically the way the connections feature works is you post a profile and list *topics* you're interested in."

"Are there pictures in the profiles?" asked Bree.

"Yes. As you can imagine, a lot of people hide their face or are heavily disguised. Some people don't care and post a clear face shot. Paige wears a mask in her profile. She only posted one photo." He moved his phone so the women could see his computer screen.

The gold mask covered the upper half of Paige's face, but her heavily lined eyes were visible through the eyeholes. Her long hair was elaborately curled and in two high ponytails. Black lipstick covered her lips, and she held a finger in front of them as if telling someone to be quiet.

She does not look seventeen.

Mercy read the adjacent bio. Paige called herself Diana989 and said she was nineteen. Her height and weight were listed, making it obvious that she was small. Her interests included bondage and discipline, breath play, dollification, age play, impact play, voyeurism, blood play, and humiliation. She was seeking a male dom and was willing to travel.

"What is impact play?" asked Bree.

"Anything that involves striking the body," said Evan. "Can be a hand or whip or paddle. Age play is taking on different-aged roles, and we've all heard of breath play. Erotic asphyxiation. It's considered one of the more dangerous activities, along with blood play."

Mercy didn't want to hear an explanation of blood play. "Dollification?"

"My understanding is that it means the person has a desire to be owned. The dom will be able to dress her as he pleases—like a doll. Heels. Makeup. Dresses. And she will be subservient."

Mercy thought of the dress Paige's brother had described. And the pink nails. "You can't show her parents this profile," she said. "Maybe just tell them about it."

"I haven't even gotten to the messages," said Evan. "It gets much worse."

"She's seventeen," muttered Bree. "How does this happen?"

"BDSM information is everywhere," said Mercy. "Teens are curious. Something about it must have struck a chord with her." She eyed the picture of Paige. "Consenting adults can do whatever they want. We're not here to kink shame, and I can see how this site is a resource for certain communities. But damn, clearly it can become a hunting ground for predators."

"There are safety warnings all over the site," said Evan. "To open an account you have to agree not to hold CuffMe or its parent company liable for any injuries, libel, and another dozen issues. It also requires you to agree that you're over the age of eighteen.

"Paige's account was deleted a whole month before she disappeared. Obviously she thought she was covering her tracks, but we've been given access to her entire activity history." He changed his screen to a list of accounts that Paige had messaged. "She talked to sixteen people," Evan continued. "She blocked and deleted fifteen of them, but one she simply deleted their message history."

"That's got to be our guy," said Mercy.

"I agree. In my subpoena, I requested account information for everyone she talked to. The company didn't want to comply with that and dragged their feet, citing their clients' privacy." He raised a brow. "I—and the judge—made it clear that we consider the company responsible for allowing a seventeen-year-old on their site who has vanished. They reluctantly relented to our demands, and sometime this morning I expect to receive the men's account info."

Mercy scanned the list of usernames who had chatted with Paige.

Kinkplay492

NumberOneNiceGuy!!

SonOfJor-el

TheMaster232

CommanderSpanky27

BabyBoi457

KhalDrago3058

"We need to investigate all the men she talked to," said Bree. "Even if she did block them."

"I'm one hundred percent certain the man we want is the one she didn't block," said Evan.

His confidence surprised Mercy. "Why do you say that?"

"I'll show you in a minute. But first take a look at some of her conversation with him." He clicked on TheMaster232. "It's long. They talked for days."

Mercy started to quickly scan. "He's very polite," she said, slightly surprised. "It reads like a get-to-know-you at a dinner party."

"Exactly," said Evan. "He's courteous and attentive. Letting her guide the conversation. The other men who messaged her jumped right into abrupt questions, sex talk, and requests for naked photos. Most of them she blocked the first day she spoke with them. This guy's style is to approach very carefully."

Mercy continued to read. "You're right. His questions are all soft-balls. She's the one who asks him what he is looking for . . . and he states it very civilly."

> I'm a kind and giving person. I have a lot of respect
> for the people who are interested in the life we enjoy.
> I appreciate you taking the time to ask about my
> needs.

"He's a 'kind person.' Bullshit," said Bree. "He knew exactly how to rope her in."

Mercy continued to read. As the days passed, their banter grew more friendly and personal. He told her his name was Mark, and Mercy shook her head as Paige gave her real name. They discussed TV shows, movies, and favorite foods. Mercy could tell Paige was growing more and more interested in Mark as a person. She started to bare her soul.

> I'm looking for a new start. I feel stagnant here. Your
> life sounds really wonderful.

Even though you're across the United States, you feel close. I wish we could meet.

"No, Paige. *Don't even think about it*," said Mercy. She wanted to grab the girl and shake some sense into her.

"I think it's too late to tell her what to do," said Bree. "Or what not to do."

Then the pictures started. Without being asked Paige sent him a selfie. No mask but with heavy makeup. A few seconds later Mercy exclaimed as a selfie of Mark showed up in the chat.

"I already checked out the photo," said Evan. "A reverse image search pulls that up as a stock image. 'Man taking selfie.' But I think the photos he sends later are actually him. I didn't find them online."

Mercy rapidly scrolled and then yanked her gaze away. "Jesus, Evan. You could have warned us."

Mark had moved to nudes. None showed his face, but Mercy agreed with Evan that they were probably Mark, suspecting the man couldn't resist showing Paige his real junk.

Bree made a gagging noise. "I've never understood why men think women want to see this."

"Paige makes it sound like she does," said Mercy. "She's full of praise." She exhaled as Paige started sending her own nude photos. Some extremely graphic.

"This whole thing reads as if it should be on a *Dateline* special," said Mercy. "His manipulation is subtle. I have no doubts he's done it before."

"Definitely," said Bree. "To Vanessa and Tisha. And maybe others."

In the chat Mark suggested they switch to texting. Paige agreed, and he sent his phone number.

It was the number from the burner phone that had led Mercy to New York.

That was the final message.

TheMaster232's account was listed as having been deactivated on the same date as Paige's account.

Mercy sat back in her chair. "You're right, Evan. There's no doubt that this is him. Damn! We need his account information ASAP. I'm sure it's a bunch of bull, but there's got to be something in there we can use. Did you notice all the time stamps are late at night? If that's Pacific time since this is Paige's account, and our guy is in New York, he was communicating with her at two or three in the morning."

"Has a day job?" speculated Bree. "Or a spouse? Waits until she's asleep?"

Evan had turned his phone's camera back to himself. "I hate to take this to the Holcrofts without the man's account information first. I know they'll immediately want that info. If we had a lead from his account, maybe it would distract them a bit from the pictures."

Mercy didn't envy Evan. It would be painful presenting this to Paige's parents.

Paige sent him at least a dozen naked photos.

"One thing we haven't looked into is the local BDSM scene here," said Bree. "I doubt it goes on just behind closed doors. There's got to be a group or organization around here . . . most likely in Albany. Scarlet Falls might be too small." She frowned as she thought. "I'm not sure where to start, though. I guess search on the internet. That's what someone looking for like-minded people would do."

"Hang on," said Evan. His screen blurred as he opened something on his phone. "This is it! They emailed the account information for Mark."

Bree held up crossed fingers, and Mercy joined her.

"Oh, nice," said Evan. "They included an IP address. That won't tell us exactly where he is, but we can get a general area—I'll look it up in a second. The account lists his name as Mark Verney. The phone number is the one we have from the burner phone, but there's a physical address in Scarlet Falls, New York. Hopefully that's not a fake."

Our killer is close.

Evan rattled off the address, and Mercy popped it into her laptop. "Registered owner of the home at the address is Sylvia Verney. She's seventy-nine," she said.

"The IP is from the Scarlet Falls area," said Evan. "It's a big location but it does include the home address."

"Mark Verney is listed under names associated with that address," said Mercy. "Sylvia might be his mother."

"I've got an expired driver's license under Mark Verney," said Bree, looking at her computer. "Age is forty-five. Same address."

"We gotta go, Evan," said Mercy, closing her laptop.

"I can look at who else Mark Verney communicated with," said Evan. "Maybe one of your victims is on here."

Mercy stood and looked at Bree. "Ready?"

"I'm more than ready."

Chapter 30

Him

Disappointment hits me hard. I couldn't wait to get home, but the girl just cowers in her cage. The door is open, yet she hasn't come out. She hasn't moved at all. She's like a doll. I realize quite suddenly that I don't care. Our sessions have become almost mundane. With her being obedient and silently crying when disciplined for an infraction I had to trick her into committing. It's almost like she doesn't even want to be punished.

What the hell?

True submissives crave their masters' attention. But when I ignore her, she seems relieved. This is not how this is supposed to go.

Is she another failure? Or have I simply done my job too well and made her the perfect submissive in a short amount of time?

Whatever the reason, I'm beginning to tire of her.

Maybe I need an older woman, someone with life experience, someone who craves the punishment I seek to give. Someone who will make the game more interesting.

I open my laptop and turn on the VPN. I begin with a general search for new articles and videos about me that have hit the internet over the past day. So many links! Major stations are taking an interest in me. People are fascinated. I'm becoming a national star.

Many of the articles and videos are rehashing previous stories. I scan the dates for new entries. Clips from the town hall are amusing. I like watching the sheriff and FBI agent get metaphorically smacked over and over. Whose idea was it to put two females on the case? Why not send a man from the FBI to take charge? These two are out of their element.

Bright side: I seem brilliant in comparison. I'm yanking their strings over and over, and they are reacting exactly as I predict. I'm not just the Master—I'm the Puppet Master. They are fun to manipulate. I can't wait to see what they do with my next surprise.

Maybe someday one of them could be in my cage. Neither of them would cower for hours on end. Of that I am sure.

I flex my fingers before taking to the keyboard again.

As I type, temptation takes hold. I stare at the submissive. Has she even moved an inch? Disinterested, I turn back to the laptop. There are so many more women willing to take her place. My fingers type the letters before I can stop them. I read the link in the search bar. CuffMe.com. Desire to engage swims inside me. I could find a new, more interesting target.

I glance at her again. She is a zombie, hunched over, staring at the floor of the crate.

Boring. The only thing that would make her more interesting is her actively dying. For a few seconds, I let the image play. Then I shut it down before it controls me. It's too soon. I won't rush her finale. I will savor it.

My hand hovers over the Enter key.

I shouldn't.

It's risky.

I deactivated that account for a reason.

And yet . . . I can't help myself.

Fuck it. I need to do something. My current situation isn't working.

I press Enter.

Chapter 31

MERCY

"This is a nice neighborhood," said Mercy, eyeing the houses, trying to distract herself and slow her heart rate as Bree drove to Sylvia Verney's home. Her thoughts were wrapped up in the possibility of finding their killer that morning.

And hopefully Paige.

The homes were older, stately colonials on acre lots. The streets turned with gentle curves, and huge old oak trees lined the roads. The calm neighborhood was a contrast with her crackling state of mind.

"Yeah." Suspicion filled Bree's answer.

"What's wrong?"

"I don't like to think that our killer has a nice life. I want him living in a shithole."

"Maybe the home is a shithole inside."

Bree pulled to the curb. "Our backup is still a minute out, but this is the address."

Not a shithole.

The Verney home was one of the smaller homes on the street, but the yard was impeccable and the white paint crisp and fresh. The two-story home was symmetrical, balanced with its front door in the very center and an identical pattern of windows to each side.

It didn't look like the home of someone who tortured women.

"Is that a swing set?" Bree asked as they sat in the SUV, waiting for a deputy to arrive.

Mercy leaned forward. The home had a single-lane driveway that led to a detached garage behind the home. Next to it she saw what was definitely one end of a swing set. "Yes. Kids live here? Creepy."

"Think of the BTK Killer. Family man. Prominent in his church. I bet our guy has a different location where he keeps his women. There's our backup." The two women exited Bree's vehicle.

A squad car with two deputies had pulled up across the street. The driver raised a hand at Bree as they stepped out and met the women.

"If you two can watch the north and south sides of the home," said Bree, "we're going to knock."

The deputies nodded and split, each heading for an opposite side.

Mercy's stomach churned and small stars of pain flashed across her ribs as she and Bree went up the stone walkway to the front door.

No one is expecting us.

But she acknowledged that those were the situations that could turn deadly in an instant.

Under the portico, they each stepped to one side of the blue door and Bree knocked. Mercy heard a woman's voice inside, possibly that of an older woman.

The door opened and a tall angular woman with white hair looked at them with curiosity. Her thick lenses enlarged her eyes, and they grew bigger as she noticed Bree's uniform and Mercy's vest. "What can I do for you, officers?" She wore a thick cardigan with her slacks, and a wave of cooled air flowed from the home into the warm morning. Her gaze went past them to the two county vehicles in the street. "Did something happen?"

"Good morning," said Bree. "Are you Sylvia Verney?"

"I am." Lines formed between her brows.

"We were hoping to speak with Mark Verney. Is he here?" asked Bree.

Sylvia cocked her head. "He is . . . May I ask what this is about? Did he get in trouble for something? He's been here all morning."

"We'd just like to ask him some questions," said Mercy, giving her warmest smile. "Won't take long."

"Hmmm." Suspicion entered her gaze. She wasn't pleased.

For a moment, Mercy thought Sylvia was going to refuse. Instead the woman turned and yelled, "Mark! Can you come here for a second?"

Mercy noted she wore hearing aids.

Sylvia faced them again and gave the women a look that should have been stern, but lacked power because her glasses made her eyes so big. "I'm going to be right here the whole time."

"Not a problem," Mercy lied, speaking a little louder because of the hearing aids. If they felt Mark wasn't being forthcoming, they could ask for privacy. Or request Mark come to the station. Behind Sylvia, fast footsteps sounded on stairs and Mercy tensed.

A second later a young boy with wide blue eyes and a ton of freckles stared at them. He couldn't have been more than ten years old. His eyes widened as he spotted their holstered weapons. "What, Grandma?" He glanced up at Sylvia and then continued to stare at the guns.

Sylvia looked at Mercy and Bree and raised a brow. *Well?*

"I'm sorry," said Bree. "We're looking for an older Mark Verney. Who's around forty-five." She smiled at the boy. "You must also be Mark."

Sylvia's face lost all expression, and she set her hands on Mark's shoulders. "That would be my son. He passed away six years ago." Her fingers tightened, and the boy looked up at her again.

He's dead?

Mercy met Bree's gaze.

Now what?

"I'm very sorry for your loss," said Bree. "Maybe we have the wrong name. Is there another male in your family that's . . . older than Mark here?"

"Not anymore," she stated. "My husband has been gone for nearly twenty years. Mark was our only son. His wife lives a few miles away, and I watch my grandson several times a week while she works."

Mercy's thoughts shot in a dozen different directions. The Verney name was a lie. The home address was a lie.

Another dead end.

Bree stepped off the porch and waved at the deputies. "Go ahead and head out. We're good here." The two acknowledged and headed for their vehicle. Bree returned. "We're sorry to have bothered you. It appears someone tried to mislead us."

Sylvia nodded and gently turned Mark around. "You can go back to your TV show now."

But the boy twisted back to face Bree with eager eyes. "Have you ever shot anyone?"

"Mark!" Sylvia turned him again and gave a push. "Go!" The boy sped off, his feet pounding on the stairs once more. She sighed, crossed her long arms, and eyed them. "I don't like this. Who would send you here looking for my dead son? That's horrible. Is that someone's idea of a joke?"

"We're not sure," said Mercy. "But—"

"You're not *sure*? So what happens now? Is a SWAT team going to break down my door one day and then say they have the wrong address? What is going on?"

Mercy took a half step back, startled by the woman's sharp tone.

"No one is going to break down your door, Mrs. Verney," Bree said calmly. "This lead ends with us. No one will be back."

"Figures. When I want the police, no one comes. But you two show up on a mistake."

Bree raised her chin. "I'm sorry. What did you not get a response on? Can I do something for you?"

Mercy suspected the Verney house was within the Scarlet Falls PD jurisdiction. But she knew Bree wouldn't let that stop her from offering help.

Sylvia waved a hand. "They said my issue only qualified to file a report over the phone, so they did that instead of sending an officer. But I'd really expected someone to at least come take fingerprints. How do you catch crooks if you don't take fingerprints?" The woman looked disappointed.

"Was something stolen, Mrs. Verney?" Bree was the picture of patience.

It was the CSI effect. People expected a forensics team for every little problem and then believed the trace evidence would lead to instant results. The real world was very different.

"Nothing was stolen. Not that I can tell, but twice now I've found my back door unlocked when I was positive I locked it the night before."

Oh, brother.

"That sounds very unnerving," said Bree, sincerity in her tone. "Did you check with your grandson?"

"He wasn't here the nights it happened. I live alone, and the only person with a key is my daughter-in-law. I asked her if she'd been in the house overnight, and she thought I'd lost my marbles." Indignation crossed her face. "And now the lock is damaged. I can't get my key in it from the outside, so it needs to be replaced."

Mercy glanced at Bree. It did sound like the lock had been fooled with. Considering the woman lived alone, it had to be stressful for her.

"Would you like me to take a look at it?" asked Bree.

"Please do. The locksmith is coming tomorrow, but I think some photos and fingerprinting would be a good idea. You can't be too safe."

"How long ago did this happen?" asked Mercy, who was glad to hear about the locksmith.

"The first time was a month ago. And then last week."

"There's probably been too many hands on it since then to lift prints," said Bree. "But I'll take some photos."

Bree's police radio crackled. "All units. We have a report of a kidnapping at the Scarlet Falls Mall. All units in the vicinity respond."

"That's near us." Bree pressed the mic at her shoulder. "10-4. Taggert responding." She looked at Sylvia. "I'm sorry, we need to go. I'll try to come back." She and Mercy raced for her unit.

"Report of a woman being forced into the trunk of a car," said the dispatcher as Bree and Mercy slammed their doors shut.

Shit. Could it be?

Mercy met Bree's gaze. "I assumed the call would involve a child. Do you think . . . ?"

"It's possible." Bree was grim. "Hang on."

The SUV flew down the street.

Chapter 32

BREE

Bree ran with full lights and sirens, pushing the SUV to its limit. Tires squealed as she took a turn at the maximum speed. It felt as if two tires left the pavement for a second. Then the vehicle settled back on all four again. She straightened the wheel, her heart hammering as she pressed down on the gas pedal even harder. Next to her, Mercy held the chicken strap with a white-knuckle grip.

She slowed as traffic thickened near the mall. Cars ahead pulled over to let them pass. Bree's hands ached from the tight hold on the wheel.

A single mantra kept rolling in her head.

He's got another one. He's got another one he's got another one.

How could this be happening again? Her stomach rolled with mental images of the two dead women, then the photos on the CuffMe site, Paige with the heavy makeup, the nudes, and the dick pics from TheMaster. She had been a cop for over fifteen years. She knew all about abduction and human trafficking, but seeing it still made her physically sick.

It was that easy to grab a woman. Even a senator's daughter wasn't immune. Was there anywhere women were actually safe?

She swallowed hard and shouted over the sirens, "There are times when the frustration of not being able to prevent a crime feels overwhelming."

"This is definitely one of those times," said Mercy.

On the radio, dispatch coordinated deputies and SFPD patrol units. "All units in the vicinity of the Scarlet Falls Mall. Suspect is driving a white Audi sedan, four-door." That was all they had?

Bree used her radio to update dispatch. "Sheriff Taggert, ETA one minute."

Other units in the vicinity responded with their expected arrival times. No reports of the white Audi came in.

"Looks like we'll be the first on scene." Bree braked, then accelerated through a turn. "We were closest." She scanned their surroundings for the suspect's vehicle.

Mercy leaned with the roll of the vehicle. "Let's hope we get there fast enough to make a difference."

But they both knew the call had specified a woman had been kidnapped, past tense.

"He could be a few miles away from the mall by now," Bree said.

Mercy put a hand on the dashboard to steady herself. "We don't even know that this incident is related to our case."

"Nope. We don't know anything."

The agent's comment was a good reminder not to make assumptions, but any potential kidnapping deserved the same amount of attention, even if it was unrelated.

Bree made the sharp turn into the parking lot entrance. She cut across the empty rows until she spotted a security guard waving his arms. She pulled up next to him, barely shoving the shifter into park before leaping out. Mercy kept pace with her.

The guard ran closer, pointing toward the other side of the parking lot. It was Don Dutton. But instead of the semibored guard in his air-conditioned office, he was a mess. His face was red with exertion.

One of his shirttails hung out. Sweat gleamed on his forehead and stained the armpits of his uniform.

"What happened?" Bree yanked her notebook out of her pocket.

Dutton's breath was ragged. He inhaled hard, then began, the words coming out in a rush. "I was doing my rounds inside the mall. Heard a scream. Looked outside. Saw a woman struggling against a big man. He had her by the wrist and was dragging her toward a sedan. I ran out the door and yelled for him to let go of her, but I couldn't get there fast enough. He took her."

"The vehicle?" Bree tapped her pen on the paper. He'd already given a make and model, but maybe he could remember more now that he was processing the incident.

Don pressed a fist to the center of his chest and made an attempt to regulate his breathing. "It was an Audi sedan, four-door, white, fairly new. I didn't get the plate. The car was facing the wrong way, and I was too far away. I wasn't close enough to see the guy's face either, but he was tall—I'd say at least six feet—and blond. He was wearing dark pants and a light-blue shirt." He stared at the pavement for a few seconds, then shook his head. "That's all I can remember."

Bree wrote down the details. "How about the woman?"

"Didn't see her face either. She seemed small—or at least a lot smaller than the guy—and she had a long ponytail. Brunette." Don closed his eyes, as if trying to summon more details. Opening them, he nodded. "She was wearing denim shorts and a blue shirt." He turned up a palm and put it just above his waist. "One of the short ones that show some stomach."

"A crop top?" Mercy asked.

Don shrugged. "I guess. I don't know what they're called."

"You didn't see her face?" Bree asked.

"No." He shook his head and propped his hands just above his belt. "But she was screaming bloody murder and trying to resist, using her whole body as deadweight. Like this." Don demonstrated, extending a hand in front of him and sinking his butt toward the ground. "But he was bigger. He just scooped her up, threw her over his shoulder, and tossed her in his trunk." He shuddered. "I tried to stop him. I really did, but I wasn't fast enough."

"What about shoes?" Bree prompted.

Dutton rubbed his forehead. "I don't know what the guy was wearing on his feet. I think the girl was in white sneakers, but I'm not sure."

"Which way did he go?" Mercy asked.

"That way." Don pointed.

"West." Bree hurried back to her SUV and updated the BOLO on the vehicle and driver to include more details. They still didn't have enough information to issue an Amber Alert. When she returned to Don, Mercy was asking him if he had security footage.

"We should," he said, brightening, as if the thought of being helpful eased some of his guilt for not stopping the abduction.

More sirens approached. A sheriff's department patrol unit pulled into the lot. Behind it were two Scarlet Falls PD cars.

"Before we go to your office, show us exactly where his car was parked," Bree said.

Don led them to a parking spot near the end of the row. "He was under the light."

Mercy turned in a circle. "Where was the woman going? I don't see another vehicle parked near here."

Don gestured across the lot to a glass-walled bench. "Probably the bus stop. Next bus comes in about ten minutes."

"Have you ever seen the woman before?" Bree asked.

"I don't think so," Don said. "But I didn't get a good look at her face, so I can't be a hundred percent sure."

Mercy jerked a thumb at the mall. "Her shorts and top didn't look like a uniform or the typical clothes of any of the employees of the stores inside?"

Don considered the question with a tilt of his head. "I don't know. You're thinking she worked here?"

"It's possible." Mercy nodded.

Don lifted a shoulder. "She looked more like a typical older teen, young twentysomething shopper to me, but there are a couple of stores that sell clothes like what she was wearing."

Bree updated the responding officer and directed Deputy Zucco to tape off a square of pavement around the overhead light. "Go over every inch of pavement in case either one of them dropped something."

"Yes, ma'am," Deputy Zucco said. The two SFPD cops pitched in immediately.

"Let's see that video feed." Bree turned toward the long building.

The three of them hustled across the hot pavement. Sweat soaked Bree's uniform by the time they entered the mall. Mercy's face shone, and the hair around her face was damp.

An overhead air-conditioning vent gave Bree goose bumps. Don shoved into the security office and rushed back to his desk and bank of monitors. Bree and Mercy stayed close. The three of them crowded behind the desk to view the screens. His hands shook as he called up the image. When they'd seen him previously, he'd seemed calm and collected, but the incident had clearly rattled him.

A video feed appeared on-screen, gray, grainy, and full of static.

"Fuck!" He pounded a fist on the desk, jolting the equipment. The feed was blank. "I know that camera was working when we ran our checks a few days ago." He swept a hand over his sweat-damped buzz cut. Then he returned to the mouse and keyboard. "See? It was working yesterday. The camera went out at midnight last night." He clicked a few more buttons. "There are three more cameras out." He swore again. "I didn't have a chance to run any diagnostics today. I started with my rounds." He sighed and rubbed the bridge of his nose. "I should have, though. Sometimes this job is too easy, and we get a little complacent.

Usually, we don't see much beyond a little vandalism or shoplifting. Occasionally, a car gets stolen."

"Check the video of people exiting the mall at the doors closest to the spot she was taken," Mercy suggested.

"Good idea." Dutton worked his keyboard. Then he pointed to three windows on his screen, each showing a door. "Here are the three closest exits." He clicked on the REWIND button to move the feed backward in time. "I don't see anyone who looks like her." He put an elbow on the desk, looking confused, then he straightened. "Maybe she was coming *to* the mall. She could have gotten off a bus or someone could have dropped her off."

"Let's go look at the cameras," Bree said.

Don's steps were slower as he led them back outside. The heat hit Bree like a slap. Another deputy and several more SFPD cars had arrived. The responding patrol vehicles were parked at angles around the abduction location.

Bree stared up at the camera mounted high on the pole. She could see the broken camera lens from the ground. "Looks like someone took it out with a rock or a BB gun or something like that."

Mercy looked around. "Could have been a regular handgun. Is this area busy overnight?"

"Not very, and gunshots can sound like a car backfiring." Bree turned toward Deputy Zucco walking toward her.

"We found some litter on the ground." She gestured. "A cigarette butt, some gum, and a hamburger wrapper. Also, the SFPD captain is here."

The captain was second-in-command to the Scarlet Falls chief of police.

"The trash is probably unrelated, but let's bag and tag it anyway." Bree always erred on the side of caution. You couldn't go back and recover evidence after a day's worth of mall shoppers walked across the same ground.

The SFPD captain approached, and Bree faced him. Technically, even though the mall was in the SFPD's jurisdiction, Bree could have demanded to run the operation. She outranked the captain as the highest law enforcement officer in the county, but she'd rather play nice. Besides, they needed more bodies for legwork. Cooperation could be key for an investigation of this size. The incident could have been an entirely separate crime: an angry boyfriend or a run-of-the-mill human trafficker. In which case, Bree was happy to let the SFPD run the investigation.

She filled him in on what had happened so far. "We need to canvass the stores in the mall. See if anyone knows a woman who meets her description. I know it's vague, but we have to try."

The captain nodded. "I'll put men on that. We'll also contact the bus company and get their surveillance tapes of the buses that let off passengers here today."

"Great. Keep us posted?" Bree asked.

"Of course." He turned away.

She caught up with Mercy just as the first news vans appeared. "There's Ken."

Mercy pursed her lips. "He must have someone manning the scanner 24/7."

"What do you think of all this?" Bree circled a hand in the air.

"I don't know." Mercy scanned the area. "We know he lured Paige, but we don't know how he nabbed the other women. He could have used a variety of methods."

"We don't know how many victims he's taken." Bree surveyed the chaotic scene. People had gathered outside the mall doors to watch the police activity.

Ken Wells climbed out of his van, smoothed his hair, and approached Bree. "Has another woman been kidnapped?"

"That's what we're trying to find out." Bree held up a palm, stopping the reporter in his tracks. "Please back up. This is a crime scene."

She turned away from the press.

Unless proven otherwise, they would treat this incident as a possible kidnapping by the killer.

The noise, heat, and activity suddenly felt overwhelming.

"I need some water." She headed for her vehicle. Mercy fell into step beside her.

Bree slid behind the wheel and started the engine. A pathetic stream of warm air leaked from the vents. She grabbed a bottle of water and drank. "How many women could he kill before we stop him?"

Mercy didn't answer, just drank from her own bottle.

For the first time in her life, Bree wondered if she was up to the job.

Chapter 33

MERCY

Mercy paced around the table in the conference room. Ever since the kidnapping hours ago, she and Bree had been working nonstop, but all the tasks were slow and tedious. The nonglamorous side of police work.

A number of Scarlet Falls PD officers and county deputies were reviewing video of the dozens of indoor mall cameras, seeking a glimpse of the woman with the long ponytail in denim shorts. So far there had been no results. Bree had pulled a list of white Audi registrations in a fifty-mile radius. Mercy had wanted to look at a wider area, but Bree's report already listed more than three hundred vehicles. Mercy had scanned the list.

I don't know what I'm looking for. John Q. Kidnapper?

The BOLO had resulted in two white Audis being pulled over. The first had four teenagers in it and the second was a young mom with a toddler in a car seat.

"Do you think he picked the woman beforehand?" asked Bree, scanning more video from the mall. "Or had rolled the dice, hoping the right woman walked into his trap?"

Mercy mulled it over. "He knocked out three cameras ahead of time. He would have had to hang around that area for quite a while before the right person appeared at an opportune moment. Doesn't sound like our man. I think he had picked her out beforehand, which most likely means she had a predictable routine."

"She's an employee at the mall," stated Bree. "She has to be. She must regularly use those doors and take that bus. And he knew it."

"The footage from the bus company hasn't helped."

"They need to go back, not just look at today's," said Bree. "Check footage for that bus at that time of day for several days. I bet she walks that route a few times a week when she gets off work. Maybe she doesn't ride the bus to work, so that's why she's not showing up in their review. Maybe she gets a ride to work."

"We need to get word to the officers canvassing the stores," said Mercy. "Employers need to account for all of their female employees with long brunette hair."

Bree picked up the phone to contact the sergeant heading the canvass. "What about her clothes? It didn't sound like she was dressed for retail work."

"Maybe she changed after work," suggested Mercy. "It's stupid hot out. She put on shorts for the bus ride home." Bree nodded and made her call.

Mercy turned to their list of suspects on the board, her gaze going to the booking photo of Jimmie Elkins. Jimmie still hadn't turned up since getting out on bail.

Jimmie wasn't blond. The mall security guard had been positive about the suspect's hair color.

Jimmie didn't drive an Audi either.

He could have bleached his hair and borrowed or stolen a vehicle.

But she couldn't see scrawny Jimmie wrestling a woman into a trunk.

She sighed and looked at the next photo. Rick Mullen. Vanessa's ex-husband. Blond.

"We need to go talk to Rick Mullen," said Mercy as Bree hung up the phone. "Find out where he was when the kidnapping happened—even though there is no Audi registered to him. I wonder if the security guard got the car make wrong."

"He pays attention to detail," said Bree. "He gave us a good description of the victim. I lean toward him having the correct car—but let's not take it as set in stone."

"Definitely," said Mercy. "We still need to ask Rick about the life insurance policy he has on Vanessa too."

"I agree," said Bree.

Mercy looked at her, hearing the doubt in Bree's tone. "You don't feel him for this."

"I'm trying not to make any assumptions," said Bree. "I suspect seeing him with those kids makes me hope he's not capable of this."

"I need to get out of this room," said Mercy. She'd been staring at her computer screen for hours since the kidnapping, looking at video and car registrations. "Let's take a drive to the Mullens' home."

The day was becoming another scorcher, the sky hazy instead of the clear blue from earlier in the week, and possible thunderstorms were in the forecast. Judging by the browning of Rick's lawn, rain was sorely needed. Twenty minutes later, Mercy knocked on Rick Mullen's door. One of the children was wailing inside. Bree frowned and stepped farther to the side of the door. A few seconds later the door was opened by the neighbor woman who'd taken the kids the first time they'd visited and who they'd seen supporting Rick at the town hall.

They looked like a couple at that meeting.

She looked frazzled. The youngest was on her hip, his face red and his cheeks soaked with tears. Recognition flashed in her eyes as she took in Mercy and Bree. "Can I help you?"

"We're looking for Rick," said Bree. "Is he home?"

"No, he had to go into the office for a meeting today."

"*Juuuuulia!* My game is stuck!" hollered Rick's daughter from some-where in the house.

"I'll be there in a minute," the woman yelled back.

"Are you expecting him back soon?" asked Mercy. "We have some follow-up questions."

"Have you found his ex-wife's killer yet?" She bounced the boy, who had shoved a fist in his mouth as he stared at the women with sad eyes.

"Not yet." Mercy paused. "I'm sorry, what's your name? You live across the street, right? I know you help watch the kids sometimes."

The woman's gaze narrowed. "My name's Julia. And since I know you're wondering, Rick and I are in a relationship. He and Vanessa haven't been together for years," she added defensively. "And I thought he'd be home by now. I expected him closer to lunch."

We'll go pay a visit.

They knew where Rick worked from his background check.

"Thank you for your help," said Bree, handing Julia a card. "Have him give us a call when he's back."

She and Mercy walked away. "Time for a pop-in?" asked Mercy.

"Absolutely."

◆ ◆ ◆

Rick Mullen hadn't shown up for his meeting.

The receptionist at the small accounting firm had been very cooper-ative after Mercy and Bree showed their IDs. She said they'd called Rick when he didn't show up for his meeting but had reached his voice mail. The meeting had been that morning from nine to one. Lunch included.

"It's not like him," the woman had said. "I figured something was up with one of his kids."

"Do we talk to Julia again?" asked Mercy as they got in Bree's SUV to leave.

"She seemed convinced he was at the meeting," said Bree. "Do you think she was lying?"

"Lying to law enforcement?" Mercy grinned. "Never."

"You noticed Julia fits the killer's type, right?"

"I did."

"I don't really want to wait around until he returns," said Bree. "We could be here a long time and we have stuff to do."

Bree's radio crackled. "All units. Report of shots fired at the Shady Acres Motel."

Mercy met Bree's gaze. The sheriff was already starting the vehicle. "10-4, Taggert responding."

"Maybe Jimmie showed up," said Mercy.

They arrived at the motel and saw the deputies hovering outside one room. During the drive over, the dispatcher had informed Bree that there was one DOA on the property. No injuries and no suspect.

"That's Jimmie's room," said Bree as they got out of her vehicle.

Shit.

Civilians were grouped at one end of the lot, deputies taking notes as they spoke with them one on one. Mercy spotted the motel clerk with a Big Gulp in hand. Bree headed to Jimmie's room, and Mercy pulled the clerk aside.

"Thought you were told to let the police know when Jimmie showed up."

"Haven't seen Jimmie." His gaze darted to one side.

"When did he come back?" asked Mercy.

"Said I didn't see him."

Mercy said nothing.

"I heard one shot and called 911 without looking outside. I saw nothing." Sweat started beading on his temples.

"You didn't check if anyone needed help?"

"Fuck no. Someone had a gun. I'm not getting shot for this job."

"You see anyone after?"

"No. I was on the floor behind the counter until I heard the police show up."

"Cameras?"

He stared at her, an *are you kidding* look on his face.

I didn't think so.

She walked away and was surprised to see the medical examiner, Dr. Jones, pull in. "You must have gotten the call immediately," Mercy said.

"I was in my car headed home. The call came through and I figured I'd get it out of the way. You been in there already?"

"Not yet. I'll follow you."

A minute later Mercy didn't know what to say as she, Dr. Jones, and Bree stared at Jimmie Elkins.

Jimmie was in his motel bathroom, propped between the side of the toilet and wall, a gunshot wound above his right temple. A revolver near his hand. The wall was a colorful pattern of blood, skull fragments, and hair. Mercy carefully stepped forward and took a closer look at the revolver.

"Charter Arms," she muttered. "Cheap gun."

She glanced back at Bree, who had been quiet since they entered the bathroom, and Mercy did a double take. "You good?" The sheriff was white. Bree didn't meet her gaze and spun around and left.

Mercy glanced at the ME, who shrugged. She looked back at Jimmie.

I've seen worse. I'm sure Bree has too.

She backed out of the way and let the ME take a closer look.

"Hmmm," said Dr. Jones under her breath. "Did you shoot yourself?"

Mercy eyed the gun and obvious entry wound with heavy stippling. Assuming Jimmie was right-handed, suicide was a definite option. "Shell's behind the toilet," she said, spotting the brass among the grime.

Mercy snapped a pic of the shell, and then turned it slightly with her pen so she could read the end. "Thirty-eight plus P."

"That so?" said Dr. Jones. "Lotta power there." She turned Jimmie's head. "Exit wound is low. If that's the through and through I suspect it is, there's no way Jimmie could shoot himself at that angle." She easily slid a pinkie into both wounds, the gruesome sight making Mercy look away. "Yeah, unless he had rubber arms, he couldn't achieve this angle. Someone had to be standing above him and shooting down. Don't quote me yet," she said with a glance at Mercy. "I'll confirm on my table. Unless you've got a long, thin poker handy for me to run through the wound."

"I don't need to see that right now," said Mercy.

It was enough to know that Jimmie had most likely been murdered.

Who'd you piss off, Jimmie?

Mercy studied the bathroom, remembering all the drugs that had been floating in the toilet a few days before. She wondered if there were more drugs to be found in the room.

Is someone upset that Jimmie didn't have money for the stash we confiscated?

Her thoughts went to Vanessa.

Or is this related to her?

She wondered what had happened to Bree. Mercy left the medical examiner to her musings and stepped out of the bathroom. Bree wasn't in the motel room.

Mercy moved to the doorway and spotted Bree standing alone behind her SUV with a water bottle.

Something's up.

Chapter 34

BREE

Bree could barely focus on the dark road. Her brain kept replaying the sight of Jimmie's blood and brains sprayed on the wall of the motel. The arcs of red. Gray matter. Bits of skull. She clutched the wheel. She couldn't drive and rehash the scene, so she tamped it down and drove on autopilot.

Mercy sat in the passenger seat. As if reading Bree's mind, Mercy didn't say a word.

After parking at the farm, Bree slid out of the vehicle. Mercy followed her into the barn and helped check the horses and turn them out for the night. There had been some lightning but no rain to break the heat.

They worked as a team, silently. In the house, the dogs greeted them as if they hadn't seen a human for ages, even though Bree's brother had cared for them earlier. The dogs seemed to sense Bree's distress, because they stuck close, flanking her and pressing against her legs.

Bree stood in her kitchen, unable to settle. Exhaustion and stress were finally catching up with her. When had she slept for a whole night? The house felt still and empty. Loneliness crushed down on her like a weight. "There's food in the freezer if you're hungry."

"I'm not," Mercy said.

Feeling closed in, trapped, Bree headed for the back porch. The night air was cloying and hot, but she drank in the scents of grass and manure, anything to wipe out the smell of her own fear. She pulled out her phone and tried to call Matt. The call went right to voice mail. He must be out of cell range. She lowered the phone, not sure what frightened her more: having him not available or the way she needed to talk to him. Dependence was not something she accepted easily. But she sent him a text, asking him to call her when he could.

That doesn't sound too pathetic.

The door opened behind her, and Mercy walked out. She offered her a glass of wine. "I hope you don't mind. I helped myself."

Bree accepted the glass. "Thanks. Make yourself at home."

"It's been a day."

"No kidding."

"Ready to talk about what happened at the motel?" Mercy asked, leaning against the railing.

Bree sipped her wine, barely tasting it. "My father was an abusive drunk. But more than that, he was a psychopath. Most people can't fathom evil unless they've lived with a person who embraced cold rage as a state of being. My mother, my siblings, and I all lived in fear of him. I spent most of my first eight years learning to be invisible. One night, he started on my mother. Him beating her wasn't unusual, but there was something about that night. Something different." She paused, thinking, remembering. The focused, mean look on his face. Nearly three decades later, she could still see the intensity in his eyes. She felt it burning through her, the threat as palpable as the humidity in the air tonight.

"I called 911. Adam started to cry. He was just a baby, but even he could sense the danger. My father went for him." Terror dried Bree's throat. She drank some wine. She could see Adam as an infant, standing in his crib, red-faced. Her father reaching for the baby. "My mother attacked him. She'd never done that before. Just launched herself at him. He was so much bigger, so much more aggressive. She didn't stand a chance, but she gave us one. He had no choice but to turn back to her." Bree's pulse skyrocketed, and cold sweat dampened her skin.

To pause the replay, to gain control, she gulped more wine. "I grabbed my brother, found my sister hiding under the table, and took them out of the house. The last time I saw my mother, he had her pinned to the wall by the throat."

She stopped, breathed. Her lungs hurt as if she'd sprinted up a steep hill. Warm night air, not freezing cold. "I had a hiding spot because he went off frequently and invisibility was survival. There was a loose board under the porch. I took Erin and Adam there. It was winter, snowy, bitter cold. We were in pajamas, and we couldn't stop shivering. Adam kept crying. I had to make him stop. If he found us, he'd kill us. I don't know how I knew, but I did."

Bree saw her mother's face again. Daddy's hand around her neck, her eyes sad, determined, and resigned. "My mother knew too. I don't think I ever saw that so clearly before. I blocked a lot of that night—and my whole childhood—until recently. She distracted him, sacrificed herself so we could run, hide—survive."

"And you did."

"We did."

Her glass was full again. Mercy must have refilled it, but Bree hadn't seen her. Hadn't noticed that she'd brought the bottle outside. Bree had been back in those terrible moments, reliving them, probably more clearly than ever before. "I didn't see him die, but I saw a crime scene photo. He was found leaning against the wall, bullet hole in the side of his head, gun next to his hand. Blood and brains splattered the wallboard behind him. He hadn't been able to kill us, but he shot himself before the sheriff arrived."

"I don't know what to say," Mercy said. "Except I wish he'd just taken himself out and left the rest of you alone."

"Yeah. That wasn't his style. Inflicting damage was his superpower." Bree wondered how different her life would have been if her father had turned his rage inward instead of outward.

"We should eat something," Mercy said.

"Probably." Bree looked out over the pasture, watched the dark shapes of the horses moving in the night, breathed in the warm night air. She had survived. Maybe now that she had Matt and the mutual trust and personal security they shared, she was able to handle details of her past—she was finally able to process the full reality of her parents' deaths.

"The one thing I've always remembered about that night was the sheriff. He found us under the porch. Coaxed me out. Wrapped me in his coat. I knew I was safe with the same instinct I'd sensed the danger my father presented."

"And that's why you became a cop." Mercy pushed off the railing.

"It's pretty obvious." Bree carried her wine back into the house. She opened the freezer. Nothing appealed. She went to the pantry and opened a bag of potato chips.

"Now you know my deep, dark secret." Bree tilted the bag toward Mercy.

"Definitely deep and dark. I'll give you that." Mercy grabbed a handful of chips.

"Anyway. I'm OK. It helps to talk about it—which I've just learned." Bree's laugh felt lopsided. From the wine or the enormity of her emotions?

Who knows?

Both.

"Anyway," Bree said. "Thanks for listening."

"I get it." Mercy paused, unease flickering in her eyes. "Carrying around dark secrets eats away at your soul. You don't realize it until you find someone you trust enough to share them and suddenly you feel lighter."

Bree eyed her.

Someone has her own soul-eating secret.

She didn't want to pry. She took a big sip of her wine and pried anyway. "Your face doesn't hide anything, does it?"

Mercy grimaced. "It's a curse. Although my husband likes it. Says he knows everything I'm thinking." She emptied her glass.

Is that her first or second glass?

"What soul-eating thing are you thinking about?" Bree tipped the wine bottle over Mercy's glass. A small dribble of wine came out. Empty. It must have been Mercy's second glass too. "Need more?"

"If we're going to keep talking about this, definitely."

Bree grabbed another bottle and the opener and focused on the cork. "Tell me."

"My father never hurt us. For the most part, he was a good man—but he had old-fashioned, stubborn opinions about women's roles in life . . . which essentially boiled down to women belong in the kitchen and education was wasted on them. But I was thinking how lucky me and my four siblings were compared to you. We knew we were loved and grew up feeling secure. It was my father's attitude about a particular event that drove me away at eighteen. It estranged me from my entire family for fifteen years."

"I'm sorry," Bree said, realizing Mercy must have put herself through college and joined the FBI with no support from her family. "Did you have a good group of friends? That can make all the difference." She filled Mercy's glass.

"No." Mercy swirled the wine in her glass, her gaze locked on the red fluid. "I was a loner. I trusted no one. I simply did what I needed to do."

I don't think she's gotten to her soul-eating secret.

"That takes strength." Bree tipped her head and started toward her sofa, and Mercy followed with the potato chip bag and wine in hand. They settled into the soft cushions. "Do you talk to anyone in your family now?"

"Yes. A few years ago, an investigation brought me back to my little hometown and face-to-face with everyone. For the most part, we're on good terms now. But my brother Levi . . ."

Bree saw her eyes fill.

"He was murdered during my investigation and died in my arms." She took a heavy draw on the wine.

Bree stilled, thinking of her sister and wishing she'd been there when Erin had passed. Instead, her sister had died alone.

"Worst of all, it was completely my fault. If I hadn't left at eighteen, he'd be alive." Her tone grew thick. "Hidden secrets, you know? Mine and Levi's. We fucked up. And it led to his death fifteen years later."

Bree held her breath, waiting.

Mercy looked her in the eye. "I can't tell you what we did. As law enforcement, you'd have an obligation to turn me in."

She killed someone.

"You were eighteen?" asked Bree, wondering if she could set aside her legal responsibilities if Mercy told her what happened.

"Yes. And told no one for fifteen years." A half smile touched her lips. "Then I met Truman. He broke down my walls and got it out of me. He says I was justified . . . but that afterward I—and Levi—handled it wrong in many ways."

"And now you're raising his daughter?"

"Yes." Mercy's eyes lightened. "His last words were a request that I take care of her. Ollie also lives with us. That's a long story, but he came into our lives recently and is now Truman's son. We call ourselves a patchwork family." A genuine smile filled her face.

"I have one of those myself." And Bree thought they were perfect. "Sometimes the family you choose are the ones who create a home in your heart and help heal past pain."

Mercy lifted her glass to Bree. "Truth."

Bree clinked her glass and they both drank. Mercy exhaled and sank deeper into the cushions. Bree sensed the agent's tension evaporate.

Mine is gone too. Mostly.

It's been a fucked-up day.

It'd felt good to tell the agent about her past. Bree didn't open up to many people—just Dana.

Mercy caught her gaze. "I don't share with anyone what I told you."

"I was just thinking the same thing."

The two were silent for a long moment. Guilt touched Bree as she realized that she'd momentarily forgotten about Jimmie.

"We probably should go back to the case," Bree said.

"Shit. Yes." Mercy's eyes were underscored with deep shadows. The case was taking a toll on her too.

"So Jimmie is dead." Bree felt a little self-centered for focusing on her own past when a man had been killed. "What does that mean to our investigation?"

Mercy tapped a finger on the bowl of her glass. "It's either unrelated—he led a dangerous life—or it *is* related. But how?"

"Can he still be our killer and coincidentally got himself killed in a drug deal gone bad?"

"I hate coincidences."

"Same." Bree's mind churned. "Was he killed by the serial killer? If yes, then why?"

"His death makes no sense in respect to our case."

"And yet it happened." Bree shuddered, the motel room scene popping into her mind like a full-color glossy. Since brain bleach didn't exist, it would be there forever.

"The day has been so . . ." Mercy paused, clearly searching for a word.

Bree supplied it. "Fucked?"

"Yeah. And I just realized something I hadn't thought of earlier today, so maybe the wine is clearing my head."

"I doubt that." Bree's head was definitely fuzzy at the moment.

Mercy set down her wine. "What if our killer doesn't keep more than one girl at a time, and now he's taken another captive. Does that mean he's killed Paige?"

Bree stared at her. "Shit."

Chapter 35

MERCY

Day 7

"You're up early," Mercy said as she answered Evan's phone call and stifled a yawn. It was eight a.m. on the East Coast, and she and Bree had dragged themselves into the office an hour ago after a late night of heavy talk and more wine than expected.

We deserved to blow off a little steam.

The image of Jimmie dead in the filthy bathroom was still fresh in her mind. "Have you read my report on the shooting of Jimmie Elkins?" she asked Evan.

"Our suspect reactivated his CuffMe account last night," Evan stated, ignoring her question.

Mercy blinked, her brain trying to catch up. Across the conference table, Bree met her gaze and raised a tired brow. Mercy knew the dark circles under her eyes matched the sheriff's. "Evan, I'm putting you on speaker. Bree is here too."

"Morning, Sheriff," said Evan. "Our suspect's CuffMe profile has been reactivated," he repeated. "We still have access to it, and we can see he's communicating with other women. I'm not seeing any meetings being planned in the conversations. He's blocking most accounts after a few sentences. He's clearly looking for something specific."

"That has to mean that Jimmie definitely wasn't our killer—unless someone else is using the account," said Mercy, swallowing hard. "Does him trolling online mean he's already disposed of the victim from the mall and is looking for someone new?"

"Maybe the mall victim turned out to not be acceptable or he wasn't the kidnapper," said Bree. "It also emphasizes the question of whether or not Paige is still alive."

Are we too late?

"I don't know what it means," said Evan. "I've been speaking with one of the company's lawyers. CuffMe is very uptight about protecting their clients' privacy—"

"Their killer's privacy," snapped Bree.

"But he confirmed again that TheMaster232 account's IP address is still somewhere in the Scarlet Falls area, and the name on the account is still Mark Verney. I went through everyone TheMaster communicated with in the past and sent a list of profile names to the lawyer. He had someone check those accounts and verified that the names Vanessa Mullen and Tisha Talbot were not the owners of any on that list. He also said there are no accounts with the company period with those names as the owner."

"They could have used fake names," Mercy pointed out.

"True," said Evan.

"We know he met Paige on CuffMe," said Mercy. "I still think he could have met Vanessa or Tisha there with fake names on their accounts, but I'd assumed he'd met them around here as they were sometimes local prostitutes." She looked at Bree. "Do we need to put out a warning to that community? Interview some women about their johns? Maybe some have dealt with a man who uses a ball gag."

"Communicating with those women is not as easy as it sounds. The last person they want to listen to is the police," said Bree. "Let me think about how to approach them."

"It drives me crazy that our guy is hiding behind a computer screen," said Evan.

Mercy pulled up the site, wanting to look at TheMaster232 profile, only to find she couldn't even get in without creating her own account. "Evan, can you somehow give us access to his conversations?"

"I can't. CuffMe gave only me access."

Mercy thought for a long moment.

We could . . .

"You've gone quiet," Evan said.

"I have an idea," said Mercy.

"I suspect I know what it is," Evan said dryly. "And I don't like it."

Mercy gestured at the CuffMe home page on her screen. "We could set up a profile to get him to talk to us. We know exactly the kind of woman he wants." She looked eagerly at Bree. "We could draw him in."

"He talked to Paige for a long time before meeting her," said Bree. "We don't have months."

Paige doesn't have months.

If we're not already too late.

"We don't need him to agree to meet," said Mercy. "We just need a crumb of information that could lead us to him. We know TheMaster is in the area here somewhere. If he said something like . . . *I often visit the library—*"

Bree made a derisive noise.

"Or *I shop at Whole Foods, not Hannaford. Something.* We could ask about his plans for the evening. If he thinks our fake profile is in another state, maybe he'd feel comfortable enough to let some local references slip through." She was warming to the idea, a subtle excitement growing. It felt like a good possibility.

On the phone, Evan was silent, and she could tell Bree was mulling it over.

"We can do this," Mercy stated. "It can't hurt. Evan can let us know if he sets something up in conversations with other women. It'll be like we're watching him from two different angles."

"I like the thought of yanking him around," said Bree, nodding resolutely. Her cell phone buzzed, and she glanced at the screen. "It's Dr. Jones. She probably has a prelim on Jimmie Elkins."

"Evan, you never answered if you read my report about Jimmie," said Mercy as Bree answered her phone.

"I did. Sorry, I was focused on the CuffMe information."

"Dr. Jones," said Bree. "You're on speaker with Agent Kilpatrick and Detective Bolton."

There was a pause. "Who is Detective Bolton?" asked Dr. Jones.

"Detective Bolton is with the Deschutes County Sheriff's Department in Oregon," said Mercy. "He is investigating an aspect that may be tied to Jimmie Elkins's death."

"In that case, I can confirm that Jimmie Elkins's death was a homicide," said Dr. Jones. "Clearly someone tried to stage it as a suicide, but like I speculated at the scene, the angle of the shot was physically impossible for him to achieve. He had a perimortem crack on the posterior aspect of his skull, which could explain why he was on the ground when he was shot."

"Someone slammed him into the tile wall," commented Mercy. "Possibly a physical altercation happened before the shooting."

"I took his nail scrapings for forensics—maybe you'll get lucky. The only other thing that might interest you was that he had a low level of methamphetamines in his system. You'll have my full report in a few hours, but those are the highlights."

"Thank you, Doctor," said Bree.

"Good luck." Dr. Jones ended the call.

"A low level of meth was probably SOP for Jimmie," said Mercy.

"I'll have my chief deputy contact the surrounding counties and see if we can get a line on who Jimmie's supplier was in addition to the evidence we'll have from the weapon," said Bree. "I can't help but feel this was the result of a dispute—most likely drugs or money. It was fast and harsh." She tipped her head toward Mercy's laptop. "Our killer doesn't appear to do anything quickly."

"I'll start setting up the CuffMe profile," said Mercy, already searching online photo sites for pictures that would catch their suspect's interest. "He likes them petite with long dark hair. Young too."

"I'm getting in the shower," said Evan on speaker. "I'll check in with you two later."

Mercy ended the call and considered a photo. "Too sexy?" she asked Bree.

"You can't use stock photos," said Bree. "He'll run a reverse image search and find them immediately. We need private pictures."

"Crap, you're right," said Mercy, thinking hard. "How are we going to get pics for the profile? I don't have any photos to share—I'm too tall anyway."

"Same," said Bree. "Maybe we could—I know!" She pulled out her phone and tapped her screen a few times. "I think I can catch her before she leaves her house."

"Who?" asked Mercy.

"Deputy Zucco. She was at the kidnapping scene yesterday," she said, holding the phone to her ear. "She's new to Randolph. Came out of NYPD recently. I know she did some undercover work for them."

"I remember her. She's definitely the right size."

"Yep. She's got the right hair too. Don't let her size fool you. She's tough." Bree held up a finger. "Zucco? You on your way in yet?" Bree paused. "OK. Hang on. I'm putting you on speaker with Special Agent Kilpatrick. We have a request."

"Just name it," said a woman with a New York accent.

Mercy nodded at Bree.

"I know you did undercover work at the NYPD," said Bree. "One was a prostitution sting, right?"

"I did several of those."

"We need someone of your stature and looks for pictures to post on a BDSM site. We're creating a fake profile."

Zucco was silent.

"I know that sounds awful," said Mercy. "We'll keep the pictures clean—we just need them to be appealing. We can cover your face as much as possible. We know the types of photos that have caught his attention before."

"You have an online target?" asked Zucco. "Is this related to the suitcase women?" Her tone grew sharp.

"Yes and yes," said Bree. "Any chance you have some clothing that would work?"

Zucco laughed. "Do I have some sexy clothing? You bet I do. I'm in. I'll do anything to help catch that asshole."

"Can you bring in the clothes this morning?" asked Bree. "We'll do a quick photography session. I'd like to get this up and running ASAP."

"I'll be there in fifteen. This sounds like fun." She gave a rich laugh. "Looking forward to it."

Bree ended the call. "I knew she'd be on board."

"I'll fill out the bio while we're waiting." Mercy checked the box on the screen to swear she was eighteen and then a half dozen other boxes that basically said CuffMe wasn't responsible for anything and people needed to use common sense. Then she was instructed to set up her profile. "I need a username." Mercy wrinkled her nose, remembering the suggestive names of the men Paige had chatted with.

"Something that sounds submissive," said Bree.

"Paige's profile and interests came across that way. I remember dollification was one of them because I'd never heard of it," Mercy said. "How about YourDoll?" She typed it in. "Of course, it's in use." She randomly added 945 to the end and it was accepted.

"I'll do twenty-five for her age. And located in Boston, Massachusetts. That should be far enough away to make him feel relaxed, but close enough for him to consider meeting her."

"He went across the country for Paige," said Bree.

"That was crazy, wasn't it? I wonder what made the appeal so strong."

"Hopefully we can get his attention."

"I'll include all the interests Paige had listed in hers. I can list that our woman is willing to travel too. What else do we know about him to help capture his attention?"

"He likes ball gags," muttered Bree.

"It'd be great if we could get one in a photo with your deputy."

"You'll have to go to the adult store," said Bree. "I don't keep them around the department."

Mercy grinned. "Maybe someone else does."

"I don't want to know about it."

Mercy sat back in her chair. "That's all I can do until we have photos."

An hour later they had photos.

Deputy Renata Zucco had walked in with a bag full of clothes. Mercy had considered a slinky black dress until she saw something pink in the bottom of the bag. Bree spotted it at the same time and pulled out an off-the-shoulder blouse. She met Mercy's gaze.

Pepto-Bismol pink.

Some smoldering eye makeup and pigtails completed the look. "Am I to be sexy or a schoolgirl?" Renata had asked.

"Yes," Mercy and Bree had answered in unison.

"Got it."

Mercy uploaded five photos. Bree had taken some great angles that were revealing and coy at the same time, Renata's face only partially visible in each one. A tease for the observer. The shots were just enough for it to be obvious that she was beautiful. She wore the black dress in one full body shot, her dark hair covering one eye, while the other eye stared into your soul.

Renata and Bree watched over Mercy's shoulder as the profile took shape.

"You look amazing," said Bree.

Renata shrugged, pulling her hair into a severe ponytail and took a makeup wipe to her eyeliner. The siren from a few minutes before was now in uniform.

"Ready?" said Mercy, her cursor hovering over the Post button.

"Go for it," said Bree.

Mercy clicked.

Please work.

Chapter 36

HIM

This time, I have no hesitation using my Master profile. The cops are clueless. I scroll through the options. It's amazing, really, how many women are dying to be my submissive. They want to be owned. It just goes to show that submission is the natural state for females. Paige is in her cage. I opened the door when I came home, yet she hasn't moved. I bet she wouldn't even come out if I left the house.

Maybe I should try that. I could set a trap for her. Then I'd have a legit opportunity to punish her. At least she'd give me some pleasure before I kill her.

Can't do that yet.

As a senator's daughter, she has value. Her father's position was a bonus to my pride—a feather in my cap, to be cliché. I'd already selected her before I learned what he did. Now, that ego bonus might come in handy in a very practical way. I might need her as a hostage or to extract ransom from her rich daddy. I won't spare her, though. Her time will come. I've put too much effort into her transformation. I've earned the pleasure of her death. For now, I'll enjoy the anticipation.

Then what?

On one hand, I applaud the way I've modified her behavior. She was a huge step up from the prostitutes I practiced on. Using the site gave me a quality woman, the kind of female I deserve. On the other hand, as I scroll through the responses to my post and click to look at the profiles, I see that I can do better.

I can find a quality woman who is less of a child. I know that Paige lied about her age. At first, I thought I'd like a young one, but now I know a little experience might make for a better challenge. Let's see. What are my options?

Clicking through to each profile, I study their photos. Too old, too young, too blonde. I pause on the image of a dark-haired woman. She's gorgeous in an innocent-looking way. Do I want innocence? I had that with Paige, and she bored me in just a couple of weeks. I make a note and stick her on the maybe list. The next is butt ugly. Hard pass. I have standards.

This one has potential. Her eyes are almost downcast, but there's a glimmer of fire in them. Interesting. She's a definite maybe. The next is a bit older, looks to be in her midthirties, but she's still plenty attractive.

I check several more profiles before I narrow my list down to three women. My choices are innocent, fiery, and experienced. I'll think about them awhile, then decide which ones to message.

I'd forgotten how much fun this is. The opening gambit of the game. The lure, the setting of the trap, the snap of its jaws. I can't wait.

With some profiles selected, I turn to a fresh internet search for, well, me.

I spend a few minutes scrolling through new articles and videos. Headlines grab my eye: Another Woman Kidnapped in Randolph County, Woman Nabbed from Scarlet Falls Mall, Serial Killer Strikes Again.

I read through a couple of articles. I actually laugh out loud at the article describing the abduction and asking for help in identifying the woman who was taken.

Such chaos. The sheriff and FBI are completely stumped. The local cops are useless too. I am pulling all the strings, and they are doing exactly as I predict. Every time.

I am in control.

The thought of me jerking around three separate law enforcement agencies gives me a surge of pleasure. I have outsmarted them at every turn. I'm playing chess, and they can't even organize their checkers. Their investigation is a joke. They have no idea what is going on. Excitement rushes through my blood. I can't wait to see how they respond to what I've planned next.

Chapter 37

BREE

Bree sat at her desk. Her head ached, and her stomach felt sour. It was a little sad that just a few glasses of wine put her into such a state, but she rarely drank. The coffee wasn't helping her stomach, but it was definitely necessary for her brain. She popped an antacid and picked up her phone to view her messages. That morning, Dana had sent her a few pictures of the kids on the boardwalk. Their smiles did more for Bree's physical state than the TUMS, and she was once again grateful that they were far away from home.

Her phone vibrated in her hand. She read Matt's name on the screen. Her heart leaped as she pressed ANSWER. "Hey."

"Hey," he said. "What's wrong?"

"You can tell from one word?"

"I guess so." He sounded almost surprised. Dogs barked in the background.

She snorted. "And I was just thinking it was ridiculous how much I've missed you."

"Back atcha." His voice went husky.

"The work with the dogs is good?"

"It's great. But I still miss you. We just hit some cell reception. I checked the news. I'm sorry I'm not there. The case sounds like it's gone sideways."

"I wish you were here too." The feeling in her gut could only be described as yearning, but the word made her mentally roll her eyes. "*Sideways* is a mild way to describe this case."

"You need me to come home? I'm sure I can get a copter ride from somebody."

"No. The FBI is assisting, so I have support." *But it's not the same.*

"How is the fed?" Matt asked.

"She's solid, and she brings resources to the table."

"The federal budget is a little bigger than Randolph County's?"

"Just a little." Bree laughed. Just hearing his voice brightened her mood, which she admitted had been pretty bleak.

Static broke up Matt's response. "I'm losing reception. I love you."

"I love you too." She hoped he'd heard her.

The line went dead, and she stared at the phone for a minute, feeling bereft. How had she managed before him? The same way she would work this case. It would be harder without him, but she would do the job.

Marge poked her head in the doorway. "There's a woman in the lobby I think you should talk to."

Bree raised her brows. She trusted her assistant's instincts, but she was already swamped. "OK, but why?"

Marge leaned on the doorframe. "She says her friend went missing a few months ago, and the Redhaven police refused to investigate."

Bree waited.

Marge paused. "They're both prostitutes."

"Oh." Bree felt the sigh come from deep inside. Missing persons cases rarely generated substantial law enforcement responses unless the individual was a child or there were clear signs of foul play or exigent circumstances. Adults were free to come and go as they pleased. They were not required to report their location to family members. Families with missing adults were often forced to hire PIs when the trails went quickly cold. Given the lifestyle of a prostitute, it was even harder to track them. Other prostitutes and potential pimps didn't like to cooperate with law enforcement. Drugs were often involved. Clients didn't want to admit they frequented sex workers.

"You think this is related to the case?" Mercy asked.

"Maybe," Marge said.

"Someone got that fourth tattoo," Bree said. "We'll talk to her in room one." She put her palms flat on the table and pushed to her feet.

Marge nodded. "Her name is Shelly Fox."

Bree and Mercy made their way down the hall to the interview room. Bree peered through the doorway.

The woman inside was thin. Her long blonde hair was damaged at the ends, greasy and dark at the roots. She stood in the corner of the room, her arms wrapped around her waist. She ripped off a piece of her thumbnail with her teeth. When Bree and Mercy entered the room, she whirled, every muscle in her body tense. She'd backed herself into a corner, poised for flight with nowhere to run, which was a fair summation of the life of a prostitute.

"Ms. Fox?" Bree stopped in the doorway, taking care not to press on her personal space.

The woman gave her a tight nod back.

"I'm Sheriff Taggert. This is Special Agent Kilpatrick. Would you like some coffee?"

"Yeah. That'd be good." Shelly didn't move.

Bree leaned into the hall, spotted Marge, and gestured for her to bring coffee. Then Bree and Mercy eased into the room. Bree pulled out a chair, letting Shelly keep the table as a barrier. Mercy took the chair next to Bree.

Marge brought a tray with three steaming coffee mugs, packets of sugar and cream, and a few donuts she must have pilfered from the break room. Shelly looked like she hadn't eaten in some time, but then, the tracks on her arms suggested she chose drugs over food. Bree let the donuts draw Shelly closer. She sank into a chair, her gaze darting to Bree and Mercy and back again.

Bree slid a mug in front of her and took a donut. "These are fresh. Help yourself."

Shelly's eyes shifted to hunger. Bree wondered when she'd eaten last. Shelly selected a donut and ate it in three bites.

Bree waited for her to finish. "Tell me about your friend."

Shelly wiped her mouth on the back of her hand and doctored her coffee with two packets of sugar and a tiny tub of creamer. "Her name is Missy. Missy Star."

Bree jotted it down. "Do you know if that's her real name?"

Shelly shook her head.

"When was the last time you saw her?" Mercy asked.

Shelly jerked a shoulder. "Dunno exactly. About three or four months ago. She used to be on the same corner as me every night. Then she just wasn't."

"Which corner?" Bree opened her notebook.

Shelly paused, her eyes worried.

"It's OK," Bree said. "We won't arrest you."

Shelly looked unconvinced. She licked her lips, and her next words were almost a whisper. "Cops lie."

The accusation hit hard. There was no law against cops lying to suspects. Bree had done it herself to gain information and solve cases. But there was clearly a downside: lack of trust.

Bree went with the most honest response she could. "I can't make you trust us, but we're trying to stop a killer. If this is related, we need to know."

"You think that killer got Missy?" Shelly's mouth flattened, but she wasn't surprised at the thought.

Bree turned up both palms in a *who knows* gesture. "We won't know unless we look for her."

Shelly chewed on another nail. She wasn't going to have a single one left at this rate. "Oak and Fifth in Redhaven."

"Was Missy worried about anything in particular?" Mercy leaned her forearms on the table.

Shelly raised her hand and bit off another nail. "Yeah. A client. He was into weird bondage shit. There are always guys into that, but this one was different." Shelly cocked her head. "He scared her. He wanted more than just handcuffs and some spanking. She said it felt like he really wanted to hurt her."

Bree made a note. "Did he do anything specific?"

"He choked her," Shelly said. "But not like erotic . . . erotic . . . I can't remember the term."

"Erotic asphyxiation," Mercy supplied.

"Yeah." Shelly nodded. "She said it wasn't like that. Usually, *they* want to get choked to increase their pleasure. But with him, it wasn't like that. *He* liked choking *her*, if you know what I mean."

"Yes." Bree exchanged a look with Mercy. "We understand."

Shelly splayed a hand at the base of her throat. "She had bruises around her neck. Dark ones."

Mercy sat up straighter. "Did she describe him?"

Shelly shook her head. "He was strong. That's all she said."

Disappointment filled Bree.

Mercy's eyes sharpened. "Did he engage Missy more than one time?"

"Yeah," Shelly said. "He paid well, and she said he was a little weird the first couple of times. Wanted to tie her up and liked it rough. But each time, he got rougher. She was afraid he was gonna go off and actually kill her."

"Do you or Missy have a manager?" Bree asked.

Shelly shook her head. "Every girl I know who does gets beat by him and the clients."

"Fair assessment," Bree agreed. "Would you please wait here for a few minutes? I'll be right back."

She left the room and hurried to the squad room to find Todd at his desk. "Get me five random male photos for an array." She stopped in the conference room and pulled photos of the men in the serial killer case. With the stack of photos, she returned to the interview room.

"Have you seen any of these men?" She dealt out pictures of Jimmie, Tisha's father, Rick Mullen, and Pete Conrad, intermixing them with the photos of the random men.

Shelly leaned over the table and examined the men carefully. She stopped and went back, tapping the table below the picture of Pete Conrad. "I might have seen him around recently."

"Did he solicit your services?" Mercy asked.

She chewed her lip. "Maybe."

"Could he be the same man who got rough with Missy?" Bree asked.

"I don't know." Fear flashed in Shelly's eyes. "Do you think it's him?"

"We don't know. Did he get rough? Or use anything like, say, a ball gag?"

"No." Shelly shook her head. "He likes to talk dirty. He never asked for any bondage-type stuff."

Mercy frowned. "Was he around when Missy disappeared?"

Shelly's forehead furrowed. "I've only seen him the past month or two, but I can't say he wasn't around then. Just that I didn't see him then."

"Do you remember anything else?" Bree asked.

Shelly finished her coffee. "No."

"Where did Missy live?" Mercy asked.

"She rented a room at the Grand on Fourth." Shelly's hand trembled. She clasped it with the other to still the shakes. From drug withdrawal or nerves? Could be both, Bree decided.

"How did you get here today?" Bree asked.

"My brother brought me," Shelly said.

"Do you need a ride back?" Bree offered.

"No, he's waiting for me." Shelly stood.

Bree showed her to the door. She wrote her cell number on the back of a business card. "If you see anything or hear anything, please call me."

"Sure." But Shelly's voice didn't sound promising. She looked at the door. "Thanks for listening. You're the first person to actually care about Missy."

After Shelly left, Bree finished her donut. "What do you think?"

Mercy frowned at Pete Conrad's photo. "We already know he solicits local prostitutes, so I'm not sure her recognizing him matters."

"Except that he's still doing it, even though he's already facing charges."

"We could pick him up," Mercy said.

"Might be worth talking to him again," Bree agreed. "I'll have a deputy bring him in. I'll meet you back in the conference room in five. We need to find another lead while we wait for Pete."

Chapter 38

MERCY

Mercy checked their CuffMe profile in the conference room while she waited for Bree. TheMaster232 had not taken the bait.

Yet.

She opened the messages from other men who had messaged her fake profile and grew nauseated. Like many who had contacted Paige's profile, they'd immediately launched into graphic sex talk. One by one, Mercy blocked them.

No, she did not want a pearl necklace.

No, she would not let him watch her with other men.

Scat play? She'd done a quick Google search, afraid she knew what he wanted, and then blocked him. Bathroom activities needed to stay in the bathroom.

So did vomit.

How do people come up with these ideas?

"No luck yet," Mercy said as Bree walked in.

"What if he has more than one account?" asked Bree. "He could be one of these men. He was polite with Paige, but maybe he's like all these other guys on another account."

Mercy had wondered the same thing. "We'll take our chances. If he doesn't message by the end of the day, we can send him a message. But he contacted Paige first . . . If he wants a submissive, he won't like us making the first move. I don't want to ruin it."

"This isn't going to work," said Bree, an impatient look on her face. "We can't be wasting time on this profile. We have things to do."

Mercy raised a brow. "You've made a dozen phone calls this morning, talked to Shelly Fox, put out feelers for Jimmie's drug dealer, and now I'm about to review more video from the Scarlet Falls Mall. We're not wasting time—there is so much to dig into. If one of us is called out, we can go. Laptops are portable, you know. We're not stuck here."

"You're right."

Mercy opened the new mall videos. A few more stores had sent their videos from the day before, and Mercy searched each one, looking for someone who fit the description of the victim who'd been nabbed in the parking lot. "Think the kidnapped woman was from out of town?" she asked Bree. "Could be why no one has reported her missing yet."

"I think we can toss our theory about her being an employee. We would have heard by now if an employee was missing. Out-of-towner is a possibility, but I still feel he was expecting someone specific."

A ping made Mercy return to CuffMe. Her heart shot up into her throat. "It's him."

Bree rolled her chair around the table and they both stared at the screen.

TheMaster232: Good morning, beautiful

"Polite," mumbled Mercy. "That's our man."

YourDoll945: Good morning to you too, Master

Mercy had started to comment that she liked his photos but worried the sentence was too forward and deleted it.

Be submissive.

"Say something else," whispered Bree. "Keep his interest."

"I think he's testing me," said Mercy. "Seeing if I'll wait for his direction."

"I *hate* mind games," grumbled Bree.

A full minute passed before another message came through.

TheMaster232: Pink is lovely on you

"Oh, my God," said Mercy. "What is his hang-up with that shade of pink?"

YourDoll945: I'm glad it pleases you

Bree made a retching noise. "Good thing you're typing. I wouldn't be able to hold back."

TheMaster232: How is the weather in Boston today?

"Checking," said Bree. "Sunny and clear. Humid."

"I remember that was one of the first questions he asked Paige too," said Mercy, trying to remember how Paige had answered the question. "She mentioned bikes," she muttered.

YourDoll945: A clear blue day. Somewhat humid, but I'll definitely get in a bike ride

They waited.

"Was that too much?" asked Bree, fidgeting in her chair. "Just how sensitive is this guy?"

Mercy said nothing as she realized she was holding her breath.

TheMaster232: Where do you like to bike?

"Crap," said Mercy. "How specific do I have to be? I don't know Boston." She looked at Bree, who was scanning her phone.

"Deer Island," said Bree, scrolling a Boston bike path website. "Say you take the ferry."

YourDoll945: Today I think I'll go to Deer Island. It's a nice day for a ferry ride

They waited for his reply.

And waited.

The conversation vanished.

Mercy sucked in a breath. "He blocked us! What did I do wrong?" She slumped back in her chair. *"Shit."*

"Was it because you had an opinion about the weather? Or that bike plan was too adventurous for the submissive woman he wants? Damn it!"

She and Bree continued to stare at the screen as if hoping he'd reappear, that it'd been a mistake.

"It was worth a try," said Bree. "Maybe *bike* is a euphemism we don't know, so we answered completely wrong."

Mercy laughed. "Should we set up a new profile? Clearly we know how to write one to snag him. We can't use Renata again. We'd have to find someone else."

"That won't be easy."

Mercy thought on it, hating to let the profile idea go. They'd been lucky with Renata, and finding another woman of the right look who was also willing to be posted would take time. She picked up her phone. "I'll let Evan know our experiment is over."

"Mercy?" he answered. Background noise indicated he was driving.

"Our profile got blocked by TheMaster, Evan. I don't think I said anything wrong, but there was something he didn't like."

"It was worth a try. And from what I've seen while monitoring his messages, he quickly blocks almost all the conversations. Most of the women immediately start discussing sex, and it appears that is not what he wants to hear."

"Yes. It took a while with Paige before their conversations went there."

"I'm keeping an eye on two conversations. SweetLittleGirl29 and DaisyMae455 are having slow, drawn-out conversations with him that haven't veered into anything sexual yet. For some reason, he likes to take his time."

"Can you find out who they are?" asked Mercy.

"The conversation needs to go further before CuffMe sees it as a problem and shares their account information. According to the lawyer I'm dealing with, there's nothing here yet, and I think he's right. If TheMaster takes as long as he did with Paige, we've got a lot of waiting to do."

"We can't wait," said Mercy. "We need to find Paige. Now."

"I know, Mercy."

"Sorry." Mercy rubbed her forehead. "I think I'm disappointed the profile failed. Let me know if anything else happens."

"I will." Evan ended the call.

"TheMaster is communicating with someone on the website?" asked Bree, who had been closely following Mercy's side of the conversation.

"Yes. Two women. But the conversations are nonsexual and slow. The site won't share their info with Evan because of that."

"Something could still come out of it."

"It won't do much good." Mercy slumped back in her chair. "TheMaster switched to texting with Paige before he made any plans with her. He'll probably go offline again if he finds someone he's interested in. And even if CuffMe does share a woman's account information, it'll probably be fake like TheMaster's name and address were."

"We'd still check out any account information," said Bree. "Maybe we'd get lucky."

I doubt it.

Chapter 39

BREE

Bree turned to stare at the murder board and studied the photos strung along the top. The faces of the dead women—and the senator's daughter—stared back at her. She knew she was imagining the accusation in their eyes. The criticism came from within. She blamed herself for lack of progress on the case, which wasn't fair, but the world was hardly fair, was it?

Mercy rubbed her temples. "We've gathered a board full of information, but it feels like we still don't know anything."

"Having him block us on CuffMe hurt," Bree admitted.

Someone knocked on the conference room door. Since the case details had been leaked to the media, Bree had been militant about keeping the door closed and locked at all times, with only those directly involved in the investigation being granted access.

Marge opened the door. "That reporter, Ken Wells, is in the lobby. He's asking to see you. I told him you weren't available, but he won't leave. He says it's urgent."

Bree and Mercy shared a look. Mercy's brows rose.

Why would a reporter want to see us?

"Take him to room one," Bree said.

Marge nodded and withdrew.

"I wonder what Mr. Anonymous Source wants?" Mercy stood.

"Let's find out." Bree was just as curious.

She locked the conference room door after she and Mercy left. They went down the hall to the interview room. The door was open, and Bree could see Ken Wells sitting at the table, spinning a can of Coke between his palms. When they walked into the room, Ken jumped to his feet. Bree pulled back in surprise. For the first time, the reporter didn't look as perfect as his Mattel namesake. His face was flushed, his hair mussed, and his suit wrinkled.

Bree didn't bother with a polite greeting. She and Mercy faced the reporter across the table.

Ken lowered himself slowly into the chair. "You must be wondering why I'm here."

Neither Bree nor Mercy responded.

Ken swallowed, then reached for a briefcase on the chair next to him. He pulled out a manila envelope. "When I got home today, this was inside my storm door." He opened the clasp. His hands shook as he dumped out a regular letter envelope.

The hairs on Bree's neck quivered as she read the block lettering, neatly printed in blue ink. *KEN WELLS*. Instinctively, she knew not to touch it. "What is it?"

"I think it's from him." Ken's voice trembled.

Bree left the room for a pair of gloves. After donning them, she handled the envelope by the edges. Inside was a piece of plain white paper, trifolded. She slid it out, careful not to disturb any possible prints. A small card fell out onto the table. Not a card, a driver's license. Bree turned it over to reveal Tisha Talbot's DMV photo.

Her lungs froze for two heartbeats. Mercy gasped softly.

Bree took a breath and unfolded the paper. The words on the paper were written in the same blue ink and neat print as the reporter's name on the envelope.

Dear Ken,

Hello again. I have some new information for you. Guess who is in my house right now? Her name is Paige, and she's the daughter of US Senator Adam Holcroft. I didn't kidnap her, though. She chose to come to me with her own free will. The sheriff and FBI have been keeping her disappearance a secret, but now you know. Don't you think it's time the public knows as well?

I've enclosed a little something just so you know it's really me. Also, release this information today or you'll end up in your own suitcase. I know where you live.

The Master

"Again?" Bree asked Ken. "This isn't the first communication you've received from him?" He avoided eye contact, and she knew the answer.

Ken studied the laminate tabletop. "I think I've heard from him before, but I didn't know it was him at the time."

A burst of outright hostility heated Bree's belly. She did not blurt out the first question flashing in her mind like a neon sign: *How dare you keep potentially valuable evidence from the investigators of a serial murderer case?* Instead, she gritted her teeth and spit out one word. "How?"

Ken sniffed and clasped his shaking fingers on the table in front of him. "Papers like this one, but they came to my office, not my home." He paused. "And they weren't personal like this. They were just a sentence or two."

Bree stared at the note. "Same paper, same envelope, same ink?"

"Yes."

"Did you keep the other letters?" Mercy asked, her words strained with the effort of keeping control.

"Yes," Ken muttered.

Fury lowered Bree's voice. "Where are they?"

Ken reached for his briefcase again. He pulled out two envelopes. Fucking two! Bree donned another pair of gloves, then opened them, handling the pages by the edges.

> The sheriff is holding back. The victims both had pink nail polish and long dark hair.

> Once again, law enforcement is keeping important information from the public. There were four matching tattoos, not two.

Bree couldn't speak for a full minute as she processed the letters. "He's been feeding you information since the beginning."

"I didn't know it was him!" Sweat dampened Ken's hairline. "I thought it was someone in your department."

Bree lowered the papers. "So having women in danger is fine, but now that you feel threatened you want to cooperate?"

Ken didn't respond.

"We need your prints for elimination purposes on these notes," she said. "Though I doubt he left prints behind." She gathered the papers and jerked her chin toward the door for Mercy to follow her. On the way out, Bree shot Ken a glare. "You don't move."

In the hallway, Bree summoned Todd and Juarez. She dropped the letters and the gloves she'd used to handle them into an evidence bag. She asked her chief deputy to process the evidence, then she asked Juarez to grab the background info on Ken. She grabbed another deputy and assigned her to watch the interview room door. "He stays put."

Bree and Mercy retreated to the conference room. Bree closed the door and leaned on it. "Thoughts?"

"Selfish bastard!" Anger flashed in Mercy's eyes.

"Agreed."

"How did the killer know that we knew about the four tattoos?" Bree asked.

Mercy threw her hands into the air. "Who knows? Maybe he didn't. Maybe he was just trying to make trouble. I don't think he's concerned with honesty."

"Good point," Bree said.

Mercy paced. "The killer has Paige. This is the confirmation we've been waiting for."

"Now what?" Bree asked.

Mercy walked the short length of the room and back. "I'll call Evan and then I'll call my boss. We need more agents here. Now. They need to pull everyone off the leads in the other states. No one else could know that Paige is missing. Enclosing Tisha's driver's license makes it clear the information is coming from the actual killer. And that he's definitely here. Hang on." She pulled out her phone and dialed.

Bree stepped away as Mercy talked to Detective Bolton and then called the FBI. She closed her eyes and took several yoga breaths. After a few minutes, Mercy finished her calls and rejoined her.

"The Albany FBI office has been notified. They're going to pull every available agent and send them here. We need the manpower."

"I don't like the notes to Ken," said Bree.

"It wouldn't be the first time a serial killer utilized the press."

"No."

"But I don't like that Ken kept the source a secret," Bree said. "Did he really not think about where the information was coming from?"

"Maybe he's not that bright."

Juarez opened the door and came into the room. "Ken Wells's background check." He handed the pages to Bree.

She glanced down, her focus riveting on two words. She looked up at Mercy. "Guess what Ken drives?" She waited one heartbeat. "A white Audi."

"So we have a blond man who knows too much about the serial killer who drives the same kind of vehicle just used to abduct a young woman?"

"Seems like too big of a coincidence."

Mercy's tone went flat. "The leaks and letters could be a ruse. We already know our killer is interested in the investigation. He set us up in an ambush." Her hand went to her ribs, the move seeming like an unconscious reminder of her cracked ribs.

"I wonder if the Audi is outside in the lot," Bree said.

"Do we have enough evidence for a warrant?" Mercy asked, sounding doubtful. "Doesn't seem like it."

"No, but maybe Ken will be arrogant enough to let us look."

"Can't hurt to ask." Mercy shrugged.

Bree led the way back to the interview room. Ken stiffened as they entered.

Instead of sitting across from Ken, Bree perched on the table, looming over him.

Ken leaned back, the move an instinctual response to her invading his personal space.

Bree leaned an inch closer. "So, Ken. You know an awful lot about these crimes."

"I—I've been following the case since the beginning," he stammered, his Adam's apple bobbing.

Mercy chimed in. "You know things only the police and the killer know."

"Because he told me." The sweat stains under Ken's armpits expanded.

Bree didn't respond. She let the silence spin—and Ken sweat.

"You don't think . . ." His eyes went wide. "You don't think it's me?" His gaze jumped from Bree's to Mercy's.

Bree shrugged. Mercy checked her fingernails.

"You have to believe me." Ken gripped the arms of the chair.

"You withheld information from an active investigation," Bree said. "Why?"

Ken gulped. "Because I wanted the scoop. It was dumb and greedy. I know that now."

"Is that the real reason?" Mercy asked with a tilt of her head.

Ken nodded like a bobblehead. "Yes. I swear."

"The girl at the mall was abducted and shoved in the trunk of a white Audi yesterday. That's what you drive, isn't it?"

Ken's mouth dropped open. "It wasn't me."

Bree held eye contact—and her breath.

He broke gaze first. "You can look in my trunk. It wasn't me. I didn't do anything, and you have to find him."

"Because he knows where to find you now, right?" Disgust curled Mercy's lip.

Ken looked away, his face flushing. Shame?

"You can wait here." Bree pointed to Ken.

"No way!" He leaped to his feet. "If you're looking in my car, I'm going too."

Bree conceded. "All right. Let's go."

Bree and Mercy flanked Ken as they walked out of the station. The parking lot was quiet for a change. Neither the press nor the protesters could camp out there 24/7. Thankfully.

Ken's Audi was at the back, parked under a tree. No air moved outside, and the sun was too intense for that late in the day. Far-off thunder gave a low rumble, and the blacktop felt sticky in the heat. They crossed the lot, and sweat trickled down Bree's spine and gathered at the small of her back.

"Open the trunk," Bree said.

Ken reached into his pocket for his key fob. He pressed a button. The trunk popped open.

"Please stand over there," Mercy said, pointing at the tree.

Bree handed Mercy a pair of gloves and donned a fresh pair herself. She shined her flashlight in the trunk. After five minutes of searching, she hadn't found anything. Disappointment crashed down on her.

Then Mercy said, "Look here."

The beam of her light shone on the lip of the trunk. Caught in the rubber edging were a half dozen strands of long dark hair.

"How fast can you get a DNA test on that?" Bree whispered.

"I can have it in less than twenty-four hours," Mercy whispered back. "Rapid tests in Albany. We have three women's DNA profiles to compare it to, and you now have enough on Ken to hold him until we have results."

"I'll send it with a deputy to Albany."

"It could belong to the woman kidnapped at the mall."

"Then we'll have a DNA profile ready to compare when we figure out who she is."

Bree strode toward Ken, removing the cuffs at her belt. "Place your hands on your head."

We might have our man.

Chapter 40

MERCY

"For someone whose appearance is always so perfect, his house is a surprising mess," said Mercy as she stood in Ken Wells's kitchen two hours later.

Beside her, Bree stared at the overflowing sink of dirty dishes. "I don't understand. He has a dishwasher. Isn't it just as easy to put them in there?"

"Ollie and Kaylie would disagree with you." Mercy had begged the kids not to stack dishes in the sink. It would work for a few weeks, and then the problem would start again. She sniffed at Ken's stack. "Something is fermenting."

Ken was in the county jail for the night. Mercy had referred to it as the Hotel Taggert, which Bree hadn't found amusing. He'd protested over and over that he had nothing to do with any of the women's disappearances. To which Bree had replied, "Then you've got nothing to worry about."

Now the women and three deputies were searching Ken's house. His home was a one-story older building that sat on a street where the only difference in the houses was the paint color and the vehicles in the driveways. A quick hunt for occupants in the home and garage had turned up nothing, so they began a deeper search.

"What exactly are we looking for?" asked the youngest deputy, Juarez.

In Mercy's opinion, Juarez didn't look old enough to drink.

"Anything related to BDSM or that indicates a woman might have been held here. Our warrant includes electronics, but don't unplug any computers. Forensics will do that. Keep an eye out for additional cell phones too," said Mercy. The other two deputies nodded and started in their assigned rooms. Juarez hesitated, his gaze going from Mercy to Bree.

Damn, he looks young.

"Whips, handcuffs, ball gags, chains," Bree rattled off, seeing his confusion. "Not the frilly pink types in your parents' bedroom drawers. Hard-core items. Maybe evidence of blood. Got it?" She raised a brow.

Deputy Juarez nodded and headed to the bedroom he'd been assigned.

"Surely he knows about . . . stuff," Mercy muttered. "Doesn't he watch movies?"

"Who knows? He's a nice young man but a little naive." Bree pointed at a cupboard. "I'll start on this side of the kitchen."

Mercy opened a drawer on the other side. "Junk drawer." She ran a gloved hand through the random items and moved on to the next. "Another junk drawer."

Ken had four of them.

In the last drawer she found three older cell phones. She was tempted to power them on, but knew to leave that for forensics, so she photographed and bagged them. Bree looked over.

"I have at least three old cell phones lying around," Bree commented. "Probably five."

"Me too."

They made quick work of the kitchen and sped through the dining nook and living room.

"Sheriff?" called Juarez. "I've got some stuff here."

Mercy and Bree followed the voice to a bedroom, where Juarez had opened a drawer in a nightstand. Inside was an array of sex toys.

"I don't see pink frills," said the deputy, his eyes serious.

Mercy took a photo of the drawer. "No pink, but still rather vanilla, I'd say. Let forensics collect them." Even with gloves on, she didn't want to touch. "Anything else in this room?" He shook his head.

Another deputy pointed out a desktop computer in Ken's office. She told them she'd checked the desk drawers and that the filing cabinets were locked. "There's a handgun in the bottom desk drawer."

Bree looked. "Glock 19. Could be the gun he used to shoot you."

Mercy's spine twinged in memory.

"Look at these." Bree indicated several nicely matted and framed eight-by-ten photos on the wall. Each one was of Ken, his microphone in hand. Three were of him interviewing people. Four others framed him with striking scenery in the background, and the last was a snowstorm with Ken barely recognizable under his hat and coat. Bree pointed at the first photo. "That's the governor. The second is one of our senators, and look, my favorite person, Madeline Jager, is in the last."

"Isn't she just a councilwoman or something?" asked Mercy. "Seems a little odd considering the other two images are of important people."

"Hmmm. Good point. Why you, Madeline?" Bree frowned at the photo, and then her face cleared. "I bet I know why. Look at Ken in this one compared to the other photos."

Mercy studied them and then grinned. "That's a really good angle on him, isn't it? Too good not to hang on his wall for visitors to see. It has nothing to do with your archenemy. I'm surprised he didn't crop her out."

Bree snorted. "What do you think about the locked filing cabinets?"

"I think we need to ask Ken for the key." She looked at the deputy. "No random keys in the drawers or under something?"

"No. I looked specifically for that when I discovered they were locked."

"We need to check his credit cards," said Bree. "See where he was when Paige was taken. Although I suspect he's too smart to have used them on that trip."

"We could see if he was on the air at all that day and the days surrounding it. That should be easy enough."

"I'll get Marge on it," said Bree, taking out her phone.

"It's almost nine p.m."

"Marge doesn't care. She likes this sort of thing." She left the room to make a call.

All the deputies had congregated and were now looking at Mercy. "Nothing else?" she asked. All shook their heads. "To the garage."

She followed the group.

It didn't feel like two people lived in the home. The covers on one side of his big bed were rumpled, and the pillow dented and smushed into a ball. The other pillow lay perfect, undisturbed. The other bedroom had a double bed that looked like it hadn't been touched in years. Dust covered the headboard and nightstands.

Where could Paige be?

If she's still alive.

Mercy swallowed hard, trying not to think of the family photos of Paige in contrast to her sexy profile picture on CuffMe. The girl had gotten in over her head.

In Ken's detached single-car garage, Mercy smelled mildew, oil, and gasoline. There was no room for his white Audi. Stacks of boxes and general garage crap filled two-thirds of the area. A rusty lawn mower turned out to be the source of the gasoline smell.

"Do we have to look in every box?" asked Juarez.

"Yes," said Bree. "With the five of us, it will go fast. Why don't you start with his workbench? Photograph everything before you open it," she instructed the other deputies as she took video of the entire inside.

Mercy hadn't even noticed the workbench hidden behind the stacks. It was a simple high wood table with a pegboard above it. Dozens of tools hung on the pegs. "Don't touch the tools," she told Juarez. "But look closely for anything that could be blood." She turned to the closest cardboard box and flipped it open. A cloud of dust made her sneeze. Another sneeze echoed from Bree.

"This crap hasn't been touched in years," Mercy stated, surveying the small garage space. "I don't see anything that could rapidly create this level of dust. Even if he left the doors open all the time, it wouldn't accumulate like this in six months."

For a long time there was only the sound of scraping cardboard and sneezing.

"Sheriff?" asked the female deputy. A small metal box sat on the palm of one gloved hand. "It was tucked back on that shelf. Take a look inside." Her tone told Mercy she'd found something very interesting.

Bree poked around in the box as Mercy looked over her shoulder at the contents. "Jewelry," she stated, spotting several bracelets and rings.

"Yeah." Bree hooked a necklace with one finger and lifted.

Mercy sucked in a breath, her gaze locked on the name in cursive silver metal. "Paige."

More confirmation that she's in New York.

He has her.

"I've seen that necklace," said Mercy. "She's wearing it in one of the formal family photos in our files."

Bree nodded, anger in her face. "You're right." She met Mercy's gaze. "But where is she?"

Mercy shook her head, eyeing the jumble of jewelry in the box. "Is the rest Paige's or . . . do these belong to other women?"

"There's at least twenty pieces in here."

"Are there missing women we don't know about?" Mercy whispered. Her hands went icy as an idea occurred to her, and she strode out of the garage to the home's dark backyard. Two motion sensor lights suddenly flooded the yard. The area had a tall fence and trees blocking all views from the neighbors' homes. Mercy circled the yard, noting the numerous beds of shrubs and flowers.

Bree stood in the doorway of the garage, watching, comprehension on her face. "He dumped two of them along the road," she said. "It doesn't fit his MO to bury them."

"Maybe the roadside dump was the change from his MO," said Mercy. "We need a cadaver dog. Or GPR."

Ground-penetrating radar.

"I'll call Deputy Collins and have her bring her K-9, Greta, tonight. We can get GPR, but it will probably be tomorrow," said Bree, pulling out her phone and heading back into the garage.

Mercy slid her phone out and called Detective Bolton.

It's only six o'clock back home.

"Mercy. What's up?" answered Evan.

"We've got him, Evan." Mercy's voice shook. "We decided to look at Ken Wells, the reporter who brought in the notes I called you about earlier. We found long dark hairs in his car and five minutes ago we found Paige's necklace in his garage—the necklace with her name."

"But . . . did you find Paige?"

"No. But Ken has been sitting in jail since this afternoon. If she's still alive, he can't hurt her now. We'll question him again on her whereabouts and press harder. He's been denying everything, but he can't deny this." Her voice dropped. "I think we might be too late, Evan. Paige's necklace was with a lot of other jewelry. I'm worried they're trophies from other victims."

"Damn," said Evan. "This will be hard to tell her parents, but I know they won't give up hope until Paige is found."

"I'm working on it." Mercy ended the call. Her mind was whirling with a million tasks to strengthen their case and how to pressure Ken to tell them where Paige was.

So much to do.

Four SUVs suddenly pulled up and parked in front of Ken's home. A fifth vehicle blocked the driveway. Mercy knew what the fleet of SUVs meant.

The cavalry's here.

Mercy was pleased the Albany FBI office had sent a team so quickly. And thank goodness it was a large one. They needed more hands and brains to explore all the new details of the investigation. To find Paige and more evidence against Ken, they needed all the help they could get. The case had suddenly erupted into too much for just her and Bree.

Bree stepped out of the garage, a frown on her face as she studied a man in slacks and a polo shirt striding up the drive, the headlights from his SUV at his back.

"Agent Kilpatrick?" he asked.

"That's me," said Mercy, holding out her hand. "We're glad you're here."

"Sam Martinez. I'm the SAC out of Albany."

Special agent in charge. They sent the biggest gun.

Martinez shook her hand and did the same with Bree. "Sheriff Taggert. We went to the sheriff's department but were told you were out here. I left two agents to question Ken Wells again." He looked at the home. "How much have you been able to search?"

Mercy and Bree gave him a rundown as four other agents joined and listened. The necklace and small box of other jewelry was passed to a gloved agent, who gingerly accepted it as if it were an explosive.

"It's possible he didn't hold any of the victims here," said Mercy. "We've found no evidence of Paige Holcroft's or any other victim's presence on the grounds. I suspect he kept them at another location. We can use your help to dig into Ken's records to figure out where that could be. Maybe a relative's home or a rental or—"

"We'll take care of all of that," said Agent Martinez. "We'll get the senator his daughter back."

Mercy's phone buzzed. She didn't recognize the number and sent it to voice mail.

"The backyard needs to be checked. We've got the county K-9 coming in tonight and hopefully can get GPR by tomorrow," said Mercy. "Based on the amount of jewelry, there may be other victims. This yard can't be seen from any of the neighbors and has several flower beds. An easy place to— Excuse me."

Her phone had rung with a second unfamiliar number. She sent it to voice mail too. "As I was saying—"

Bree's phone rang, and she stepped away to answer it.

"Send me your notes, Kilpatrick." He looked at two of his agents. "You two start in the home."

Mercy paused, an odd feeling rising in her stomach. "I'm happy to go over our investigation with you, Agent Martinez. We have a conference room at the sheriff's department and—"

"I know," said Martinez, looking past her at Bree's deputies, who were watching the conversation from several yards away.

His inattention bothered Mercy, and her skin prickled on the back of her neck.

What is going on?

Bree returned. "We've got a new issue," she announced, looking at Mercy and Agent Martinez. "The media is now aware that Senator Holcroft's daughter has been missing." She stared accusingly at Martinez. "Not sure how the word suddenly got out."

Mercy opened the voice mail on her phone, reading the messages. Both were from reporters asking about Paige. Another call came through and she ignored it.

How did they get my direct number?

"Shit," she muttered. "This adds a whole new element to our investigation. A pain-in-the-ass element."

"Don't worry about it, Kilpatrick," said Martinez. "We have it in hand. You can head home."

Mercy couldn't move.

Does he mean . . . ?

"You've done a good job here," said Martinez, still looking past her. "And I'm sure you're exhausted. Albany is taking over from this point, so you can head back to Oregon."

"What the hell?" snapped Bree. "You can't sweep in and kick her out. You have no idea of how this investigation has progressed. You *need* her."

"Sheriff Taggert." Martinez looked Bree in the eye. "What matters now is how this investigation moves forward. Our suspect has been caught. We'll build the case."

"Caught thanks to us," stated Mercy, heat growing in her chest. "You don't know—"

"That's enough, Kilpatrick." He moved his gaze to meet Mercy's, and she found she preferred it when he looked past her. "*Go home.* Ken Wells is our problem now." He looked at Bree again. "It's late, Sheriff. Why don't you get some sleep too?"

A slow smile crossed Bree's face, and Mercy knew she was pissed. "You can order Special Agent Kilpatrick around all you want, Martinez. But you *can't* tell me what to do. This is my county, and you are here at my discretion."

Martinez blinked.

He didn't expect that.

"The FBI has rank here," he stated. "This involves a US senator."

"Yes, it does," said Bree. "So you should take advantage of every bit of knowledge you can get. Special Agent Kilpatrick—"

"Is going home," he said. "We will handle Ken Wells."

Mercy caught Bree's eye and gave a small tip of her head.

There is no point in arguing with him tonight.

Bree pressed her lips together, her eyes full of fire.

"Let's go," said Mercy, touching Bree's arm. The two of them headed down the driveway.

"Are you nuts?" Bree hissed. "Who can you call to talk some sense into him?"

"Let's deal with it tomorrow. If they want to be up all night collecting evidence and questioning Ken, let them. We'll get some sleep and come at it fresh in the morning."

"I won't be able to sleep."

"I hope I will," said Mercy. "I'll address the Martinez issue in the morning. I suspect he is hoping for glory and big headlines if he returns Paige to the senator."

Her words and tone were confident, but in her gut she suspected she was permanently off the case.

Fuck me.

Chapter 41

PAIGE

Day 8

He's distracted.

He's barely talked to me in the last twenty-four hours. I can see in his gaze that he's moved on. When he looks at me, surprise flashes in his eyes. As if he's forgotten I'm here.

He won't let me live.

I know this in the depths of my soul.

It's up to me to survive.

In the beginning we slept in the same room. He'd lock the bedroom door from the inside, the key always hidden. But lately, he sleeps in the living room and locks me in the bedroom. I refuse to sleep in that bed, so I sleep on the floor with the pad from my crate.

This morning he unlocked the bedroom door so I could use the bathroom, and then he ordered me into the crate, but left its door open. I waited for my breakfast, but I think he forgot it again.

I don't care; I'm not hungry.

I hear the clank of his coffee cup as he sets it in the sink. I know this means he'll shower next. I close my eyes and curl my legs closer inside the crate. His steps pause at the bedroom door, and I feel his heavy gaze on me. I stay still, my mouth slightly open as if in sleep, but I worry he can hear my heart pounding.

The bathroom door closes, and I open my eyes.

Now.

I crawl out of the crate and silently dart into the living room. I don't dare take time to dress. I've seen him slip the keys into the pocket for remotes on the side of his easy chair. I plunge my hand into the pocket.

Nothing.

I shove both hands in, checking the corners.

Where are they?

Breathing hard, I yank open all the kitchen drawers searching for the keys, careful to be as quiet as possible. I hear the shower start, and I know he showers quickly. Maybe two minutes at the most. I glance at the front door. Three locks.

What if they're not all on the same key ring?

I've never seen him unlock the front door. But the key ring has several keys. They must be for those other bolts.

I find nothing in the drawers. I start on the cabinets, peeking into everything that could possibly hide a set of keys. Again I end up empty-handed. Tears stream down my face, and I brush them aside.

The fridge.

I shake my head. I can't do it. Surely the keys are somewhere else. Maybe he took them into the bathroom. I refuse to consider that possibility. I open the hall closet and check the pockets of every coat. No keys.

The fridge.

I freeze. Every cell in my body screams for me to stay away from the tall appliance.

The shower goes silent.

I'm going to die.

I turn off my thoughts, stride to the fridge, and open it, my gaze locked on the containers in its door. A plastic butter tub rattles as I shake it. My fingers tremble as I pry off the lid and grab the keys. I thrust the tub back into the fridge door and push it shut. I tear over to the front door, fumbling through the keys. There are eight. Two are vehicle keys. I single out the first key that looks right and shove it into the top lock.

It won't turn. I try the next lock. No movement. I try the third lock. No movement.

I choose the next key. It slides open the top bolt, and a bubble of celebration explodes in my chest. The following key is useless in the remaining two locks. Same with the next.

Two keys and two locks left.

The next key fits the second lock.

The bathroom door opens.

My fingers refuse to cooperate, and I drop the keys. I snatch them up as his roar fills my ears. His steps shake the floor as he races toward me. I can't breathe. In my head, I'm screaming as my hands seem to move in slow motion.

I plunge the last key into the last lock, slide the bolt, and rip the door open.

Go!

On my second step out the door, he grabs my hair and yanks. My scalp burns, but I fling my weight to the side, still screaming. My feet shoot out from under me, and his fingers sink into my upper arm.

Go!

I land on my knees on the porch, but his hands still have hold of my hair and arm. I swing at his face, but it's too far away, and he slaps me, knocking my scream into silence. He drags me backward, my scalp and face in pain. I fight for breath as my butt slides across the doorstep, back into the house of hell.

I'm going to die.

Chapter 42

BREE

The next morning, Bree sat in the conference room. Shoulder to shoulder, she and Mercy studied the murder board. Ken's picture now hung front and center. Lines connected him to various incidents and pieces of evidence. They'd been searching Ken's house until late and had gotten to the office later than usual. Bree hadn't slept well and had woken up in a mood.

Was still in a mood was a more accurate description. Anger crawled up the back of her neck when she replayed Martinez's douchebag maneuver from the night before. "I still can't believe the Albany office just took over your case."

Mercy huffed. "Yeah. The FBI has its share of political climbers."

"Still sucks."

"It does." Mercy frowned at Ken's photo. "Why do you think he came to you with the note?"

Bree lifted both palms. "I suppose he wanted to manipulate the investigation."

Mercy shrugged. "The killer has been doing that all along, so that does make sense."

"True." But the outcome didn't settle in Bree's gut.

"I shouldn't even be here. I'm supposed to go back to Oregon." Irritation sharpened Mercy's voice.

"No rush, right?"

"My boss might disagree, but I hate being pulled off the case before Paige is found." Mercy turned and picked up her take-out coffee cup. She drained it, crushed it, and hurled it into the trash can with force.

"Understandable," Bree said. "You've been looking for her from the beginning. You're invested in her life."

Is she even alive?

"Damn it!" Mercy pulled out her phone. "I need to book a flight home. I can't change the SAC's decision. There's no point in pretending otherwise. The only thing continuing to work the case will do is get me suspended."

Bree hated to lose her FBI ally. Mercy was a valuable resource and an excellent investigator. Bree had grown to trust her, while it was clear SAC Martinez was not a team player.

Marge opened the conference room door. "Sheriff? You need to see this." She brought an iPad into the room and stood it on the table. On the screen, Madeline Jager faced a bank of reporters. "I can confirm that the serial killer has been arrested. Ken Wells has been arrested . . ." A photo of Ken appeared in the corner of the screen. Jager gave details on Ken and his job as a reporter.

Fury roiled in Bree's belly. "She's making an announcement on the arrest without consulting with anyone in law enforcement?"

"She doesn't know anything about the case." Mercy's voice rang with disgust. "This is a total political hijacking. She wants credit with the voters, even if she had nothing to do with said arrest. This"—Mercy waved a hand—"makes it seem as if she solved the case, even if she never says that. The triumph is all over her face."

Bree couldn't argue. Jager was an attention seeker. Her whole life was the adult version of *look at me.* "On the bright side, she also excluded the FBI. If Martinez's move was also political and media-seeking, this might make his head explode."

"Is *irony* the right word for that? Or is it *karma?*"

"Both?"

On the iPad, Jager continued. "Evidence linking Ken Wells to the victims was found in his home."

Bree gestured toward the screen. "Nothing I can do about it now."

"Hold your own press conference," Mercy suggested. "Jager let you take the heat for issues with the case. It seems unwise to let her take the credit for the resolution."

"Agent Kilpatrick is right," Marge said. "You'd better nip this in the bud. This type of victory will encourage Jager. She'll be even worse going forward."

"I hate politics." Bree rubbed her forehead. "You're right. Jager needs to be controlled. But I'm not ready to announce Ken Wells is our serial killer."

"Why not?" Marge asked.

"I can't explain it right now. We have evidence, but until we find Paige, the case just doesn't feel . . ." Bree searched for the right word.

Mercy supplied it. "Complete."

"Exactly. But I do need to think of a way to counter Jager's power play." Bree really did hate the political aspects of her job. Her phone buzzed, and she didn't recognize the number on her phone screen. She stabbed the ANSWER button with a forefinger and pressed the phone to her ear. "Sheriff Taggert."

"Sheriff, this is Sylvia Verney." She sounded breathless. "I'm looking out my window, and the man who lives across the street just dragged a woman into his house."

"Are they still outside?" Bree asked.

"No."

"Did he strike her?"

"Yes. They struggled, but he's bigger and stronger. He won."

Unable to recall the house number, Bree reached for a sticky note and pen. "Give me your address."

Mrs. Verney recited the information.

Bree pulled the note off the pad. "A car is on the way. Call back if you see anything else."

"All right," Mrs. Verney said in a shaky voice.

Bree ended the call and used her radio to request a patrol car in the area. Then she turned to Mercy. "That was the older woman whose son's name and address were used to open TheMaster's CuffMe profile." Bree summarized the call.

"That's in Scarlet Falls, right?" Mercy asked, rising.

"Right, but it's in my jurisdiction." Bree normally didn't impose herself on the local PDs, but this was different. "This sounds like a domestic disturbance, but I don't like that she's already been involved in the case or that I left the situation with her back door unresolved." Bree headed for the door. "I don't like coincidences in general."

"I don't like them either." Mercy followed. "I'm in."

Bree ran with lights and sirens to Mrs. Verney's pretty neighborhood, but radio chatter informed her that a patrol vehicle reached the house two minutes before she screeched to a stop.

The SFPD patrol car was at the curb, and the officer was speaking with Mrs. Verney on her front stoop. Though it was hot outside, the older woman wore a cardigan and slacks. Nervous fingers toyed with a button on her sweater.

Bree and Mercy joined them on the stoop. The officer and Bree exchanged nods. He was in his late fifties, with a salt-and-pepper buzz cut. Bree had seen him around, but they'd never worked together. His name tag read O'BRIEN.

Mrs. Verney pointed at the house across from hers, a neat one-story with a two-car garage. "That's the house." The sun glinted off her thick glasses. Behind them, her eyes were huge with worry.

"Who lives there, ma'am?" The officer poised his pen over a notepad.

She adjusted her hearing aid, producing a faint, high-pitched feedback sound. "Could you repeat the question?"

O'Brien did, louder and slower.

Mrs. Verney frowned. "His name is Don Dutton. He's a security guard at the mall."

Bree froze. *Don Dutton?*

Mercy emitted a rush of audible breath.

"I'll have a word with him." Officer O'Brien tucked his pad and pen back in his pocket.

"The girl was naked," Mrs. Verney whispered.

O'Brien turned and walked down the driveway. He looked over his shoulder and gave Bree a quizzical look as she and Mercy tagged along.

Bree said, "We've met Dutton."

"We might be able to help," Mercy added.

O'Brien shrugged. "I hate domestics. Happy to have backup."

Domestic disturbances were some of the riskiest calls.

O'Brien went to the door and knocked. The door opened, and Don Dutton stepped outside. He raised his brows. "Um, can I help you? Is something wrong?" His eyes lingered on Mercy, then stopped on Bree. "Sheriff?"

"Hello, Mr. Dutton," Bree said. "We're responding to a call from a neighbor."

O'Brien cleared his throat. "We received a report of an altercation outside."

"Altercation?" Don's head tilted, as if he were confused.

"Did you have a physical altercation with a young woman on your front step a few minutes ago?" O'Brien asked. "Is there a female in the house, a girlfriend, wife . . . ?"

"I live alone." An *aha* look crossed Don's face. "I know what this is about." He laughed and stepped outside, closing the door behind him.

He went to the driveway. After he pulled out his phone, he opened an app and tapped on the screen. The overhead garage door rolled up. Inside, a gray Dodge Charger occupied the far side of the garage. The spot nearest the interior door stood empty, except for what appeared at first glance to be a woman, sprawled on the concrete, arms and legs akimbo.

It took Bree a few seconds to process what she was seeing: a blow-up sex doll. Unfortunately, she'd seen one before. This one was fairly life-like, except for ridiculously exaggerated sex organs.

Bree glanced at Mercy, who rolled her eyes.

Don blushed and gestured to the door. "I just bought it. It's a gag for a bachelor party. She's awkward to maneuver, and I accidentally locked the garage interior door and had to carry her in the front door. My bad."

O'Brien chuckled.

Dutton raised both hands in a *surrender* gesture. "It's not my thing, but the groom's brother wants to bust on him."

"Poor guy." O'Brien barked out a laugh, waving toward the doll and moving his hands over his own body to mock the enormous breasts. "That's hilarious."

"Right?" Don shook his head. "Should be a good time."

The two men stared at the doll for a few more seconds.

O'Brien slapped Dutton on the shoulder. "Why isn't there a pregnant Barbie? Because Ken came in a different box."

Irritation crept up the back of Bree's neck. She shared a look with Mercy, who also looked annoyed at the inappropriateness of the conversation.

Bree cleared her throat, loudly. O'Brien started, turning back as if he'd forgotten she and Mercy were there. Bree made direct and prolonged eye contact to signal her displeasure with his behavior.

"Sorry." But O'Brien didn't look sorry. He looked annoyed that she'd called him on the comment. "I think we've seen all we need to see here. Enjoy the party." He nodded to Dutton.

"I'd like to take a quick look inside the house," Bree said.

O'Brien glanced at Bree over his shoulder. "I don't see any reason to."

"Me either," added Dutton.

And Bree couldn't force the issue, not without a warrant.

O'Brien headed back toward Mrs. Verney's house without a second look back at Bree. Frustrated, she gave Dutton a nod, then she and Mercy left him in his garage.

Mrs. Verney hadn't left her stoop.

"Ma'am, what you saw was a doll. A life-size one." O'Brien appeared stumped as to how to describe a sex doll to the older woman.

"That's bull." Mrs. Verney wasn't buying his explanation. "The girl was fighting back. She took a swing at him. He dragged her by the hair."

O'Brien shook his head. "It was a doll, ma'am. No doubt it's a little awkward to maneuver." He echoed Dutton's comment.

"It was *not* a doll." Mrs. Verney crossed her arms and glared at the cop.

O'Brien tapped his face next to his eye. "Maybe you should have your vision checked." With that comment, he sauntered away.

Mrs. Verney looked to Bree, then Mercy. "You believe me, right?"

O'Brien hadn't handled the situation well, but Bree didn't know what to think. "There's no proof of what you saw. Mr. Dutton lives alone. He said there was no one else in his home."

"Of course he said that," Mrs. Verney said in a disgusted voice. "Aren't you going to search his house? He's weird. A while back, his car smelled so bad, like he was carrying rotting garbage around in the trunk."

"Ma'am, we can't search a citizen's home without a warrant, and there's no evidence to support getting one. Mr. Dutton provided a reasonable explanation for what you saw. There's nothing we can do. It's his word against yours."

"The police don't do anything these days. You never came back to follow up on my ruined lock." Mrs. Verney's cheeks flushed. "It could have been one of those gangs trying to break in. This neighborhood is going downhill. Did you see the graffiti at the playground? Disgraceful! I don't feel safe anymore."

"Yes, ma'am." Bree ended the old woman's rant, which she sensed could have gone on for some time. "You have my number if you need any further assistance. If you see something questionable, you can record it on your phone. Then it isn't your word against someone else's."

Mrs. Verney humphed, then stepped inside her house and closed the door with a firm and telling slam.

Bree walked to her vehicle, her gaze drawn back to Dutton's house. He'd closed the garage door.

Back in the vehicle, Mercy stared out the windshield. "I don't like it."

"Me neither," Bree said. "He said he just bought that doll, right? Did it look new to you?"

"Nope. There was a layer of dust on it."

Bree didn't want to think about what else could be on a not-new sex doll. "That's not enough to get inside his house."

"It is not." Mercy fastened her seat belt. "What now?"

"I don't know." Bree drummed her fingers on the steering wheel. "Dutton has popped up multiple times in this investigation. This feels too coincidental, and yet, everything that has happened with him is completely plausible."

"You think he might be involved?"

Bree cracked her knuckles. "I think we need to find out more about Don Dutton. For now, I'll reserve judgment."

"What about Ken?"

"The FBI has Ken covered, and they're looking for Paige in all possible places related to Ken. But if they're wrong . . ."

Mercy finished. "They won't find Paige."

"I'm going to have a deputy in an unmarked car watch Don's place, just in case he has Paige inside. I want to know if he goes anywhere." Not wanting the maneuver put out on the radio, she used her cell phone to make the request of Juarez. "I'll have a full background check run on Don. If there's something to be found, we'll find it."

The radio crackled and the dispatcher announced the report of a wildfire.

Bree frowned. "Not good. The woods are like kindling."

Mercy's phone rang. "It's Detective Bolton," she told Bree. She hit the speaker button. "Hey, Evan. Sheriff Taggert is in the car with me."

"Good. You both need to hear this."

Bree's hands tightened on the wheel. The detective sounded stressed.

"TheMaster just sent his phone number to a woman and then deactivated his CuffMe account."

"Shit," Mercy and Bree said simultaneously.

"They'd alluded to possibly meeting up but then agreed to switch to texting," said Evan. "Which is the same pattern he used with Paige."

"Can we get her account information?" asked Mercy. "She needs to be warned."

"I've called my CuffMe contact three times," said Evan, his voice tight. "I've left a voice mail each time stating what happened. I don't know if I'm being ignored, or if he doesn't want to tell me that the company won't share the woman's account information."

"Do you know where she lives?" asked Bree.

"She told him Syracuse," Evan said. "We have no way of knowing if it's true."

"Syracuse is less than an hour from here," Bree said. "Which woman has he chosen?"

"DaisyMae455," Evan answered.

"Evan . . . if TheMaster's been online, there's no way he can be Ken Wells. Ken is sitting in jail." Mercy met Bree's gaze.

"Crap," said Evan. "Now what?"

"The Albany FBI is running with Ken Wells as the killer," said Mercy. "It's been announced to the media. I bet TheMaster is feeling pretty comfortable with that news out there."

"But who is he?" asked Evan.

Mercy pressed her lips together. "We'll continue to investigate," she said. "We've got a short list."

Bree nodded.

"Keep pressuring the CuffMe site," said Mercy. "Someone needs to contact DaisyMae455."

"I'll do what I can. Keep me in the loop." Evan ended the call.

"Now what?" asked Bree. "All we have is suspicion."

"I know," said Mercy. "But I might have an idea. Let's get back to the station to put it together."

"I hope whatever you're planning doesn't take too much time. I feel like he's going to move fast on DaisyMae455."

"I agree. If we're right—she'll walk right into his trap."

Chapter 43

Him

New beginnings are so full of promise. They're almost as fulfilling as proper endings. I ease off the gas pedal as I approach the park. Excitement hums through my veins, like three shots of espresso but better, so much better. I'm not into drugs, but I imagine this is what cocaine feels like. The anticipation of a fresh hunt is exhilarating.

Trees surround the parking area, shielding it from the road. I can't see the asphalt rectangle until I turn into the entrance. But then, seclusion is why I picked this park. The lot is empty. Perfect. Air-conditioning blasts from the dashboard vents as I select a parking spot under a tree, hoping the shade will keep the interior of my car from turning into an oven. I reverse into the spot so I have a comfortable view of the entrance. I want my vehicle positioned for a quick exit if necessary.

My new plaything, Daisy Mae, should be here soon, and I'm hoping she's as perfect as her name.

I like to arrive a few minutes early, to get the lay of the land, so to speak, and make sure the location is clear. As I suspected, the day is simply too hot for most people. At noon, the temperature is already in the nineties, with the humidity hovering at sauna level.

A few dark clouds hover on the horizon as I step out of the car and walk a lap around the picnic area. The air smells faintly of smoke from a distant wildfire. In the shade of a few trees, four long wooden tables with attached benches are arranged in the dusty brown weeds. On a slab of concrete under a small roof, two vending machines sell water, Gatorade, soda, and snacks. On the other side of the vending machines, a trail map marks the hiking and bike trails that branch off from this location. A small cinder block restroom in the corner of the clearing smells foul in the heat, even from a distance. I inspect it quickly. There are two single restrooms. Both doors are propped open. Both rooms are empty. In between the restrooms is a door marked MAINTENANCE. It's locked. I turn away.

The wind kicks up, sending a low cloud of dust across the parched ground. I see a flash of heat lightning in the distance. A storm would be welcome to break the heat and cut down on the dust. I scan the area. No people. No cameras. I am completely alone.

Satisfied that we won't be interrupted, I return to my car and lean on the hood to wait. She should be here in a minute or two. Being late—or early—isn't acceptable. I made that clear in her instructions. Sweat drips down the back of my neck. I check the time. She has another minute. A quick burst of anger warms my gut.

I hear the grate of tires on sandy blacktop. Right on time! Daisy Mae knows how to follow directions. I watch the compact gray SUV pull into the lot. The car matches her vehicle, Pennsylvania plates and all. She's here! I wonder if she is as excited to meet me as I am to see her.

And how she will feel in a few more days.

She said she's been a submissive before, so punishment won't come as a shock to her, like it did with Paige. I swear that one didn't even know what the word *submissive* means. Daisy Mae has some experience. Hopefully not too much, though. I like to deliver some surprises.

A few scenarios run through my head. I picture Daisy Mae as the lead role in my own private movie, and my pulse accelerates. My blood pounds, heady and ready. I forcibly contain my enthusiasm. The Master must maintain his composure at all times—at least on the outside.

I distract myself with the thought of Ken Wells sitting in a jail cell, his entire life being dismantled by the FBI. My setup worked perfectly. Ken is an idiot. The sheriff and FBI aren't any smarter. None of them suspect the evidence in Ken's trunk and garage was planted. The only piece of jewelry that matters is Paige's necklace. The rest were just random, but the cops will be searching for bodies for weeks. They're convinced they have their man. I'm in the clear—free to resume my hunt for the perfect woman. Maybe I'll plant Paige's body near Ken's house.

I've learned so much since I began this journey. I had little trouble manipulating authority figures from a very early age. If you can stare a person in the eyes and lie without blinking, they believe you're sincere. My parents were always easily fooled. As long as I can remember, I've taken pleasure in others' pain. I bullied weaker kids in school—not because of a tormented past. I picked on smaller kids because it was fun, and I enjoyed their helplessness.

I have never experienced the slightest bit of remorse. The more I hurt others, the more I like it. Childhood bullying escalated and women took the places of my classmates. Admittedly, I made some mistakes that cost me a career. I didn't expect those bitches to challenge me. I equated physical weakness with emotional. Since then, I've learned to break both the body and the mind. Both are satisfying. These inclinations—and my growing appetite—led me to BDSM, where women signed up to let me hurt them. At first, I played by the rules. Now I make my own.

The gray SUV approaches slowly. Sunlight reflects on the windshield, obscuring my view of the driver. The vehicle turns into a parking spot on the other side of the aisle. I see a sweep of long dark hair. Daisy Mae in the flesh. I push off the car and stand facing her, my weight evenly distributed, my posture strong.

Like a Master.

The door opens. A foot appears. She's wearing the stilettos I requested. She steps out and straightens. The dress clings to every inch of her incredible body. The skirt is short, revealing long, long legs. I congratulate myself on my choice. Her shoulders are hunched, and her face tipped downward. She definitely understands what it means to be submissive. Her hair falls forward in a shiny curtain and blocks my view of her face.

When she speaks, her voice is timid and soft, childlike. "Are you the Master?"

My hand drops to my pocket. I feel the outline of my stun gun. I won't risk a scuffle in a public location. I'm also carrying a real gun, a utility knife, and plastic ties in case she resists. She comes with me willingly or she comes unwillingly. By showing up at this meeting, she forfeits any ability to change her mind. She's seen me. There's no going back to her previous life.

I walk toward her. "I am."

She doesn't move but waits for my command. *Oh. Yes.* She is perfect. And she is all mine.

"Come here," I order with a snap of my fingers.

She approaches. Her eyes remain appropriately downcast. My hand leaves my stun gun. I won't need it. She is as compliant as can be. My left hand seeks one of the plastic ties. She might be the perfect submissive, but I can't risk having her unrestrained while I drive. I pull out the ties. "You'll need to wear these in the car. Hands behind your back."

"Yes, Master." She starts to turn. Her hands drop. She whips back around, her body pivoting on one five-inch stiletto like an erotic dancer. Instead of putting her hands behind her back, she reaches beneath her dress to yank something from under the hem and produces a gun. "Sheriff's department! Show me your hands!"

What is happening?

Shocked, I can't process what I'm seeing. Even the gun pointed at my chest doesn't feel real.

The wind blows her hair away from her face, and I finally see her. Not Daisy Mae. Disbelief floods through me. It's the woman behind the YourDoll945 profile. My instincts were right. There had been something off about her. But a cop? I didn't suspect that.

She points it at me, the submissiveness in her posture evaporating, her voice commanding instead of babyish. "Don Dutton, you are under arrest."

A door bangs open. I freeze, my body burning with anger as I recognize the sheriff bursting out of the locked door near the restrooms, her gun aimed directly at me. She taps the mic on her lapel and yells, "Go! Go! Go!"

Bodies move in my peripheral vision. I'm focused on Daisy Mae, but I see uniforms. Of course Daisy Mae—or whatever her name really is—wouldn't come alone.

Moving only my eyeballs, I spy the FBI agent among the cops closing in. I don't move, but fury rages in my chest.

Those bitches played me.

Chapter 44

BREE

Heart pounding, Bree walked away from the maintenance closet where she'd been hiding to watch the meeting. She approached Dutton, gun in hand and aimed directly at his center mass. "Sheriff's department!"

In her peripheral vision, she saw Mercy, Todd, and Juarez converge on Dutton from three different locations in the trees, AR-15s raised and ready. Their vehicles were parked in the woods, out of sight. Three more patrol units were down the road and would be here in a few minutes.

Dutton had walked right into *their* trap for a change.

Don Dutton is *TheMaster.*

She wasn't at all surprised. Instead, a sick feeling rolled around in her gut. The deputy who'd been watching Dutton's house had reported when he'd left his home twenty-five minutes before.

After the conversation with Detective Bolton, Mercy and Bree had messaged DaisyMae455 from their fake profile. They'd convinced her to call the sheriff's department. Once she'd learned she could be communicating with a murderer, she'd gratefully agreed to cooperate. She'd given them the details of her proposed meeting with TheMaster, and Deputy Zucco had taken her place.

Mercy had informed SAC Martinez that the sheriff's department had set up a meeting with the man they believed was the real killer. Martinez had insisted the FBI was building a strong case against Ken Wells. Martinez had refused to allow the Albany office to join the sheriff's action. Then he'd told Mercy—again—to go back to Oregon.

Instead she'd joined the hunt. Bree respected the hell out of Mercy's decision to disobey orders and put finding Paige over her own career.

Bree studied Dutton as she and her team closed in. His palms faced Zucco in a standard surrender posture. A plastic zip tie dangled from one hand. His pockets bulged. He was probably carrying a weapon or two. He hadn't moved, but his eyes were tracking each of their movements. He licked his lips. What was he thinking? Was he plotting a counterattack? Planning an escape?

Didn't matter. They had him.

Zucco didn't waver. Her Glock stayed level on Dutton. "Put your hands on your head!"

Dutton slowly moved both hands and rested them on his scalp. Bree's pulse kept hammering. She would not relax until he was in handcuffs and behind bars.

A bell dinged. Tires ground on gravel. Bree's heart stuttered. Someone was coming. *Shit.*

A boy yelled, "Woo-hoo!"

A woman called, "Timothy Andrew Stafford, get back here."

Everyone froze as a bright-blue, child-size mountain bike shot out of the woods. A heartbeat later, two adults emerged from the narrow trail. The boy was about seven or eight years old. With his head bent low over the handlebars, he pedaled like an Olympic cyclist. Spider-Man decals adorned his helmet. His parents' faces locked in shocked, horrified stares as the boy cut right through the center of the deputies.

Bree and her team stood helpless. None were close enough to intercept him. All they could do was watch the child pedal into a circle of drawn weapons—straight at a serial killer.

Dutton lunged at the boy and yanked him off his bike. The bike clattered to the blacktop while Dutton clutched the child to his chest, using him as a shield and backing toward his Dodge Charger.

After an initial squeal of surprise, the boy screamed and kicked. His sneakered feet flailed against Dutton's legs. "Let me go!"

Dutton pulled a gun from his pocket and pressed the muzzle under the kid's chin. "Stop it, or I'll shoot you."

The boy went limp, his skinny legs dangling. A wet stain spread across the front of his khaki shorts. Tears and snot ran down his face, and his pallor went ghostly white. His lips moved in a silent *Mommy*.

Panic crushed Bree's heart. She pictured her niece, maybe a year or two older.

Fuck fuck *fuck*.

"Put him down!" Bree shouted. Everyone still had their weapons trained on Dutton, but they didn't dare shoot him for fear of hitting the boy.

"Back away. All of you." Dutton held the boy close.

The parents threw their bikes to the ground. The father charged.

"Don't do it!" Dutton warned. "I'll kill him."

The father skidded to a stop, his face a wild blend of fear and rage. Just behind him, the mother wailed. "No! My baby!"

Dutton whirled, his gaze darting around. "Nobody move, or the kid dies." He continued to shuffle toward his car.

Bree held her breath. Her heartbeat echoed in her ears. In her peripheral vision, she saw Mercy, Todd, and Juarez all following Dutton's movements with their weapons.

Dutton set the boy's feet on the ground and whispered something in his ear. The boy's face turned even paler. He didn't move, except for the visible trembling of his entire body, as Dutton reached behind him and opened the car door. Dutton backed his ass into the driver's seat, keeping the boy in front of him.

In a single breath, he moved the gun and fired one shot around the child's body. Juarez went down. Then Dutton pulled the boy onto his lap, closed the door, and took off with the screech of tires on pavement.

Bree yelled into her radio mic. "Shots fired! Officer down!" After requesting an ambulance, she warned her nearby deputies, asked for assistance from all surrounding local, county, and state police agencies, and provided a description of Don, his vehicle, and the boy for an Amber Alert.

Bree waved Todd and Zucco toward Juarez. The young deputy was down, a bloodstain spreading rapidly on his thigh. Zucco knelt next to him, her palms overlapped, pressing on the wound to stem the bleeding. Todd raced for the woods. His vehicle—and first aid kit—were hidden in the trees about fifty feet away.

"He's bleeding too much." Bree hesitated. She wanted to stay with Juarez, but Dutton had a child. Her heart stumbled again.

Juarez waved a weak hand and spoke through pain-gritted teeth. "You have to save the boy."

Kids come first.

"We've got him," Zucco said, her hands and uniform covered in Juarez's blood, her eyes fierce. "Go get that motherfucker."

Chapter 45

MERCY

"Ken Wells is not our killer!" Mercy shouted into the phone to be heard over Bree's sirens as they sped to Don's home. "It's Don Dutton!" she told SAC Martinez, who was speechless on the other end of the line. She gave him a brief rundown of the shit show at the park while keeping both eyes on the road and traffic as Bree drove like a maniac.

The sheriff had just watched her officer get shot.

And had to leave.

What is Don doing with that boy?

"We're almost to his house," she told Martinez. "I doubt he went there because we know where he lives, but Paige might be inside."

"We're on our way, Kilpatrick."

Mercy ended the call. "Your deputy will be OK," she said to Bree, who blew out a breath.

"I know. He's in good hands. But damn it was hard to leave him." She glanced at Mercy. "I hope Paige is in Don's house."

I hope Paige is alive.

Bree sped down Don's street.

"I don't like that he tried to meet a new woman," said Mercy. "That can't mean anything good for Paige." Bree blocked Don's driveway with the SUV and let dispatch know they'd arrived.

No sightings had come in on the BOLO for Don's vehicle.

Mercy scanned the front of the one-story house. "I can't believe we were just here. That bastard shut his front door and took us to his garage so we wouldn't see inside the home. I knew that blow-up doll was bullshit."

"Let's go." Bree stepped out of the vehicle, and Mercy followed suit, her weapon in hand, appreciating the weight of the tactical vest even in the hundred-degree heat. A haze had settled over the area, and Mercy caught the faintest hint of smoke. She glanced to the east, noting how the haze in the sky was dense with an orange-gray tint. The wildfire was closer than she'd like.

Bree gestured for the two deputies who'd followed them to the scene to go to the back of the house. "Garage first," she stated to Mercy, who nodded, knowing if Don's Charger wasn't in the garage, then he most likely wasn't in the house. She followed two steps behind Bree and to her left to the side door of the garage. They each stepped to one side.

Bree raised a brow at Mercy, who shook her head. *My back,* she mouthed to Bree, knowing the door required a solid boot thrust near the handle, and her back pain would hamper her kick. Bree moved in front of the door, took two steps, and powered her boot against the hollow wood door. It splintered near the handle and swung inside the garage. Mercy slipped in and covered the area to the left as a second later Bree did the same, covering the right.

The Charger wasn't in the garage.

Bree used her mic to notify the deputies behind the home.

"There's nowhere to hide someone in here," said Mercy. "Bare walls and concrete pad." She eyed the blow-up doll, remembering how the men had laughed about it earlier. "Let's clear the house." She mentally crossed her fingers that Paige was inside and alive. The women moved out of the garage and to the home's front door.

Out of the corner of her eye, Mercy saw a small group of neighbors gathering across the street to watch. "Shit. They need to get out of here." Don could be armed in the home or nearby. They didn't need another innocent bystander taken hostage or shot.

"Get inside your homes!" Bree hollered in a much louder voice than Mercy expected. "This is a dangerous police action! Our suspect is armed!"

They immediately scattered at Bree's last shout. People were curious until they knew they could get shot.

"Randolph County Sheriff! Open the door!" shouted Bree.

They took the same positions at the front door as they had at the garage. They paused for a few seconds, looked at each other, and shook their heads at the same time.

No one would be coming to the door.

Bree told her deputies to hold their positions at the back of the house and then drove her boot into the front door. She stumbled backward with a grunt as the door held firm.

"It didn't move at all," said Mercy, studying the door. It was solid and heavy, unlike the hollow-core door of the garage. She touched the painted frame. *Metal?*

To keep someone inside.

"I have a battering ram in my vehicle."

"Maybe the back door isn't as strong?" asked Mercy. Bree nodded and spoke into her mic to ask the deputies what the back door was like.

"I think it's a sliding glass door," came the answer. "But it's covered with plywood. So is every window on the back of the house."

Bree met Mercy's gaze.

We're in the right spot.

Mercy took a few steps to the side to study the closest window. Some sort of wood shutter inside blocked her view. "This looks easier to breach than trying to rip off plywood."

"Be right back." Bree ran to her vehicle, returning a moment later with the battering ram and two sets of eye protection. She handed one to Mercy, who slipped them on. The window was large, designed to give the living area an expansive view of the outdoors.

Bree swung the battering ram and broken glass fell to the ground. She continued until one large pane was cleared and then focused on the wooden shutter slats inside. Mercy had stepped back, watching behind them and keeping an eye on all other windows.

The wooden shutters were no match for the ram. Bree notified her deputies that they were entering and gestured at Mercy, who bent over and stepped through the pane, leading with her weapon, scanning all corners of the living area. "Clear."

Bree was a half step behind. "Randolph County Sheriff!" she yelled again.

Inside was dim. All the windows were covered with locked shutters, and only the overhead lights in the kitchen were on. They were in a room separated from the kitchen by a small island. It had a large sectional, a TV, and a few easy chairs.

"Smells like bad cheese," whispered Mercy, switching to breathing through her mouth.

"And old fish."

Mercy's stomach twisted. "Go," she whispered. Bree led the way with Mercy behind, resting one hand on Bree's shoulder, keeping them in tune with the other person's movements. They cleared a hall closet and a filthy bathroom with a disgusting tub. Next down the hall was a small dark bedroom. Bree flipped the light switch, and they found cardboard boxes nearly stacked to the ceiling along one wall and a battered desk. The room's window was covered with plywood on the inside.

"Plywood inside and out?" muttered Bree. "This house is a cage."

"Computer is gone," Mercy said, nodding at the distinctive clean rectangle visible in the dust. Bree cleared the closet and they moved to the next bedroom. Again, plywood had been nailed inside the window. A weight bench, its padding split, and a few stacks of weights were the only items in the room. Bree opened the closet and found a large gun safe, its door ajar.

Four guns were in a neat row, and the small shelves were packed with ammunition and three handguns. Mercy's gaze locked on the weapons, wondering if one had been fired at her. Bree was already leaving the room. Their goal was to check for people; evidence could be collected later.

The farthest door down the hall was closed. Three bolts locked it from the outside.

"Jesus," Mercy breathed.

Was Paige locked inside?

"Randolph County Sheriff!" Bree yelled at the locked door. "Stand back! We're coming through!" She nodded at Mercy, who slid the bolts and thrust the door open. Bree entered, covering the left of the room, and Mercy behind, covering the right. The light was already on in the room.

Mercy held her breath. The room smelled as if a sweaty football team had been locked inside for a month.

A dog crate.

The large wire cage was empty, and a stained pad lay halfway out its open door.

Bree cleared the closet and Mercy checked under the large bed. "That's it," she said to Bree, her voice oddly high. "There's no one here."

Bree spoke into her mic, telling the deputies the home was clear. "How's the backyard?" she asked.

"Chain-link fence," said someone. "No outbuildings."

"Is it all grass? Flower beds?" She met Mercy's gaze.

The radio was silent for a long moment. "Overgrown with weeds and grass," said the deputy. "No recently disturbed dirt."

He'd known what Bree was asking.

Now what?

"We have to figure out where he took her," stated Bree. She strode out of the room.

Mercy lingered, unable to look away from the dog crate, knowing Paige had likely been locked inside. On the floor of the room were a pile of clothing—most of it pink—and two pairs of spiked heels. A few lipsticks were on the floor, lined up end to end next to a half dozen pink hair accessories in a neat row.

Dollification.

"He treated her like his personal toy," Mercy said out loud to no one, trying not to think of how destroyed Paige must have felt when her dream man and new life turned into piles of dirty junk on the floor. She spun around and blindly left the room.

We're too late.

"Mercy." Bree's voice coming from the main room sounded strained. On edge, Mercy drew her weapon and slowly moved down the hall until she saw Bree in the kitchen, leaning against the small island.

"Are you OK?" Mercy asked as she checked the room with the TV again. Clear. She holstered her weapon.

Bree shook her head and wiped her cheeks, staring at the floor.

Outside the voices of the other deputies came through the broken window.

"I'll unlock the front door in a moment," Mercy yelled back. She joined Bree, realizing the sheriff was seriously rattled. "We're going to find her," Mercy told Bree, feeling as if she were telling the biggest lie of her career.

"No . . . no . . . not that." Bree wouldn't look at her. She gave a futile gesture at the fridge.

Confused, Mercy slipped on a glove, grabbed the fridge handle, and pulled.

She lost her breath as she stared.

No . . . no . . . no!

It was a dead naked woman. The fridge's shelves had been removed, and she sat with her back against a side wall, folded into the small space with her knees nearly in her face.

Mercy slammed the door shut and fought to find her breath.

How could he? How?

She steeled her stomach and slowly opened the door again. Long dark hair covered most of the woman's face, and her skin had an odd texture—too dry. Her flesh had shrunk and pulled tight to her bones.

"Like Vanessa Mullen," she whispered, remembering the partially mummified corpse at the medical examiner's. Behind her, Bree made a small sound.

Pink fingernails . . . and toenails.

Mercy made herself reach in and draw the hair out of the victim's face. Her hand trembled as she exposed the heart-shaped tattoo above the woman's withered breast. She forced herself to study the profile. "I don't think it's Paige," she said softly. "The shape of her jaw and her forehead is all wrong. And I think she's been dead a lot longer than Paige has been missing."

She sensed Bree move closer, her stressed breathing growing louder.

"Oh, my God," said Bree. "There's fucking food on the door shelves. *He still used it for food!*" The sheriff whirled away and vomited in the sink.

Mercy fought to keep her stomach under control, bile rising in the back of her throat. She gently closed the door, hating to put the woman back in the dark. But she and Bree needed time to pull themselves together.

"Hey, boss?" came a voice at the window again. "All good in there?"

"Just a minute," Mercy answered in a hoarse voice. She set a hand on Bree's back as the sheriff leaned on her forearms over the sink. "We'll get him," she said firmly. "We'll lock up his ass."

Bree spit in the sink. "If I don't shoot him first."

"You just created quite the scene contamination," Mercy said.

Bree's torso shook with silent laughter. "Shall I rinse it away or leave it for forensics?"

Mercy reached over her and turned on the water. "I assume you don't want a glass from his cupboard to rinse your mouth?"

"Fuck no," said Bree. She cupped her hand in the stream to drink and then rinsed the sink and ran the disposal. "There's enough evidence in this shithole to lock him up. I think they can overlook me barfing in the sink." She straightened, her eyes still damp. "That's one of the worst things I've ever seen . . . especially since we have a good idea what that woman went through." She sniffed and wiped her eyes with the back of her hand. "I bet it's Missy Star. The prostitute that Shelly Fox reported missing."

"You're probably right," said Mercy. "I'm going to open the front door now. You good?"

"Yeah."

Mercy went to the front door and stopped. "He added three locks to this door," she said in disgust. "And they have to be unlocked with a key from the inside. He must have gone out the front door, because none are engaged. Only the standard bolt is locked . . . which has to be done with a key from the outside."

"Of course he went out the front door," commented Bree. "Every other exit is boarded up."

Mercy opened the door to the impatiently waiting deputies.

"Get a crime scene unit out here," Bree told the deputies, command back in her voice. "And cordon off the property. No one comes near."

Mercy wandered back down the hall, still trying to calm her stomach. She wanted to get out of the stinking house, but felt as if she'd be abandoning Paige . . . and the woman in the fridge. She returned to the room with the dog crate and a burst of anger wiped away her nausea.

"There's a closet right there," she muttered, eyeing the hanging menswear. "He wouldn't even let her hang up her clothes." She squatted and gently sorted through Paige's wrinkled clothing pile, stopping on a stretchy, short black dress.

The slut dress.

Finn's description of his sister's dress.

And her red spiked heels.

Mercy took a deep breath, glad it was Evan's job to update Paige's parents.

The pile of clothing smelled as if they'd never been washed. Mercy found a dog collar under the pile and a pair of handcuffs.

That poor girl.

Her gaze went to the lipsticks and hair accessories. It looked like the collection of a ten-year-old girl who loved pretty things and lined them up neatly with care and pride. Unlike the clothes.

Maybe he made her organize them. He seems like the type that wants things a certain way.

Mercy froze as she noted the lipsticks weren't parallel with the hair things. The row of end-to-end lipsticks angled away . . . as if pointing at the crate. Her heart beating hard, Mercy shoved the crate aside.

Paige had left a message on the floor in lipstick.

Chapter 46

PAIGE

One hour earlier

"Get out."

He unlocks the crate and I crawl out, careful not to make eye contact.

I reach for my lipstick.

"No makeup."

I grab my black dress in my pile of clothes, but he shoves a pair of shorts and a tank top at me with his foot. "No dress. No heels. Wear these. Hurry up!"

Then he strides out of the room.

I freeze.

What does that mean?

He insists on lipstick almost 24/7. And never lets me wear shorts or a tank.

An aura of excitement and eagerness had hovered around him. I haven't seen him like this since we first met. Then I understand.

He's done with me.

I shouldn't have tried to escape.

He'd been furious after he dragged me back in the front door. Stomping and screaming at me. I'd waited for the whip but it never happened. Instead he locked me in the crate—like usual.

I was stupid to hope he would put me on a plane back to Oregon. I was expendable. Like that other woman. Terror racked me. The day I'd known was coming had arrived.

Why doesn't he just kill me here?

But he'd told me to get dressed, and now I hear him rustling in the bathroom, putting things in a bag. We're going somewhere, and he doesn't care how I look, so it must be somewhere without people.

The cabin.

He's constantly obsessed about the cabin, even showing me pictures of the place surrounded by tall pines and near a river. Talked about how great life would be when away from everyone else. He would quit his job, and we'd live off the land. I nodded and made the appropriate noises.

But there was a catch; the cabin wasn't his.

It belonged to a neighbor who'd let him use it a few times. He'd said the neighbor had broken his leg, so it had sat empty most of the year. He'd mentioned several times that he wanted to drive me there and take it over, claim squatter's rights, which made no sense to me. I'd simply nodded some more, pretending to understand.

Tears stream down my face as I pull on the shorts and wonder how anyone could ever find me in the woods. At least at his house there was a slim chance I could somehow signal a neighbor. Although my almost-escape this morning caught no one's notice.

Nobody will look for me at the cabin.

They'll find my body someday. Maybe.

I think of my parents, forever looking and searching for me, never having answers.

How can I let them know I'm sorry?

"You done?" he yells from the bathroom.

"Almost, Master." I frantically scan the room for the millionth time, hoping to find something . . . anything to save myself. It is futile.

My gaze falls on my lipstick. The bright red that looked so much like blood. I grab it and shove the crate aside. *CABIN*, I write. Then I stop. I have no idea where the cabin is.

What is the owners' last name?

He'd made fun of them.

"Hurry up!"

I move to smear the word, terrified he'll beat me when he sees it.

Clinton.

He'd joked that the neighbors were the most unpresidential people he'd ever met.

I scribble the name and yank the crate back over it. With shaking hands, I arrange my lipsticks in a line leading to the crate. I can't make an arrow. He'll notice. I quickly straighten the hair bows and headbands so the lipsticks won't appear odd to him.

"What's taking so long?"

He is right behind me. Fear races through my veins, and I lift a headband, not meeting his gaze. "Is this one acceptable?" I ask in a meek voice.

"Doesn't matter." He hauls me to my feet, and I drop the band. "Put your hands together."

I obey, and he puts on zip tie cuffs.

He's put metal cuffs on me before, but the zip ties are new.

Another clue that today is different.

Twenty minutes later, sweat coats every inch of my body as I lay cramped in the trunk of his car.

The salt runs into my eyes, making them burn.

It's so hot in here.

I need water.

The car stops, and I hear him get out and slam his door. Then there is silence. The temperature in the trunk steadily grows. I reach up, my hands still zip-tied together, and touch the lid of the trunk and yank my hand back. Even through the thin lining under the lid, it is hot. Much hotter than when we first left the house.

Is this the end? Is he leaving me here to die? Baked in this oven of a vehicle?

The trunk stinks. Like something has rotted and seeped into the mat. I've been breathing through my mouth to keep from vomiting.

How long will it take me to die?

Will I just fall asleep? Or will I suffer?

I don't think we're at the cabin. I know the distance is much farther than he has driven, so I wonder if he's getting supplies.

Do I tell him how hot I am?

He'll beat me for speaking up.

Distant yelling reaches my ears.

Is help coming?

I'm about to shout for help when I hear his voice close by. "Nobody move, or the kid dies."

I freeze. My words stick in my throat. I can't help it. When he's near, I'm trained to be silent. I hear his car door open and more talking.

Someone whimpered. A child.

I jump as a gun fires close by, and his car door slams. I'm thrown backward as his tires spin, and the car lurches forward. Shouts fade in the distance. But the whimpers in the car continue.

"Shut up or I'll shoot you," he yells.

He's kidnapped a child.

Images of what he could do to a child assault my brain. The things he's done to me. I pull tight into a ball and press my knuckles against my mouth to keep from screaming.

Chapter 47

BREE

"There's a bright side. This message suggests Paige is still alive." Bree stared at the message written under the dog crate in lipstick: *Clinton cabin.* "Does that mean he took her to a cabin?"

Mercy said, "That would be my guess."

"But where is it?" Bree scanned the room, then pulled out her cell phone and called Marge. "I need you to pull real estate records for Don Dutton. Find out if he owns any other property, maybe a cabin somewhere?"

"Will do," Marge said. "And I have that background information you asked for on Dutton."

"Putting you on speaker so Agent Kilpatrick can hear." Bree lowered the phone and tapped the button.

Marge continued. "You're not going to believe it. A little over ten years ago, Dutton was a cop."

In Bree's mind, pieces of the case clicked into place like LEGOs. "Actually, that makes perfect sense. He knew how to play us because he was one of us."

"It made framing Ken easy for him," Mercy added. "He knew exactly what to do."

"I couldn't get his personnel file, of course, but I made some calls." After working for the county for more than three decades, Marge knew everyone. "Dutton was fired for inappropriate conduct. He had multiple excessive-force complaints against him. Several women he arrested claimed he sexually assaulted them. My source says he used to go to strip clubs on his lunch hour—in uniform. My source also said it took forever for them to fire him."

Bree pictured Dutton with O'Brien from the SFPD after Mrs. Verney's call, the inappropriate jokes about the sex doll, the shoulder slapping, the knowing grins, the general air of familiarity between the two men. "Did he work for the SFPD?"

"He did," Marge confirmed. "I'll get on this property and tax record search right now."

"Thanks." Bree ended the call.

A deputy came through the door. "Sheriff? I talked to all the immediate neighbors. No one is aware of Dutton owning any other property or where he might have gone. They all said he keeps to himself."

I'll bet he does.

"Call over to the mall and talk to the other security guards he works with," Bree said.

"Yes, ma'am," the deputy said.

"It's hard to have close friends when you keep prisoners in your house," Mercy said.

"Right?" Bree agreed. "And you can't really invite neighbors over for a beer if you have a dead body in your fridge."

She scrambled for ideas. She kept picturing the poor woman folded up in Don's refrigerator and superimposing Paige's face on the body. If they didn't find him, would Paige end up the same way?

Where did he take you, Paige?

"Ma'am?" The deputy gestured to the lipstick message. "The next-door neighbors' last name is Clinton. I just talked to them." He pointed to one side of the house. "That side."

Bree headed toward the door. "Let's go."

Mercy was already halfway to the door.

They rushed outside. The air was hazy from the local wildfire but it was still refreshing after the stink of Dutton's house. The Clintons—a couple in their sixties—were watching the police activity from their front porch.

Bree approached them and introduced herself and Mercy. "Do you own any other property?"

Mr. Clinton leaned on a pair of crutches. "We have a cabin on the Scarlet River. We haven't been able to get out there since I broke my leg." He gave them the address, which was a rural route number.

"Thank you." Bree turned away, her blood zinging with the new lead. "That has to be it," she said to Mercy.

"Yes." Mercy fell into step beside her. "Are we going there?"

"We? You're in?"

"I am."

"OK, then." Bree summoned two deputies. "You're both with me."

The K-9 unit pulled up to begin their search in case there were any other bodies stashed or buried on Don's property. Bree issued orders and left her people to do their jobs. She and Mercy climbed into the SUV. Two deputies followed in a patrol unit. Sirens screaming and lights flashing, Bree sped toward the cabin. She reported their destination to dispatch and asked for any available deputies to assist.

In the passenger seat, Mercy spoke on the phone with SAC Martinez, who was not pleased but now on board and coordinating FBI backup.

How could he not be? The body in Dutton's fridge had been undeniable.

Fourteen minutes from their destination, Mercy lowered her phone. "I'll bet Dutton fabricated the kidnapping at the mall."

"He knew just what to do. He probably took out the parking lot security cameras himself." Bree leaned over the steering wheel and scanned the horizon. "The air's gotten really smoky."

Radio chatter turned to an update on the wildfire, which had grown. Bree spotted thick black smoke over the trees. "Whoa! I don't like the looks of that."

Mercy tapped her phone on her knee, then froze. She pointed through the windshield. "What's that on the side of the road?"

A tiny figure sat on the roadside.

Chapter 48

Him

Smoke clogs my throat and fills the air with floating gray particles. An ember lands on my arm. I swat it off, but it's left a small red dot. I can see the fire over the treetops now. Orange flames reach for the sky through a thick haze of black smoke. My phone—which I would ditch if I didn't need updates on the fire—shows the wildfire has changed direction. It's headed straight for me at locomotive speed.

I'm sure the authorities can track my phone, maybe even my car. But the fire might help me. The road to the cabin is closed. No one can follow me here.

"Move!" I tighten my grip on Paige's wrist and drag her across the yard. She pulls back. I'm not sure if it's fear or defiance, but she's going to get me killed.

My getaway plan would have been perfect if the fucking wind hadn't shifted direction. My neighbor broke his leg and can't use his cabin. It's sitting empty, and I won't be connected to it—a perfect place to hide. I know there's a boat here. My stupid neighbor is always yammering on about it. So I'm not trapped.

But who would have predicted a fucking forest fire?

I should just let Paige go like I did the boy. I didn't want to deal with two hostages, and kids are a pain in the ass. Besides, I hope retrieving the boy will slow down anyone on my tail.

Paige won't get away. The fire is everywhere. The forest is going up like a giant pile of straw. From the looks of what's coming, the only way out is the river. If I leave her here, Paige will burn for sure. I'd like the pleasure of killing her, though. I've earned it. Paige also makes a useful hostage. Her father's money and position give her value. Thanks to the sheriff, I can't return to my house. I'll need to start over. New name. New location. New vehicle. The works. Cash will be necessary to obtain this new identity.

Lots and lots of cash.

New documents aren't cheap these days.

Daddy the Senator should be willing and able to pay a nice ransom for his spoiled little princess. Maybe enough to set me up. It's my best option.

My only option.

I need this little bitch. I yank harder. She resists. Her feet slide in the dust. Paige is small, but uses her weight instinctively, sinking her ass toward the dry weeds and patches of dirt on the ground. Too bad I'm bigger. I haul her forward. She stumbles across fifty feet of dry ground between the cabin and the old wooden dock. At the end of it, a fishing boat bobs on the water. The river looks calm, but I know the current is swift. The neighbor has told me more than I ever wanted to know about his fishing trips.

I thought luck was with me when the kid pedaled into the trap the cops set. Now I hope it hasn't changed, that I'm not trapped, that Paige and I will float away from the fire—away from the authorities. I'll toss my phone in the river. No one will be able to track us.

Paige sits down on the dock.

What the fuck? Does she want to die?

"Get up." I reach for her other arm and lift her. She doesn't weigh much. I toss her over my shoulder, fireman-style. Paige thrashes, throwing me off balance. I'm forced to put her down.

"Get on the boat," I order, giving her a shove. Momentum carries her forward. She has no choice but to jump onto the boat. I untie the lines. I toss the stern line onto the boat. The water immediately pulls the aft end of the boat away from the dock. The current is stronger than it appears on the surface. I wrap the bowline around a post once. With the line in hand, I prepare to climb aboard. But Paige is on her feet. She steps onto the sidewall and leaps back onto the dock. Anger and frustration swell as I grab her wrist with my free hand.

She whirls and strikes out with a bare foot. Paige has no leverage. Her kick is weak, but it connects with my balls. Not much strength needed there. I double over. Nauseating pain radiates through my whole body. My legs fold, and I go down on my knees on the dock. I drop the rope. The boat drifts away from the dock. I try to snag the rope, but it slithers out of my reach, landing in the water.

My breaths rasp. I choke on a mouthful of smoke. Paige breaks free, squirming backward on her ass, her bound hands making her movements awkward. She flips onto her hands and knees and finally scrambles to her feet. She sprints down the dock, away from me.

The dumb bitch leaves the dock and runs straight into the woods. Straight at the fucking fire.

I turn to the boat, but the current is carrying it away. Even if I jump into the water and manage to swim fast enough to catch up, it's damned hard to climb into a boat that large from the water, especially while it spins and drifts with no one at the helm.

How am I going to get out of this?

Chapter 49

BREE

Bree slowed. "It's the boy!"

"Oh, my God." Mercy pressed a hand to her mouth.

Relief burst in Bree's chest as she reported to dispatch and stopped the vehicle on the shoulder. Her deputies stopped behind her. The boy sat cross-legged in the full sun. She got out of the vehicle. The wind that hit her face was hot and dry and heavy with the smell of smoke. Tiny particles blew through the air.

She slowly approached the boy. "Hey, Timothy."

He turned his flushed red face to Bree. "He told me not to move."

"You did good." She crouched in front of him and held out a hand. She didn't have time to waste, but he was traumatized. She wouldn't rush him. "But it's OK now. You're safe. Let's get you out of the sun. Are you thirsty?"

He nodded, then launched himself into her arms and sobbed against her chest. She let him cry for a minute, then pulled back. "Timothy? Did you see a young woman in the car with the man?"

"It was just him in the car." Timothy shook his head. "I don't want to think about him right now."

"I understand. Can I ask you one more question?"

"OK," he said in a tiny voice.

"Did he say where he was going?"

"He didn't talk at all." Timothy shuddered.

Bree smoothed the damp hair away from his face. "OK. Thanks. I have to go, but you did great."

He rubbed a hand across his wet face. "You're gonna catch him?"

"I'm going to try my best."

"Mommy says that's all we can do."

Bree held back the hot prick of tears. "Your mommy is very smart." She stood and steadied him on his feet. He walked beside her, clutching her hand, as they approached the patrol unit. The deputies stood by their vehicle.

Bree bent down to the boy's level. "These nice deputies are going to take you to see your mommy and daddy. You're safe with them. That I can promise."

"OK." Timothy squeezed her hand, then released it.

After he was safely loaded into the patrol car, Bree turned back to Mercy and the job at hand. "The smoke is much worse."

"It is."

Over the trees on the horizon, gray and black smoke plumed into the sky.

"That's not good." Bree assessed the wind. "The wind is blowing the smoke toward us."

"Not good at all."

Bree checked in with dispatch on the status of the fire.

"Last report says the fire is headed south at a fast pace," the dispatcher said. "The fire chief says proceed with caution."

"Roger that."

Then she and Mercy got back into the SUV. In the rearview mirror, Bree watched the patrol unit turn around and head back toward town. She shifted into drive and glanced at Mercy. "Any word on FBI backup?"

Mercy checked her phone. "They're about ten minutes behind us."

Bree punched the gas pedal. "Same for the state troopers. I'm out of deputies, and there aren't any local PDs out here. I really appreciate you coming with me." Otherwise, Bree would be alone.

"I wouldn't miss this."

"Let's hope backup catches up with us."

At a cue from the GPS, Bree turned onto a narrow dirt road. She slowed the vehicle to navigate the rutted lane. The air had turned gray.

"I don't like this smoke," Mercy said.

The radio squawked. The wind had shifted suddenly—and so had the fire. Crews reported thick smoke and downed trees. State police closed the highway they'd just left.

Bree checked the map on the dashboard computer. "The fire is headed right toward us."

"The cabin is on the river." Mercy traced the river with her finger. "I don't see a bridge or a way out. If we keep going, we'll be trapped."

An ember blew onto the hood.

"We could turn around." Bree didn't want to quit, but getting burned alive wasn't on her to-do list either.

Mercy shook her head. "He dropped the boy on his way. This is where they went. Paige wasn't at his house. She must be with him."

"She could have been in the trunk of his car." The smoke thickened, forcing Bree to slow the vehicle. She lowered her window and could hear the crackling of fire. Light shifted among the trees, and she saw the glow of flames. Wind blew through the branches. Embers soared through the air, and smoke rose from small fires in the underbrush.

It's moving too fast!

"Shit." Mercy pointed out the passenger window. "I see fire!"

"Do we go back?" Bree took her foot off the gas pedal. Three deer and a rabbit bounded across the lane, no doubt fleeing the fire. A loud crash shook the ground. A minute later, Bree's vehicle crept up on a giant downed oak tree across the lane. She hit the brakes and slammed a fist on the steering wheel. "The woods are too thick to go around. We have to go back."

Mercy gestured toward the radio, then swiveled to look out the rear window. "We can't. The fire is behind us now."

"We have to keep moving forward." Bree reached for the door handle. "We'll have to continue on foot."

Mercy tapped the map on the dashboard computer and switched to satellite view. "We're almost at the cabin. There are a bunch of homes and cabins on the river. I see docks. Where there are docks, there should be boats."

Bree glanced behind them. The woods were black with shifting smoke. A lick of flames reached through the trees. "Let's move." She reported their location and intended direction to dispatch.

The radio crackled as the dispatcher responded. "The chief says the fire hasn't jumped the river. If you can get to the other side, you should be all right."

"Roger that." Bree dropped the mic and fished a flashlight and Leatherman tool from the console. She handed both to Mercy. She jumped out of the vehicle, hurried to her cargo hold, and grabbed her backpack. They'd have to move fast. Survival equipment only. The air was hot and foul. They both coughed. Bree reached into her crime scene kit and fished out a few N95 respirators. She slipped one over her face, handed one to Mercy, and tucked the remaining ones into the cargo pocket of her pants.

Mercy grabbed several water bottles and stuffed them into her pockets.

They moved around the SUV and broke into a jog. They rounded a bend in the lane and the cabin appeared. They stopped at the edge of the clearing. Dutton's Dodge Charger was parked in front of a tidy cabin.

Bree glanced behind her, but all she could see was smoke. "If we can't find a boat, we're trapped."

Mercy jerked a thumb at the Charger. "But so is he."

Chapter 50

PAIGE

Run!

 Run!

I won't stop.

His shouts flood my ears, and terror drives my feet, my bound wrists throwing off my balance. I don't know what I'm running toward and it doesn't matter. I'm simply running away from him. As far away as possible. My knees ache where I scraped them on the dock, but I ignore it. Pain radiates from my bare feet, rocks and sticks jabbing them. I move my legs as fast as I can.

 Run!

 Run!

My lungs burn. The smoky air makes me pant, my body craving more oxygen. I'll run until my feet are raw and bleeding to get away from him. I weave among the firs and scramble up a small rise, using my bound hands against the ground to keep from falling on my face in the dusty dirt. A crackling fills my ears and I look to my right.

 Fire.

The fir trees are burning. The treetops glow orange, and smoke clouds the sky as the fire ravages them. Small embers ride the strong winds, but most turn to ash before they reach me. The forest is sprinkled with a light dusting of gray ash and it gets thicker as I run. I spit as a large snowflake of ash blows into my mouth.

Too much smoke! Go another way!

I veer to my left and lose sight of the burning trees. But I still hear the fire, and the air full of ash doesn't dissipate. I veer again, seeking cleaner air. I skid to a stop as I crest a small rise. Before me is a sharp, rocky drop.

Shit.

I can't go down. I change direction again, running parallel to the embankment. I've lost all sense of direction and worry I'm running back to the Master. Pain shoots up one leg and I stumble, trying to avoid the tender underside of that foot. I fall to one side, landing on an elbow. Pain races through the nerves in my arm, and I grit my teeth to keep from crying. I check my foot. Both feet are bleeding from numerous cuts. But the new slice is deep. I look around and take a deep breath. The ashy air makes me cough and nearly gag.

I have to keep going.

If I stop, I'll die.

I awkwardly push to my feet. It's incredibly hard with the zip ties. Something brushes my leg, making me jump and nearly fall again. A rabbit rushed by. I watch as it leaps its way down the steep embankment and up the far side before it vanishes into the brush. I wonder if its instincts are guiding it to safety or if it's running blindly from the fire.

Like me.

I spin in place, searching the woods for a sign of which way to go. There's no possible way I can get down the steep drop like the rabbit. I study the trees and brush on the other side. The sky above them is less smoky compared to the darkening, swirling sky above me. I continue to follow the top edge of the gully. Maybe the drop-off will ease, and I can get to the other side.

I'm trusting a rabbit?

My pace has slowed. I hobble. Every step feels as if I'm walking on glass shards, and I want more than anything to sit and rest. But I fear if I stop, I'll never get up. I was moving faster before I looked at my feet. I wipe my wet cheeks. Tears and ash create a gray muck that coats my hand. The air is hot and the noisy crackle of the fire has escalated.

It's getting closer.

I don't want to burn alive.

I'm bawling now, hating myself for leaving my home and blundering into the hell that began with Don and will now end with death. A painful death. I jerk as an ember lands on my arm, causing a spike of pain. I'm unable to brush it off with my bound hands, so I blow at it, and tear-filled spit comes out of my mouth.

Keep moving.

The embankment isn't as steep now, but there's no way I can get down it and keep my balance with my hands tied. I'll fall and crack my head open on one of the huge, jagged rocks. Movement catches my eye, and I spot a dog speeding along the bottom of the gully.

Not a dog. A red fox.

It rushes up the far side and vanishes.

That must be the way I need to go.

Motivation fills me and I push on. Far ahead, the slope down to the gully eases. I lock my gaze on an area that looks manageable and stumble toward it. I'm coughing as I reach it, and I pause as I fight not to retch. But inside I'm cheering because I'm confident I can get down this slope. I'll tackle getting up the other side once I'm down.

I'm sure it's easier to breathe down there too.

I turn sideways and start to shuffle-step down the hill, my clasped wrists raised in front of me, ready to catch me if I fall.

My head jerks back, and I fall on my ass. Don stares down at me, his hand wrapped in my hair, my scalp burning.

"Stupid bitch. You thought you could escape?" He smirks.

Relief at seeing a human—any human—flashes through me for a brief second, but dread and fear drive it away.

I'd rather burn in the fire.

Chapter 51

MERCY

Mercy's eyes burned from the smoke, sweat dripped inside her mask, and she wished she could ditch the heavy, hot tactical vest. But she was thankful that Bree was prepared for the emergency. The sheriff's stash in the back of her SUV had rivaled Mercy's survival bags in her personal vehicles back home. She held her weapon in both hands, breathing hard, and nodded to Bree on the other side of the cabin door.

"Randolph County Sheriff!"

Bree didn't wait for an answer and kicked in the door. They entered, covering each side of the big room. The cabin was dim and quiet. They quickly cleared the main room, bedroom, and bath.

"I don't think he came inside," said Mercy, pulling down her N95 and sucking in the cleaner air of the cabin. "There're no bags in the bedroom or personal things on the bathroom counter. The kitchen is bare."

"He's around here somewhere. He can't get far if he tries to leave," Bree said, a grim look in her eyes.

Because we can't get far either.

Mercy glanced at her phone. No signal. Bree's radio had been their only source of communication for the last half hour. "I'd hoped Paige would be here," she said softly.

"Same. Let's check for outbuildings," said Bree. "Maybe that's where Don is too."

Mercy nodded and replaced her mask. The women stepped out of the cabin, where the dustings of ash swirled through the air. They scanned the area. Fire flamed in treetops not too far away, and the hot wind blew directly in their faces. The cabin was surrounded by tall trees and dry brush. No one had ever preventatively cleared the perimeter. It was ripe to burn.

The fire is blowing straight at us.

"If there aren't any outbuildings, we need to get to the river," said Mercy, brushing ash off her face. "We'll have to swim if there's no boat nearby." She raised a brow at Bree.

"I'm a good swimmer," said the sheriff, who plucked at her tactical vest. "But this won't help." She lifted a booted foot. "These will have to go too."

They abruptly stilled, gazes locked.

"Did you hear that?" asked Mercy. It'd sounded like faint screams. Female screams.

"Yes." Bree was already moving.

Mercy followed her around the corner of the cabin, her weapon gripped in both hands. The sheriff passed Don's car and headed for a trail between the trees. The screams turned to shouts, and it sounded as if the woman were cursing. The trail was short and opened up to a clearing, giving a wide view of the river. And the dock where Don wrestled with a woman.

Paige?

The woman was on her back, kicking at Don with her feet and shrieking at the top of her lungs. Her hands were clasped in front of her in zip tie cuffs. He stepped aside and yanked her by her hair and shoulder to a sitting position, and then dragged her down the dock toward the water.

Mercy and Bree darted down the embankment to the first boards of the dock, weapons trained on the man who'd shot Mercy and Bree's deputy.

"I don't have it," said Bree, and Mercy knew she meant she didn't have a shot. With Don bent over behind the woman, it was too risky.

"There's no boat," said Mercy. "What's he planning to do?"

"Nothing good," said Bree as they stepped forward on the wood dock. "Randolph County Sheriff! Let her go, Don!"

Don and the woman looked up, startled by the newcomers fifty feet away.

"That's Paige." Mercy's knees went rubber for a split second as she realized the girl was still alive.

She made it.

Don crouched lower behind Paige's back. He kept his grip on her hair, but drew a gun and held it against her temple.

"Shoot him!" Paige shrieked.

"I still can't," whispered Bree.

Mercy glanced down at the boards of the dock. Don and Paige's struggle had created an uneven path through the light ash layer, but there was something smeared on the wood. Mercy sucked in a breath and squinted at Paige. Her feet were bloody and dark clumps of wet ash stuck to the bottoms. She was also bleeding from her knees and a split lip, where he'd probably hit her.

But she continued to fight.

"Let her go!" Bree shouted again as she and Mercy slowly moved forward.

We have no cover.

The former cop could most likely shoot them from this distance, but his right hand was twisted in Paige's hair, and her struggling made it impossible to keep his left hand still.

Please be right-handed.

"I'll put a bullet in her brain unless you leave," Don shouted.

"What if we don't?" Mercy yelled back. "Then you'll go for a swim?" The crackle of fire grew louder behind them, and its heat was hot on the back of her head. Their time on the dock was ticking down. "Let her go! You haven't done anything irreversible yet. The consequences aren't as bleak as you think!"

Don shouted with laughter. "You think I don't recognize that line from every police negotiator's handbook? Next step is to grant me a small request to try to gain my trust. I know the drill." He shook his head. "Fucking idiots."

Bree spoke into her mic. "Suspect is in sight. Has hostage. We are on the dock at location."

"Understood," said dispatch. "Fire is nearly to the river. Can you cross?" Concern filled the dispatcher's usually calm voice.

"We're aware of the fire," Bree answered ruefully. "Not sure what will happen."

"Leave!" Don yelled.

"No one's leaving!" shouted Mercy. "The fire has blocked all roads out. It's just you and us."

As if on cue, a large gust blew heavy ash over the four of them, sending Don and Paige into coughing fits.

Did he really think we could all leave?

"I've got another mask," yelled Bree over the sounds of the fire. "Let her go and it's yours."

He shook his head and dragged Paige backward toward the edge of the dock.

"Her fucking wrists are bound." Mercy feared what he'd do.

Will he throw her in the water?

"He knows we'll go in after her," Bree says. "He thinks he can get away if we're too busy saving her."

"If Paige goes in, let me get her." Mercy put a hand in her pocket, checking for the Leatherman tool she'd stashed. "I can cut her—"

"Go!" shouted Bree as Don lunged backward off the deck with Paige. The girl's scream was cut off as both of them hit the water.

Mercy sprinted to the edge. Don had vanished. Paige thrashed, fighting to keep her head above water with her useless arms. At the dock the river was deep, and panic filled the girl's eyes. Mercy holstered her gun, ripped her mask from her face, and her fingers scrambled to unlace her heavy boots.

"Where is he?" yelled Bree, her weapon pointed at the water as she scanned.

For an instant after ditching the boots, Mercy considered ripping off her vest. *He's armed.* Instead she grabbed her Leatherman, opened a blade, and jumped in.

Cold water shocked her, stealing her breath. The current had carried Paige several yards, and Mercy lit out after her with strong strokes. She reached the panicking girl and grabbed her bound arms, turning Paige away and wrapping an arm around her chest as she treaded water. It was harder than expected, and Mercy's head dipped underwater several times.

I should have taken off my vest.

Mercy spit water. "Hold still! I'm going to cut your ties." Paige stopped thrashing her arms, her breaths loud and fast, her back against Mercy's chest. They both treaded water, unavoidably kicking each other, trying to keep their heads out of the water while upright. Mercy's vest and clothes continued to pull her down. She had to paddle with her free hand holding the Leatherman to stay above water.

This won't work.

"Paige! I need you to float on your back. I'll be right beside you. I know it's hard but relax!"

The young woman stopped kicking, tilted her head back, and raised her legs as Mercy removed her arm from Paige's chest but kept her close with a grip on her tank top. Mercy kicked and paddled to stay afloat.

"Good! Lift your hands."

They were moving farther and farther from the dock. The river appeared calm on the surface, but Mercy felt its strong current against her legs. Twice her feet had banged against huge rocks hidden below the surface.

Several gunshots sounded, and from the corner of her eye, she saw that a barefoot Bree had fired into the water. Now she pointed past them, yelling something Mercy couldn't understand. Mercy scanned the river for Don.

He must be swimming underwater, and Bree fired when he came up for air.

His head suddenly popped up, facing Mercy from several yards away. He paused for a second as they made eye contact and then went under again.

I think Bree's shots missed.

Chapter 52

BREE

I missed.

He's going after them.

Bree secured her weapon in its holster and dived into the water. She'd removed her boots but left on her body armor. It would hamper swimming, but Don had a gun. Know what else hindered swimming? Bullets.

The vest might also offer protection from debris in the water.

The momentum of her dive propelled her toward Don. She needed to intercept him before he reached Mercy and Paige. She opened her eyes under the water, but she didn't see him. The water was murky, and she could see only a few feet in front of her. She surfaced, spitting out water and taking in a huge gulp of air. The cold water chilled her hot skin. She turned her head. She treaded water, scanning the river all around as the current swept her downstream. Tiny waves lapped against her face. She shook water out of her eyes.

Where is he?

Ahead, the river narrowed, and the current increased. Boulders rose out of the river, patches of white water frothing between them. Mercy and Paige were about to pass through the small bottleneck.

A flash of movement caught her attention. She spun and spotted a disturbance on the surface of the water, almost a wake, as if something were moving below. She took a breath and ducked under, looking for Don. Hands grabbed her legs and pulled her deeper. She struck out at him, but the water slowed her movements and lessened the impact of her blows. She kicked, catching a part of him that felt soft, his midsection maybe. Her lungs burned. She needed oxygen. But so did he. His grip loosened, and she stroked toward the light. Her head broke the surface, and she inhaled, filling her lungs.

The current picked up, sweeping her toward the rocks. Don surfaced next to her, his eyes gleaming with hate and desperation. He reached for her. His fingers caught the vest at her shoulder. She kicked out at him, then jabbed a hand at his throat, her knuckles striking his Adam's apple. He choked and coughed, wheezing for a few seconds before a hand flailed out and snagged her uniform again.

He dragged her under. She thrashed at him, exhaustion weakening her blows. Her foot landed on his leg. She pushed up, getting her face above water long enough to suck in some air.

If she wasn't going to make it, damn it, she'd take him down with her and make sure that Paige and Mercy had a chance. A mental image of Kayla and Luke flashed into her eyes. Then Matt's face.

Matt would take care of the children. His family would help. She knew this without question, but sorrow burst through her before an equally strong surge of rage.

Fuck you, Don Dutton.

Mercy

"Get them off!" Paige begged.

"Hang on! We've got to get past this rough part first!" The river had narrowed as it sped toward a bottleneck between boulders, and Mercy had to pay attention to keep the two of them from smashing their heads on the huge rocks. She took a tight grip on Paige, and they both went underwater as they passed through the short passage. Mercy's rib cage and hip slammed against a boulder, and she saw stars. If her ribs hadn't been broken before, they were now.

On the other side of the passage, the river widened and calmed.

Now.

Mercy kicked hard to tread water with just her legs, took a deep breath, and thrust the blade between the girl's wrists and jerked up. The tie partially broke, and Mercy's head dropped below the surface. She kicked again, came back up, and then repeated the maneuver.

Got it.

Paige immediately flipped over and grabbed Mercy, clawing at her shoulders and hips, sinking her underwater. Mercy batted the girl's hands away and struggled until her head broke the surface. She gasped for air. "Don't grab me! Can you swim?"

"Yes." Paige was crying, her face wet with tears, snot, and river water.

She's exhausted and terrified.

So am I.

"I need you to turn over and float again. I'll pull you to the shore."

Still sobbing, the girl raised her feet and tipped her head back again, her arms making slow strokes at her sides. Mercy grabbed the back of Paige's tank top and settled into an awkward sidestroke toward the far side of the river, shocked at how weak her limbs were. She had a ways to go.

I've got to take off the vest.

One-handed, she tore at the strong Velcro. It took a half dozen pulls, and then she yanked on the front zipper and pulled each arm through. She let the vest sink.

Mercy exhaled, feeling fifty pounds lighter.

I'll buy the sheriff's department a new vest.

Looking back, she saw the cabin on fire. The blaze had burned all the trees and brush surrounding it, exposing it to the river. Beside it, Don's car was in flames. The fire had rushed down the riverbank and now licked at the first boards of the dock. The sky was invisible, smoke choking the air and rolling across the river.

She focused ahead, the opposite riverbank calling her, its fire-free shore a beacon of safety.

We can make it.

She paused to catch her breath and looked for Bree. And then continued to twist and look for what felt like forever, dread building in her chest. "Do you see Bree? Did she come through the rocks?" she asked Paige. Water filled Mercy's mouth and she spit. *"Do you see her?"*

The girl twisted her head to look but stayed on her back, maintaining her float. "I don't see anyone."

Where is Bree?

Bree

Bree's lungs screamed for air. The river had become choppy. Her back smashed into a rock. She was grateful that even with all its extra weight, the body armor vest absorbed some of the impact.

She tilted her head backward but still couldn't keep her face above water long enough to take a full breath without inhaling water. Dutton's face turned toward her. A stream of bubbles trailed from his nose and mouth. She thrust her fingers into his short hair, cupped his scalp like a basketball, and shoved his head under the water. He pulled away, took a breath, then wrapped his arms around her. His greater body weight dragged her under.

She fought for air again. Then the water swirled around them, and an eddy sucked them both down. Bree struck a boulder, pain surging through her arm and shoulder. She tumbled and smashed against a huge rock, her body rolling, helpless, like clothes in a washing machine.

Her hand caught between two rocks, the current yanked at her body, and pain exploded through her wrist as the bone snapped. Bubbles escaped her mouth, and her vision dimmed. Blackness tunneled her view. Agony crescendoed, radiating from her wrist through her whole arm. She thought of her family. *I'm sorry.*

No!

No giving up. If she died, she'd at least go fighting.

She planted a foot on the boulder and tried to pull in either direction. The pain turned white hot, threatening to render her unconscious. Confusion clouded her thoughts. She floated for a second, the current pulling her body away from her trapped hand. She could see brightness, the orange fire reflecting on the surface of the river.

A hand tapped her shoulder. She turned. *Mercy!*

Mercy grabbed Bree's vest. With both feet planted against the boulders, she pulled at Bree's arm in the opposite direction. Bree's hand, and some skin, scraped free. Blood plumed in the water.

Mercy stomped on the rock again. This time her effort sent them upward. Toward the brightness. Toward air.

Their heads broke the surface. Water spewed from Bree's mouth at the same time air flooded in. She couldn't tell which she was inhaling. But her lungs worked like bellows. Sucking in more and more. Four breaths later, her lungs ached with fresh air. She coughed. Her vision cleared.

Her feet found the bottom. The water became shallow. She fell to her knees and crawled. Mercy stumbled beside her. They were both alive. *Halle-fucking-lujah.*

Cradling her broken wrist, Bree sat back on her haunches, still coughing. River water poured from her nose. She wheezed out two words. "Where's. Paige?"

Mercy, also coughing and wheezing, rose onto her knees like a meerkat. "No!"

Bree's head turned.

Twenty feet away in the shallows, Don held Paige's head underwater.

Mercy

Mercy pushed to her feet, stumbling toward Don. Her legs were weak, and the exertion made her choke and spit, water still in her lungs. He screamed at Paige as she thrashed in the water, his back to Mercy. She reached for her weapon.

My gun is gone.

Somehow in the struggle with Paige or when she took off her vest, something had tripped both levels of her holster's weapon retention. Her gun was at the bottom of the river.

Doesn't matter.

She stalked toward the man, bending to grab the biggest rock she could carry with one hand, never taking her gaze off him.

I won't let him kill Paige.

He was on his knees in two feet of water, leaning his weight on Paige's head and neck. He looked back as Mercy approached and then let go of Paige and lunged at Mercy's legs, knocking her to one side. She landed hard in the water, slamming her head into a boulder and dropping the rock in her hand, her breath gone at the pain in her ribs. He threw himself on top of her stomach, trying to turn her face into the shallow water.

No!

She shoved to push him off, her legs splashing, but he was too heavy. His face was close to hers, his eyes crazy, and he shouted things she couldn't process. Her brain was overloaded, struggling to keep her alive. She took a breath and lowered her hands. He immediately twisted her neck, forcing her face underwater, leaning his weight on her neck and head like he had with Paige. Mercy ran her hands along the gritty river bottom, failing not to panic at the water covering her face.

Where'd it go?

Her fingertips grazed her rock, and she wrapped her hand around it. Focusing all her waning strength, she swung her arm out of the water and crashed the rock against Don's temple. His hands let go of her head, and he collapsed on top of her, his body limp. Her head burst through the water's surface, and she sucked in a sputtering breath as she shoved him aside. She rolled over and crawled out of the water, her head down, her waterlogged body and clothing impossibly heavy.

"Mercy!"

She looked to the side and saw Bree attempting to pull Paige to shore one-handed, her other hand limp at her chest. "She's not breathing!"

Mercy flung herself to her feet and stumbled to the women. She grabbed Paige's other arm and hauled her to dry ground. "Is your hand OK?" she asked Bree as she tipped Paige's head back, put her ear by the girl's mouth, and watched for her chest to rise. She pressed her fingers into the girl's cold neck, hoping for a pulse.

Come on, Paige!

"I think my wrist is broken," said Bree.

Her heart pounding, Mercy heard no breaths and saw no rise of Paige's chest. She immediately pinched the girl's nose and gave her two rescue breaths. "You can't do chest compressions with a broken wrist," she told Bree. "Take over breaths." Bree nodded and knelt on the other side at the girl's head. Mercy stacked the heels of her palms on Paige's chest and started compressions. After counting out thirty, she nodded for Bree to give breaths.

There was still no pulse.

Exhaustion swamped Mercy, but she started more compressions.

I won't stop until someone comes.

Bree gasped, her eyes wide, staring past Mercy.

Mercy looked back. A few yards away, Don pointed a gun at Mercy. His gaze locked with hers.

I can't move.

Bree

On her knees, Bree fumbled for her weapon with her left hand. She trained in shooting with her off hand, but these were hardly firing-range conditions. Pain, exhaustion, her soaked uniform, her slippery hand—they all worked against her.

Please work. Please work. Please work.

In her head, she knew her Glock should fire wet.

Should.

But sometimes, they didn't.

One-handed, she leveled the gun at Don's chest and pulled the trigger. The gun bucked, the shot ringing out.

Thank you.

She adjusted her aim and fired again. Dutton's body jerked. Blood bloomed on his chest. Bree pulled the trigger again and again, not stopping until he ass-planted and collapsed into the water. Even then, she kept the gun trained on him. She still had a couple of bullets left. Right? Actually, she had no idea how many times she'd fired. Her brain had simply reverted to her training. *Shoot until the threat is neutralized.*

She spared a glance at Mercy. "Did he shoot you?"

Returning to her compressions, Mercy shook her head. A moment later Paige coughed, and her body arched. Mercy rolled the girl onto her side, and Paige vomited river water and then started to cry.

Exhausted, Mercy collapsed next to the girl, one hand on Paige's side.

"I've never been so happy to hear someone cry," said Mercy, wiping her own eyes.

Bree lurched and stumbled to her feet. With her handgun still pointed at Don, she approached him, using a foot to roll him to his back. His eyes were open, staring at nothing. He looked dead, but she handcuffed him anyway—awkwardly, with one hand—before pressing two fingers to his throat.

Yep. Dead.

She turned to check on Mercy and Paige.

Both alive.

She looked over them, toward the river. On the other side, the fire raged. But it hadn't crossed the water. Bree's knees folded with relief and her butt hit the ground. It was almost too hard to believe they were safe.

Chapter 53

MERCY

Day 9

Don Dutton was dead.

Mercy was glad. She, Bree, and Paige had almost died. Instead, justice had been served.

Paige had shaken and cried for the longest time as the women comforted her on the shore. They'd tried to keep her from seeing Don's body, but she'd insisted. In fact, she'd limped over to look at him a few times as they waited, saying she needed to be certain he was dead. Her injured feet had looked like raw meat.

As they'd waited in the smoky air, watching the forest burn across the river and wearing the wet respirators, which had survived the soaking in Bree's pocket, Mercy had told Paige how she'd followed a lead across the country to find her.

Paige had been racked with guilt, sobbing about hurting her family. "My dad doesn't need this," she'd said as tears streamed down her face. "He's important. My stupidity might keep him from being reelected. He's going to be so *angry*."

Mercy had hugged her tighter, wincing at the pain in her ribs. "Believe me, your father does not care about that at all. He just wants you back safe."

Paige had choked out a few stories as they waited. She shared how she'd tried to escape, not caring that she was naked, and he'd pulled her back into the house by her hair. And another about finding a woman in the refrigerator. "He said there were others," she whispered.

"If that's true, we'll find them," Bree had told her.

Would there be more bodies?

Helicopters working the fire had spotted them on the riverbank, and the women waited only a few hours before a truck of firefighters showed up to rescue them.

They had eventually arrived at the hospital. The struggles in the river had left Bree with a broken wrist that needed to be set and Mercy with a concussion and broken ribs—which she'd known were broken, but they were hurting much worse now, and yes, she'd like pain medication.

Lots of pain medication.

Paige's cut feet had to be treated. The hospital staff had told them that she would be OK.

Mercy had known that wasn't quite true. Paige's physical wounds would heal, but her psychological wounds would affect her for years.

After their injuries were addressed in the emergency room, Mercy and Bree had spent a loopy, drugged night in a shared hospital room. Mercy had jerked awake several times with terror in her soul as Don shot her in her dreams.

"You saved my life," she told Bree during a painkiller-fueled, tear-filled moment at two a.m., as the shock of the previous day set in.

"You'd already done the same for me." Bree had held up her bandaged hand, and Mercy flashed back to that moment underwater when she'd jerked Bree's hand free from between the rocks.

I didn't think I'd succeed.

Bree could be as dead as Don.

Her drug-affected emotions overtaking her, Mercy had cried again, and Bree joined her.

This morning Mercy's brain was still foggy from the drugs, and exhaustion was heavy in her limbs as she lay in her hospital bed. Bree said she felt as if she'd never be able to get out of bed. Their conversations wandered off on odd tangents as both struggled to focus and stay awake. They gave up trying to act coherent and blearily watched TV, agreeing on *Ted Lasso*, both desperately needing a happy distraction.

Mercy had to constantly remind herself that the fire and peril were over. They'd rescued Paige, and Don Dutton was dead. As they lay in their white and clean hospital room, it felt as if they'd been magically transported from yesterday's fiery and dangerous hell to a different world. A quiet, safe world of peace.

Bree's chief deputy, Todd Harvey, stopped by and told them that the fire was 80 percent contained, and so far there didn't appear to have been any deaths.

We were almost that death statistic.

Mercy knew she'd have nightmares about being trapped in the fire.

The deputy also told them that ballistics had linked a drug supplier's gun to Jimmie Elkins's murder. "Probably killed him because we confiscated the drugs Jimmie was supposed to sell," Bree had said, slightly slurring her words and looking sad. "Too bad for Jimmie." Her voice cracked, and she started to cry.

Mercy had nodded, feeling sorry and tearing up for the man who'd made too many bad decisions.

Deputy Harvey stared in disbelief at Bree and then at Mercy as they sniffed and wiped their eyes about murdered Jimmie Elkins. "How much pain medication did they give you two?"

The deputy confirmed that the woman in the fridge had been identified as Missy Star—whose real name was Elizabeth Stewart, the woman Shelly Fox had nervously reported as missing. Missy had lived on the streets for so long, her family hadn't even realized she was gone.

Bree fell asleep while he was talking. The deputy shook his head at his tired boss and then said goodbye to Mercy. She promised to update Bree when she woke.

But she fell asleep too.

"Mercy."

Sounds like Truman.

"Mercy. Wake up."

Her eyes flew open. Truman was sitting on the side of her bed, a worried look in his brown gaze. She lunged up, squawked in pain, and then threw her arms around her husband, ignoring the fire in her ribs and the pain lighting up her skull.

He came.

"Careful," he said, hugging her gingerly. "There's a reason they kept you overnight in the hospital."

"You're here!" she said, burying her nose in his neck and inhaling the scent of him as happiness flooded her. "I didn't expect you until tomorrow."

"I got an earlier flight. I couldn't stand it anymore." He pulled back and looked her up and down. "You look like you've been beat up." He started to touch a bruise on her forehead but pulled back.

"You should see the rest of me."

"Eventually," he said, a promise in his gaze. He pushed her back onto the pillows. "I love you so much. You have no idea how much I've missed you." He leaned forward and kissed her lightly.

"I love you too." She sighed, soaking in the feel of him and the sight of his face.

"We were told what you two went through," said Truman. "My God, Mercy. Both of you should be dead. And Paige too." Pride filled his eyes. "But you did it. You found the girl and got her out safe. I'm so fucking proud of you." He touched her cheek—one of the few places on her body that didn't hurt.

"I couldn't stop until we found her," Mercy admitted. Then she realized someone else was speaking in the room. A man was talking to Bree. Like Truman, he sat on Bree's bed, concern in his gaze as they spoke in quiet tones. "That must be Matt."

"It is," said Truman. "I met him outside your room. He seems like a good guy. Left whatever he was doing to come to her."

Mercy studied Matt, curious what type of man he was. It wasn't easy to be with someone in law enforcement.

Does he know what he has in her?

The look on his face said he did, and she figured Bree knew what she was doing.

Paige suddenly appeared at their room's door. Her hair in a neat ponytail, she wore a summer dress and leaned on crutches. It took Mercy a full second to recognize the cleaned-up girl, and then she realized that Paige's parents were right behind her. The senator strode across the room, his hand out to Mercy. "Agent Kilpatrick, I—I can't thank you enough."

Mercy took his hand. In the week since she'd seen him, he'd lost a lot of weight. But the haggard and guilty look in his eyes was gone. He'd found peace.

"Yes, Agent Kilpatrick—" started Denise.

"Call me Mercy, please. And this is my husband, Chief Daly."

Paige's mother's eyes were red rimmed, and she had one arm tight around Paige's shoulders. "Thank you for saving our daughter. I'm so thankful she is safe. We came so close to losing her."

"I glad she's safe too. That's Sheriff Taggert," Mercy said, gesturing at the next bed. "Bree, this is Senator Holcroft and Denise Holcroft."

The parents immediately approached Bree, who held out her left hand to shake. Mercy studied Paige as her parents fervently thanked Bree. The young woman had dark circles under her eyes, but there was a calm aura around her that hadn't been there yesterday. Mercy waved Paige over, and the girl slipped out from under her mother's arm. She sat on the other side of Mercy's bed and gave Truman a shy smile.

"How did it go with your parents?" Mercy asked in a low voice, referring to Paige's concern that they would be angry with her.

"Good." Her eyes lightened, knowing what Mercy meant. "You were right. They're just happy I'm back."

"I'm glad to hear it." She eyed the bandages on Paige's knees and feet. "The hospital's letting you leave?"

"Yes. They were worried about a concussion, but I'm fine. Just cuts and bruises. I need to stay off the foot with the huge gash for a while. When we leave here, we're heading to the airport. And the first thing I'm going to do when I get home is find someone to remove this tattoo." Paige shuddered, gently touching her chest where the chain-link heart hid under the dress. "I don't need more memories."

"The memories will get more manageable. Time makes it easier, gives you distance, but it will never completely go away. Maybe you could have a different tattoo put over that one? One that represents something you love?"

"Maybe." She looked at her hands and then at Mercy, uncertainty in her gaze. "Could we have coffee when you get back? I'd like to talk more."

"Of course." Mercy didn't know how mentally healthy it would be for Paige to connect with her—a link to Don Dutton—but meeting once shouldn't hurt. Her mother left Bree's bedside and gently told Paige that it was time to leave. The young woman gave Mercy a very careful but lingering hug. The parents gave emotional goodbyes, and the trio left to return to Oregon and what would hopefully be a normal life.

"That's a lucky family," said Bree. "The other victims' families had horribly sad endings." She squeezed Matt's hand, holding his gaze as she tipped her head at Mercy. "Matt, that's Mercy. She knows her shit."

Mercy and Truman both snorted. "Right back at you," said Mercy. "And nice to meet you, Matt. I would trust Bree to watch my back anytime." Mercy leaned deeper into the pillow, tired out by the small amount of socializing. Her eyes struggled to stay open and she gave in.

Truman squeezed her hand. "I'm not going anywhere," he whispered.

She smiled, her eyes still closed. "I know."

Chapter 54

BREE

Day 10

Bree sat on the back porch, a mug of coffee in her left hand. An ice pack balanced on the cast on her right wrist. The morning was warm, but an overnight thunderstorm had broken the excessive heat wave.

Sitting next to her, Mercy sipped her own coffee and leaned on an ice pack of her own. "When do your kids come home?"

"Tomorrow." Bree couldn't wait to see them. Her ice pack slipped, and she bobbled her coffee, nearly spilling it. "I can shoot left-handed, but everything else is a giant pain in the ass."

"You train shooting."

"I guess I should have trained off-hand shirt buttoning and tooth brushing." Bree's morning routine had been nearly comical. Hooking a bra one-handed had been ridiculously hard.

The barn door opened, and Matt led Beast to the pasture. The dogs trailed behind him and the horse. He slipped off the horse's halter and released him. Beast spun, kicked up his heels, and bucked across the grass like a colt. The other horses wisely gave him space.

Bree laughed. "A two-thousand-pound puppy."

"He's gorgeous." Mercy sighed. "I will miss your farm. I'd forgotten how relaxing farm life is."

"You're welcome to visit anytime. Next time, we'll plan on a ride." Mercy smiled. "I'd like that."

"I'm grateful the wildfire didn't come anywhere near here."

"Me too."

Matt approached the back porch, worry in his eyes. Bree's night in the hospital had been restless. Exhaustion and the pain meds had knocked her out as soon as she'd climbed into her own bed last night. The few times pain had woken her, he'd been up in a second to bring her a glass of water, a pill, or a fresh ice pack. Now, his eyes searched hers, clearly looking for signs of discomfort. "Todd called this morning. He's going to stop by. Are you up for it?"

"Yes. I want to know everything," she said.

Matt sent a text, then brought out some toast with peanut butter and refilled Bree's and Mercy's coffee mugs. By the time they'd eaten, Todd drove up in his patrol vehicle. He walked up onto the back porch and sat on the railing. "How are you both?"

"Alive is good enough," Mercy said.

"I'm fine." Bree managed to keep a straight face. Though she knew with her cast, bruises, small burns, and abrasions, she looked terrible. "Maybe not fine, but definitely better than I look."

Todd shook his head. "I'll catch you up so you can take a nap or something." He took a breath. "The evidence from Dutton's house has been processed. There's so much DNA, and the body, he had pictures . . . There's no doubt he killed the two women from the suitcases and the one in the refrigerator. Paige gave plenty of details in her interview as well." He exhaled. "Did the DA call you?"

"He did," Bree said. "I'm clear. Shooting Dutton was justified."

The DA had taken care of that immediately. The protesters had disappeared, and the public seemed to have shifted their loyalty from the board of supervisors back to Bree. Madeline Jager was scrambling to manage public criticism.

Todd nodded. "The press has been calling the station nonstop. Marge says you should do a major interview ASAP to counter Jager's disaster of a town hall."

"Marge is always right," Bree said. Reporters had been calling her directly as well. "I'll do it." If not for any reason other than to stick it to Jager, which felt petty, but then so did most political moves. Still, that woman brought out the worst in Bree.

"Lastly, we reviewed Dutton's financial and cell phone records. He tried to cover his tracks with the burner phone, using cash, et cetera, but he rented a car a few weeks ago. The dates of the rental match up with Paige's disappearance, and we have Paige's testimony, so the kidnapping ends are tied up."

"Good," Bree said.

Todd continued. "They found a lockpick kit in his garage, and Dutton's fingerprints were on the Clintons' back door. The lock was damaged as well. So that's probably how he stole the keys to their cabin and boat."

Bree sat up straighter. "Mrs. Verney's back door had scratches as well."

Mercy shifted her ice pack. "Why would he break into her house?"

"Who knows?" Bree removed the ice pack from her wrist. "But it's been too long to recover prints, so we'd never be able to prove it anyway."

"We don't have to," Mercy said. "He's dead."

There was no trial to prepare for. Bree still liked to tie up loose ends, but sometimes you had to accept the limitations of reality.

Todd shifted on the railing. "Also, some employees at the mall said his car smelled horrible for at least a week."

"Mrs. Verney also complained of that." Bree scratched the skin between the bandages over the abrasions on the back of her hand and the edge of her cast. Underneath the cast, her wrist and forearm itched like crazy.

"Yeah," Todd said. "We think he drove around with the bodies in the suitcases for a while."

Bree pictured it. "Then he just dropped them on the side of the road?"

Todd lifted both palms to the sky. "He's dead, so we can't ask him, but that's how it seems. The only good thing is that we didn't find any evidence of additional victims. That's all I have for you for the moment."

"Keep me updated."

"I will." He pushed off the railing. "Get some rest. There's no reason to rush back. Mostly, we're doing paperwork from the fire and Don's death."

"I won't rush back," Bree said. "I know you have it handled."

It felt good to have confidence in the team she'd built.

"Then I'll get back to it." Todd walked away.

A few minutes later, the back door opened and Truman came out, carrying his and Mercy's bags. He loaded them into the rental car, then returned to the porch.

Mercy stood. "Thanks for letting us crash here last night."

They hadn't been able to get a flight out until that morning, and Mercy hadn't been in any condition to sit on an airplane anyway. As it was, her flight would be very uncomfortable.

Mercy set her mug on the railing, one hand braced against her injured ribs. Her back was a hot mess.

Bree was considering going back to bed after they left. She felt like she could sleep for a week. But Matt helped her to her feet, and they walked Mercy and Truman out to their vehicle.

Truman and Matt shook hands. Bree wrapped her good arm around Mercy's shoulders and gave her a gentle—very gentle—squeeze. "Thanks for everything. I couldn't have done it without you." She felt the hot prick of tears in the corners of her eyes.

"Same." Mercy's eyes went misty. She pulled back, wincing.

"Keep in touch?" Bree asked.

"You bet." Mercy turned. Matt opened her car door and offered a helping hand. With a final thanks, she eased into the passenger seat.

Truman gave Bree a kiss on the cheek. "Thanks for having her back."

"You're very welcome, but she did the same for me." Bree stepped back.

Matt slid an arm around her shoulders. "Tell me if I hurt you, OK?"

"My shoulders are all right." Bree leaned on him, and they watched Mercy and Truman drive away.

Matt steered her back toward the porch and into the house. "I agree with Todd. You should take a nap."

"It's the only thing on my agenda except for eating and icing my wrist." She dropped her ice pack into the freezer, then headed for the stairs. The dogs followed, and they all piled into bed.

Matt brought her fresh ice and a pain pill. Bree took both, then stretched out. Matt slipped two pillows under her cast to elevate her wrist. The dogs arranged themselves around her legs. Ladybug tried to crawl up next to her, but Matt blocked her. "Sorry, this is my spot today."

He pressed against Bree. "I love you."

"I love you too." She rested her head on his shoulder.

Matt turned on the TV and selected a baking competition.

Bree's eyes grew heavy. "Now I want a cupcake."

"My dad is coming over later to check on you." Matt's dad was a mostly retired doctor. "I'll have him bring some." Matt covered her left hand with his own. "I'm sorry I wasn't here."

"Me too, but I'm grateful I had the feebie to fill in for you." Bree's brain began to drift. The pain in her wrist ebbed. "I'm so glad you're home—I don't think I could relax if you weren't here—but if I had to have someone else cover for you, Mercy did a fine job."

As Bree drifted off, she had a feeling she would see Mercy again. But she hoped their next meeting didn't involve murder.

Acknowledgments

This book is entirely a work of fiction, but it was inspired by a real case we learned about at a conference. We had created two new worlds of characters in our Rogue River and Widow's Island series, but we had occasionally discussed how to bring together individual characters from our own novels. We couldn't figure out how to make it work. Kendra's characters live on the West Coast; Melinda's live on the East.

As we sat in the conference with our good friend author Lee Goldberg, a murder case was presented that involved two law enforcement agencies many states apart. We looked at each other, struck by the same thought. *This setup could work!* Melinda leaned over to Lee and whispered, "Dibs!" Previously we had generously ceded dibs to Lee on a case that inspired his successful Eve Ronin series.

For four years, we discussed this idea. Life's curveballs and working around our individual publishing schedules kept us from writing the book. In 2023, we found time. It was a new writing process for us—very different from our novellas—and we discovered we loved it. We enthusiastically attacked the story, and *Echo Road* was quickly born. We brought together two of our favorite—and fan-favorite—characters and discovered Mercy and Bree had a fantastic chemistry.

This book wouldn't have been written without the support of our Montlake publishing team. We've worked with Montlake for more than a dozen years and wouldn't go anywhere else. Thank you to our agents, Meg Ruley and Jill Marsal, two other amazing women who came together to work as a team. Thank you to our editor Anh Schluep for waiting four years and her never-ending excitement about this project. Big thanks to our developmental editor Charlotte Herscher, who we *swear* we will never write a book without. She's shaped nearly all our individual projects with skilled hands and tactful advice. Thank you to our readers who have loved Mercy and Bree for years and beg for more stories. And of course thanks to Lee Goldberg for respecting dibs.

Will there be another Mercy and Bree novel? It's being discussed . . . Stay tuned.

About the Authors

Photo © 2014 Marti Corn Photography

Kendra Elliot has landed on the *Wall Street Journal* bestseller list multiple times and is the award-winning author of the Bone Secrets and Callahan & McLane series, the Mercy Kilpatrick novels, and the Columbia River novels. She's a three-time winner of the Daphne du Maurier Award, an International Thriller Writers Award finalist, and an RT Award finalist. She was born and raised in the rainy Pacific Northwest but now lives in flip-flops. Visit her at www.kendraelliot.com.

Melinda Leigh is the #1 Amazon Charts and #1 *Wall Street Journal* bestselling author of the She Can series, the Midnight Novels, the Scarlet Falls series, the Morgan Dane series, and the Bree Taggert series. Melinda is an International Thriller Award finalist for best first book.

Her novels have garnered numerous other awards, including two RITA nominations. She holds a second-degree black belt in Kenpo karate and has taught women's self-defense. Melinda lives in a messy house with her family and a small herd of rescue pets. For more information, visit www.melindaleigh.com.